GOD'S SPY

JUAN GÓMEZ-JURADO is an award-winning journalist who has worked in radio and television. Published in more than thirty-five countries worldwide, *God's Spy* is his first novel. He lives with his wife and daughter in Spain.

"Impressive."   —*The Tampa Tribune*

"Juan Gómez-Jurado is the new pope of Vatican intrigue."

—*Qué Leer* (Spain)

GOD'S SPY

✝

Juan Gómez-Jurado

TRANSLATED BY
JAMES GRAHAM

A PLUME BOOK

PLUME
Published by the Penguin Group
Penguin Group (USA) Inc., 375 Hudson Street, New York, New York 10014, U.S.A. • Penguin Group
(Canada), 90 Eglinton Avenue East, Suite 700, Toronto, Ontario, Canada M4P 2Y3 (a division of
Pearson Penguin Canada Inc.) • Penguin Books Ltd., 80 Strand, London WC2R 0RL, England •
Penguin Ireland, 25 St. Stephen's Green, Dublin 2, Ireland (a division of Penguin Books Ltd.) •
Penguin Group (Australia), 250 Camberwell Road, Camberwell, Victoria 3124, Australia (a division
of Pearson Australia Group Pty. Ltd.) • Penguin Books India Pvt. Ltd., 11 Community Centre,
Panchsheel Park, New Delhi – 110 017, India • Penguin Group (NZ), 67 Apollo Drive, Rosedale,
North Shore 0632, New Zealand (a division of Pearson New Zealand Ltd.) • Penguin Books
(South Africa) (Pty.) Ltd., 24 Sturdee Avenue, Rosebank, Johannesburg 2196, South Africa

Penguin Books Ltd., Registered Offices: 80 Strand, London WC2R 0RL, England

Published by Plume, a member of Penguin Group (USA) Inc. Previously published in a Dutton edition.

First Plume Printing, March 2008

10 9 8 7 6 5 4 3 2 1

Originally published in Spain as *Espia de dios* by Roca Editorial.

Map by Jeffrey L. Ward

 REGISTERED TRADEMARK—MARCA REGISTRADA

The Library of Congress has catalogued the Dutton edition as follows:
Gómez-Jurado, Juan.
  [Espía de Dios. English]
  God's spy / by Juan Gómez-Jurado ; translated by James Graham.
     p. cm.
  ISBN 978-0-525-94994-7 (hc.)
  ISBN 978-0-452-28912-3 (pbk.)
  I. Graham, James, 1955–   II. Title.
  PQ6707.O54E8713 2007
  863'.7—dc22   2007004079

Printed in the United States of America
Original hardcover design by Carla Bolte

PUBLISHER'S NOTE
This book is a work of fiction. Names, characters, places, and incidents either are the product of the author's imagination or are used fictitiously, and any resemblance to actual persons, living or dead, business establishments, events, or locales is entirely coincidental.

The scanning, uploading, and distribution of this book via the Internet or via any other means without
the permission of the publisher is illegal and punishable by law. Please purchase only authorized electronic editions, and do not participate in or encourage electronic piracy of copyrighted materials. Your
support of the author's rights is appreciated.

BOOKS ARE AVAILABLE AT QUANTITY DISCOUNTS WHEN USED TO PROMOTE PRODUCTS OR SERVICES. FOR INFORMATION
PLEASE WRITE TO PREMIUM MARKETING DIVISION, PENGUIN GROUP (USA) INC., 375 HUDSON STREET, NEW YORK, NEW YORK
10014.

FOR KATU, LIGHT OF MY LIFE

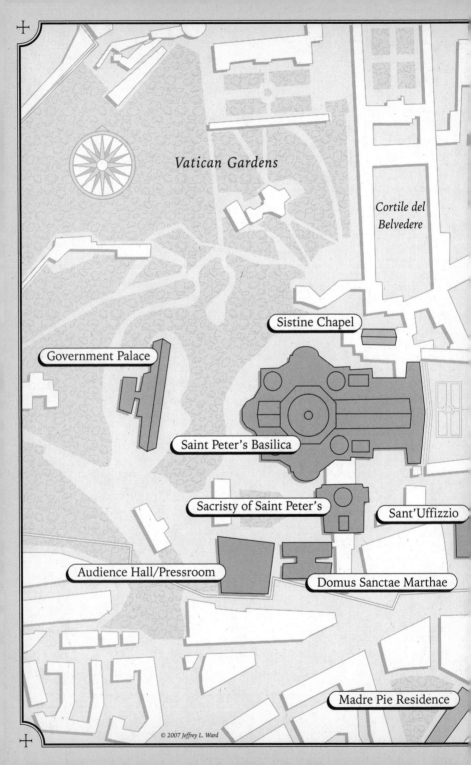

Vatican Gardens

Cortile del Belvedere

Sistine Chapel

Government Palace

Saint Peter's Basilica

Sacristy of Saint Peter's

Sant'Uffizzio

Audience Hall/Pressroom

Domus Sanctae Marthae

Madre Pie Residence

© 2007 Jeffrey L. Ward

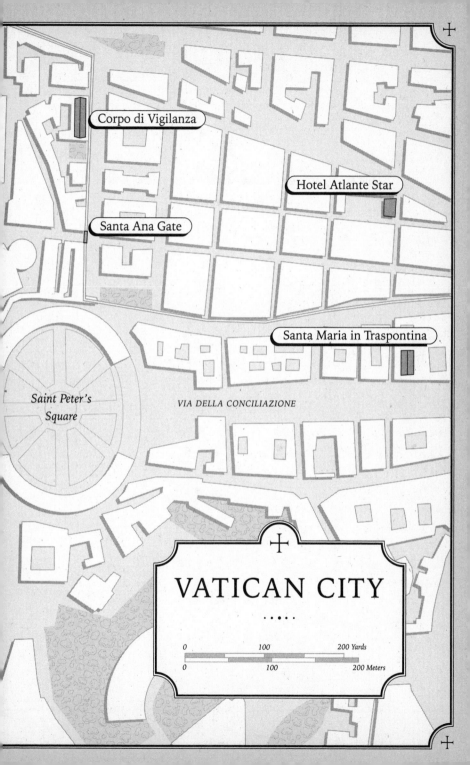

And I will give unto thee the keys of the kingdom of heaven . . .

—Matthew 16:19

PROLOGUE

THE SAINT MATTHEW INSTITUTE

(center for the rehabilitation of Catholic priests with a history of sexual abuse)

Sachem Pike, Maryland

July 1999

Father Selznick awoke in the middle of the night, a fish knife pressed against his throat. Victor Karosky had come into possession of the knife by mysterious means, and he made use of the endless nights in solitary confinement to sharpen it on the edge of a tile he pried loose from the floor of his cell.

That was the second time he had successfully squeezed out of his wretched little six-by-ten-foot cell, letting himself down by a chain that he fastened to the wall with the cartridge of a ballpoint pen.

Selznick had insulted him. He had to pay.

"Don't try to talk, Peter."

Karosky's firm, gentle hand covered Selznick's mouth while the knife caressed the fresh stubble on the face of his priestly brother. Up and down it went in a macabre parody of shaving. Selznick watched him, paralyzed with terror, his eyes wide open, his fingers clutching the edge of the sheet, feeling the other man's weight pressing upon him.

"You know why I have come, don't you, Peter? Blink once for yes and twice for no."

Selznick had no reaction until he saw the fish knife stop in midair.

He blinked twice.

"Your ignorance is the only thing I find more infuriating than your utter rudeness, Peter. I have come to hear your confession."

1

A faint glimmer of relief passed over Selnick's face.

"Do you repent for your abuse of innocent children?"

Selznick blinked once.

"Do you repent for the stain you laid on your priestly ministry?"

A single blink.

"Do you repent for having scandalized so many souls, defrauding our Holy Mother Church?"

Another blink.

"And last but not least do you repent for interrupting me during group therapy three weeks ago, an act that considerably set back my social reintegration and my eventual return to serving God?"

A strong, unwavering blink.

"I am happy to see you repent. For the first three sins, I impose a penitence of six Our Fathers and six Hail Marys. For the last sin . . ."

The expression in Karosky's cold, gray eyes was unwavering as he lifted the knife and inserted it between the lips of his terrified victim.

"Peter, you have no idea how I am going to enjoy this."

Selznick took almost forty-five minutes to die, and he did it without making a sound, without alerting the watchmen who stood guard a hundred feet away. Karosky let himself back into his cell and shut the door. That was where the Institute's petrified director found him sitting the next morning, covered in dried blood. But that was not what most disturbed the elderly priest.

What completely unhinged him was the absolute indifference, cold and very believable, with which Karosky asked for a towel and a washbasin. "I've spilled something on myself" was all he said.

DRAMATIS PERSONAE

PRIESTS

ANTHONY FOWLER, former officer in U.S. Air Force Intelligence, American

VICTOR KAROSKY, priest and serial killer, American

CANICE CONROY, former director of the Saint Matthew Institute, deceased, American

SENIOR CIVILIAN OFFICIALS IN THE VATICAN

JOAQUÍN BALCELLS, Vatican spokesman, Spanish

GIANLUIGI VARONE, the sole judge in Vatican City, Italian

CARDINALS

EDUARDO GONZÁLEZ SAMALO, camerlengo, the pope's chamberlain, Spanish

FRANCIS CASEY, American

EMILIO ROBAYRA, Argentine

ENRICO PORTINI, Italian

GERALDO CLAUDIO CARDOSO, Brazilian

The 110 other cardinals present for the conclave

MEMBERS OF RELIGIOUS ORDERS

Brother FRANCESCO TOMA, Carmelite, Parish of Santa Maria in Traspontina

Sister HELENA TOBINA, director of Saint Martha's House, Polish

CORPO DI VIGILANZA, THE VATICAN POLICE FORCE

CAMILO CIRIN, inspector general
FABIO DANTE, deputy inspector

ITALIAN POLICE

Unità per l'Analisi del Crimine Violento (UACV, or Department for the Analysis of Violent Crime)
PAOLA DICANTI, inspector and psychiatrist, head of the *Laboratorio per l'Analisi del Comportamento* (LAC, or Laboratory for Behavioral Analysis)
CARLO TROI, director general of UACV, Paola Dicanti's boss
MAURIZIO PONTIERO, detective
ANGELO BIFFI, forensic sculptor and digital image expert

CIVILIANS

ANDREA OTERO, freelance reporter writing for *El Globo*, the Spanish daily newspaper
GIUSEPPE BASTINA, courier for Tevere Express, Italian

SOME PERTINENT FACTS
ABOUT VATICAN CITY

(taken from *The CIA World Factbook*)

Surface area: .17 square miles (the smallest country in the world).

Borders: 1.99 miles (with Italy).

Lowest point of elevation: Saint Peter's Square, 62.34 feet above sea level.

Highest point: Vatican gardens, 246.06 feet above sea level.

Climate: Moderate, rainy winters from September to mid-May; hot, dry summers from May to September.

Land use: 100% urban area. Cultivated land, 0%.

Natural resources: None.

Population: 911 citizens with passport. 3,000 workers during the day.

System of government: Ecclesiastic, absolute monarchy.

Rate of birth: 0%. No births at any time in the course of its history.

Economy: Based on charitable donations and the sale of stamps, postcards, prints, and the management of its banks and finances.

Communications: 2,200 phone lines, 7 radio stations, 1 television channel

Annual income: $242,000,000 (in dollars).

Annual expenses: $272,000,000 (same).

Legal system: Based on the Code of Canon Law. Although it has not been officially applied since 1868, the death penalty remains in effect.

Special considerations: The Holy Father has tremendous influence over the lives of more than 1,086,000,000 believers around the world.

☩

APOSTOLIC PALACE
Saturday, April 2, 2005, 9:37 P.M.

The bedridden man was no longer breathing. His personal secretary, Monsignor Stanislaw Dwisicz, who had spent the last thirty-six hours clinging to the dying man's right hand, burst into tears. The doctors on duty had had to use force to pull Dwisicz away during the hour they spent trying to bring the old man back to life. Their efforts went above and beyond. As they undertook one and then another attempt to preserve the man's life, the doctors knew they had to do everything in their power, if only for the sake of their own consciences.

The supreme pontiff's private apartment would have surprised more than one uninformed observer. The ruler before whom the world's leaders respectfully bowed their heads lived in conditions of utter simplicity. His private quarters were inexplicably austere, the walls bare except for a crucifix, the furniture no more than a chair, a table, and the hospital roll-away that, in the last few months of his illness, had replaced the bed. Stationed around it, the doctors did everything they could in the effort to revive him, while large drops of sweat fell onto the immaculate white sheets. Four Polish nuns changed the sheets three times a day.

Dr. Silvio Renato, the pope's personal physician, put an end to their pointless efforts. Waving his hand, he ordered the nurses to cover the timeworn face with a white veil. He asked everyone to leave, remaining alone with Dwisicz. He wrote up the death certificate then and there. The cause of death was obvious: the man's heart had collapsed, as had his circulatory system, both of which were further aggravated by inflammation of the larynx. He wavered when it came to filling in the elderly man's name, although finally, to avoid confusion, he chose the name the man had been given at birth.

Once he had filled out and signed the document, the doctor handed it to Cardinal Samalo, the pope's chamberlain, who just then entered the room. The cardinal, dressed in his red robes, had the distressing task of certifying the death officially.

"Thank you, Doctor. With your permission, I will proceed."

"It's all yours, Your Eminence."

"No, Doctor. From here on in, God is in charge."

Samalo slowly drew close to the deceased man's bed. At seventy-eight years of age he had many times prayed to God not to have to witness this scene. He was a tranquil man, one not likely to lose his head, and yet he was well aware of the heavy load, the multiple responsibilities and duties, that now descended upon his shoulders.

Samalo examined the body carefully. The man had arrived at eighty-four years of age, in the course of which he had overcome a bullet to the chest, a colon tumor, and a complicated appendicitis. Parkinson's had worn him down a little bit every day, leaving him so weak his heart finally gave out.

From the window on the third floor of the Palace, the cardinal could see nearly two hundred thousand people spilling into Saint Peter's Square. The rooftops of the surrounding buildings were overflowing with antennas and television cameras. In just a short while there will be even more, Samalo thought. What's coming will overwhelm us. The people adored him; they admired his sacrifice, his iron will. It is a hard blow, even if everyone has been expecting it since January . . . and more than a few prayed for it. And then we have another problem to deal with.

A noise was heard from the other side of the door, and the Vatican's head of security, Camilo Cirin, walked into the room at the head of the three cardinals who had the task of certifying the pope's death. Worry and lack of sleep were etched on their faces as the three men in their red robes drew close to the bed.

"Let's get started," said Samalo.

Dwisicz held a small, open case at Samalo's side. The chamberlain lifted the white veil that covered the face of the deceased, and opened a tiny phial containing holy oils. He began the age-old ritual in Latin.

"*Si vives, ego te absolvo a peccatis tuis, in nomine Patris, et Filii, et Spritius Sancti. Amen.* If you are alive, I absolve you of your sins in the name of the Father, the Son, and the Holy Ghost. Amen."

Samalo made the sign of the cross over the deceased's forehead and continued.

"*Per istam sanctam Unctionem, indulgeat tibi Dominum a quidquid. Amen.* With this sacred oil, God forgives you the sins you have committed. Amen."

With a solemn gesture, he invoked the apostolic benediction.

"By the power which the Holy See has placed in me, I hereby grant you full forgiveness for and remission of all sins, and I bless you. In the name of the Father, the Son, and the Holy Ghost. Amen."

With the chamberlain holding the case open, he took a silver hammer out. Three times he tapped the forehead of the deceased man, each time gently, and each time asking, "Karol Wojtyla, are you alive?"

There was no response. The chamberlain looked at the three cardinals who stood by the bed, all of whom nodded.

"The pope is dead. There is no doubt."

With his left hand, Samalo removed the fisherman's ring, the symbol of his authority in this world, from the dead man's right hand. Using his right hand, he once again shrouded the face of John Paul II with the veil. He took a deep breath, and looked at his three companions.

"We have a lot of work ahead of us."

CHURCH OF SANTA MARIA IN TRASPONTINA
Via della Conciliazione, 14
Tuesday, April 5, 2005, 10:41 A.M.

Inspector Paola Dicanti closed her eyes briefly and waited until they were accustomed to the darkness as she stood in the entrance to the building.

It had taken her almost half an hour to get to the scene of the crime. If Rome is always a vehicular chaos, after the Holy Father's death it was transformed into an auto inferno. Thousands were arriving every day in the capital of Christendom to bid their last farewell to the body lying in state in Saint Peter's Basilica. This pope had gone to the next world with the fame of a saint, and there were already volunteers moving around the streets collecting signatures to begin the process of beatification. Every hour, eighteen thousand people passed in front of his mortal remains. "A smashing success for forensic medicine," Paola commented to herself ironically.

Her mother had warned her, before she left the apartment they shared on the Via della Croce.

"It will take too long if you go by Cavour. Go up Regina Margherita and down Rienzo," she said as she stirred the semolina porridge she was cooking for her daughter, just as she had done every morning for thirty-three years.

So Paola had of course gone by Cavour, and had lost a good deal of time.

The taste of semolina lingered in her mouth. It was always the first thing she would eat in the morning. During the year she spent studying at FBI headquarters in Quantico, Virginia, she had missed it so badly it almost became an obsession. She ended up asking her mother to send her a big box of the porridge, which she heated in the microwave in the Behavioral Sciences Division's dining area. The taste wasn't the same, but its presence made it easier to be far from home during a year that was both so difficult and so rewarding. Paola had grown up two steps from Via Condotti, one of the most exclusive streets in the world, but her family was poor. She never even knew the meaning of the word until she went to the United States, a country with its own measure for everything. She was over-joyed to return to the city she had hated so fervently when she was growing up.

In Italy, the Department for the Analysis of Violent Crime (the UACV, or Unità per l'Analisi del Crimine Violento) was created in 1995, with a specific focus on serial killers. It seems incredible that at such a late date the country that ranked fifth in the world in the number of psychopaths lacked a unit organized to track them down. Inside the UACV there was a special department known as the Laboratory for Behavioral Analysis (LAC, or Laboratorio per l'Analisi del Comportamento) founded by Giovanni Balta, Dicanti's teacher and mentor. Balta died at the beginning of 2004 after a sudden and massive heart attack, at which time *Dottoressa* Dicanti became *Ispettore* Dicanti, the head of the LAC's Rome office. Her FBI training and Balta's excellent reviews were her references. Upon her supervi-sor's death, LAC found its personnel drastically reduced: Paola be-came the entire staff. Even so, the department was part of the UACV, and they were able to count on technical support from one of the most advanced forensic units in Europe.

Nevertheless, as of that moment, they had yet to solve a single case. In Italy there were thirty serial assassins running around free, unidentified. Of these, nine cases were considered "hot" since they were connected to the most recent deaths on record. No new bodies had turned up since Dicanti became head of LAC, and the absence of definitive evidence increased the pressure, so that her psychological profiles became at times the only thing available to lead the police to a suspect. "Castles in the air," Carlo Troi called them. Troi was a physicist and mathematician by training, a man who spent more time on the phone than in the laboratory. Unfortunately, Troi was UACV's director and Paola's immediate boss, and every time they passed in the hall he gave her a sarcastic look. "My pretty little novelist" was his nickname for her when they were alone in his office: a mocking allusion to the abundant imagination in Dicanti's profiles.

Paola was desperately hoping her work would begin to bear fruit, just so she could stick it in her boss's face. He was an old goat, and she had made the mistake of giving in and sleeping with him one night. The long hours of work were piling up, her guard was down, her heart was overwhelmed by an emptiness with no name . . . and then came the time-honored, morning-after regrets. Especially when she reminded herself that Troi was married and nearly twice her age. He had been a gentleman, hadn't gone on about the subject at length, and was careful to keep his distance, but he never let Paola forget it either, hinting at it with phrases halfway between sexist and charming. God, how she hated the man.

And now finally, for the first time since her promotion, she had a case she could tackle from the outset, one where she wouldn't have to work with shoddy evidence gathered by dimwitted agents. She had taken the call in the middle of breakfast, and immediately hurried into her room to change. She combed her long, dark hair, tied it up in a bun, put away the pants and jersey she was going to wear to the office, took out an elegant suit with black jacket. She was intrigued: the call had not supplied a single detail, except that a crime had been committed that fell within her expertise, and they summoned her to Santa Maria in Traspontina "with utmost urgency."

And there she stood in the doorway of the church. Behind her, a surging mass of people milled about in a line that stretched for almost two and a half miles, coming to an end just short of the Vittorio Emanuele II Bridge. Paola looked worriedly out over the scene. The people had spent all night on line, but those who might have seen something were already far away. The pilgrims glanced in passing at the discreet pair of carabinieri standing at the entrance to the church. The police diplomatically assured the occasional group of believers that the building was undergoing repairs.

Paola took a deep breath and crossed the threshold of the darkened church. The church had one nave, with five chapels on either side, and the air inside was full of ancient, musty incense. The lights in the church were dimmed, no doubt because that is how it had been when the body was discovered. It was one of Troi's mottos: "Let's see it the way he did."

She looked around, her eyes trying to pick things out in the darkness. Two men conversed in low tones in the rear of the church, their backs to her. A Carmelite friar, nervously saying the rosary at the foot of the baptismal font, stared at her as she surveyed the scene.

"Beautiful, isn't it, signorina? It dates from 1566. Constructed by Peruzzi, its chapels . . ."

Dicanti interrupted him, without losing her smile.

"I am afraid I have no interest in art at right this moment. I'm Inspector Dicanti. Are you the parish priest?"

"Indeed. I was the one who discovered the body. I'm sure that's of more interest to you. Blessed is the Lord in days such as these. . . . A saint departs and leaves us with devils in his stead!"

The Carmelite looked very old. He wore tortoiseshell glasses with thick lenses, and the traditional brown habit, with a large scapular knotted at the waist; a thick white beard covered his face. He took several steps around the small fountain, enough for her to see that he was hunched over and limping slightly. His hands nervously thumbed his prayer beads, shaking uncontrollably at odd moments.

"Calm down. What is your name?"

"Francesco Toma, *Ispettore*."

"Tell me in your own words what took place today. I know you've gone through it six or seven times already, but it can't be helped. Take my word for it."

The friar exhaled.

"There's not much to tell. In addition to the parish, I am charged with care of the church. I live in a small room behind the sacristy. I woke up as I do every day, at six in the morning, washed my face, put on my robes. I crossed the sacristy, and entered the church through a hidden door at the foot of the large altar. I went to the chapel of our Lady of Carmen, where I say my prayers every day. I noticed that there were candles burning in front of the chapel of Saint Thomas, yet when I went back to my room they had all gone out. That's when I saw it. I started running towards the sacristy, scared to death because at that point the killer could still be in the church. I called 113."

"You touched nothing in the crime scene?"

"No. Nothing. I was frightened out of my wits, may God forgive me."

"And you didn't try to help the victim?"

"He was clearly beyond any sort of earthly help."

A figure moved toward them down the main aisle of the church. It was Detective Maurizio Pontiero, from the UACV.

"Dicanti, hurry up. They're going to turn on the lights."

"Just a second. Take this. It's my card. My mobile phone number is at the bottom. Call me anytime if you remember anything else."

"I will. Here's a gift for you."

The Carmelite handed her a small, brightly colored card.

"Santa Maria del Carmen. Take it with you wherever you go. It will help you find the right road in these uncertain times."

"Thank you." Dicanti accepted the card from the old friar without giving it a second look, and slipped it into the breast pocket of her coat.

The inspector followed Pontiero through the church to the third chapel on the left, which was cordoned off by the UACV's classic red-and-white crime scene tape.

"You got here late," Pontiero said, reproaching her.

"The traffic was murder. It's a big circus out there."

"You should have taken Rienzo."

Even if, in the hierarchy of Italian police, Dicanti occupied a higher rung than Pontiero, he was the agent in charge of UACV Field Investigations, and for that reason he outranked any laboratory researcher, even someone like Paola, who was the head of her department. Pontiero was fifty-one years old, trim and hot tempered. His face, which resembled an old raisin, wore a perennial frown. It was quite clear to Paola that Pontiero adored her, but he took care not to show it.

Dicanti was about to cross the line when Pontiero's arm shot up to stop her.

"Hang on a second, Paola. Nothing you have ever seen will prepare you for this. It's absolutely demented, I promise you." His voice was trembling.

"I'm sure I'll know how to handle it, Pontiero. But thanks."

She walked into the chapel. A technician from the UACV had arrived before her, taking photographs. At the rear of the chapel, against the wall, was a small altar adorned with a painting of Saint Thomas at the moment he pressed his fingers into Jesus's wounds.

The body sat underneath.

"Holy Mother of God."

"I warned you."

It was a spectacle straight out of Dante. The dead man leaned against the altar. His eyes had been torn out, leaving in their place two gaping wounds the color of dried blood. From the mouth, left wide open in a horrendous, grotesque grimace, hung a grayish brown object. In the sudden flash of a camera bulb, Dicanti saw the worst: the victim's hands had been severed and were resting one on top of the other near his body. Cleansed of any bloodstains, they sat together on a strip of white linen. One of the hands was adorned with an unusually large ring.

The dead man wore the black robes with the red sash and piping of the cardinals.

Paola's eyes widened.

"Pontiero, tell me it's not a cardinal."

"We don't know, Dicanti. We are investigating, although there isn't much left of the face. We held things up for you so you could take a look at the place and see it the same way the killer did."

"Where is the rest of the team from Crime Scene Analysis?"

The Analysis team were UACV's big shots. All of them were highly skilled pathologists, specializing in the recovery of traces, prints, hairs, and anything else a criminal might have left behind. They worked according to the rule that in every crime there is an exchange: the killer takes something and he leaves something.

"They're on their way. The van is stuck in traffic on Cavour."

"They should have gone by Rienzo." The technician put in his two cents.

"No one asked for your opinion," Dicanti snapped back.

The photographer left the chapel muttering unpleasant things about Paola under his breath.

"You have got to get that character of yours under control."

"Why in God's name didn't you call me earlier, Pontiero?" Dicanti asked, completely ignoring the detective's recommendation. "This is a very serious case. Whoever did this is really sick in the head."

"Is that your professional analysis, *Dottoressa*?"

Carlo Troi strolled into the chapel, directing one of his mocking glances her way. He was enamored of surprise entrances like that. Paola realized now that he was one of the two men talking with their backs turned in front of the baptismal font when she entered the church; she blamed herself for having let him catch her unprepared. The other man was standing near the director, but he never uttered a word and he didn't enter the chapel.

"No. My professional analysis will be on your desk as soon as it's ready. I simply put forward the observation that, whatever else we might say, the man who committed this crime has a few screws loose."

Troi was about to say something, but at just that moment the lights of the church came on. And then all of them saw something that they had missed: written on the floor of the church, close to the body of the dead man, in letters of no great size, was

$$EGO\ TE\ ABSOLVO$$

"Looks like blood," Pontiero said, putting into words what everyone was thinking.

A mobile phone began playing the chords of Handel's "Hallelujah" Chorus. The three looked at the man who was standing near Troi, and who with great seriousness took the cell phone out of his coat pocket and answered the call. He hardly said a word, little more than a dozen ahas and mmms.

After he hung up, he looked at Troi and nodded.

"It's what we feared," UACV's director said. "Dicanti, Pontiero, needless to say, this is a very delicate case. The body we have here is the Argentine cardinal Emilio Robayra. If the assassination of a cardinal in Rome is in and of itself an indescribable tragedy, it is that much greater at the present instant. The victim was one of one hundred and fifteen men who in the next few days will participate in the conclave that will choose the next supreme pontiff. The situation is consequently extraordinarily delicate. This crime cannot reach the ears of the press for any reason whatsoever. Imagine the headlines: 'Serial Killer Stalks the Papal Election.' I don't even want to think about it."

"One moment, Director. You said a serial killer? Is there something we don't know?"

Troi cleared his throat and looked at the mysterious person who had come in with him.

"Paola Dicanti, Maurizio Pontiero, let me introduce you to Camilo Cirin, inspector general of the Corpo di Vigilanza, the police force in the independent state of Vatican City."

Cirin nodded as he stepped closer. When he spoke, he did so with effort, as if he strongly disliked having to use words at all.

"We believe this man is the second victim."

$$\maltese$$

THE SAINT MATTHEW INSTITUTE
Sachem Pike, Maryland
August 1994

"*Come in, Father Karosky, come in. Take your clothes off behind the screen, if you would be so kind.*"

The priest started to remove his cassock. The technician continued to talk to him from the other side of the white screen.

"*No need to worry about the test, Father. It's the most normal thing in the world, right? Very normal.*" *The technician laughed under his breath.* "*Maybe you've heard other residents here talking about it, but the lion isn't as fierce as they make him out to be, as my grandmother used to say. How long have you been with us?*"

"*Two weeks.*"

"*Time enough to get acquainted with the test, yes, indeed. Played any tennis yet?*"

"*I don't like tennis. Can I leave now?*"

"*No, Father, put on the green nightshirt so you don't catch cold.*" *The technician laughed again.*

Karosky walked out from behind the folding screen with an oversized green shirt on.

"*Walk over to the examining table and lie down. That's right. Hang on, let me adjust the support for you. You have to be able to focus on the image on the television screen. Can you see?*"

"Perfectly."

"Great. Hang on, I have got to make some adjustments to the dials on the machine, and then we can get started. What we have here is a really fine television, wouldn't you say? A thirty-two-inch screen. If I had something like this at the house, for sure my old lady would show me a little respect, don't you agree?" Once again, the technician laughed at his own joke.

"I'm not sure."

"Ha. Certainly not, Father, certainly not. That harpy wouldn't show a little respect to Jesus Christ himself if he slipped out of a package of Golden Grahams and slapped her on her flabby ass. Ha ha ha."

"You ought not take God's name in vain, my son."

"Right you are, Father. OK, everything is ready. You've never had a penile plethysmograph before, correct?"

"No."

"Of course you haven't. What a joke. Did they explain to you what the test consists of?"

"In general terms."

"Okay, now I'm going to put my hands under your nightshirt so I can attach two electrodes to your penis. Is that all right? This will help us to measure your level of sexual response to various stimuli. Good, I am now proceeding to attach them. Done."

"You have cold hands."

"Yeah, it's a little chilly in here, isn't it? Are you comfortable?"

"I'm fine."

"Then let's begin."

One image after another began to appear on the screen: The Eiffel Tower. Dawn. Mist in the mountains. Chocolate ice cream. Heterosexual coitus. A forest. Trees. A woman performing oral sex on a man. Tulips in Holland. Homosexual intercourse. Las Meninas by Velázquez. Sunset on Mount Kilimanjaro. Two men engaging in oral sex. Snow on the rooftops in a Swiss village. A young boy performing oral sex on an older man, the child with sad eyes looking straight into the camera as he sucks on the adult's member.

Karosky stands up. His eyes are full of rage.

"Father, you cannot stand up. We aren't finished yet—"

The priest grabs the man around the neck and forces his head down against the instrument board again and again, until blood begins to splash onto the various dials, soaking the technician's white lab coat and Karosky's nightshirt and finally bathing the whole world in blood.

"Never commit impure acts like this ever again, do you understand me? Do you understand me, you dirty little piece of shit? Do you?"

CHURCH OF SANTA MARIA
IN TRASPONTINA
Via della Conciliazione, 14
Tuesday, April 5th, 2005, 11:59 A.M.

The silence immediately after Camilo Cirin spoke became even more pronounced when the bells in nearby Saint Peter's Square began ringing the Angelus.

"The second victim? They've torn another cardinal to pieces and we just find out now?" Pontiero's expression made his opinion of the situation absolutely clear.

Cirin, unmoved, stared straight back at him. He was, no doubt about it, an unusual man. Medium height with brown eyes, uncertain age, wearing a plain suit and gray overcoat—nothing about him called attention to itself, which was in itself extraordinary: he was a paradigm of normality. He used as few words as possible, as if by doing so he took himself out of the picture, something that fooled none of those present: all of them had heard talk about Camilo Cirin, one of the most powerful figures at the Vatican, in charge of the smallest police force in the world: the Vatican Vigilanza. A team of forty-eight agents (officially), less than half that of the Swiss Guard, but infinitely more powerful. Nothing took place in his tiny country without Cirin knowing about it. In 1997, a man had tried to outshine him: Alois Siltermann, the newly chosen commander of the Swiss Guard. Two days after his appointment, Siltermann, along with his wife and a corporal of irreproachable reputation, was found dead. They had been killed at gunpoint. The blame fell on the corporal, who, after he supposedly went mad, had shot the couple and then put his "regulation firearm" in his mouth and squeezed the trigger. The entire explanation would make sense if not for two small details: corporals in the Swiss Guard do not carry weapons, and the corporal in question had his front teeth destroyed. All of which leads one to believe that the pistol was brutally forced into his mouth.

A police colleague told Dicanti the whole story. After the event took place, he and his fellow police officers set out to give all possible assistance to the members of the Vigilanza, but they had barely set foot on the crime scene when they were cordially invited to return to the inspectorate and close the door from the inside, without so much as a thank-you for showing up. The dark legend of Camilo Cirin traveled mouth to mouth in police precincts across Rome, and UACV was no exception.

The three of them stood there, just outside of the chapel, stupefied by Cirin's declaration.

"With all due respect, *Ispettore Generale*, I think that if it was clear to you that a killer capable of committing a crime similar to this one was running around loose in Rome, you had a duty to report it to UACV," Dicanti said.

"Absolutely right, and that is exactly what my distinguished colleague did," Troi responded. "He communicated it to me personally, and we both agreed that this is a case that has to be kept in the strictest secrecy, for everyone's benefit. And we both agreed about something else. The Vatican has no one capable of going hand-to-hand with a criminal so, how shall I say, idiosyncratic as this one."

Surprisingly, Cirin interrupted.

"Let me be honest, signorina. Our work consists in containment, protection, and counterespionage. In those fields, I guarantee we are among the best. But with a guy—how did you put it?—who has a few screws loose, we are outside our field of competency. We were thinking about asking for help when we received news of this second crime."

"It's our conclusion that this case requires a much more creative grasp of the subject, Dicanti." Troi was speaking. "Which is why we don't want you to limit yourself to producing profiles, as you have done up to now. We want you to direct the investigation."

Paola kept her peace. This was work for a field agent, not for a criminal psychologist. Certainly she could do the job as well as any field agent, what with the training in the subject she had received in Quantico, but that such a request should come from Troi, and at that very moment, astonished her.

Cirin spun around toward a man in a leather jacket who had walked up to the group.

"Here you are. Let me introduce Fabio Dante, deputy inspector of the Vigilanza. He will be your liaison with the Vatican. He will bring you up to speed on the first murder, and you'll work together on this one, since it's all one case. Anything you ask of him is the same as asking it of me. And the reverse holds as well: anything he refuses you, it's as if I myself refuse you. In the Vatican we have our own rules, which I hope you can understand. And I hope you catch this monster. A man who kills two princes of the Holy Mother Church cannot run around on the loose."

And without a single word more, he walked out.

Troi moved very close to Paola, so close he made her uncomfortable. Their romantic adventure was still fresh in her mind.

"You heard it, Dicanti. You just now made contact with one of the most powerful men in the Vatican, and he has given you a very specific assignment. I have no idea why he settled on you but he expressly mentioned your name. Do what you have to do. Give me reports every day, short, sweet, and to the point. Above all else, collect the irrefutable evidence. I hope your 'castles in the air' amount to something this time. Bring me something, and soon."

Turning on his heels, he headed for the exit in pursuit of Cirin.

"What utter bastards," Dicanti blurted out when she was certain the others were out of earshot.

"Keep going, don't hold back." Dante, the most recent arrival, was laughing.

Paola blushed and held out her hand.

"Paola Dicanti."

"Fabio Dante."

"Maurizio Pontiero."

Dicanti made use of Pontiero and Dante's handshake to study the latter closely. Barely forty-one years old, he was short and well built, his head of dark hair sitting on top of barely two inches of thick neck. A mere five feet six inches in height, the superintendent was attractive, even if he was hardly good-looking. His eyes were olive green, so characteristic of the south of the Italian peninsula.

"I take it 'bastards' includes my superior, *Ispettore?*"

"In truth, yes. I believe an undeserved honor has befallen me."

"We both know it isn't an honor but a terrible pain in the neck. And it isn't undeserved. Your track record speaks volumes of your readiness for this. A pity you have no results to go along with it, but that's about to change, right?"

"You read my job history? Isn't anything confidential around here?"

"Not for Him."

"Listen, you pretentious little . . ." Pontiero had smoke coming out his ears.

"*Basta,* Maurizio. It isn't necessary. We are at the scene of the crime, and I am the responsible party. Let's get down to work, and we can talk later. We will leave the field to them."

"Fine. You're in charge, Paola. The boss has spoken."

Waiting a prudent distance on the other side of the red line were two men and a woman sheathed in dark blue overalls. They were the team from Crime Scene Analysis, specialists in evidence recovery. Dicanti and the two others exited the chapel and walked toward the central nave.

"So we agree on that, Dante. Tell us everything you know," Dicanti said.

"Sure. The first victim was the Italian cardinal Enrico Portini."

"No way!" Dicanti and Pontiero blurted out in unison.

"Take my word for it, my friends. I saw it with my own eyes."

"The great candidate of the reform wing. A church liberal. What a mess it would be if the news media got hold of this."

"No, Pontiero, it would be a catastrophe. Yesterday morning George Bush arrived in Rome with his whole family. Another two hundred representatives and international heads of state are lodging in your country but they will be in mine for the funeral on Friday. We're on maximum alert, but you know what the city is like. A very complex situation, and the last thing we want is to spread panic. Come outside with me. I need a smoke."

Dante led them out to the street, where the crowd was constantly growing larger and more tightly packed. The Via della Conciliazione was completely swamped with human beings. Every flag was represented: French, Spanish, Polish, Italian, and dozens of others. Young people playing guitars, the faithful with candles lit, even a blind man with his Seeing Eye dog—two million people would attend the funeral of the pope who had changed the map of Europe. The worst environment in the world to work in ever, Dicanti thought. Any scrap of evidence would be lost in the whirlwind of pilgrims.

"Portini was staying at the Madre Pie residence, on the Via de Gasperi," Dante said. "He arrived Thursday in the morning since he knew in advance about the pope's grave condition. The nuns say that everything was completely normal when he dined on Friday evening, and that he stayed a long while in the chapel, praying for the Holy Father. No one saw him go to bed. There was no evidence of a struggle in his room. No one slept in his bed, unless the man who kidnapped him remade it perfectly. He never came down for breakfast on Saturday, but people think he must have continued his devotions at the Vatican. It's not clear to us what happened on Saturday, but Vatican City was one big mess. Do you understand? He disappeared in the middle of the street in the Vatican."

He stopped, lit a cigarette and offered one to Pontiero, who turned him down reluctantly and took out one of his own. Dante went on.

"His body showed up yesterday morning in the chapel at the residence, but just as it was here, the lack of blood indicates that the setting was well prepared. Luckily the man who discovered the body was an honorable priest who called us right away. We have photographs of the place, but when I suggested that we should call you, Cirin told me he would be in charge. And he ordered us to clean up absolutely everything. The cardinal's body was taken to a location deep inside the Vatican, where it was incinerated."

"What! They destroyed the evidence of a serious crime on Italian soil! This I do not believe."

Dante stared at them, defiant.

"My boss made the decision, and perhaps it wasn't the best response. But he called your boss and explained the situation. And here you are. Are you aware what we have on our hands? We are not prepared to handle something like this."

"Which is precisely why you should have left it to professionals." Pontiero interjected, a hard look on his face.

"You still don't get it. We cannot trust anyone, which is why Cirin, a good soldier of our mother Church, did what he did. Don't look at me with that face, Dicanti. Try to understand the reasons for what he did. If Portini's death was all we had to deal with, we could have gone looking for any excuse, and the subject would be buried. But it didn't turn out that way. It's nothing personal, please understand."

"What I understand is that we were invited to the second course of the meal. With half the evidence. Fantastic. Is there anything else we should understand?" Dicanti was really furious now.

"At this moment, no," said Dante, who once again hid behind an ironic smile.

"Shit, shit, shit. We've got a terrible mess on our hands, Dante. From now on I want you to tell me everything. And I want one thing to be very clear: I am in charge. They've ordered you to help me with everything, but I want you to understand that more important than the fact that the victims are cardinals, both crimes have taken place in my jurisdiction. Is that clear?"

"Crystal clear."

"It had better be. The modus operandi was the same?"

"As far as my detective talents take me, yes. The body was stretched out at the foot of the altar. His eyes were gone. The hands, just like here, were cut off and placed on a piece of canvas alongside the body. Repugnant. I myself was the one who put the body in a bag and carried him to the crematory furnace. I spent all night in the shower, take my word for it."

"It would have been a good idea to have stayed a little longer," Pontiero muttered.

Four long hours later they finished working on Robayra's body and could start to remove it. On the express orders of Director Troi, it was the very same men in Analysis who put the body in a plastic bag and carried it off to the morgue, so that no one from the sick bay would see the cardinal's clothing. It was made clear to everyone that this was a very special case, and the identity of the dead man had to continue to be a secret.

For everyone's benefit.

$$\dagger$$

THE SAINT MATTHEW INSTITUTE
Sachem Pike, Maryland

September 1994

Transcription of Interview #5 Between
Patient No. 3643 and Doctor Canice Conroy

Dr. Conroy: Good afternoon, Victor. Welcome to my office. Feeling better?

No. 3643: Yes, Doctor. Thanks.

Dr. Conroy: Do you want anything to drink?

No. 3643: No, thank you.

Dr. Conroy: Well, a priest who doesn't drink—a real novelty. It won't bother you if I. . . .

No. 3643: Go ahead, Doctor.

Dr. Conroy: It's my understanding that you have spent some time in the infirmary.

No. 3643: I picked up a few bruises a week ago.

Dr. Conroy: Do you remember how these bruises came about?

No. 3643: Yes, Doctor. It was during an altercation in the observation room.

Dr. Conroy: Tell me what happened, Victor.

No. 3643: I went there to undergo a plethysmograph, on your recommendation.

Dr. Conroy: Do you recall the purpose of the test, Victor?

No. 3643: To determine the causes of my problem.

Dr. Conroy: Exactly, Victor. You recognize that you have a problem, and this is no doubt progress.

No. 3643: I always knew I had a problem, Doctor. I remind you that I am here in this center on a voluntary basis.

Dr. Conroy: That is a subject I certainly want to take up with you in our next session. But for now keep telling me about the other day.

No. 3643: I went into the room and took off my clothes.

Dr. Conroy: That made you uncomfortable?

No. 3643: Yes.

Dr. Conroy: It's a medical procedure. You have to take off your clothes.

No. 3643: It isn't necessary, if you ask me.

Dr. Conroy: The technician has to attach the instrument that measures your reaction on a part of your body that is normally hard to reach. Which is why you had to take off your clothes, Victor.

No. 3643: I don't think it's necessary.

Dr. Conroy: Very well, just go along with me for a moment and agree that it is necessary.

No. 3643: If you say so, Doctor.

Dr. Conroy: What happened next?

No. 3643: He attached the electrodes down there.

Dr. Conroy: Where, Victor?

No. 3643: You know where.

Dr. Conroy: No, Victor, I don't know and I want you to say it.

No. 3643: On my thing.

Dr. Conroy: Can you be more explicit, Victor?

No. 3643: On my . . . penis.

Dr. Conroy: Very good, Victor. That's it: The masculine member, the male organ whose purpose is for copulation and urination.

No. 3643: In my case, only for the second function, Doctor.

Dr. Conroy: Are you sure, Victor?

No. 3643: Yes.

Dr. Conroy: It was not always like that in the past, Victor.

No. 3643: The past is over. I want to change that.

Dr. Conroy: Why?

No. 3643: Because it's God's will.

Dr. Conroy: Do you really believe that God is involved with that, Victor? With your problem?

No. 3643: God's will is involved in everything.

Dr. Conroy: I'm a priest too, Victor, and I believe that God sometimes lets nature run its course.

No. 3643: Nature is an intellectual construct that has no place in our religion, Doctor.

Dr. Conroy: Let's go back to the observation room, Victor. Tell me how you felt when the technician attached the electrodes.

No. 3643: He had cold hands.

Dr. Conroy: Just cold, nothing else?

No. 3643: Nothing else.

Dr. Conroy: And when the images started to appear on the screen?

No. 3643: I felt nothing then, either.

Dr. Conroy: You know, Victor, I have the results from the plethysmograph and they show specific reactions here and here. Do you see those spikes?

No. 3643: I felt disgust when I saw certain images.

Dr. Conroy: Disgust, Victor?

[Conversation pauses for more than a minute.]

Dr. Conroy: Take all the time you need to answer, Victor.

No. 3643: Sexual images disgust me.

Dr. Conroy: Anything specific, Victor?

No. 3643: All of them.

Dr. Conroy: Do you know why they disturbed you?

No. 3643: Because they offend God.

Dr. Conroy: Nevertheless, when you observed particular images, the apparatus registered tumescence in your masculine member.

No. 3643: It isn't possible.

Dr. Conroy: To put it in vulgar terms, they gave you a hard-on.

No. 3643: Language like that offends God and the dignity of his priests. I have to . . .

Dr. Conroy: What do you have to do, Victor?

No. 3643: Nothing.

Dr. Conroy: Are you having a violent seizure, Victor?

No. 3643: No, Doctor.

Dr. Conroy: Did you become violent the other day?

No. 3643: Which other day?

Dr. Conroy: Right. Forgive my lack of clarity. Would you say that the other day, while you were beating the head of my psychologist against the control board, that you had a violent seizure?

No. 3643: That man was tempting me. "And if thine eye offend thee, pluck it out and cast it from thee," says the Lord.

Dr. Conroy: Matthew, chapter 18, verse 9.

No. 3643: Precisely.

Dr. Conroy: And what of that eye? Of the agony of that eye?

No. 3643: I don't understand.

Dr. Conroy: The man's name is Robert. He has a wife and a daughter. You sent him to the hospital. You broke his nose, seven teeth, and gave him a severe concussion. Thank God, the guards managed to subdue you in time.

No. 3643: Maybe I became a little violent.

Dr. Conroy: Do you think you could become violent now, if your hands weren't strapped to the sides of the chair?

No. 3643: If you want to, we could find out, Doctor.

Dr. Conroy: I think we'd better stop the interview right here, Victor.

✝

MUNICIPAL MORGUE
Tuesday, April 5, 2005, 8:32 P.M.

The autopsy room was a chilly place, painted a jarring grayish mauve that did nothing to lighten the atmosphere. A light outfitted with six bulbs hanging over the autopsy table lent the cadaver a few last minutes of fame in the eyes of the four spectators staring down at him. It was their job to find out who was responsible for his untimely demise.

Pontiero clamped his hand over his mouth when the coroner lifted Cardinal Robayra's stomach onto the tray. A putrid odor permeated the autopsy room as the examiner proceeded to cut the stomach open with his scalpel. The smell was so strong it overwhelmed even the formaldehyde-and-chemical cocktail the doctors used to disinfect the tools of their trade. Dicanti asked herself why coroners kept their instruments so clean before putting them to use. An absurd idea. It wasn't as if the dead man was going to pick up an infection.

"Eh, Pontiero, do you know why the dead baby crossed the road?"

"Yeah, Doc, because he was stapled to the chicken. You've told me that one six, no seven, times. Know any others?"

The coroner was humming quietly as he went about making his

35

incisions. He was a good singer, with a hoarse, smokey voice that made Paola think of Louis Armstrong, above all because he was humming "What a Wonderful World." He interrupted the song only to torment Pontiero.

"The real joke is watching you struggle not to puke, Pontiero. Don't think I don't find that funny. This one got what he had coming."

Paola and Dante glanced at each other over the cardinal's dead body. The coroner, a recalcitrant Communist, was an old hand at his job who at times lacked respect for the dead. He thought Robayra's demise terribly humorous, something Dicanti didn't find the least bit amusing.

"Doctor, could you limit yourself to an analysis of the body and just leave it at that? Both our invited guest, Deputy Inspector Dante, and I find your attempts at humor offensive and out of place."

The coroner glanced at Dicanti out of the corner of his eye and went about examining the contents of Robayra's stomach. He gave up the satirical jabs, but between his teeth he cursed everyone in the room and everyone's family as far back as the third generation. Paola stopped listening to him, being more preoccupied with the look on Pontiero's face, which at that moment was a shade halfway between white and green.

"Maurizio, I don't know why you torture yourself like this. You've never been able to stand the sight of blood."

"Shit, if this phony little saint can take it, I can too."

"You would be surprised to know how many autopsies I've attended, my delicate colleague."

"Really? Well, I remind you that there's at least one more waiting for you, although I think I will enjoy it more than you."

Here they go again for Christ's sake, Paola thought, while she tried to mediate between the two. They had carried on like this all day. Dante and Pontiero had felt a mutual repulsion from the moment they met, but to be fair to Pontiero anything in pants that came closer to Dicanti than ten feet wound up on his bad side. She knew he regarded her like a daughter, but he took it too far sometimes. Fabio Dante was the frivolous type and he certainly wasn't the brightest bulb in the box, but he was not deserving of the nastiness her coworker was lavishing upon him. What she could not figure out was how a man like Dante had come to occupy the position he did in the Vigilanza. Bad jokes, one after the other, followed by harsh putdowns, all of it in sharp contrast to Inspector General Cirin's closely guarded, colorless character.

"Perhaps my distinguished visitors can muster the refinement necessary to lend their attention to the autopsy they've come here to watch."

The coroner's raspy voice dragged Dicanti back to reality.

"Go ahead, please." She shot a cold look at both cops to get them to knock it off.

"OK, the victim had not eaten anything since breakfast, and everything indicates he ate very early because all I can find are a few scraps."

"So maybe he skipped a meal or he fell into the killer's clutches before lunch."

"I doubt he passed on a meal. . . . He ate well, as you can see. Alive, he weighed a little over two hundred pounds, at six feet tall."

"Which tells us the killer was physically fit. Robayra was hardly light as a feather," Dante interjected.

"And it's one hundred and thirty feet from the church's doorway to the chapel," said Paola. "Someone would have to see the killer bringing the body into the church. Pontiero, do me a favor. Send four cops you trust into the area. Send them in plain clothes, but with their badges. Avoid telling them what happened. Just say that there was a robbery at the church, and you want them to find out if anyone saw anything during the night."

"Hunting around with the out-of-towners is a waste of time."

"So don't do it. Talk to the people who live nearby, especially the old people. They get by on very little sleep."

Pontiero nodded and hurried out of the autopsy room, visibly pleased at not having to stay on. Paola watched him exit, and when the doors had slammed shut behind him, she looked straight at Dante.

"What exactly is going on with you, Mr. Vatican? Pontiero is a good cop, he simply cannot stomach the sight of blood. That's all. I'm asking you to cease and desist the inane verbal jousting."

"You said it. So we have more than one big mouth here in the morgue." The coroner was laughing to himself.

"Mind your own business, Doctor. Let's keep going. Do I make myself clear, Dante?"

"Calm down." Dante raised his hands in self-defense. "I don't think you understand what's happening here. If tomorrow morning I had to go into a burning building with a pistol in my hand, shoulder to shoulder with Pontiero, there's no doubt I'd do it."

"So can you tell me why you keep picking on him?" Paola was utterly dismayed.

"Because I enjoy it. And I'm sure he enjoys being pissed off at me too. Why don't you ask him?"

Paola shook her head, muttering unflattering things about men under her breath. "Let's keep going, shall we? Doctor, do you know the hour and the cause of his death?"

The coroner scanned his notes.

"I remind you that this is a preliminary report, but I'm pretty sure. The cardinal died around nine o'clock at night yesterday, Monday. Margin of error, one hour. His throat was slashed. The cut was made from behind, by someone I believe was the same height. I can't tell you anything about the weapon, except that it was at least *six* inches long, a straight edge, and very sharp. It could be the kind of razor a barber uses. I don't know."

"What about his wounds?" said Dante.

"The extraction of the eyes took place antemortem, before he died, as did the mutilation of the tongue."

"He pulled out the tongue? Christ almighty." Dante was disgusted.

"In my opinion he did it with a pair of pliers. When he was done, he stuffed the recess with toilet paper to staunch the hemorrhage. He later removed it, but a few traces of cellulose were left behind. But listen, Dicanti, you surprise me. It really doesn't seem as if this is affecting you very much."

"I've seen worse."

"So let me show you something I am sure you have never seen. I have never come across anything like it, and I have been at this for many years. He stuffed the tongue in the rectal cavity with astonishing expertise. Then he cleaned up the blood around it. I would have missed it if I hadn't looked inside."

The coroner showed them photographs of the tongue, cut into pieces.

"I put it on ice and sent it to the laboratory. Get me a copy of the report when it comes in. I still have no idea how he did it."

"Don't worry, I will see to it personally," Dicanti assured him. "What about his hands?"

"Those were cut off postmortem. Not a clean job. There are hesitation marks here and here. Probably it was difficult for him or he was standing in an uncomfortable position."

"Anything under the nails?"

"Fresh air. The hands are impeccably clean. I suspect he washed them with soap. I believe my nose detects a trace of lavender."

Paola was thinking.

"Doctor, in your opinion how long did the killer need to inflict these wounds on the victim?"

"I hadn't thought about it. Let's see. Give me a second."

The old man let his hands slide up and down the corpse's forearms, the sockets of the eyes, and the mutilated mouth while he thought it over. He was still singing to himself quietly, this time something by the Moody Blues. The name of the tune eluded Paola.

"Well, gentlemen . . . He needed at least half an hour to remove the hands and clean them, and something like an hour to wash the rest of the body and put the clothes back on. There's no way to say how long he tortured the victim but it looks like he took his time. I'm certain he spent at least three hours at it, probably more."

Some place quiet, unknown. Private, far away from prying looks. Soundproof, because Robayra certainly had to have screamed. How much shouting is a man going to do if somebody is pulling out his eyes and his tongue? A great deal, no doubt. They had to come up with a time frame, establish how many hours the cardinal had been in the killer's possession, then subtract the time he spent in doing what he did to his victim. That way they could reduce the scope of the search, if they were lucky and the killer had not had all the time in the world.

"I know the boys have yet to find any fingerprints. Did you come across anything out of the ordinary before cleaning him, anything you sent to be analyzed?"

"Nothing much. A few fabric fibers, a few traces of something that could be makeup on the shirt collar."

"Makeup? Interesting. From the killer?"

"Look, Dicanti, maybe our cardinal had a few secrets," Dante said.

Paola looked at Dante. She was caught off guard. The pathologist gritted his teeth, laughing mischievously.

"I'm not going there," Dante hurried to say. "I just want to say that it's possible he took a great deal of care with his image. He was, after all is said and done, a man of a certain age."

"Still, it's a remarkable detail. Any traces of makeup on his face?"

"No, but the killer must have cleaned it, or at least dried the blood from the eye sockets. I'll give it a closer look."

"Doctor, send a sample of the makeup to the laboratory, just in case. I want to know the brand and the exact shade."

"That could take some time unless they have a data bank already set up to compare with what we send them."

"Write on the order that they can go through an entire perfume shop if they have to. It's the type of assignment that really appeals to Troi. What do you want to tell me about blood or semen? Did we get lucky?"

"No chance. The victim's clothes were spotless, and there were only a few traces of a blood, the same type as the victim's. Definitely his own."

"Anything on the skin or in the hair? Spores, anything?"

"I found small traces of adhesive in what was left of the wrists, which makes me suspect the killer stripped the cardinal, bound him with duct tape before torturing him, and afterwards put his clothes back on. He washed the body, but not in a bath. See this?"

The pathologist pointed to a thin white line of dried soap on Robayra's side.

"He used a sponge with water and soap, but without much water in it or he wasn't being very careful in this area because he left a lot of soap on the body."

"What kind of soap?"

"That's easier to identify than the makeup, but it's less useful, too. It appears to be ordinary lavender soap."

Paola leaned over the body and took a deep breath. Lavender it was.

"Anything else?"

"There's some adhesive on the face too, but a minute quantity. That's it. And definitely, the deceased was very shortsighted."

"And what does that have to do with the matter at hand?"

"Dante, pay attention. He is not wearing his glasses."

"Of course he isn't wearing his glasses. The killer tore his eyes out, what does he need his damn glasses for?"

The coroner was clearly annoyed by Dante.

"Fine. Listen, I'm not telling you how to do your job. I'm just telling you what I see."

"That's good, Doctor. Call us when you have the complete report."

"Of course, *Ispettore*."

Dante and Paola left the coroner bent over the body, whistling his versions of the jazz classics, and stepped out to the hallway, where Pontiero was barking short, concise orders over his cell phone. As soon as he was finished, Dicanti spoke to both of them.

"OK, this is what we're going to do. Dante, you go back to your office and write out a report of everything you can remember from the scene of the first crime. I prefer you do it alone, which will make it easier. Put in all the photos and pieces of evidence your wise and knowing leader has let you keep. And then come back to UACV headquarters as soon as you're done. I'm afraid this is going to be a long night."

FBI

BEHAVIORAL SCIENCES DIVISION

NATIONAL CENTER FOR THE ANALYSIS OF VIOLENT CRIME

INTERNATIONAL TRAINING PROGRAM

FINAL EXAM: VICTIMOLOGY

Student: DICANTI, Paola

Date: July 19, 1999

Grade: A+

Single Question: Describe in 100 words or less the importance of TIME in the creation of a criminal profile, using the Rosper method. Make a personal evaluation by connecting the variables with the perpetrator's level of experience. You have two minutes counting from the time you turn the page.

Answer: The perpetrator has given himself the time necessary to:

  a) *kill the victim*

  b) *interact with the body*

  c) *remove any traces of himself from the victim and dispose of the body*

Comment: According to my deductions, variable a) is limited by the perpetrator's fantasies, variable b) helps to reveal his hidden motivations, while c) defines his capacity for analysis and improvisation. In conclusion, if the perpetrator dedicates more time to

  a) *he has a moderate level of experience (3 crimes)*

  b) *he is an expert (4 crimes or more)*

  c) *he is a beginner (this is his first or second murder).*

✝

UACV HEADQUARTERS
Via Lamarmora, 3
Tuesday, April 5, 2005, 10:32 P.M.

"Let's see. What do we have?"

"Two cardinals murdered in the nastiest way imaginable."

Dicanti and Pontiero ate sandwiches and drank coffee in the laboratory's conference room. For all its modernity, it was a gray and depressing space. The only spot of color came from the hundreds of crime scene photos spread out in front of them on an enormous table, with four plastic bags full of evidence in a pile at one end. At that moment it was all they had. They were waiting for Dante to bring them the leftovers from the first murder scene.

"All right, Pontiero. Let's start with Robayra. What do we know about him?"

"He lived and worked in Buenos Aires. Arrived on an Aerolineas Argentinas flight Sunday morning, with an open ticket he'd bought several weeks before. The flight was not reserved until one in the afternoon Saturday. With the time difference, I figure that was when the Holy Father died."

"Round-trip?"

"Just coming."

"Strange . . . either the cardinal failed to plan ahead or he came to the conclave with high hopes. Maurizio, you know I'm not particularly religious. What have you heard about Robayra's chances to become pope?"

"Not much. I read something about him a week ago, I think in *La Stampa*. They thought he was well positioned but not one of the great favorites. In any case, you know how the Italian media is: they only pay court to our cardinals. Portini I have read about, and plenty too."

Pontiero was a family man, impeccably honest. He was, from what Paola knew, a good husband and father who went to mass each Sunday without fail. And his invitations to Dicanti to accompany the family were just as punctual, forcing her to come up with one excuse after another. Some were good, some bad, but none of them held up. Pontiero knew that in Dicanti's heart of hearts faith didn't play a large part. That had taken leave with her father, ten years before.

"Something bothers me, Maurizio. It's important to know what sort of frustration connects this killer to the cardinals. If he detests what the cardinals stand for, if he's a seminarian who isn't playing with a full deck, or if he just hates their little red hats."

"Their *cappellos cardenalicios*."

"Thanks for clearing that up. I suspect there's something which ties the victims together, something bigger than the hat. Basically, we're not going to get very far down this road unless we are in contact with an authentic source, someone who can speak with authority. It's Dante's job to open doors for us, so we have access to someone high up in the Curia. And when I say high up, I mean very high up."

"Won't be easy."

"That we will see. But for now, let's focus on what we know. For starters, Robayra died somewhere else other than the church."

"There really wasn't much blood. He must have died in another location."

"Clearly the killer had to keep the cardinal in his power a certain amount of time in a secluded place no one else knew about, where he could take his time interacting with the body. We know that he had to gain his victim's confidence in some way, so that the victim would enter the secluded place of his own free will. From there, he moved the body to Santa Maria in Traspontina, obviously for a reason."

"What about the church?"

"I spoke with the parish priest. It was closed up like a drum when he went to sleep. Remember that he had to open it for the police when they arrived. But there's a second door, very tiny, which lets out onto the Via Corridori. That's probably how they got in. We checked it out?"

"The lock was in good shape, a new one. It wouldn't give. But even if the door was swinging on its hinges, I don't see how the killer could have gotten in."

"Because?"

"Do you have any idea how many people were standing in the main door, on Via della Conciliazione? And on the street behind, even more. Jesus. It's crammed with people here for the funeral. They're in the street, blocking traffic. Don't try to tell me that our killer walked in with a body in his arms in full view of the entire world."

Paola thought for a few seconds. Maybe that tide of humanity was wonderful camouflage for the killer, but still, how had he entered without forcing the door?

"Pontiero, let's make sure that how he got in is among our priorities. Tomorrow we'll talk to the friar. What was his name?"

"Francesco Toma, a Carmelite." Pontiero nodded his head slowly as he jotted in his notebook.

"That one. On the other side of the margin we have the macabre details: the message on the floor, the severed hands resting on the canvas . . . and these bags here. Go ahead."

Pontiero started reading the list while Inspector Dicanti filled out the evidence report with a ballpoint pen. An ultramodern office, and they still had relics from the twentieth century like these antiquated forms.

"Evidence, item number one. Priest's stole. Embroidered cloth, rectangular, worn by Catholic priests during the sacrament of confession. Found hanging from the dead man's mouth, soaked in blood. Blood type is the same as that of the victim. DNA analysis in progress."

That was the brownish object they had been unable to make out in the half-light of the church. The DNA analysis would need at least two days, and even that was because one of the world's most advanced laboratories was at UACV's disposal. Dicanti broke out in laughter whenever she watched the American show *CSI*. If only evidence could be processed as quickly as it seemed to be on television.

"Evidence, item number two. White canvas. Origin unknown. Material, cotton. Presence of blood, minimal. The severed hands of the victim were found sitting on top of it. The blood type is that of the victim. DNA analysis in progress."

Dicanti hesitated. "One thing. Robayra is written with a *y*, not an *i*?"

"With a *y*, I'm pretty sure."

"Good. Keep going, Maurizio, please."

"Evidence, item number three. A crumpled piece of paper, approximately one-and-a-quarter-inch square. Found in the left eye socket of the victim. The type of paper, its composition, weight, and percentage of chlorine are all being studied. Written on the paper, by hand with a ballpoint pen, the letters

"MT 16," Dicanti said. "An address?"

"The paper was found covered with blood and crushed into a ball. It's clearly a message from the killer. The absence of the victim's eyes could be not so much a punishment as a sign. . . . As if he were telling us where to look."

"Or that we are blind."

"A killer who does it for his own amusement. The first one to show up in Italy. That's why I think Troi wanted you to be in charge, Paola. Not your usual detective but someone who thinks creatively."

Dicanti reflected on Pontiero's words. If it were true, the risks doubled. The profile of a killer who taunts the police typically corresponded to an extremely intelligent person, one much harder to catch as long as he never tripped up. Sooner or later they all tripped up, but in the meantime the morgue was standing room only.

"OK, let's think for a minute. What streets do we know with those initials?"

"Viale del Muro Torto."

"No go, it runs through a park, and it has no street numbers, Maurizio."

"In that case Monte Tarpeo is out too. It's the street that crosses the Palazzo dei Conservatori gardens."

"And Monte Testaccio?"

"In Parco Testaccio . . . that might be it."

"Wait a minute." Dicanti picked up the phone and dialed a number in the police department. "Documents? Ah, Silvio, hello. Take a look for me and see if there is a number 16 on Monte Testaccio. And bring us a map of the city streets here in the conference room. Thanks."

While they waited, Pontiero continued on with the list of evidence.

"And the last, for now: Evidence, item number four. Crumpled paper, one-and-a-quarter-inch square. Found in the victim's right eye socket, in identical condition to that of item number three. The kind of paper, its composition, weight, and percentage of chlorine are being investigated. Written on the paper, by hand, with a ball-point pen, the word *undeviginti* and an arrow."

UNDEVIGINTI

⟶

"*Undeviginti*. Damn, it's a fucking hieroglyph." Dicanti was exasperated. "I just hope it's not the continuation of a message that he left on the first victim, because the first part went up in smoke."

"I guess we have to resign ourselves to what we have, for now."

"Stupendous, Pontiero. Why don't you tell me what *undeviginti* is, so I can resign myself to it?"

"Your Latin isn't what it used to be, Dicanti. It means nineteen."

"It's true, dammit. They were always throwing me out of school. And the arrow?"

At that moment one of the assistants from Documents entered the room with the street map of Rome.

"Here you are, *Ispettore*. I looked for the street you asked me about: there is no 16 Monte Testaccio. That street only has fourteen distinct residences."

"Thanks, Silvio. Do me a favor: stay here with Pontiero and me and we will go over all the streets in Rome that begin with *MT*. It's a blind shot but I've got a hunch."

"Let's hope you're a better psychologist than fortune-teller, *Dottoressa* Dicanti. You'd do better if you looked in the Bible."

Their three heads spun around to the entrance to the conference room. A priest in his street clothes was standing on the threshold. He was tall and thin in a wiry frame, and noticeably bald. He looked to have lived about fifty well-preserved years, and his features were forceful, even hard, evidence of many mornings he had spent outdoors watching the sun come up. Dicanti's first thought was that he looked more like a soldier than a priest.

"Who are you and what do you want? This is a restricted area. Please do us the favor of leaving immediately," said Pontiero.

"I am Father Anthony Fowler. I'm here to give you a hand." His Italian was grammatically correct but ever so singsong and unsteady.

"This is part of the police department and you've entered without authorization. If you want to help us, find a church and pray for our souls."

Pontiero started to walk toward the new arrival, in the spirit of inviting him to make his exit whether he wanted to or not. Dicanti had already turned back around to study the photographs when Fowler spoke again.

"It's from the Bible, the New Testament to be precise."

"What's that?" Pontiero was surprised.

Dicanti raised her head and looked at Fowler.

"Mind explaining yourself?"

"MT 16. The Gospel according to Matthew, chapter 16. Did he leave another note?"

Pontiero looked upset.

"Listen, Paola, you are not really going to get yourself involved with this guy—"

"We're listening."

Fowler stepped into the conference room. He carried a black overcoat draped on his arm, which he then laid over a chair.

"As everyone knows, the Christian New Testament is made up of four principal books, one for each of the Evangelists: Matthew, Mark, Luke, and John. In the Christian bibliography the book of Matthew is abbreviated MT. The number which follows represents the chapter. And the next two numbers indicate a citation in that chapter, between two verses."

"The killer left this."

Paola put piece of evidence number four, wrapped in plastic, in front of him. The priest studied it closely. He gave no indication that he recognized it, nor did the blood upset him. He simply looked it over thoroughly and then said:

"Nineteen. How appropriate."

Pontiero was just about to boil over.

"Are you going to tell us what you know now or are you going to make us wait around for it, Father?"

"*Et tibi dabo claves regni coelorum,*" Fowler recited. "*Et quodcumque ligaveris super terram, erit legatum et in coelis; et quodcumque solveris super terram, erit solutum et in coelis*. And I will give unto thee the keys of the kingdom of heaven; and whatsoever thou shalt bind on earth shall be bound in heaven; and whatever thou shalt loose on earth shall be loosed in heaven. Matthew 16, verse 19. That is to say, the words with which Jesus confirmed Peter as the leader of the Apostles, and awarded him and his successors power over the whole of Christendom."

"*Santa* Madonna," Dicanti said out loud.

"Considering what is just about to take place in this city, ladies and gentlemen, I think that you ought to be worried. Very worried."

"Shit, some vagabond who lost his marbles slits the throat of a priest and you're ready to sound the alarm. Doesn't sound so scary to me," said Pontiero.

"No, my friend. The killer isn't just a homeless person who's lost his mind. He's a cruel man, methodical and intelligent, and he's terribly conflicted. Take my word for it."

"Really? Seems like you know a good deal about what's motivating him, Father." Pontiero was mocking their visitor.

"I know much more than that, gentlemen. I know who he is."

✝

ARTICLE REPRINTED FROM THE DAILY MARYLAND GAZETTE

July 29, 1999, Page 7

AMERICAN PRIEST ACCUSED OF
SEXUAL ABUSE COMMITS SUICIDE

SACHEM PIKE, Maryland (wire service)—As the sexual abuse scandal continues to rock the Catholic Church in North America, a Connecticut priest accused of sexually abusing minors hung himself in his room at an institution for troubled clergy, according to a report police made to the American Press wire service last Friday.

Peter Selznick, 61 years old, relinquished his position as parish priest at Saint Andrews in Bridgeport, Connecticut, April 27 of last year, just one day after authorities in the Catholic Church interviewed two men who claimed Selznick abused them over the course of several years from the end of the 1970s to the early 1980s, according to a spokesman for the Bridgeport Diocese.

The priest was being treated at the Saint Matthew Institute in Maryland, a psychiatric center, which takes in members of the clergy accused of sexual abuse or with "problems in sexual orientation," according to a statement from the institution.

"Hospital personnel knocked on his door several times and attempted to enter his room, but something was blocking the door," Diane Richardson, Prince George police department spokesperson, stated at a press conference. "When they entered the room, they found the body hanging from one of the exposed beams in the ceiling."

Selznick hanged himself with a bed sheet, Richardson stated, adding that his body was taken to the mortuary for an autopsy. At the same time, she categorically denied rumors that the body was found nude and mutilated, rumors which she characterized as "completely unfounded." During the press conference, reporters cited "eyewitnesses" who stated that they had seen the mutilations. The spokeswoman stated that "a nurse who works for the County's medical team was under the influence of marijuana and other drugs when those declarations were made." This particular municipal employee has been suspended from his job without pay until his case is resolved. This newspaper made contact with the nurse who started the rumor, who refused to say anything further than a brief "I was wrong."

The Bishop of Bridgeport, William Lopes, stated that he was "profoundly saddened" by Selznick's "tragic" death, adding that the scandal which preoccupies the North American branch of the Catholic Church has "many victims."

Father Selznick was born in New York in 1938, and was ordained in Bridgeport in 1965. He served in various parishes in Connecticut and for a brief time worked as a priest at the parish of San Juan Vianney in Chiclayo, Peru.

"Every person, without exception, has dignity and value in the eyes of God, and everyone needs and deserves our compassion," Lopes stated. "The disturbing circumstances which surround his death cannot eradicate all the good that he did," the Bishop said in conclusion.

The Director of the Saint Matthew Institute, Father Canice Conroy, refused to speak to this publication. Father Anthony Fowler, director of New Initiatives at the Institute, apologized for the absence of a statement from the Director, explaining that Father Conroy was presently "in a state of shock."

✝

UACV HEADQUARTERS
Via Lamarmora, 3
Tuesday, April 5, 2005, 11:14 P.M.

Fowler's declaration was like a shot to the solar plexus. Dicanti and Pontiero were frozen in their tracks. They stared at the priest.

"May I sit down?"

"There are plenty of empty seats, " Paola said. "Take any one you like."

She made a sign to the staffer from Documents, who quickly left the room.

Fowler laid his small black suitcase down on the table, its edges scratched and frayed. The suitcase had seen a good part of the world, and its condition was a testament to the many miles its owner had carried it around. He opened it and took out a thick stack of papers from a cardboard carton whose edges were bent and coffee stained. He set the papers on the table and sat down across from the inspector. Dicanti watched him carefully, noting his economy of movement and the energy radiating from his green eyes. The question of where exactly this strange priest came from very much intrigued her, but she made a firm decision not to let herself be overwhelmed, much less on her own turf.

Pontiero grabbed a seat, spun it around, and sat to Fowler's left, his hands resting on the support. Dicanti made a mental note to remind him to knock off imitating old Bogart movies: Her second in command must have watched *The Maltese Falcon* three hundred times. If he considered someone suspicious, he inevitably sat to this person's left, compulsively smoking one Pall Mall nonfilter after another.

"Go ahead, Padre. But show us something that proves who you are."

Fowler took his passport out of his breast pocket and handed it to Pontiero. He made a gesture to show his displeasure at the cloud of smoke billowing from Pontiero's cigarette.

"I see, I see. A diplomatic passport. So you have immunity, eh? Who the hell are you? Some sort of spy?" Pontiero asked him.

"I am an official in the United States Air Force."

"Holding what rank?"

"Major. Would Detective Pontiero mind if I asked him to stop smoking right next to me? I gave it up years ago and have no desire to start all over again."

"He is addicted to tobacco, Major Fowler."

"Padre Fowler, Dr. Dicanti. I am . . . retired."

"Wait a second. How is it you know my name, or the *Ispettore's*?"

The specialist in criminal affairs smiled. She found herself both curious and entertained.

"Maurizio, I suspect that Padre Fowler is not so retired as he says."

Fowler returned Dicanti's smile, but with a tinge of sadness.

"I have recently gone back to active service, it's true. And strangely enough, the reason for that is the work I did in civilian life." He grew quiet, waving his hand to push the smoke away.

"And? So tell us, if you're so clever, who and where the son of a bitch is who did what you see here to a cardinal in the Holy Mother Church, so that we can all go home to bed."

The priest did not react, as unflappable as his starched collar. Paola suspected the man was simply too hardened to fall for Pontiero's little act. There was no doubt life had sown terrible trials in the creases on his skin, or that his eyes had confronted worse things than a small-time cop and his smelly tobacco.

"Enough, Maurizio. And kill the cigarette."

Pontiero threw the butt away. He was pissed.

"As you like, Padre Fowler," Paola said as she shuffled the photographs on the table, her eyes bearing down on the priest. "You've made it clear to me that, for now, you're in charge. You know something I don't, something I need to know. But you're in my neck of the woods, on my turf. It's up to you to say how this turns out."

"What do you say to starting off with a profile?"

"Can I ask you why?"

"Because in this case there's no need to create a profile in order to know who the killer is. I can tell you that. In this case we need a profile in order to know where to find him. And those are two different things."

"Is this an exam, Padre? Do you want to know exactly how good the person sitting across from you is? Are you going to be the judge of my deductive capacities, just like Troi?"

"I think that at this moment the only person judging you is you yourself."

Paola took a deep breath and mustered every bit of self-control to keep from shouting. Fowler had put his finger right in the wound. And just when she thought she was about to lose it, her boss showed up in the doorway. He stayed there without moving, carefully studying the priest, who looked back at him equally intently. Several seconds later, the two greeted each other with nods of the head.

"Padre Fowler."

"*Direttore* Troi."

"They let me know about your arrival by, shall we say, an unfamiliar channel. It goes without saying your presence here is an imposition, but I recognize that you can be of some use to us, if my sources are accurate."

"They are."

"Then please keep going."

From earliest childhood Paola had had the discomforting sensation she had arrived late to a world already under way, and at that instant the feeling returned. She was fed up with the fact that everyone there knew things she did not. She could ask Troi for an explanation when she got the chance later, but right now she decided to turn things to her advantage.

"Padre Fowler here has told Pontiero and myself that he knows the identity of the killer, but it seems he wants a free psychological profile before he reveals his name. It's my personal opinion that we're losing precious time, but I've decided to play along with his game."

She leapt to her feet, which staggered the three men who were watching her. She walked over to the blackboard that took up almost all of the back of the room and started to write.

"The killer is a white male, between the ages of thirty-eight and forty-six. He is of medium height, with a strong body, intelligent. His studies took him as far as the university, and he's gifted with languages. He is left-handed, he received a strict religious education, and he endured difficulties or abuse in his early life. He's immature, his work subjects him to pressure over and above his affective and psychological stability, and he suffers from an intense sexual repression. He most likely has a history of considerable violence. This isn't the first or even second time he has killed someone, and, obviously, it won't be the last. He thinks very, very little of us, the police, as much he does of as any of his victims. And now, Padre, why don't you give your killer a name?" Dicanti spun around and tossed the chalk into the priest's hands.

She glanced at her audience. Fowler watched her, a look of surprise on his face; Pontiero beamed; Troi remained the skeptic. Finally it was the priest who spoke up.

"Well done, *Dottoressa*. Ten out of ten. I may be a psychologist, but I can't figure out how you came to your conclusions. Could you explain a little further?"

"The profile is only provisional, but the conclusions should be somewhat close to reality. That he is a white male is shown by the profile of his victims, since it's very unusual for a serial killer to kill someone from a different race. That he's of medium height, since Robayra was tall and the angle and location of the cut in his neck indicate that someone about five feet nine inches tall took him by surprise. That he's strong is obvious; otherwise it would have been impossible for him to get the cardinal as far as the interior of the church, because even if he used a car to transport the body to the door, around back there is still a distance of some one hundred and thirty feet to the chapel. His immaturity is directly proportional to the thrill killer type: he has a profound disrespect for his victim, considers him an object; the same goes for the police: he considers them inferior beings."

Fowler interrupted her by politely raising his hand.

"Two details in particular grabbed my attention. First, you said that it's not the first time he committed murder. Did you deduce that from the involved handiwork at the scene of the crime?"

"Exactly. This person possesses a basic familiarity with police work. He's carried this off on more than one occasion. Experience tells me that the first time is very messy and spur of the moment."

"The second was when you said, 'His work subjects him to pressure over and above his affective and psychological stability.' I'm at a loss to explain how you came to that conclusion."

Dicanti, still standing, blushed. She crossed her arms and gave no answer. Troi took the opportunity to intervene.

"Ah, good old Paola. Her great intelligence always leaves a small crack for her feminine intuition to slip in, isn't that so? At times Dicanti arrives at purely emotional conclusions, Padre. I have no idea how. Of course, she would have a great future as a writer."

"More than you know. Because she hit the bull's-eye," said Fowler, getting up from his chair at last and striding toward the blackboard. "*Ispettore*, what is the correct name for your profession? Profiler, isn't that it?"

"Yes," Paola said, still embarrassed.

"When did you receive your degree as a profiler?"

"Once I had finished the course in Forensic Criminology and after a year of intensive studies at the FBI's Behavioral Sciences Division. Very few candidates manage to pass the entire course."

"Can you tell us how many qualified profilers exist in the world?"

"At present, twenty. Twelve in the United States, four in Canada, two in Germany, one in Italy, and one in Austria."

"Thanks. Is everyone clear on that, gentlemen? Only twenty people in the world are capable of drawing a psychological portrait of a serial killer with any kind of certainty, and one of them is in this room. And believe me, if we want to catch this man. . . ."

Fowler turned around and wrote a name on the blackboard in a large hand, with firm, thick letters:

VICTOR KAROSKY

". . . We are going to need someone capable of getting into his head.

"Now you have the name you asked me for. But before you race to the phone to bark out orders for his arrest, give me a chance to tell you everything else I know about him."

+

CORRESPONDENCE FROM
EDWARD DRESSLER, PSYCHIATRIST
TO CARDINAL FRANCIS CASEY
[Excerpts]

Boston
May 14, 1991

[. . .] Your Eminence, we no doubt find ourselves in the presence of a
born recidivist. From what I am told, this is the fifth time he has been
reassigned to a new parish. The tests we carried out over the course
of two weeks confirm that we cannot take the risk of sending him to
live in close proximity to young children without putting them in
danger. [. . .] By no means do I doubt his desire to repent, because it
is strong. But I doubt his ability to control himself. [. . .] We cannot
permit ourselves the luxury of having him in a parish. It would be
better if we clipped his wings before he loses all control. Otherwise, I
cannot hold myself responsible. I recommend a period of internment
of at least six months in the Saint Matthew Institute.

Boston
August 4, 1993

[. . .] I have tried for the third time with him [Karosky]. [. . .] I have
to say that the "fresh air" as you called it, when you moved him from
parish to parish, has not helped at all; rather the opposite. He is

beginning to lose control with greater frequency, and I detect strains of schizophrenia in his behavior. It is very possible that at some moment he will completely cross the line and become another person. Eminence, you know my devotion to the Church, and I understand the present overwhelming lack of priests but to lower the bar so very close to the ground! [. . .] 35 of these men have passed through my hands so far, Eminence, and I have seen, in some of them, the possibility that they might recover their autonomy [. . .] Karosky is definitely not one of those. Cardinal, only on rare occasions has Your Eminence followed my advice. I beg you to do so now: persuade Karosky to enter Saint Matthew's.

UACV HEADQUARTERS

Via Lamarmora, 3

Wednesday, April 6, 2005, 12:03 A.M.

Paola sat down, bracing herself to listen to what Fowler was going to say.

"1995 was when it all began, for me anyway. At that time, after I'd retired from the Air Force, I worked under the direction of my bishop. He wanted to make use of my training in psychology to send me to the Saint Matthew Institute. Anybody heard of it?"

All three answered in the negative.

"I'm not surprised. The very existence of the institution is a secret to a majority of the informed public in North America. It officially consists of a residence center set up to attend to priests and nuns with 'problems,' located in Sachem Pike, Maryland. The reality is that ninety-five percent of its patients have a history of sexual abuse of minors or problems with the consumption of drugs. The Institute's facilities are without question luxurious: thirty-five rooms for the patients, nine for the medical personnel (nearly all interns), a tennis court, two paddleball courts, a pool, recreation room with billiard table . . ."

"Sounds more like a health resort than a psychiatric institution," Pontiero interjected.

"Well, the place is a mystery on many levels. It is a mystery to the outside world and a mystery to those who live there, who at first see it as a place where they can retire for several months, where they can rest, although little by little they discover that it is something very different. All of you know the enormous problem the Church in my country has had with certain Catholic priests over the last few years. From the point of view of public opinion, it wouldn't be well received that persons who have been accused of sexual abuse with minors were celebrating paid vacations in a luxury hotel."

"And they were getting away with it?" asked Pontiero, who seemed very affected by the subject, perhaps on account of his two children, both of them teenagers.

"No. I'll try to recount my experience there in the most succinct form possible. Upon my arrival I found a profoundly secular place. It didn't look like a religious institution: no crucifixes on the wall, none of the members of the various orders wore habits or robes. I've spent many nights in the open air, on an expedition or at the front, and I never took my clerical collar off. But everyone there came and went just as they pleased. Faith and self-control were obviously in short supply."

"And you never communicated this to anyone?" Dicanti asked.

"Of course. The first thing I did was to write a letter to the bishop responsible for that parish. He accused me of being too influenced by my time in the armed forces, by the 'rigidity of the military atmosphere.' He advised me to be more 'adaptable.' Those were tricky times for me; my career in the Air Force was a roller-coaster ride. I have no intention of getting into that; it has nothing to do with the case at hand. I'll just say that I had no desire to add to my reputation for being intransigent."

"You don't have to justify yourself."

"I know, but I've got a bad conscience about what happened there. They cured neither minds nor souls in that institution; they simply gave their patients a little push in the direction of least resistance. What took place there was exactly the opposite of what the diocese hoped would happen."

"I don't follow," said Pontiero.

"Nor do I," Troi chimed in.

"It's complicated. To begin with, the only psychiatrist with a university degree on staff at the center was Father Conroy, at that time the Institute's director. None of the others had graduate university training beyond nursing school or a technical degree. And they were allowed the luxury of making psychiatric evaluations!"

"Insane." Dicanti was amazed.

"Completely. The one endorsement you had to have to get hired was to belong to Dignity, an organization which promotes the priesthood for women and sexual freedom for male priests. I personally do not agree with them about anything, but . . . it's not my place to judge. What I can do is make some estimate of the professional capacity of the personnel, and that was very, very wanting."

"I don't see where all this is taking us," Pontiero said, lighting another cigarette.

"Five minutes more and you will. As I was saying, Father Conroy, a great friend of Dignity and very liberal when it came to people's inner life, managed Saint Matthew in a completely erratic manner. Honest priests arrived there, men confronted with baseless accusations, and thanks to Conroy they relinquished the priesthood that had been the light of their lives. Others he urged not to struggle against their nature but to simply live life. He considered it a success when a religious person gave up his or her vows and began a homosexual relationship."

"And you see that as a problem?" asked Dicanti.

"No, not if the person really wants it or needs it. But the patients' needs didn't matter to Conroy in the slightest. First, he established his objective and then he applied it to the person, without any prior knowledge of him or her at all. He played God with the hearts and minds of those men and women, some of them with terrible conflicts. And then he washed it all down with a fine single malt. Washed it down well."

"Good Lord," said Pontiero, feigning being scandalized.

"Take my word for it: He was not on the premises. But that was not the worst. Owing to grave errors in the selection of candidates, many young men in my country who were unfit to be the shepherds of men's souls entered Catholic seminaries during the seventies and eighties. They weren't even fit to take care of their own souls. It's a fact. With time, many of these young men gave up the cloth. They did a great deal of damage to the good name of the Catholic Church and, what is worse, to many children and young men. Many priests accused of sexual abuse, guilty of sexual abuse, never went to jail. They disappeared from view; they were moved from parish to parish. And some of them finally ended up at Saint Matthew. Once there, and with a bit of luck, they were directed towards civilian life. Shamefully, many returned to the ministry when they should have been behind bars. Tell me, *Dottoressa* Dicanti, what sort of chances are there for the rehabilitation of a serial killer?"

"Absolutely none at all. Once he crosses the line, there's no way to bring him back."

"It's the same for a compulsive pedophile. Sadly, the unambiguous certainty you possess does not exist in our field. They know that they have a monster within reach, someone who must be caught and caged. But it is much more difficult for the therapist who works with the pedophile to know if he has crossed the line for good or not. I know of only one case where I never had the slightest doubt. And that was a case where, beneath the pedophilia, there was something else."

"Let me guess: Victor Karosky. Our killer."

"The same."

Troi cleared his throat before interrupting. An irritating habit, which he repeated every so often.

"Padre Fowler, would you be so kind as to explain to us why you are so sure that this is the man who has torn Robayra and Portini to pieces?"

"Certainly. Karosky turned up at the Institute in August 1994. He had been moved around various parishes, with his superior shunting the problem from one place to the other. In every one of them there were complaints, some more serious than others, although none of an extremely violent nature. According to the testimony we collected, we believe he abused eighty-nine children in all, although the number could be higher."

"Fuck."

"You said it, Pontiero. Look, the root of Karosky's problems is located in his childhood. He was born in Katowice, Poland, in 1961. There—"

"Hold on, Padre. He is forty-four years old now?"

"That is correct. He stands five feet eight and a half inches tall and weighs one hundred eighty-seven pounds. He has a strong build, and IQ testing reveals an intelligence between 110 and 125, depending on when he took the test. He took seven in all at the Institute. He found them entertaining."

"Pretty high IQ."

"You are a psychiatrist, while I studied psychology and was never an especially brilliant student. I encountered the most extreme psychopaths too late to read the subject's bibliography. So tell me: is it true that serial killers are extremely intelligent?"

Paola smiled, half-ironically, and glanced at Pontiero, who looked at her with the same expression.

"I think that the detective here can respond more forcefully to the question."

"'Hannibal Lecter does not exist and Jodie Foster should stick to costume dramas.' Dicanti says it all the time."

Everyone laughed, not because the joke was funny but simply to let some of the tension out of the room.

"Thanks, Pontiero. Padre, the popular figure of the super-psychopath is a myth fashioned from the novels and the movies. In real life, someone like that does not exist. There have been serial killers with high IQs and others with low IQs. The big difference between the two is that the ones with the high IQs tend to carry out their crimes over a longer period of time because they are more cautious. What without a doubt the academics all agree on is the serial killer's great talent for killing people."

"And among those who aren't academics?"

"Outside the academy, I've noticed that some of these bastards are more clever than Satan himself. Not intelligent but clever. And there are some, a minority, who have a high IQ, an innate aptitude for their despicable task and for dissimulation. And in one case and one case only until now do these three characteristics exist in a criminal who was also a person of great culture. I'm talking about Ted Bundy."

"A well-known case in my country. He strangled and then sodomized something like thirty women with a tire iron."

"Thirty-six. That we know about," Paola corrected him. She remembered the Bundy case in great detail, in as much as it was required study material in Quantico.

Fowler nodded sadly.

"As I was saying, Victor Karosky came into the world in 1961 in Katowice, ironically just a few kilometers from where Karol Wojtyla was born. In 1969, the Karosky family, composed of himself, his parents, and two brothers, emigrated to the United States. His father found work in the General Motors plant in Detroit, and according to all the records, he was a good worker but very hard to handle. In 1972, there was a cutback owing to the gas crisis, and Karosky senior was the first worker out the door. The father had by then received his American citizenship, so he made himself comfortable in the tiny apartment he shared with his family, drinking up the severance pay and the unemployment insurance. He really went at it, gave himself over to the task. He became another person, and he started to sexually abuse Victor and his older brother. The brother's name was Beria. When he was fourteen years old, he walked out of the house one day and never came back."

"Karosky told you all this?" Dicanti asked, intrigued and puzzled at the same time.

"Only after intense regression therapy. When he arrived at the Institute, his story was that he came from a model Catholic family."

Paola, writing everything down in the tiny script of a public worker, rubbed her eyes with her hand. She wanted to dislodge every speck of exhaustion before she started talking.

"What you are telling us fits perfectly into the common registers of first-level psychopaths: personal charm, absence of irrational thinking, a lack of trustworthiness and of remorse, a great talent for dissimulation. The blows from his father and the general consumption of alcohol by his parents have also been observed in more than seventy-four percent of known violent psychopaths."

"So it's the probable cause?" Fowler asked.

"More likely it's one determinant among many. I can cite thousands of cases of people who were brought up in chaotic households much worse than the one you've described and they've advanced in life to a relatively normal maturity, if such a thing actually exists."

"Hold on. We've barely scratched the surface. Karosky told us about the death of his younger brother in 1974, from meningitis, without anyone paying much attention to the fact. I was greatly surprised by how cool he was when he related that particular episode. Two months after the child died, the father mysteriously disappeared. Victor never explained whether he had something to do with the disappearance, although we did not think so, since he was only thirteen years old. But we do know that it was at this time that he began to torture small animals. Still, the worst thing for him was to remain at the mercy of an overbearing mother, obsessed with religion, who even went so far as to dress him up as a girl so they could 'play together.' It seems like she fondled him under his skirt, and was accustomed to telling young Victor that she would cut his 'little packages' so his disguise would be complete. The result: Karosky still wet the bed at fifteen years old. He wore discount clothes, out of fashion or torn—they were, after all, poor. At school he had to undergo insults and was very isolated. . . . One time in high school a friend made an unfortunate comment about Karosky's attire as they passed in the corridor. Karosky, furious, beat the other kid in the face repeatedly with a heavy textbook. The kid wore glasses and the lenses shattered in his eyes. He was left sightless."

"The eyes . . . just like the cadavers. So that was his first violent crime."

"As far as we know, yes. Victor was sent to a reformatory outside Boston, and the last thing his mother said to him before waving good-bye was 'I should have had an abortion.' A few months later she committed suicide."

The room was utterly silent. Words were beside the point.

"Karosky stayed at the reformatory until the end of 1979. We have no information for that year, but in 1980 he entered a seminary in Baltimore. Application forms for his entrance to the seminary stated that his record was clean and that he came from a traditionally Catholic family. He was nineteen years old by then, and it seemed that he had been reformed. We know almost nothing of his stay in the seminary, except that he studied until he fainted and that he was profoundly sickened by the institution's openly homosexual environment. Conroy insisted that Karosky was a repressed homosexual who denied his true nature, but he was wrong. Karosky is neither a homosexual nor a heterosexual. He has no definite orientation. The fact that sex is not an integrated part of his personality is what, from my point of view, has caused such grave injury to his psyche."

"Care to explain yourself?" Pontiero asked.

"I may as well. I am a priest who made the decision to remain celibate. That doesn't stop me from being attracted to *Dottoressa* Dicanti," said Fowler, gesturing toward Paola, who was unable to keep from turning red. "I know I am heterosexual, but I choose chastity of my own free will. I've integrated sexuality into my personality, although in such a way that I do not exercise it. Karosky's case is very different. The profound traumas of his infancy and childhood provoked a split down the middle of his psyche. Karosky clearly rejected the part of his being that is sexual and even violent. He both hates and loves himself, simultaneously, and it crops up in outbreaks of violence, schizophrenia, and finally in the abuse of minors, duplicating his father's abuses. In 1986, during his pastoral year, Karosky had his first incident with a minor. The victim was a young kid, fourteen years old, and there were kisses and petting, nothing else. We believe the minor did not consent to it. In any case, there's no official proof the bishop heard about this episode, because in the end he ordained Karosky as a priest. From that day on he had an insane obsession with his hands. He washes them between thirty and forty times a day and takes exceptional care of them."

Pontiero searched hurriedly among the hundreds of macabre photographs spread over the desk until he found the one he was searching for and spun it in the air to Fowler. The priest made an effortless two-fingered catch, an elegant move that Paola quietly admired.

"Two hands, severed and washed, placed on white canvas. White canvas is, in the Church, a symbol of respect and reverence. There are many references to it in the New Testament. As you know, Christ in his sepulchre was covered with a white canvas."

"It's not quite so white now," Troi said in jest.

"I'm sure you would be delighted to apply your gadgets to the canvas in question," Pontiero commented.

"No doubt about that. Continue, Fowler."

"A priest's hands are sacred. With them he administers the sacraments. That stayed very firmly in Karosky's mind, as we'll see. In 1987 he worked at a school in Pittsburgh, where his first abuses took place. His victims were young men between the ages of eight and eleven. He is unfamiliar with any type of adult consensual relationship, homosexual or heterosexual. When the complaints began to reach his superiors, they at first did nothing. Later they transferred him, parish to parish. Very soon there was a complaint of an attack on an altar boy, whom he struck in the face without any lasting consequences. . . . And finally he arrived at the Institute."

"Do you think that if they had begun to help him earlier on things would have turned out differently?"

Fowler, his whole body tense, made an irritated gesture with his hands.

"We never helped him in the slightest. The only thing we achieved was to liberate the killer lurking inside of Karosky. And then at last we made it possible for him to escape."

"It was that bad?"

"Worse. When he arrived, he was a man overwhelmed, as much by his uncontrolled emotions as by his violent outbursts. He had remorse for his actions, although he denied it many times. He simply was unable to control himself. But with the passage of time, the wrongheaded treatments, and his close contact with the dregs of the priesthood who lived alongside him at the Institute, Karosky became something much worse. He turned cold and ironic. The remorse disappeared. As you can see, the most anguished memories from his childhood were blocked out. That alone turned him into a pederast. But with the help of disastrous regression therapies—"

"Why disastrous?"

"It would have been better if the objective had been to bring a bit of peace to the patient's mind. But I greatly fear that Dr. Conroy felt a morbid curiosity for Karosky's case, reaching to immoral extremes. In similar cases, what the hypnotizer tries to do is to implant, in an artificial manner, positive events in the memory of the patient, urging him to let go of the worst things that happened. Conroy prohibited that line of action. Not only did he record Karosky, he forced him to listen to the tapes in which, in a falsetto voice, he begged his mother to leave him in peace."

"What sort of Mengele did they have running that place?" Paola was in shock.

"Conroy was convinced that Karosky had to accept himself. According to him, it was the only solution. He had to recognize that he'd had a hard childhood and that he was homosexual. As I told you before, he created his diagnosis in advance and afterwards was determined to squeeze the patient into it with a shoehorn. To top it all off, he subjected Karosky to a hormonal cocktail, much of it experimental, like a variant of the anti-contraceptive Depo-Covetan. With this drug, injected in abnormal doses, Conroy reduced Karosky's level of sexual response while he strengthened his aggressiveness. The therapy went on and on, without positive results. There were periods in which he calmed down, but just that, periods, and Conroy interpreted that as a sign of success for his therapy. By the end he'd produced a chemical castration. Karosky is incapable of having an erection, and that frustration is destroying him."

"When did you first come into contact with him?"

"I spoke with him frequently after I arrived at the Institute, in 1995. Between us we established a relationship with a certain level of confidence, which collapsed later on, as I'll tell you in a minute. But I would rather not get ahead of myself. You see, fifteen days after his arrival at the Institute, they decided to give Karosky a penile plethysmograph. That's a test where an apparatus is attached to the penis by means of electrodes. Said apparatus measures the sexual response to distinct stimuli."

"I'm familiar with that test," Paola said, like someone who had just heard about an outbreak of the Ebola virus.

"So you see . . . He took it very badly. During the session they showed him terrible images, things beyond the pale."

"Meaning?"

"Things related to pedophilia."

"Fuck."

"Karosky reacted violently, and gravely wounded the specialist running the machine. The attendants were able to restrain him; otherwise he would have killed the guy. In the wake of that episode Conroy should have recognized that he was in no condition to be treated and should have sent him off to a mental hospital. But he never did so. He hired two security muscles, and ordered them not to take their eyes off Karosky, while he started subjecting him to regression therapy. That coincided with my arrival at the Institute. As the months went by, Karosky was withdrawing into himself. His outbursts of anger disappeared. Conroy attributed it to significant changes in his personality. They lifted the watch on him a bit. And one night, Karosky forced the lock on his room."

"He was locked in?"

"They were in the habit of locking his room from the outside at certain hours, as a precautionary measure."

"And what happened then?"

"He lopped off the hands of a priest who lived in the same wing. He told everyone that the priest was an impure man whom he had seen touching another priest in an 'improper' manner. While the guards ran towards the cell where the priest was howling in pain, Karosky was cleaning his victim's hands under the nozzle of the shower."

"The same modus operandi. As far as I'm concerned, that removes the last shred of doubt," Paola said.

"To my amazement and even fury, Conroy failed to report the incident to the police. The mutilated priest received compensation, and a team of doctors in California managed to reattach his hands, although with far less maneuverability. And in the middle of all this, Conroy ordered security reinforced and built a six-by-ten-foot isolation cell. This was where Karosky lived until he escaped from the Institute. Session after session, therapy group after therapy group, Conroy was failing and Karosky was evolving into the monster he is today. I wrote several letters to the cardinal, explaining the problem. I never received an answer. In 1999, Karosky escaped from his cell and committed his first known murder: Father Peter Selznick."

"We heard about him here. It was said to be a suicide."

"Not true. Karosky escaped from his cell by forcing the lock with a ballpoint pen and he then used a metal shank he had sharpened in his cell to cut out Selznick's tongue and lips. He also sliced off Selznick's penis and forced him to eat it. Selznick hung on for three hours before he died, and nobody knew about it until the next morning."

"What did Conroy say?"

"He officially defined the episode as a 'setback.' He managed to cover it up, by coercing the county judge and the sheriff to issue a ruling of suicide."

"And they went along with it? Just like that?" Pontiero asked.

"They were both Catholics. I think Conroy manipulated them by appealing to their duty to protect the Church. But even if he hated to admit it, my boss was in fact very much afraid. He watched as Karosky's mind slipped out of his control, as if day by day it was absorbing his will. In spite of that, he refused on repeated occasions to report the incidents to a higher level, no doubt for fear of losing his position. I wrote more letters to the archdiocese but they turned a blind eye. I talked with Karosky and never encountered even a trace of remorse, and finally I realized he had become someone else completely. He broke off contact. That was the last time I spoke to him. I am not going to lie: the beast locked up in that cell scared me. And Karosky stayed right where he was, at the Institute. They set up cameras, hired more guards. Until one night in June 2000, he disappeared. Just like that."

"And Conroy? How did he react?"

"He was traumatized. He drank even more. On the third week his liver gave out and he died. A pity."

"I wouldn't go that far," Pontiero said.

"We're better off leaving him in peace. I ran the Institute on a temporary basis while they looked for a suitable replacement. The archdiocese never trusted me, I suppose on account of my continual complaints about my superior. I was in charge for barely a month, but I made the most of it. I restructured the staff as quickly as I could, hired professional personnel, and drew up new programs for the patients. Many of those changes were never put in place, but others were, so the effort was worth the trouble. I sent a concise report to an old contact of mine at VICAP by the name of Kelly Sanders. The suspect's profile and Selznick's unpunished murder greatly disturbed her. She put an agent on the job of bringing Karosky in. Came up with nothing."

"That's it? He just disappeared?" Paola had a hard time believing it.

"Disappeared into thin air. In 2001 it was thought he had resurfaced, after there was a murder with partial mutilation in Albany, New York. But it wasn't him. Most people gave him up for dead, but fortunately someone logged his profile into the computer. I found a job at a soup kitchen at a charity in Spanish Harlem in New York City. I worked there for several years, until just a few days ago. An old boss contacted me on behalf of the service, and I thought I was going to be a military chaplain a second time. I was informed that there appeared to be signs that Karosky had gone back to work after his long silence. So here I am. I brought you a dossier with the pertinent documentation I pulled together on Karosky in the five years I worked with him."

Fowler let the heavy file, almost six inches thick, flop onto the table.

"There are e-mails relating to the hormone I told you about, transcriptions of his interviews, an article in a magazine where he's mentioned, letters from psychiatrists, reports . . . It is all yours, Dr. Dicanti. You can ask me about anything in there."

Paola stretched her hand across the table to pick up the thick pile of papers, and she had just opened it when she felt terribly uneasy. Attached with a clip to the first page of the dossier was a photograph of Karosky. He had pale white skin, straight brown hair, gray eyes. In the years she had spent dedicated to studying those empty husks, void of human sentiment, that are serial killers, she had learned to recognize the vacant look behind the predator's eyes. They were men who killed as naturally as they ate a meal. There is only one thing in nature remotely similar to that look, and those are the eyes of the white shark. They look without seeing, in a terrifying manner. There is nothing else like them.

And there it was, fully reflected in Karosky's eyes.

"Shocking, no?" said Fowler, studying Paola with his eyes. "This man has something in his bearing, in his motions. Something indefinable. At first he passes unnoticed, but when, how shall I put it, his entire personality is on fire . . . it's terrible."

"And captivating, no?"

"Yes."

Dicanti passed the photograph to Pontiero and to Troi, both of whom leaned over at the same time to get a better look at the killer's face.

"What scares you more, Padre, physical danger or to look that man directly in the eyes and feel yourself scrutinized, stripped, as if he were a member of a superior race who had broken with all our conventions?"

Fowler stared at the photo a second time. His mouth was slightly open.

"My guess is that you know the answer already."

"Over the course of my career I've had the opportunity to interview three serial killers. All three produced the sensation in me I just described and others, much stronger than both you and I, have felt it, too. But it is a bogus sensation. Never forget one thing: Those men are failures, not prophets. Human waste. They do not deserve the least iota of compassion."

✝

REPORT ON THE SYNTHETIC PROGESTATIONAL HORMONE 1789

(injectable progestin class)
Commercial name: Depo-Covetan
Report classification: Confidential, encrypted

To: Marcus.Bietghofer@beltzer-hogan.com
From: Lorna.Barr@beltzer-hogan.com
CC: filesys@beltzer-hogan.com
Subject: CONFIDENTIAL: Report 45 on HPS 1789
Date: March 17, 1997, 11:43 a.m.
Attachment: Inf#45_HPS1789.pdf

Dear Marcus:

Attached you'll find an advance copy of the report you asked about.

The analysis carried out in the ALFA-area field studies has shown serious irregularities in menstrual fluid, sleep disruption, vertigo, and possible internal hemorrhaging. The report describes serious cases of hypertension, thrombosis, and cardiac disease. There has also been an increase in a specific minor ailment: 1.3% of the patients have developed fibromyalgia, a secondary effect for which tests were not carried out in the previous version.

If you compare the report with that of version 1786, which we are marketing in the United States and Europe, secondary effects have been reduced 3.9%. If our risk analysis isn't far off, we can estimate a maximum of $53 million dollars will be spent in legal damages. Therefore, we are staying within our guidelines, that is to say, an amount less than 7% of profits.

No, don't thank me . . . just give me a raise!

By the way, test results have reached the laboratory on the use of 1789 with male patients, with the goal of repressing or eliminating their sexual response. In the program, dosages sufficient to effect chemical castration were administered. From the reports and analyses examined by this laboratory, increases in the volatility of the subject in specific instances can be clearly seen, as can particular anomalies in cerebral activity. Our recommendation is to extend the bounds of the study in order to clarify the percentage of said secondary effect's appearance. It would be interesting to undertake tests with Omega subjects, such as persons whose mental capabilities are beyond hope, or prisoners on death row.

I would be happy to be in charge of those tests.

So are we going out for lunch this Friday? I've found a great little restaurant in the Village that serves absolutely divine bass from Chile.

Regards,
Dr. Lorna Barr
Research Director

✝

UACV HEADQUARTERS
Via Lamarmora, 3
Wednesday, April 6, 2005, 1:25 A.M.

Paola's harsh language silenced the room. No one said a word. The long day and the early morning hour weighed heavily on everyone and were clearly visible in everyone's eyes. It was Troi who finally spoke up.

"Tell us what to do, Dicanti."

Paola hesitated thirty seconds before she answered.

"I know it's been a long day. Let's all go home and sleep a few hours. We'll meet back here at eight-thirty this morning. Our first order of business will be the places where the victims were killed. We are going to comb through the settings, with the hope that the agents Pontiero sent into the field came up with some evidence, no matter how ridiculous that hope is. And Pontiero, call Dante and tell him when we're meeting."

"It'll be a pleasure," he answered caustically.

Acting as if she hadn't heard anything, Dicanti walked over to Troi and touched him on the arm.

"I would like to speak with you in private for a minute."

"Let's step out to the hall."

Paola exited the room in front of the older scientist, who, as always, played the part of the gallant, opening the door for her and closing it behind him. Dicanti detested her boss's deferential manner.

"So tell me."

"What exactly is Fowler's role in this investigation? I fail to understand it, and I have no faith whatsoever in his vague explanations for why he is here."

"Dicanti, have you ever heard the name John Negroponte?"

"I'm really sleepy. Some Italian-American?"

"My God, Paola, get your nose out of the criminology books every once in a while and read a newspaper. Yes, he's American, but his family was Greek. To cut to the chase, he was recently named national director of intelligence for the U.S. He's in charge of all the various agencies in the American government: the NSA, the CIA, the DEA, etcetera, etcetera. What I'm trying to say is that this man, who most certainly is a Catholic, is one of the most powerful people in the American government. Well, then, Mr. Negroponte personally called me this morning while we were with Robayra, and we had a nice, long conversation. He informed me that Fowler flew directly from Washington in order to join the investigation. He gave me no choice in the matter. It's not just a question of the fact that President Bush himself is in Rome and everyone is therefore on guard. These are Negroponte's exact words: 'I am sending you one of my closest collaborators, and we're lucky because he knows this case top to bottom.'"

"How did they find out so fast?" asked Paola, who stared at the ground, dumbfounded by the magnitude of what she was hearing.

"Ah, my dear Paola, never underestimate Camilo Cirin for even a moment. When the second victim turned up, he personally called Negroponte. According to what Negroponte told me, they had never even spoken before, and he hadn't the faintest idea how Cirin got his hands on a phone number that was only in existence for the last two weeks."

"And how did Negroponte know who to send so quickly?"

"That's no mystery. Fowler's friend in VICAP interpreted Karosky's last words before he fled Saint Matthew as an implicit threat against the persons in the Church, and as such they were communicated to the Vigilanza five years ago. When they found Robayra's body this morning, Cirin broke his own rule about washing dirty laundry in house. He made some calls and pulled the threads together. He's a well-connected son of a bitch, with contacts at the highest level. But I guess you are finding that out for yourself, my dear."

"I have a vague idea," Dicanti said, with a strong dose of irony.

"He told me, over and over again, that there is a personal interest in this case at the very highest levels of government."

"Oh, God. We're not going to have a support team this time, are we?"

"Answer that one on your own."

Dicanti was silent. If the priority was to keep the matter secret, she would have to work with what she had. Just that.

"You don't think I'm in a little bit over my head with all this?" In fact, Dicanti was extremely tired and even overwhelmed by the whole situation surrounding the case. She'd never experienced anything like it, and for a long time after she regretted letting those words slip out.

Troi's fingers stroked his chin. He forced Dicanti to look directly at him.

"We're all in a little bit over our heads, *bambina*. But let all of that go. Just focus on the fact that there's a monster killing people. And your job is hunting monsters."

Paola smiled. She was grateful and she wanted him again, one last time, right there, even though she knew it was a mistake and it would break her heart. Luckily for her, the feeling was extremely short-lived. She made an effort to recover her composure as quickly as she could. She was hoping he hadn't noticed.

"I worry that Fowler may stir up things around us during the investigation. He could be an obstacle."

"Could be. And he could also be of great use. The man was enlisted in the Air Force and is a consummate marksman. Among his other . . . talents. Not to mention the fact that he has a thorough knowledge of our suspect and is a priest. He'll be useful to you in moving around in a world you're not accustomed to, in the same way Dante will. Think about it like this: our Vatican colleague will open the doors for you, and Fowler, the minds."

"Dante is an insufferable asshole."

"I know. And also a necessary evil. All of our suspect's potential victims are in his country. Although we're only a few feet away from him, it's his territory."

"It's still Italy, which is ours. What they did with Portini was illegal, acting without us. An obstruction of justice."

The cynic in Troi shrugged his shoulders.

"What would we have gained by reporting it? We would have made new enemies, that's all. Forget about politics and whether they do something embarrassing. Right now we need Dante. As you already know, he's part of your team."

"You're the boss."

"And you're my favorite *ispettore*. Anyway, I'm going home to rest awhile. Tomorrow morning I'll be in the laboratory, running tests on every last fiber they bring me. I'll let you build your castles in the air."

Troi was already walking down the hallway when he suddenly stopped in his tracks, turned around and gave her a piercing look.

"One more little thing. Negroponte wants us to catch this son of a bitch. He asked me as a personal favor. You follow? Don't for a second doubt that I'll be overjoyed to see he owes us one."

✝

DICANTI FAMILY APARTMENT
Via della Croce, 12
Wednesday, April 6, 2005, 1:59 A.M.

"Keep the change."

"*Molto generoso*. Thanks for the big tip."

Paola ignored the driver's attempt at humor. It was the kind of crass remark you became accustomed to in the city, where even the cabdriver insulted you when his tip was a mere sixty cents. In lira that would have been . . . Enough. More than enough. Definitely. And to top it off, the cretin had his foot on the accelerator before she was even out of the cab. A gentleman would have waited until she was inside the door to her house. Two in the morning and the street was deserted, for God's sake.

It was already warm by that time of the year, but Paola shivered as she opened the front door. Was that a shadow at the end of the street? No, it was just her imagination. She was certain of it.

She pulled the door closed quickly behind her, thinking herself ridiculous for being so overcome with fear. She hurried up the three flights to her apartment, the wooden stairs groaning with every step. And yet she barely heard it: the blood was pounding in her ears and she was gasping for air when she arrived at her door. But once she had arrived, she stopped, riveted to the spot.

The door to the apartment was half-open.

Slowly, carefully, she opened her jacket and slipped her right hand under the arm of her coat. She pulled her pistol out of its holster and went into a crouch, her elbow at a sharp angle to her body. She pushed the door open with one hand as she stepped slowly into the apartment. The hallway light was on. She took one cautious step toward the interior and then moved away from the door, pointing the pistol at empty space.

Nothing.

"Paola?"

"Mamma?"

"Come on in. I'm in the kitchen."

Paola took a deep breath and holstered the gun. It was the first time in her life she had taken a pistol out in a real situation. She had done it at the FBI Academy but . . . This case was definitely making her too nervous.

Lucrezia Dicanti was in the kitchen, spreading butter on biscuits. The buzzer on the microwave went off, and with the door open, she removed two steaming cups of milk. She placed them on a small Formica table. Paola took a look around the room. Her heart was still pounding. Everything was where it should be: the little plastic pig with the wooden spoons in its back, the brightly colored wall paint that they themselves had put on, the lingering aroma of oregano in the air. She supposed her mother had made cannolis, and she also suspected that her mother had eaten all of them, which was why she was offering her cookies.

"Have a few. I can put more butter on if you want."

"Heavens, Mamma, you nearly scared me to death. Could you tell me why you left the door open?"

She was almost shouting. Her mother looked at her, concern written across her face. She removed a paper towel from the pocket of her dressing gown and used it to brush the tips of her fingers, removing the last traces of butter.

"I was up, listening to everything going on from the terrace. All of Rome is spinning around, mad with suspense about the next pope. The radio talks about nothing else. I decided to stay up for you, and then I saw you get out of the taxi. I'm sorry."

Paola instantly felt bad and apologized to her mother.

"Calm down, young lady. Have a cookie."

"Thanks, Mamma."

The younger woman sat down next to her mother, whose eyes never strayed from her daughter. From when Paola was a little girl, Lucrezia had been adept at perceiving her trials and tribulations and how best to advise her about them. But now her daughter's head was spinning with a problem that was too heavy, too complex, too too much. She didn't even know if such an expression existed.

"It's something on your job?"

"You know I can't talk about it."

"I know, and I also know that when you have that face, which looks like someone stepped on your corns, you're going to go through the whole night tossing and turning. Sure you don't want to tell me anything?"

Paola stared at the glass of milk on the table, ladling spoon after spoon of sugar into it as she spoke.

"It's just . . . It's another case, Mamma, but this one comes complete with crazy people. I feel like this damned glass of milk, which someone keeps spooning sugar into. The sugar never dissolves, it just makes the glass overflow."

Lucrezia tenderly put her open hand over the glass, and Paola poured a spoonful of sugar into her mother's hand.

"Sometimes it helps if you share."

"I can't, Mamma. Sorry."

"That's all right, my little dove. I understand. Do you want another cookie? I know you haven't eaten a thing." Her mother knew when it was wise to change the subject.

"No, Mamma, these are more than enough. My breadbasket is already bigger than the Coliseum."

"My daughter happens to have a very pretty ass."

"Right. Which explains why I'm still single."

"No, Paola. You are still single because you have a bad temper. You are pretty, you take care of yourself, you go to the gym. . . . It's just a matter of time before you meet a man who isn't scared off by your loud voice and your nasty faces."

"I don't believe that's ever going to happen, Mamma."

"And why not? What about your boss, the charming one?"

"He's married. And he's old enough to be my father."

"You love to exaggerate. Bring him to me, and you'll see I don't turn him off. Besides, in today's world, being married isn't as important as it used to be."

If you only knew, Paola thought to herself. "You really believe that, Mamma?"

"I'm convinced. Madonna but he has such lovely hands! I'd like to dance between the sheets with that one. . . ."

"Mamma! Sometimes you really shock me!"

"Since your father left us ten years ago, not a single day has passed without memories of him. Still, I don't think I'm like those Sicilian widows, dressed in black head to toe, pouring our their hearts at their husband's graves. Go on, have another and we'll go to bed."

Paola dipped another cookie in her milk, mentally calculating the calories and feeling very guilty. Lucky for her, the sensation was a fleeting one.

✝

CORRESPONDENCE FROM
CARDINAL FRANCIS CASEY
TO MRS. EDWINA MACDOUGAL

Boston
February 23, 1999

Dear Mrs. MacDougal,

In response to your letter of February 17th of this year, I want to state my concern [. . .] I respect and regret your sadness and that of your son Harry. I am conscious of the tremendous anguish and tremendous suffering he has gone through. I agree with you that when a man of God falls into sin as Father Karosky did, it shakes a person's faith to its foundations. I acknowledge my error. I should never have reassigned Father Karosky . . . Perhaps on the third occasion when the faithful, such as yourself, came to me with their complaints, I ought to have taken a different road [. . .] I was poorly advised by the psychiatrists who reviewed his case; those like Doctor Dressler, who put his professional reputation on the line when he asserted that Karosky was fit for the ministry. I went along [. . .]

I can only hope that the generous compensation we have agreed to with your lawyer has brought a measure of satisfaction to all parties [. . .] It is more than we can afford [. . .] Without, however, of course attempting to mitigate your pain with money, if I may permit myself to advise you not to speak of the case, for everyone's good [...] our Holy Mother Church has already suffered terrible calumnies at the hands of the wicked and the Satanic media [...] For the benefit of our small community, for that of your son, and for you yourself, let us act as if this had never occurred.

I bestow my blessings upon you.

Francis Casey
Cardinal
Archdiocese of Boston

THE SAINT MATTHEW INSTITUTE

Sachem Pike, Maryland

November 1995

Transcription of Interview #45 Between

Patient No. 3643 and Doctor Canice Conroy,

with the Assistance of

Doctor Anthony Fowler and Sahler Fanabarzra

Dr. Conroy: Hello, Victor. May we enter?

No. 3643: Certainly, Doctor. It's your clinic.

Dr. Conroy: It's your room.

No. 3643: Come in, please, come in.

Dr. Conroy: I see that you are in a very good mood today. Do you feel well?

No. 3643: Stupendous.

Dr. Conroy: I'm happy to see that there have been no violent incidents since your departure from the infirmary. You are taking your medications on schedule, you are participating in the group sessions . . . You are making progress, Victor.

No. 3643: Thank you, Doctor. I do what I can.

Dr. Conroy: Fine. As we discussed earlier, today is the day that we begin your regression therapy. This is Mr. Fanabarzra. He is a therapist from India, a specialist in hypnosis.

No. 3643: Doctor, I don't know if I'm comfortable with the idea of participating in this experiment.

Dr. Conroy: It's important, Victor. We spoke about it last week, do you remember?

No. 3643: Yes, I remember.

Dr. Conroy: Then we are in agreement. Mr. Fanabarzra, where do you want the patient to sit?

Fanabarzra: He will be most comfortable in bed. It's important for him to be as relaxed as possible.

Dr. Conroy: He'll lie on the bed, then. Lie down, Victor.

No. 3643: As you wish.

Fanabarzra: Very well, Victor. I am going to show you a pendulum. Could you lower the blind a little, Doctor? That's enough. Victor, watch the pendulum, if you would be so kind.

[Transcription omits Fanabarzra's process of hypnosis, at his request. Pauses between responses have also been eliminated for the sake of brevity.]

Fanabarzra: All right then . . . it is 1972. What do you remember from this period?

No. 3643: My father . . . He was never at home. Sometimes the whole family went to wait for him at the factory on Friday afternoon. Mother said he was a good-for-nothing and if we could find him we'd stop him from spending our money in the bars. It was cold outside. One day we waited and waited. We stamped our feet on the ground to keep our toes from freezing. Emil asked me for my scarf because he was cold. I didn't give it to him. My mother rapped me on the head and told me to give it to him. Finally we got tired of waiting and we left.

Dr. Conroy: Ask him where his father was.

Fanabarzra: Do you know where your father was?

No. 3643: He was fired from his job. He came back home two days later in very bad shape. Mother said he had been drinking and sleeping with strangers. They gave him a check but there wasn't much left. We would go to Social Security to get Dad's check but sometimes he got there first and he drank it. Emil didn't understand how someone could drink a piece of paper.

Fanabarzra: Did you ask for help?

No. 3643: Sometimes the parish gave us clothes. Other kids got their clothes at the Salvation Army, because they had better clothes there. But Mother said that they were heretics and pagans and it was better to wear decent Christian clothes. Beria said that his decent Christian clothes were full of holes. That's why he hated them.

Fanabarzra: Were you happy when Beria left?

No. 3643: I was in bed. I saw him walk across the bedroom in the dark, carrying his boots in one hand. He gave me his key chain with a silver bear on it and he told me that I could put the right keys in it. In the morning Emil was crying because he hadn't said goodbye to Beria, so I gave him the key chain. Emil kept crying and threw the key chain away. He cried all day. I tore up a comic book he was reading, just to shut him up. I cut it into pieces with a pair of scissors. My father locked me in his room.

Fanabarzra: Where was your mother?

No. 3643: Playing bingo at the parish hall. It was Tuesday, she always played bingo on Tuesdays. Each playing card cost a penny.

Fanabarzra: What happened in your father's room?

No. 3643: Nothing. I sat around.

Fanabarzra: Victor, you have to tell me.

No. 3643: Nothing happened. Do you understand, sir? NOTHING.

Fanabarzra: Victor, you have to tell me. Your father locked you in his room and he did something to you. Correct?

No. 3643: You don't understand. I deserved it.

Fanabarzra: What did you deserve?

No. 3643: To be punished. Punished. I had to be punished so many times so I would repent for all the bad things I did.

Fanabarzra: What bad things?

No. 3643: So many bad things. The bad person I was. The things I did to the cat. I threw a cat into a garbage can full of old newspapers all crumpled up and set the paper on fire. The cat howled. It howled with a human voice. And for what I did to the book of stories.

Fanabarzra: What was the punishment, Victor?

No. 3643: Hurt. He hurt me. And he liked it, I know that. He told me that it hurt him too, but that was a lie. He said it in Polish. He didn't know how to lie in English, he got the words all mixed up. He always spoke in Polish when he was punishing me.

Fanabarzra: He touched you?

No. 3643: He gave it to me in the rear end. He kept me from turning around. And he put something in me, something hot that hurt.

Fanabarzra: Did these punishments happen frequently?

No. 3643: Every Tuesday. When Mother wasn't around. Sometimes, when he was finished, he just lay there, sleeping
on top of me. As if he were dead. At times he couldn't
punish me and he hit me instead.

Fanabarzra: How did he hit you?

No. 3643: He spanked me until he was tired. Sometimes after he
hit me he could punish me and sometimes not.

Fanabarzra: And your brothers, Victor? Did your father punish them?

No. 3643: I think he punished Beria. Emil never. Emil was the
good one. That's why he died.

Fanabarzra: Only the good die, Victor?

No. 3643: Only the good. Bad people never do.

✝

PALAZZO DEL GOVERNATORATO
Vatican City
Wednesday, April 6, 2005, 10:34 A.M.

Pacing back and forth with short, nervous steps on the rug in the hallway, Paola waited for Dante. The day had started out badly. She had barely slept a wink, and when she arrived at her office she ran smack into a pile of insufferable paperwork and obligations. The man in charge of Civil Defense, Guido Bertolano, was throwing a fit over the ever-larger number of pilgrims who were starting to inundate the city. By now the sports stadiums, universities, and any municipal institutions with space to spare were full to the rafters. People were sleeping in the streets, the doorways, the plazas, even the vestibules of the ATMs. Dicanti had gotten in touch with Bertolano to ask for help in searching for and capturing a suspicious person, and he just short of laughed in her face.

"My dear *ispettore*, even if your suspect were Osama himself, there is very little we could do. It will have to wait until after this whole madhouse dies down."

"I don't know if you are aware that—"

"*Ispettore*—you said your name was Dicanti, right?—Air Force One is parked at Fiumicino. There isn't a single five-star hotel that doesn't have a monarch ensconced in its presidential suite. Can you imagine what sort of nightmare it is to protect these people? There are reports of possible terrorist attacks and phony bomb threats every fifteen minutes. I'm in touch with the carabinieri in towns two hundred kilometers around. Believe me, your problem has to wait. And now please stop tying up my line," he said, hanging up without another word.

Dammit! Why didn't anyone take her seriously? This case was an absolute killer headache. The silence it dictated, inherent in the nature of the beast, only contributed to the collision between what she was trying to do and the indifference everyone else felt for it. She wasted a long amount of time on the phone without finding out anything. Between the various calls, she asked Pontiero to go round to talk to the old Carmelite at Santa Maria in Traspontina while she headed off for her meeting with Cardinal Samalo, the pope's chamberlain, or *il Camerlengo* as he was known in Italian. And there she was, at the doors to the camerlengo's office, pacing like a tiger with a bellyful of black coffee.

Fowler, meanwhile, relaxed on an luxurious bench of dark red wood. He was reading his breviary.

"It is moments like this that I regret giving up smoking."

"A little bit nervous, Padre?"

"No. But you're making it hard not to follow in your footsteps."

Paola took the priest's hint, stopped walking in circles, and sat down next to him. She pretended to read Dante's report on the first murder, while thinking about the strange look that the deputy inspector had given Fowler when she had introduced them at UACV headquarters that morning. Dante had taken Paola aside and said tersely, "Don't trust him." She was worried, intrigued. She decided that the first chance she got, she would ask Dante exactly what he meant.

She turned her attention back to the report. A complete disaster. It was clear Dante didn't take assignments like this very often, which was, on the other hand, lucky for him. They would have to conscientiously go over the scene where Cardinal Portini died, with the hope of turning up some other piece of evidence. This afternoon, no later. The photographs in any case weren't so bad. She slammed the folder shut. She could not concentrate.

Paola found it difficult to admit she was frightened. There she was in the very heart of the Vatican, in a building set apart in the center of the City. A building with more than fifteen hundred offices, the Supreme Pontiff's not least among them. To Paola, the mere profusion of statues and paintings that filled the hallways was unsettling, distracting. And for the Vatican's statesmen over the course of the centuries, that was the desired result; they were well aware of the effect their city produced in visitors. Yet Paola was not about to allow herself even the slightest distraction from the task at hand.

"Padre Fowler?"

"Yes?"

"Can I ask you a question?"

"Of course."

"This is the first time I am going to see a cardinal."

"Not so."

Paola thought for a moment.

"I meant to say, alive."

"And what is your question?"

"How do you address a cardinal?"

"Typically as Your Eminence." Fowler closed his book and looked her in the eyes. "Relax. He is only a person, like yourself or me. And you are the inspector running the investigation. You are a professional. Act as you would under normal circumstances."

Dicanti smiled gratefully. Dante at last opened the door to the office's waiting room.

"Please come in."

There were two desks in the waiting room, with two young priests seated next to the telephone and the computer. They greeted the visitors with well-mannered nods of the head, and the small party continued on into the chamberlain's office. It was an ascetic room, without paintings or carpets. There was a library on one side and a sofa with small tables on the other. A wooden crucifix was the only decoration on the walls.

Unlike the empty walls, the desk of Eduardo González Samalo, the man who held the reins of the Church until the election of the next pope, was crammed with papers. Samalo, in dark red robes, got up from the sofa to greet them. Fowler kneeled and kissed the cardinal's ring in a sign of respect and obedience, something every Catholic does when meeting a cardinal. Paola hung back, hoping to be discreet. She bowed her head just a little, perhaps out of shame. She hadn't regarded herself as a Catholic for many years.

Samalo took Dicanti's rudeness gracefully. Exhaustion and regret were clearly visible on both his face and in his slumped shoulders. He was the ultimate authority in the Vatican for the next several days but judging from appearances he was not enjoying the role.

"Forgive me for making you wait. I was on the phone just now with a representative from the German delegation. They are extremely out of sorts. There are no hotel rooms to be found anywhere and the city is veritable chaos. And the whole wide world wants to be in the front row at tomorrow morning's funeral."

Paola nodded her head courteously.

"I imagine this whole commotion must be tremendously trying."

Samalo merely let out a long, injured sigh in response.

"Have you been informed about what is happening, Your Eminence?"

"Of course. Camilo Cirin has punctually kept me informed of the events as they have taken place. It's a horrible disgrace, all of it. I suppose that in other circumstances I would have reacted much more strongly to these nefarious crimes, but I must tell you in all sincerity, I just have not had the time to be horrified."

"As you know, we have to think about the security of the other cardinals, Your Eminence."

Samalo gestured in Dante's direction.

"The Vigilanza has made a special effort to gather all of them together in the Domus Sanctae Marthae ahead of time, in order to maintain the building's security.

"La Domus Sanctae Marthae?"

Dante broke in. "Saint Martha's House. A building which was remodeled at the direct request of John Paul II, who wanted it to serve as the principal residence for the cardinals during the conclave."

"A very particular use for a whole building, wouldn't you say?"

"When it isn't hosting a conclave, it is used as lodging for prominent visitors," said Cardinal Samalo. "Unless I am mistaken, Padre Fowler, even you stayed there once. Isn't that so?"

Fowler looked very uneasy. For a few moments it seemed as if there would be a short confrontation, one without blood but a battle of wills nonetheless. It was Fowler who lowered his head.

"Indeed, Your Eminence. I was invited to the Holy See once."

"I believe you had a problem with the Sant'Uffizio, the Holy Office."

"I was called to an inquiry regarding activities in which I had taken part, that much is true. Nothing more."

The cardinal seemed to be satisfied with the priest's visible discomfort.

"Ah, but of course, Padre Fowler. . . . There's no need to give me any sort of explanation. Your reputation precedes you. As I was saying, *Ispettore* Dicanti, I am at peace in regard to the safety of my fellow cardinals, thanks to the good efforts of the Vigilanza. Nearly all of them are accounted for and out of danger, here inside the

Vatican. A few have yet to arrive. In principle, residing at the Domus was optional until April 15. Many of the cardinals are spread out in various congregations or priestly residences. But we are in the process of letting them know that they have to stay together."

"How many are at Saint Martha's House right now?"

"Eighty-four. The others, up to the hundred fifteenth, will arrive in the next few hours. We've made an attempt to contact all of them to have them send us their itinerary in order to supplement security. They are the ones most on our minds. But as I've told you, Inspector General Cirin is in charge of everything. Don't worry yourself about it, dear child."

"Does that number of one hundred and fifteen include Robayra and Portini?" Bothered by the chamberlain's condescension, Dicanti dug in.

"Well, I suppose that in reality I should say one hundred and thirteen cardinals," Samalo responded resentfully. A proud man, he took no pleasure in being corrected by a woman.

"I am sure Your Eminence has already settled on a plan in that regard," Fowler added, making an attempt to mediate between the two.

"Indeed. We are sending the rumor around that Portini has taken ill at his family's country home, in Corsica. The illness will unfortunately end on a tragic note. With respect to Robayra, matters relating to his pastoral mission will prevent him from attending the conclave, although he certainly plans to travel to Rome to render his obedience to the new supreme pontiff. Sadly, he will die in a tragic car accident, something that the police will be able to thoroughly document. These stories will pass to the press only after the conclave, not before."

Paola's astonishment was more than she could bear.

"I see that Your Eminence has everything very well in hand."

The chamberlain cleared his throat before answering.

"It's one version among many. And it is one which causes no harm to anyone."

"Only to the truth."

"This is the Catholic Church, *Ispettore*. The inspiration and light that illuminates the way for millions of people. We cannot allow ourselves any further scandals. From that point of view, what exactly is the truth?"

Dicanti had a doubtful look on her face, even though she recognized the logic implicit in the old man's words. She thought of the many ways she might reply to him but understood that it wouldn't prove a thing. She preferred to return to the interview.

"I suppose the motive for their premature gathering won't be communicated to the cardinals."

"Absolutely not. I have expressly asked them not to leave the city without the company of the Vigilanza or the Swiss Guard, with the excuse that a radical group inside the city has made threats against the Catholic hierarchy. I believe they all understand."

"Did you know the victims personally?"

The cardinal's face darkened for a moment.

"Good heavens, yes. With Cardinal Portini I had less in common despite the fact that he was Italian. My work has always been very centered around the internal organization of the Vatican, and he dedicated his life to doctrine. He was always writing and traveling. He was a great man. Personally I did not agree with his politics, which were so open and revolutionary."

"Revolutionary?" Fowler leaned forward.

"Very much so, Padre. He argued for the use of condoms, for the ordination of women priests. He would have been a pope for the twenty-first century. Furthermore he was still relatively young, although he was almost fifty-nine years old. If he had sat on the throne of Peter, he would have been in charge of Vatican Council III, which many people believe the Church urgently needs. His death has been a terrible and senseless misfortune."

"You would have voted for him?" Fowler asked.

The chamberlain laughed between his teeth.

"You are not seriously asking me to reveal whom I am going to vote for, are you, Padre?"

Paola stepped back in to take the reins of the interview.

"Your Eminence, you said you had less in common with Portini. What about Robayra?"

"A great man. Totally committed to the cause of the poor. He had defects, certainly. He was very given to imagining himself dressed in white, standing on the balcony overlooking Saint Peter's Square. Of course, he never went public with his ambition. We were very close friends. We wrote to each other all the time. His only sin was his pride. He always made a great show of his poverty. He signed his letters with a *beati pauperes*. And just to rile him up, I signed mine with *beati pauperes spirito*, but he never let on that he understood my allusion. Despite his defects he was a man of state and a man of the Church. He did so much good over the course of his life. I never dreamed I would see him wearing the fisherman's sandals, but I suppose that was because I was so close to him."

As he went on about his friend, the old cardinal shrunk a little and turned a shade of gray, his voice saddened, his face revealing the accumulated fatigue in a man of seventy-eight years. Despite the fact that she did not share the man's ideas, Paola felt sorry for him. She knew that behind those words, framed as a proper epitaph, the old Spaniard regretted not having any time to be alone and weep for his friend. Damned dignity. As she was thinking this, she realized that she was beginning to look beyond the cardinal's cape and his dark red robe, to see the person wearing them. She'd have to learn to stop looking at the clergy as if they were one-dimensional beings. Her prejudice against the priesthood could easily put her work in jeopardy.

"When all is said and done, I suppose no one is a prophet in their own country. As I mentioned, we agreed on a great many things. Good old Emilio came here seven months ago. It was the last stop on his trip. One of my assistants took a photograph here in the office. I know I have it here somewhere."

The man in the dark red robes walked over to his desk and reached inside a drawer for an envelope with photographs. He looked through them, chose one, and handed the Polaroid to his visitors.

Paola looked at the photograph without much interest until something in the image suddenly grabbed her attention. Her eyes became as wide as saucers and she grabbed Dante's arm, nearly pulling it out of its socket.

"Oh, shit. Shit!"

✝

CHURCH OF SANTA MARIA
IN TRASPONTINA
Via della Conciliazione, 14
Wednesday, April 6, 2005, 10:41 A.M.

Pontiero knocked again and again on the door that led from the rear of the church into the sacristy. Following police instructions, Brother Francesco had placed on the door a sign, written in an unsteady hand, indicating that the church was closed for renovations. Beyond being obedient, the friar must also have been a little deaf, because Pontiero had now spent five minutes pounding away on the door. Behind him, thousands of people crammed the Via Corridori, in ever growing, ever more disorderly numbers. There were more people on that small street than on the Via della Conciliazione.

Pontiero at last heard sounds coming from the other side of the door. The bolts were drawn back and Brother Francesco's face appeared in a crack in the doorway, squinting into the harsh sun.

"Yes?"

"*Fratello*, I'm Detective Pontiero. Remember me from yesterday?"

The monk nodded once, and then a second time.

"What do you want? You've come to tell me that I can reopen my church now, praise the Lord. With so many pilgrims out here . . . Take a look yourself, look around," he said as he gestured toward the thousands of people in the street.

"No, *Fratello*. I need to ask you a few questions. Is it all right with you if I come in?"

"Must it be now? I was just saying my prayers."

"I won't take much of your time. Really, just a minute or two."

Francesco shook his head from side to side.

"What times these are, what times. Death turns up everywhere, death and people running around. They won't even let me finish my prayers."

The door opened slowly and then closed behind Pontiero with a loud bang.

"Padre, that is one heavy door."

"Yes, my son. At times it's very hard for me to open it, most of all when I come back loaded down from the supermarket. These days nobody helps an old man carry his bags. What times these are, what times."

"You should get a shopping cart."

Pontiero walked back and inspected the door from the inside, attentively checking the bolt and the heavy hinges that held it into the wall.

"What I meant to say is, there are no bruises on the lock. It doesn't look like it was forced at all."

"No, my son. Thanks to God, no. It's a strong lock. The door was painted about a year ago by a parishioner, a friend of mine, good old Giuseppe. He has asthma, you know, and the fumes from the paint didn't agree with him—"

"I'm sure Giuseppe is a good Christian."

"He is, my son, he is."

"But I'm not here for that. I need to find out how the killer was able to get into the church, especially if there are no other means of access. *Ispettore* Dicanti thinks it's an important detail."

"He could have come in by one of the windows, if he had the use of a ladder. But I don't think so, because they would be broken. Madre, what a disaster if he'd gone so far as to break one of the stained glass windows."

"Would it bother you if I took a look at those windows?"

"Not at all. Follow me."

The friar limped from the sacristy toward the church, illuminated only by the candles placed at the feet of the statues of the saints and martyrs. Pontiero was surprised so many of them were lighted.

"So many offerings, Francesco."

"Ah, my son, I lighted all the candles here in the church, asking the saints to carry the soul of our Holy Father John Paul straight to the heart of heaven."

Pontiero was amused by the friar's simplicity. They were standing in the central aisle, from which vantage point the sacristy door was visible, along with the main entrance and the windows at the front of the church, the only ones in the church. He slid a finger along the back of one of the pews, an involuntary gesture he had repeated during thousands of Sunday masses. This was the house of God, and it had been profaned and defiled. Today, illuminated by the flickering glow of the candles, the church took on a very different character than it had the day before. Pontiero felt an involuntary chill. The interior of the temple was cold and damp, in contrast with the heat outside. He looked up toward the windows. The one farthest down was at a height of some sixteen feet off the ground. The entire window was composed of intricate stained glass in a full spectrum of colors, no part of which had suffered so much as a scratch.

"No one came in through the window with some 200 pounds on his back. The killer would have had to use a crane. And he would have been seen by thousands of pilgrims on the outside. No, it's impossible."

Both men heard the songs the young people were singing as they stood on line to say farewell to Pope John Paul. All of them spoke of love and peace.

"Ah, young people. Our hope for the future. Isn't that so, Detective?"

"Right you are, *Francesco*."

Pontiero scratched his head. He was at a loss to think of any entrances to the building beyond the doors and the windows. He took a few steps, which set off a strong echo in the empty church.

"Listen, Francesco. Does anyone else have keys to the church? Perhaps the person who does the cleaning?"

"No, no, absolutely not. A few of the very devout parishioners help me clean the church on Saturdays very early in the morning and on Monday in the afternoon, but they always come when I'm here. In fact, I've only one set of keys, which I always carry with me. See?" And he put his left hand into an interior pocket of his brown habit and shook the key ring.

"OK, Padre, I give up. I cannot understand how he could have gotten in without being seen."

"I have nothing to add, my son. I'm sorry I haven't been of more help."

"Thanks, Padre."

Pontiero spun around and started to walk toward the sacristy.

"Unless . . ." The Carmelite seemed to reflect for a moment, and then nodded his head. "No, it's impossible. It can't be."

"What is it? Tell me. Any little thing could be helpful."

"No, forget it."

"I insist, *Fratello*, I insist. What are you thinking?"

The friar stroked his beard and brooded.

"Well, there is an underground access. It's an old passageway which dates from the time when the temple was rebuilt."

"There was another church here?"

"Yes, the original building was destroyed during the sack of Rome in 1527. It was in the line of fire from the cannons which were defending Castel Sant'Angelo. And at that time this church—"

"Can we leave the History class for later? Let's see the passage right now."

"Are you sure? You're wearing a nice, clean suit—"

"Sure I'm sure. Show me where it is."

"As you wish, Detective, as you wish," the friar said humbly.

He hobbled around the entrance to the church, near the spot where the fountain of holy water was situated. He pointed out a crack in between the stones in the floor.

"Do you see that crack? Stick your fingers in there and pull hard."

Pontiero got down on his knees and followed the friar's instructions. Nothing happened.

"Try again. Pull hard to the left."

Pontiero did as Francesco told him, but to no avail. Short and skinny as he was, Pontiero was nonetheless strong. He wasn't about to give up. On the third try, he felt the stone shift. Then it came up easily. It was, in fact, a trapdoor. He opened it with one hand. Down below was a short, narrow stairway, some eight feet high. He found a small flashlight in his pocket and shined it into the darkness. Stone steps, and they looked solid enough.

"Very nice. Let's see where all this takes us."

"Detective, don't go down there by yourself, if you would."

"Take it easy, *Fratello*. There's nothing to it. I've got things under control."

Pontiero imagined what Dante and Dicanti's faces would look like when he told them what he had found. He got to his feet and then took his first step on the stairway.

"Wait. Let me get a candle."

"Don't bother, *Fratello*. I can see all right with this torch," Pontiero shouted.

At the bottom of the stairs was a short passageway with damp walls, which in turn gave way to a room about eighteen feet square. Pontiero ran his flashlight over every surface. It looked like the basement stopped here. There were two truncated columns, each about six feet tall, both in the middle of the room. They looked very old. He couldn't identify the period they dated from; he'd never paid much attention in History class. But even so, he could see, in what was left on one of the columns, what he thought were pieces of something that should not have been there. It looked like . . .

Duct tape.

This wasn't a secret passage, it was an execution chamber.

Pontiero turned around just in time for the blow, which was aimed so that it would split his skull, but hit him on the right shoulder instead. He fell to the ground, shuddering with pain. The flashlight had rolled far away, its beam illuminating the base of one of the columns. He knew intuitively that a second blow was on its way in an arc from the right behind him, and it struck him on the left arm. He felt around for his pistol in the space between his arm and his side, and he managed to nudge it out with his left arm, in spite of the pain. The pistol felt like it was made of lead. He had no feeling in his other arm.

An iron bar, he thought. He must have an iron bar or something like that. . . .

He tried to aim but couldn't pull it off. He was hobbling toward the column when the third blow, square on the back this time, knocked him flat on the ground. He gripped the pistol even tighter, like someone holding on for dear life.

A foot on top of his hand forced him to release the gun. The foot kept pushing down hard, and while the bones in his hand began to make a crunching noise just before they broke, he heard a voice he vaguely recognized, a voice with a very distinct tone.

"Pontiero, Pontiero. As I was saying, the original church was in the line of fire from the cannons which defended Castel Sant'Angelo. And that church had in its time replaced a pagan temple which was torn down by Pope Alexander VI. In the Middle Ages it was believed to be the tomb of Romulus himself."

The iron bar descended once again, striking Pontiero on his back as he lay on the ground stunned.

"But its exciting history doesn't end there. The two columns you see here are the very ones to which Saints Peter and Paul were bound before being martyred by the Romans. You Romans, always so attentive to our saints."

Once more the iron bar struck a blow, this time on the left thigh. Pontiero howled in pain.

"You would have learned all this upstairs, if you hadn't interrupted me. But don't worry, you are going to get to know these columns really well. You will be very, very well acquainted with them."

Pontiero tried to move, but he discovered to his horror that he was unable to do so. He didn't know how badly he was hurt. He had lost feeling in his limbs. Very powerful hands were carrying him in the darkness. He could feel that happening, and a very sharp pain. He howled in pain.

"I don't recommend you try to shout. No one will hear you. No one heard the other two either. I took plenty of precautions. I don't like it when they interrupt me."

Pontiero felt his consciousness falling into a deep black hole, like that of someone who bit by bit slips into a dream. And just as in a dream, far-off he heard the sounds of young people in the street, just a few feet above him. He thought he recognized the hymn the choir was singing. It was a memory from when he was a child, a million years in the past. "If you're saved and you know, clap your hands."

"In fact, I really can't stand it when people interrupt me," Karosky said.

✝

PALAZZO DEL GOVERNATORATO
Vatican City
Wednesday, April 6, 2005, 1:31 P.M.

Paola showed the photo of Robayra to Dante and Fowler. A perfect close-up, the cardinal laughing affectionately, eyes glittering behind his oversized tortoiseshell glasses. At first Dante just stared at the photograph. He failed to see anything there at all.

"The glasses, Dante. The ones that disappeared."

Paola looked for her mobile, dialed frantically as she headed toward the door, and flew out of the office of the astonished camerlengo.

"The glasses! The Carmelite's glasses!" Paola shouted as soon as she reached the hallway.

And then Dante understood.

"Let's go, Father!"

Dante apologized hastily to the chamberlain and left with Fowler in pursuit of Paola.

Paola stopped dialing. She was furious. Pontiero wasn't answering. He must have switched his mobile off. She raced down the stairs, toward the street. She would have to run the whole length of Via del Governatorato. At that second a small car with the SCV on the license plate appeared from the opposite direction. Three nuns were sitting inside. Paola frantically waved her arms at them to stop and then jumped in front of the car. The fender jerked to a stop an inch or so from her knees.

"*Santa* Madonna! Are you mad, miss?"

Paola hurried over to the driver's side, her badge at arm's length in front.

"Please, I don't have time to explain. I have to get to Santa Ana gate."

The nuns stared at her as if she were a madwoman. Paola climbed into the backseat on the driver's side.

"You can't get there from here; you'd have to cross the Cortile del Belvedere on foot," the nun who was driving said. "If you want, I can get you as close as the Piazza del Sant'Uffizio. It's the quickest exit out of the city right now. The Swiss Guards are putting up barriers on account of the Conclave."

"Whatever, but let's get there quickly."

The nun was in first gear and quickly speeding up when the car came to a halt a second time.

"Has the entire world lost its mind?" one of the nuns blurted out.

Fowler and Dante were standing directly in front of the car, both of them with hands on the hood. As soon as the car was at a full stop, they ran around and squeezed into the trunk. The nuns in the front seat and the back crossed themselves.

"Sure, Sister, but for Christ's sake hurry it up!"

It took barely twenty seconds for the little car to cover the quarter mile that separated them from their goal. The nun with her hands on the wheel gave every impression of wanting to get away as quickly as possible from her strange, ill-timed, and embarrassing cargo. She hadn't even hit the brakes in the Piazza del Sant'Uffizio before Paola was out and running toward the black iron gates that guarded that entrance to Vatican City, her cell phone in her hand. She dialed the number for police headquarters. The operator came on line.

"*Ispettore* Paola Dicanti, security code 13897. Agent in danger, I repeat, agent in danger. Detective Pontiero is on-site at Via della Conciliazione, 14. The church of Santa Maria in Traspontina. Send as many units as you can. Possible murder suspect inside the building. Proceed with extreme caution."

Paola ran, her jacket flapping in the wind, the gun peeking out of its holster, while she shouted into her cell phone like a woman possessed. The two Swiss Guards at the entrance took one look at her and poised themselves to block her escape. When one of the guards grabbed her by her jacket, she thrust her arms back violently, losing her grip on her cell, which flew out of her hand. The Swiss Guard was left holding two empty arms on a jacket pulled inside out. He was just starting after Dicanti when Dante arrived at full speed, his Corpo di Vigilanza ID thrust in front of him.

"Let her go. She's one of us."

Fowler was close behind, clutching his suitcase. He lost a few valuable seconds stooping down to retrieve Paola's cell phone. She decided on the shortest route, straight through Saint Peter's Square. The crowds were smaller there owing to the fact that the police had set up one line crossing the square, in contrast to the incredible masses of humanity on the earlier stages of the route. She ran with her ID out so as to avoid trouble if she encountered police along the way. Once they crossed the esplanade and passed Bernini's Colonnade without too much trouble, they arrived at the Via Corridori out of breath. From there on, the mass of pilgrims was menacingly tight. Paola plastered her left arm across her chest to lessen the chances of her pistol being seen. She moved in close to the buildings and tried to make headway as quickly as she could. Dante was a few steps ahead. He served as an improvised but effective battering ram, all arms and elbows. Fowler was immediately behind.

It cost them ten excruciating minutes to arrive at the door that led into the sacristy. Two agents were waiting for them, ringing the bell nonstop. Dicanti, panting, covered with sweat, her leather holster in full view and her hair slick and shiny, looked every bit an apparition to the two police officers, who nonetheless greeted her respectfully as soon as they saw her UACV identification.

"We received your warning. There's no answer from inside. We have four officers at the other entrance."

"Can you tell me why the hell you haven't gone in yet? Are you aware a fellow officer could be trapped inside?"

The two agents stared at their shoes.

"*Direttore* Troi called. He told us to proceed with caution. Many people are staring at us, *Ispettore*."

Dicanti leaned against the wall and took five seconds to gather herself together. Shit, she said to herself, Let's hope we're not too late. "You have the 'master key'?"

One of the cops pointed to his thigh, where, cleverly concealed from outside view in an extra pocket, he carried a steel bar with two teeth on the end. People in the street were beginning to pay attention to the drama unfolding in this group that milled around the church door. Paola gestured to the cop who had showed her the door breaker.

"Give me your walkie-talkie."

The cop handed her the device, which was hooked by a cable to the holder on his belt. Paola dictated a few short, precise instructions to the team on the other side of the church. No one was to make a move until she got there, and of course no one was to go in or out.

"Could someone explain where all this is going?" Fowler asked in between gasping for breath.

"Our best guess is that the suspect is inside. I'll go over it a little more slowly now. For starters, I want you to stay outside and wait," said Paola.

The priest handed her the cell phone that had fallen out of her pocket.

"This is yours."

"Thanks, Padre." She made a gesture with her head in the direction of the human tide surrounding them. "Do what you can to distract them while we force the door. Let's hope we get there in time."

Fowler nodded. He looked around, hunting for a perch where he could stand out from the crowd. There were no cars in the vicinity; the street had been closed off. No time to waste. What he had was people, so he would have to use them to get a little leverage. A tall, rugged-looking pilgrim stood out from the crowd close by. He must have been six feet tall.

Fowler went up to him and said, "Do you think you could lift me on your shoulders?"

The young man used his hands to indicate that he didn't know Italian. Fowler used the same language of gestures to indicate what he wanted. After several tries, the pilgrim got it. He put one knee on the ground and lifted the priest up, a big smile on his face. Surveying the crowd from above, Fowler began to sing the communion chant from the Requiem mass.

In paradisum deducant te angeli
In tuo advente
Suscipiant te martyres . . .

People in the crowd began turning around to look at him. Fowler gestured for his heavily laden porter to move toward the center of the street, taking attention away from Paola and the others. Several of the faithful, friars and priests for the most part, joined in the hymn for the dead pope, in whose honor they had been standing and walking for many hours.

Making use of the distraction, the two cops were able to force open the door to the sacristy with the steel bar. They slipped in without calling attention to themselves.

"Boys, one of ours is in here. Let's proceed with utmost caution."

They entered in Indian file, Dicanti flying in, her pistol out. She left it to the two cops to search the sacristy, while she walked into the main part of the church's nave. She hurriedly searched the chapel of Saint Thomas. It was empty, still closed off by UACV's crime scene tape. She looked over the chapels on the left side, her finger on the trigger of her pistol. She signaled to Dante, who was covering the aisle on the other side of the church, checking each one of the chapels. The faces of the saints moved around restlessly, projected onto the walls by the flickering, sickly light cast by the candles burning on every available surface. The two met up in the central aisle.

"Nothing?"

Dante shook his head. No.

They saw it at the same time. There it was, written on the floor near the entrance, at the foot of the baptismal font. In large, red, twisty letters was written:

Vexilla Regis Prodeunt Inferni

"The banners of the King of Hell are coming ever closer," a voice behind them intoned.

Startled, the two agents turned around. Fowler was walking up behind them. He had brought the hymn to a close and slipped inside the church.

"I thought I told you to stay outside."

"Forget about that now," Dante interjected. His attention was riveted by the trapdoor sitting open on the floor. "I'll call the others."

Paola looked as if she had come unhinged. Her heart told her to go down below immediately, but she didn't dare go into the dark. Dante raced over to the front door and opened the locks. Two agents walked in, leaving the two others standing on the threshold. One of the cops pulled the Maglite from his belt and offered it to Dante. Dicanti grabbed it out of his hands and headed down, her back against the steps, her muscles tense, her pistol pointing straight ahead. Fowler didn't come along, staying above and murmuring a short prayer.

Paola's head emerged out of the darkness a short time later. As soon as she climbed the stairs, she raced out of the church. Dante dragged himself up the steps slowly. He looked at Fowler, and shook his head.

Paola stood on the street. She was sobbing. She got as far as she could from the doorway and threw up everything she had in her stomach. Young people, who appeared to be foreigners waiting on line, came up to her to see if she needed help.

"Are you OK?"

Paola waved them off. Then Fowler was there, lending her his handkerchief. She accepted it and wiped away the vomit and tears. Her head was spinning. It couldn't be; Pontiero just couldn't be that blood-drenched pile she'd found tied to the column. Maurizio Pontiero, detective: a good man, fit, overflowing with an always surprising and always sympathetic sense of devilish humor. A paterfamilias, a friend, a companion. On rainy afternoons, he slunk around inside his raincoat; a colleague, he always paid for the coffee they shared; he was always there. He had been there for many years. It just couldn't be that he had breathed his last, that he had been reduced to that formless hunk of flesh. She wanted to tear that image right off her retina. Her hands pressed against her eyes with terrible force.

Her cell phone rang. She grabbed it out of her pocket, disgusted, and stood there paralyzed. On the screen, the caller was identified as M. Pontiero.

Paola was dying of fright as she took the call. Fowler studied her, intrigued.

"Yes?"

"Good afternoon, *Ispettore*. How do you feel?"

"Who is this?"

"*Ispettore*, please. You yourself asked me to call whenever I remembered something useful. And I just remembered that I had to take your coworker out of the picture. I am truly sorry. He got in my way."

"We are going to catch you, Francesco. Or should I call you Victor?" Paola was spitting out the words furiously, her eyes damp with tears while she tried to keep her balance and hit him where it hurt. So that he knew his mask had been torn off.

Silence on the other end of the line. But only for a second. She hadn't taken him by surprise in the slightest.

"So you already know who I am. Well, give my best to Padre Fowler. He has lost a bit of hair since the last time we saw each other. You yourself look a little pale."

Paola's eyes opened wide in surprise.

"Where are you, you sick bastard?"

"You don't know? I'm right behind you."

Paola looked out over the thousands of people crammed into the street, some wearing hats, some baseball caps, waving banners and drinking water, praying and chanting.

"Why don't you come over here, Padre? We could have a little talk."

"No, *Ispettore*, I'm afraid I have to keep my distance from you a little longer. But don't think for a second that you have made any progress because you have unmasked good old Francesco. His life had run its course. I finally had to let him go. And don't worry, you'll be hearing from me soon. There's no need to trouble yourself over the way you treated me when we met. I've forgiven you. You are very important to me."

He hung up.

Dicanti threw herself into the crowd, pulling people apart without rhyme or reason, looking for men of a certain height and grabbing them by the arms, turning the ones looking the other way around, tearing off their hats. People scattered and moved away. She was demented, the look in her eyes was that of a lost soul, and even so, she was ready to go over every last pilgrim one by one if she had to.

Fowler waded into the heart of the crowd and, grabbing her arm, held her back.

"It won't work."

"Take your fucking hands off me!"

"Paola. Let it go. He's not here."

Dicanti started to sob. Fowler put his arm around her. On all sides, the gigantic human serpent moved slowly forward, pushing toward the public presentation of the body of John Paul II. And somewhere inside its body the serpent was carrying a killer.

✝

THE SAINT MATTHEW INSTITUTE
Sachem Pike, Maryland
January 1996

**Transcription of Interview #72 Between
Patient No. 3643 and Doctor Canice Conroy,
with the Assistance of
Doctor Anthony Fowler and Sahler Fanabarzra**

Dr. Conroy: Good afternoon, Victor.

No. 3643: Hello again.

Dr. Conroy: A day of regressive therapy, Victor.

[Transcription once again omits the process of hypnosis, as in previous reports.]

Fanabarzra: It's 1973. From here on in you will listen to my voice and no one else's. Are we in agreement?

No. 3643: Yes.

Fanabarzra: He cannot hear you, gentlemen.

Dr. Conroy: The other day we performed a Rorschach test. Victor participated in the process in a normal fashion, pointing out the usual birds and flowers. In only two did he say that he saw nothing. Take note, Father Fowler: when Victor takes no interest in something, it is because it affects him deeply. What I hope to do is to provoke that response during the state of regression, so we can learn its origin.

Dr. Fowler: I disagree about the soundness of the method, more than whether it is empirically possible. When he is in a state of regression, the patient doesn't have many defensive mechanisms at his disposal, as he would in a normal state. The risk of inflicting trauma is too high.

Dr. Conroy: Those same defenses have rendered his brain inoperable. You know that this patient suffers from a profound rejection of particular episodes in his life. We have to get past the barriers, to uncover the origins of his illness.

Dr. Fowler: At what price?

Fanabarzra: Gentlemen, please keep your discussion to a minimum. In any case, it is impossible to show the patient any images now that he cannot open his eyes.

Dr. Conroy: But we will describe them. Go ahead, Fanabarzra.

Fanabarzra: Yes, sir. Victor, it is 1973. I want us to go to a place that you like. Which one shall we choose?

No. 3643: The fire escape.

Fanabarzra: Do you spend a good deal of time on the fire escape?

No. 3643: Yes.

Fanabarzra: Tell me why.

No. 3643: The fresh air. It doesn't smell bad out there. It smells really bad inside the house.

Fanabarzra: It smells?

No. 3643: Like rotten fruit. The stench is coming from Emil's bed.

Fanabarzra: Your brother is sick?

No. 3643:	Yes. We don't know why. Nobody takes care of him. My mother says he is possessed. He can't stand light and he has shaking fits. His throat hurts him.
Dr. Conroy:	All symptoms of meningitis. Photophobia, rigidity of the neck, convulsions.
Fanabarzra:	No one is taking care of your brother?
No. 3643:	My mother feeds him sliced apples, when she remembers to. He has diarrhea and my father doesn't want to know anything about it. I hate him. He looks at me and then tells me to clean my brother. I don't want to, it makes me sick. My mother tells me to do something. I don't want to and she pushes me against the radiator.
Dr. Conroy:	We have already documented the bad treatment he received. Let's find out what makes him see the images he sees when he takes the Rorschach. This one in particular concerns me.
Fanabarzra:	Let's go back to the fire escape. Sit there. Tell me what you're feeling.
No. 3643:	Fresh air. The metal beneath my feet. I can smell the Jewish food from the store in front.
Fanabarzra:	Now I want you to picture something. A large black blotch, very big. It fills up all the space in front of you. In the lower part of the blotch there is a small white oval. Does that look like something to you?
No. 3643:	The darkness. All alone in the closet.
Dr. Conroy:	Pay attention. I think we have something here.
Fanabarzra:	What did you do in the closet?
No. 3643:	They shut me in there. I'm alone.
Dr. Fowler:	For God's sake, Conroy, look at his face. He's in pain.
Dr. Conroy:	Shut up. We are getting where we need to be. Fanabar-

zra, I am going to write further questions on this blackboard. Read them just as I write them, are we agreed?

Fanabarzra: Victor, do you remember what happened before they
shut you up in the closet?

No. 3643: Many things. Emil died.

Fanabarzra: How did Emil die?

No. 3643: They have locked me up. I am all alone.

Fanabarzra: I know that, Victor. Tell me how Emil died.

No. 3643: He was in our room. Papa was watching the television,
Mama was out. I was sitting on the fire escape when I
heard a noise.

Fanabarzra: What kind of noise?

No. 3643: Like a balloon when the air flies out. I stuck my head in
the room. Emil was very pale. I spoke to my father and
he threw a beer can at me.

Fanabarzra: He hit you?

No. 3643: In the head. I'm bleeding and crying. My father stands
up, raises his arm. I tell him about Emil. He gets really
angry, he says it's my fault. That I was taking care of
him. That I deserve to be punished. And he starts in on
it again.

Fanabarzra: The same punishment as always? He touches you there?

No. 3643: He hurts me. I am bleeding on my head and my rear.
But he stops.

Fanabarzra: Why does he stop?

No. 3643: I hear Mama's voice. She is shouting terrible things at
Papa. Things I don't understand. Papa says she knew
already. My mother screams and calls out to Emil as loud
as she can. I know Emil can't hear her and I am very
happy. Then she grabs me by the neck and throws me

inside the closet. I shout. I am afraid. I bang on the door for a long time. She opens it and shows me the knife. She says if I open my mouth, she'll stab me with it.

Fanabarzra: And what did you do?

No. 3643: I keep quiet. I am alone. I hear voices outside. Voices I don't recognize. They are there for hours. I stay in the closet.

Dr. Conroy: Those must be the voices of the emergency ambulance service taking the body of his brother away.

Fanabarzra: How long are you inside the closet?

No. 3643: A long time. I am alone. My mother opens the door. She says that I have been very bad. That God doesn't like bad little boys who make trouble for their parents. That I am going to learn God's punishment for those who misbehave. She give me an old plastic container and tells me to do my business in there. In the morning she gives me a glass of water, bread, and some cheese.

Fanabarzra: How many days were you there?

No. 3643: A long time went by.

Fanabarzra: You didn't have a watch? You couldn't count time?

No. 3643: I try to keep count, but it's too long. If I really press my ear to the wall, I can hear Mrs. Berger's transistor radio. She's a little deaf. Sometimes she listens to baseball.

Fanabarzra: How many games did you listen to?

No. 3643: I don't know, forty, maybe fifty. I lost count.

Dr. Fowler: My God, the kid was locked in the closet for almost two months.

Fanabarzra: You never went out?

No. 3643: Once.

Fanabarzra: Why did you go out?

No. 3643: I made a mistake. I kick the can with my foot and it turns over. The closet smells like death. I throw up. When Mama comes back, she's angry. She rubs my face in the filth. Then she drags me out of the closet so she can clean it.

Fanabarzra: You don't try to escape?

No. 3643: I don't have anywhere to go. Mama does it for my own good.

Fanabarzra: And when does she let you leave?

No. 3643: One day. She runs a bath for me. She says she hopes that I have learned my lesson. She says that the closet is hell and that it will be where I go if I am not good, except that then I can't ever leave. She puts on my clothes. She says that I should have been born a girl and that there's still time to change that. She touches my little packages. She says it's all pointless, that I am going to hell in any case, that there is no way out for me.

Fanabarzra: And your father?

No. 3643: Papa is no longer here. He took off.

Dr. Fowler: Conroy, stop this right now. Look at his face. The patient is very ill.

No. 3643: He's gone, gone, gone . . .

Dr. Fowler: Conroy!

Dr. Conroy: That's enough. Fanabarzra, stop the recording and take the patient out of the trance.

✝

CHURCH OF SANTA MARIA
IN TRASPONTINA
Via della Conciliazione, 14
Wednesday, April 6, 2005, 3:21 P.M.

For the second time that week the Crime Scene Analysis technicians passed through the doors of Santa Maria in Traspontina. They went about their business as unassumingly as possible, dressed in street clothes so as to avoid notice by the pilgrims. Inside, *Ispettore* Dicanti barked out orders, jumping back and forth between her cell phone and the walkie-talkie. Fowler approached one of the UACV technicians.

"Finished with the murder scene yet?"

"Yes, Padre. We are about to remove the body and start examining the sacristy."

Fowler looked at Dicanti apprehensively.

"I'll go down with you."

"Are you sure?"

"I don't want anything to get by me. What is that?"

In his right hand the priest held a small, black case.

"It contains holy oils, which we use to give extreme unction."

"Is that going to help in some way?"

"Not in the investigation, no. But for Pontiero, yes. He was a devout Catholic, wasn't he?"

"He was. And little good it did him."

"With all due respect, that's not for you to say."

The two of them started down the steps cautiously, taking pains to step around the inscription at the entrance to the crypt. They quickly moved past the short hallway and found themselves standing at the edge of the chamber. UACV technicians had installed two electric generators, with powerful lights that lighted up the room.

Pontiero's inert body, nude from the waist up, hung between the two truncated columns that supported him. Karosky had fastened his arms to the stone with duct tape, evidently the same tape he had used on Robayra. The eyes and tongue were torn out, the face horribly disfigured, while strips of bloody flesh hung from his thorax like macabre decorations.

Paola lowered her head while the priest administered the last rites. Fowler's black shoes, shined to a high polish, stood deep in a pool of slowly congealing blood. Paola swallowed hard and closed her eyes.

"Dicanti."

Her eyes opened again. Dante had joined them in the underground chamber. Fowler had finished and was tactfully preparing to leave.

"Where are you going, Padre?"

"Upstairs. I don't want to get in the way."

"You aren't. If half of what they say about you is true, you have brains to spare. They sent you to help, right? So help us out here."

"With pleasure, *Ispettore*."

She swallowed hard and started in.

"It looks as if Pontiero entered by the door to the sacristy. It's obvious that he knocked on the door and our false friar opened it for him. Nothing unusual there. Pontiero spoke to Karosky and was attacked by him."

"But where?"

"It must have been down here. If it wasn't, there would be blood upstairs."

"Why did he do it? Perhaps Pontiero smelled something?"

"I doubt it," Fowler said. "I feel more confident that Karosky saw the opportunity and seized it. I'm inclined to think he showed Pontiero the way into the crypt and that Pontiero came down here by himself, with the other man behind him."

"That sounds right. He probably ruled out Brother Francesco immediately. Not only because he looked to be an old man who had trouble moving around—"

"But because he was a religious person. Pontiero would never suspect a friar, right? The poor fool," Dante said sadly.

"Do me a favor, Dante."

Fowler glared at Dante but the Vatican cop was staring in another direction.

"I'm sorry. Go on, Dicanti."

"Once they were down here, Karosky struck him with a blunt object. We think it was a bronze candelabra. The boys at UACV have already taken it away for testing. It was left sitting on the floor close to the body. He then tied him up and . . . as you can see. What Pontiero must have gone through."

Paola's voice broke. The two men pretended they didn't hear it, and then she coughed, to conceal her emotions and try to recover her voice before she went back to work.

"A dark room, extremely dark. He's repeating the trauma of his earliest childhood, the time he spent locked up in the closet?"

"It could be. Have they found any deliberate clues?"

"We think the only message is the one upstairs: '*Vexilla regis prodeunt inferni.*'"

" 'The banners of the King of Hell are coming ever closer,' " the priest translated a second time.

"What does that mean, Fowler?" Dante asked.

"You ought to know."

"If you are trying to ridicule me, you aren't even close."

Fowler had a wistful look on his face.

"Nothing could be further from my mind. I was referring to a quotation from one of your ancestors, Dante Alighieri."

"He isn't my ancestor. It's my last name, and his first. We have nothing to do with one another."

"I apologize. I thought every Italian publicly declared himself a descendant of either Dante or Julius Caesar."

"At least we know who we're descended from."

Fowler and Dante stood their ground, glaring at each other. Paola broke in.

"If you two are finished with the xenophobic backstabbing, we can proceed."

Fowler cleared his throat.

"As I was saying, '*Vexilla regis prodeunt inferni*' is a citation from *The Divine Comedy,* from the moment when Dante and Virgil are about to enter into Hell. It's a paraphrase of a prayer in the Christian liturgy, except that it's dedicated to Satan instead of God. Many people want to read heresy into the declaration, but in reality the only thing that Dante was trying to do was to scare his audience."

"That's what he wants? To scare us?"

"He's telling us that Hell is close at hand. I don't believe that Karosky's interpretation goes any further afield. He isn't a very cultivated man, although he likes to pretend he is. Are there any other messages?"

"Not on the body," answered Paola. "He knows that we came here and he became frightened. And it's my fault he knows it, because I was calling Pontiero's cell phone nonstop."

"Any luck pinpointing the phone?"

"We contacted the phone company. The tracking system for cell phones indicates that the telephone is turned off or outside of the area of coverage. The last call recorded in this area was from on top of Hotel Atlante Star, barely a thousand feet from where we stand," Paola replied.

"Which is exactly where I'm staying," Fowler pointed out.

"Go on, I was sure you were putting up in a pension especially for priests. You know, something a little more modest."

Fowler brushed off the comment.

"Dante, my friend, at my age one learns to enjoy the good things in life. Especially when Uncle Sam is paying for it. I've already pitched my tent in plenty of places that reek of death."

"I am certain of it, Padre. Quite certain."

"What are you referring to? Whatever you are insinuating, why don't you just spit it out?"

"I'm not insinuating anything other than that you've slept in worse places because of your . . . ministry."

Dante was even more full of bile than usual, and it was Fowler's presence that brought it out. Paola didn't understand what he was up to, but she realized that it was something the two of them had to resolve, face to face.

"Enough already. Let's get out of here and breathe some fresh air."

The two men followed Dicanti back through the church. She was giving the nurses instructions on removing Pontiero's body when one of the UACV technicians approached Dicanti and began to tell her about evidence they had found. Paola nodded her head. She turned to Fowler.

"Could we concentrate a little, Padre?"

"Of course."

"Dante?"

"Why not?"

"All right, so this is what we have found. In the rectory there was a professional makeup kit and a heap of ashes on a table, which in our opinion are the remains of a passport. He poured a fair amount of alcohol on it after he lit the fire, so not much is left. The UACV team has taken the ashes, to see if there is anything solid there. The only prints found in the rectory aren't from Karosky, which means we'll have to find out who they belong to. Dante, you get the job for this afternoon. Find out who Padre Francesco was and how much time he spent here. Search among the church's regular parishioners."

"Agreed. I'll immerse myself in the senior citizen set."

"Knock off the jokes. Karosky has played with us, but he's nervous. He is hidden in the shadows, and for a certain period of time we're not going to hear from him. If in the next few hours we can manage to find out where he's been, we can perhaps find out where he's headed."

Paola secretly crossed her fingers in her coat pocket, trying to believe what she was saying. The two men put on their best stone faces, while they too pretended that the possibility was something more than an unlikely dream.

Dante came back two hours later. With him was a woman in her middle years, who repeated her story to Dicanti. When the previous parish priest, Brother Darío, died, Brother Francesco had shown up. Three years before, give or take. From that day on the lady had been helping him clean the church and the rectory. According to her, Brother Francesco Toma was a model of humility and Christian faith. He had taken thorough care of the parish. No one had a bad word to say about him.

It was, taken all together, a sufficiently frustrating statement, but it at least made one fact clear. The Franciscan Darío Bassano had died in November 2001, which confirmed Karosky's entrance into the country.

"Dante, do me a favor. Find out what the Carmelites know about Francesco Toma."

"I'll make some calls. But I suspect we won't come up with much."

Dante went out by the front entrance, in the direction of his office at the Vigilanza. Fowler was also on his way out.

"I'm going to my hotel to change. See you later."

"I will be at the morgue."

"You don't have to do it."

"Yes, I do."

They stood there uncomfortably, not saying a word to each other, their silence underscored by a hymn one of the pilgrims was singing. In the vast, turbulent crowd of people, one after another slowly joined in the chorus. The sun slipped behind the hills and Rome was slowly sinking into the long afternoon shadows. And yet the electricity in the streets was incessant.

"A song like that was probably the last thing Pontiero heard."

Paola didn't respond. Fowler had witnessed what the profiler was going through too many times before, the process that takes place after the death of a close companion. At the outset, it is a kind of intoxication, mixed with the desire for vengeance. Little by little the affected person descends into exhaustion and sadness, as he or she reckons with what happened and the shock takes on the presence of a physical wound. Dicanti would finally be left with a dull grief, a mixture of anger, blame, and resentment, which would only resolve itself when Karosky was behind bars or dead. And perhaps not even then.

The priest was about to put his hand on Dicanti's shoulder but stopped at the last second. He was standing directly behind her, and even without seeing him, she must have felt something. She turned around and looked at Fowler, a worried expression on her face.

"Careful, Padre. He knows you are here now, and that could change everything. Not only that, but we don't really know what he looks like. He's taken pains to be very clever when it comes to his disguise."

"How much can he have changed in five years?"

"I looked at the photograph that you showed me of Karosky and I saw 'Brother Francesco' with my own eyes. They don't resemble each other in the slightest."

"The church was exceedingly dark and you hardly paid any attention to that old Carmelite."

"Trust me. I know how to study people. He could be in disguise, a beard covering half his face, but he would still look like an old man, the real thing. Karosky knows how to conceal himself very skillfully, and by now he could be someone else entirely."

"All well and good. But I've seen him up close. If he crosses my path, I will recognize him. Subterfuge will only get him so far."

"It is more than just subterfuge. He's got his hands on a 9mm now, with thirty bullets to spare. Pontiero's pistol and his bullet clip are missing."

MUNICIPAL MORGUE

Thursday, April 7, 2005, 1:32 A.M.

She came to the autopsy encased in stone. Every bit of adrenaline on reserve dissolved the instant she walked into the room, and she felt more and more depressed by the second. To watch as the coroner's scalpel dissected her partner was almost more than she could take, but she made it through. The coroner attested that Pontiero had been struck forty-three times with a blunt object, in all likelihood the candelabra that had been recovered, coated with blood, at the scene of the crime. As to what had caused the cuts on his body, including the slit on his throat, he reserved judgment until laboratory personnel were finished making molds of the incisions.

Paola listened to the report through a sensory fog, which failed in the slightest to attenuate what she was going through. She stood there watching for hours, enduring a self-imposed punishment. Dante stopped into the autopsy room, asked a few questions, and quickly went on his way. Troi stuck his head in too, but it was only a symbolic gesture. He walked out immediately, stunned, in a state of disbelief, muttering in passing that he had been speaking with Pontiero just a few hours before.

When the coroner was finished, he left the body on the metal table. He was lifting the sheet over the dead man's face when Paola spoke up.

"Don't."

The coroner exited the room without saying a word.

The body was clean, but it exuded a faint coppery scent. The harsh, unrelenting light of the six bulbs made her friend, already on the short side, look very small. The bruises covered his body like medals of pain, and his wounds, huge as obscene mouths, still gave off the rusty odor of blood.

Paola looked around for the envelope with the contents of Pontiero's pockets. A rosary, a few keys, his wallet. A ballpoint pen, a lighter, a newly opened pack of cigarettes. When she saw that last object and realized that no one was ever going to smoke those cigarettes, she felt very sad, and even abandoned. And she began to accept the fact that her partner and friend was dead. As if to deny it, she shook out one of the cigarettes. The lighter's dancing flame scraped against the heavy silence in the autopsy room.

Paola had given it up after the death of her father. She repressed the urge to cough and took a heavy drag. Imitating Pontiero, she blew the smoke straight at the No Smoking sign. And she began to say good-bye.

Shit, Pontiero. Fuck. Shit, shit, shit. How could you be so clumsy? This is all your fault. Look at yourself. We haven't even let your wife see your body. He did a good job on you, fuck he really did you good. She couldn't have taken it, she couldn't have taken it seeing you like this. It's a bit shameful. Does it seem normal to you that I'm probably the last person in the world who will see you naked? I promise you this isn't the kind of intimacy I wanted to share with you. No, of all the cops in the world you were the worst candidate for a closed coffin and now you've earned it.

Everything for you. Pontiero, you lummox, you jerk, why didn't you see it coming? What the hell did you find in that underground passageway? I can't believe it. You've always been running close behind cancer of the lungs, just like my goddamned father. Jesus Christ, you've got no idea the things I think of every time I see you smoking one of these pieces of shit. I see my father in the hospital bed again, coughing his lungs out on the sheets. And there I was, studying every afternoon. In the morning at school, and in the afternoon cramming the assignments in my head to the sound of his coughing. I always thought I'd end up at the foot of your bed too, holding your hand while you went to the other part of town, accompanied by Hail Marys and Our Fathers and you with your eye on the nurse's ass. That's what was in the cards for you, but you checked out early. Couldn't you have called me, you jerk? Shit, you look like you're chuckling at me while I apologize. Or do you think it's my fault? Your wife and children don't think so now, but they will when someone tells them the whole story. But no, Pontiero, it's not my fault. It's your fault and yours alone, you imbecile. Worse than an imbecile. Why the hell did you go down into that tunnel? And screw your damned faith in anything wearing a robe. That bastard Karosky, he really played us. Well, he played me, and you've paid for it. That beard, that nose. He wore those glasses just like he was giving us the finger, just to hold us up to ridicule. A real bastard. He looked straight at me, but I couldn't see past the two bottle caps perched on his nose. That beard, that nose. Can you believe that I don't know if I would recognize him if I saw him again? I already know what you're thinking. Take a look at the scene of Robayra's murder to see if he turns up somewhere, even in the background. And I'm going to do it, for God's sake. I'm going to do it. So stop being a little wiseass. And stop smiling, you son of a bitch, stop smiling. It's just rigor mortis, for the love of God. Even though you are dead you want to keep foisting the blame on me. Don't trust anyone, you were telling me. Watch your step, you'd say. Is it permissible to know why you're giving me all this damn advice if you're not going to follow it? God, Pontiero, a nice little mess you've left me with. Because of your damned clumsiness I have got to face this monster alone. Fuck, if we're on the trail of a priest, then robes automatically become suspect, Pontiero. Don't come at me with that. Don't let yourself off the hook with the argument that Francesco looked like a homeless, crippled old man. Christ, he really did a job on you. Shit, shit. How I hate you, Pontiero. Do you know what your wife said when she was told that you had died? She said, "He can't die. He likes jazz." She didn't say, "He has two kids," or "He is my husband and I love him." No, she said that you like jazz. As if Duke Ellington or Diana Krall were a fucking bulletproof jacket. Shit, she senses you, she feels you as if you were still alive, she hears your raspy voice and the music you listen to. She still smells the cigarettes you smoke. That you smoked. How I hate you, you pious piece of shit. . . . What good is everything you prayed for to you now? The people you trusted have turned their backs on you. Now I remember that day we ate pastrami in the middle of Piazza Colonna. You said that priests are simply men with a responsibility and not angels, and that the Church doesn't realize this. And I swear to you that I will say it to the next one who stands on the balcony of Saint Peter's, I swear I will write it on a poster so big he'll see it even if he's blind. Pontiero, you goddamned idiot. This wasn't our battle. Oh shit, I'm afraid, very afraid. I don't want to end up like you. That table looks as cold as ice. And what if Karosky follows me to my house? Pontiero, you idiot, this isn't our battle. It's a battle between the priests and their Church. And don't tell me it's mine, too. I don't believe in God anymore. Or I should say, I do. But I don't believe he's a good person. My love for Him left me stranded at the feet of a dead man who should have lived thirty years more. He took off faster than a cheap deodorant, Pontiero. And now all that's left is the stench of the dead, of every dead body we've seen the last few years. Bodies that stink to high heaven before their time because God didn't know how to care for some of his creatures. And your body is the one that will smell the worst of any of them. Don't *look at me like that. Don't tell me that God believes in me. A decent God doesn't let things like this happen, he doesn't let one of his own be transformed into a wolf among sheep. You heard just like I did what Fowler said. That head case with his lower half in knots was abandoned after all the shit they threw at him and now he's looking for thrills even more powerful than raping little boys. And what do you have to say for yourself? What kind of God lets them stick a straight arrow like you in a fucking freezer with wounds big enough for your coworker to slip her hand into? Shit, it wasn't my battle before, way before I got so carried away with Troi, to catch one of these degenerates. But you can see I'm useless. No, shut up. Don't say anything. Stop protecting me. I'm not a child. Yes, I've been useless. Is it so terrible to admit it? I haven't thought clearly. It's obvious that things have overwhelmed me, but there it is. It's over. Fuck, it wasn't my battle, but it is now. Now it's personal, Pontiero. Now I couldn't give a shit about the pressure from the Vatican, from Cirin, from Troi, or from the bitch who gave birth to every single one of them. Now I'm going to go at every one, and it doesn't matter to me if heads roll along the way. I'm going to catch him, Pontiero. For you and for me. For your wife who's waiting there outside and for your two brats. But above all for you, because you're in the deep freeze and already your face isn't your face anymore. God, he really fucked you over. How fucked over he left you and how alone I feel. I hate you, Pontiero, and I'll miss you even more.*

Paola went out to the hallway. Fowler was waiting for her, sitting on a wooden bench and staring at the wall. As soon as he saw her, he stood up.

"I—"

"It's OK."

"It's not OK. I know what you are going through and you cannot be in good shape."

"I am definitely not in good shape. But for Christ's sake, I'm not about to fall in your arms a second time like some damsel reeling from the pain. Let's leave that for the movies."

She was taking off at a clip when Troi appeared in the hallway.

"Dicanti, we have got to talk. I'm very worried about you."

"You too? What a novelty. Sorry I don't have time for a chat."

Troi stepped in her path. Dicanti's head came up to her boss's chest.

"I don't understand you, Dicanti. I'm taking you off the case. There's too much at stake now."

Paola looked up. She stared into his eyes and spoke very, very slowly, her voice cold and controlled.

"Listen to me, Carlo, really listen, because I'm only going to say it once. I am going to capture the guy who did this to Pontiero. Neither you nor anyone else has any say in the matter. Did I make that clear enough?"

"What doesn't seem to be clear is who's in charge here, Dicanti."

"Maybe so. But what I know clearly is what I have to do. So please, out of my way."

Troi opened his mouth to say something but stepped aside instead. Paola stormed off toward the exit.

Fowler laughed.

"What is so amusing, Padre?"

"You, of course. You don't fool me. You didn't consider taking her off the case for a second, did you?"

The director of UACV put on a show of being shocked.

"Paola's a strong, independent woman who runs the risk of losing her balance. All the anger she's feeling can be focused, channeled."

"Words, words, words. I don't hear the truth."

"OK, I can see that. I fear for her. I'm nervous about her. I needed to know that she has the strength to keep going. Any other answer than the one she gave me, I throw her off the case straightaway. We're not up against somebody who plays by the rules."

"Now you're leveling with me."

Fowler intuited that behind the cynical politician and administrator there lurked a human being. The priest saw what kind of man Troi was at that hour, at dawn when his clothes were wrinkled and his soul rubbed raw by the death of one of his subordinates. Maybe Troi spent a good deal of time on self-promotion, but he had almost always covered Paola's back. And he was still very attracted to her, that was obvious.

"Fowler, I have a favor to ask you."

"No."

"What do you mean by that?" Troi was bewildered.

"You don't have to ask me. I'll take care of the *dottoressa,* in spite of herself. For better or worse, there are only three of us on this case. Fabio Dante, Dicanti, and myself. We'll have to make a united front."

UACV HEADQUARTERS
Via Lamarmora, 3
Thursday, April 7, 2005, 8:15 A.M.

"Don't trust Fowler, Dicanti. He's a killer."

Paola looked up from the Karosky dossier with puffy eyes. She'd only had a few hours' sleep before returning to her desk at daybreak. She was not in the habit of doing things this way: Paola liked to enjoy a long breakfast followed by a stroll to work, ready to soldier on well into the night. Pontiero had pestered her about that. "You are letting the glorious Roman morning pass you by," he'd say, and here she was at her desk now, not exactly enjoying the morning as she paid respects to her friend in her own fashion. Yet from where she sat the dawn was particularly beautiful: the sun slithering over the Roman hills at a leisurely pace, the rays of sunlight lingering on each building and cornice, saluting the art and beauty of the Eternal City. Each of the day's shapes and colors made its appearance with such delicacy it seemed to be knocking at the door to ask permission to enter. Yet who should walk into Dicanti's office without asking, with an unnerving accusation on his lips, but Fabio Dante. The deputy inspector turned up half an hour before agreed upon. With a manila envelope in his hand and a mouth full of serpents.

"Dante, have you been drinking?"

"Nothing of the sort. I'm telling you he's a killer. Remember I told you not to trust him? His name set off an alarm in my head. A memory lodged at the back of my brain, something I knew before. So I did a little investigation of your supposed military man."

Paola sipped a cup of nearly cold coffee. She was intrigued.

"And he isn't in the military?"

"Of course he is. A military chaplain. But he's not serving in the Air Force. He's in the CIA."

"The CIA? You must be joking."

"No, Dicanti. Your Fowler is not a man to be taken lightly. Listen to me: He was born in 1951, into a wealthy family. His father owned a pharmaceutical company, or something like it. He studied psychology at Princeton. He finished school at twenty years old, magna cum laude."

"Magna cum laude. The highest ranking. So he lied to me. He told me he wasn't an especially brilliant student."

"He lied to you about that and about many other things. He didn't pick up his university degree. It seems he had serious disagreements with his father and enlisted in 1971. A volunteer smack in the middle of the Vietnam War. Five months of basic training in Virginia and ten months in Vietnam, with the rank of lieutenant."

"Wasn't he a little young for a lieutenant?"

"Are you joking? A volunteer with a university degree? They certainly planned on making him a general. I don't know what was going on in his head in those years, but he chose not to return to the United States after the war. He studied in a seminary in West Germany, and was ordained as a priest in 1977. Later on, he left traces of his presence everywhere: Cambodia, Afghanistan, Romania. We know that he went to China for a visit but then hightailed it out of there at full speed."

"None of which proves he was a CIA agent."

"Dicanti, it's all here." While he was talking, Dante started showing Paola photographs, most of them in black-and-white. In them she saw a curiously young Fowler progressively losing hair as the pictures came nearer to the present day: Fowler sitting on top of a pile of sandbags, surrounded by soldiers, wearing lieutenant's stripes; Fowler in a hospital with a smiling soldier; Fowler on the day of his ordination, receiving the sacrament in Rome from none other than Paul VI; Fowler on an enormous runway, planes in the background, dressed in his clergyman's garb, surrounded by younger soldiers. . . .

"This is from when?"

Dante consulted his notes.

"1977. After his ordination Fowler returned to Germany, to the air base at Spangdahlem. As a military chaplain."

"As his later history bears out."

"Almost—but not in every respect. A report which shouldn't be in the file, but is, says that 'John Anthony Fowler, son of Marcus and Daphne Fowler, lieutenant in the United States Air Force, received a raise in rank and salary after successfully completing field training in counterespionage techniques.' In East Germany. Right in the middle of the Cold War."

Paola shrugged. She still couldn't picture it.

"Wait, Dicanti, that's not the end of it. As I said before, he traveled extensively. In 1983 he disappeared for several months. The last person who knows something about him is a priest in Virginia."

Paola began to lose heart. A military man who disappears for several months in Virginia has but one place to go: CIA headquarters in Langley.

"Go on, Dante."

"In 1984 Fowler turns up, briefly, in Boston. His mother and father are killed in a car accident in July. He attends the deposition of the will, where he instructs the lawyers to divide all his money and possessions among various charities. He signs the necessary papers and takes off. According to his lawyer, the sum total from his parents' properties and the pharmaceutical company was in excess of eighty million dollars."

Dicanti exhaled an inarticulate, out-of-tune whistle of pure astonishment.

"A fair pile of money, and even more in 1984."

"Well, he gave everything away. A pity you didn't know him back then, eh, Dicanti?"

"What are you insinuating?"

"Nothing, nothing. All right then, to finish off the craziness, Fowler takes off for Mexico and from there to Honduras. He is named chaplain of the military base at El Aguacate, now with the rank of major. And that's where he becomes a killer."

Paola looked at the next group of photographs and froze. Rows of human bodies in dusty common graves. Workers with pitchforks and face masks that only slightly hid the horror on their faces. Disinterred bodies, rotting in the sun. Men, women, and children.

"Good Lord, what is this?"

"How much do you know about history? I'm terrible myself. I had to poke around the Internet to learn about the whole damned thing. It seems that in Nicaragua the Sandinistas had a revolution. The counterrevolution, called the Nicaraguan Contras, wanted to put a right wing government back in power. Ronald Reagan's government supported the rebel guerrillas under the table, guerrillas who in many cases seemed more worthy of being called terrorists. And can you guess who was the U.S. ambassador to Honduras during that time?"

Paola was starting to connect the dots at full speed.

"John Negroponte."

"First prize for the beauty with the black hair! Founder of the El Aguacate air base, on that very same border with Nicaragua, the training base for thousands of Contra guerrillas. According to *The*

Washington Post, El Aguacate was "a clandestine center for detention and torture, more like a concentration camp than a military base in a democratic country." Those lovely, graphic photos I showed you were taken ten years ago. There were men, women, and children in those unmarked graves. And it is believed that there are still an indeterminate number of bodies, as many as three hundred, buried out in the mountains."

"Jesus, this is terrible beyond belief." Nevertheless, the photos didn't stop Paola from giving Fowler the benefit of the doubt. "It doesn't prove anything."

"He was there. He was the chaplain at a torture camp, for God's sake! Who do you think attended the people who were shot before they died? How could he not be in the picture?"

Dicanti looked at him without saying a word.

"All right, *Ispettore,* you want more? Here is the material from the envelope. A report from the Sant'Uffizio, the Holy Office. In 1993 he was called to Rome to testify regarding the assassination of thirty-two nuns seven years earlier. They had fled from Nicaragua and ended up at El Aguacate. They were raped, taken for a ride in a helicopter, and then ka-blam! You've got a nun pancake. In the process he also testified about twelve Catholic missionaries who had disappeared. The root of the accusation was that he knew about everything that was going on but never protested those flagrant cases of the violation of human rights. In which case, he was as guilty as if he himself had piloted the helicopter. Something which, by the way, he does in fact know how to do."

"And how did the Holy Office decide?"

"Well, there wasn't sufficient proof to charge him. He got off by the skin of his teeth and left the CIA of his own free will, I'm pretty certain. For a while he was at loose ends, and then he turned up at the Saint Matthew Institute."

Paola spent a good while looking at the pictures.

"Dante, I am going to ask you a very serious question. As a citizen of the Vatican, would you say that the Holy Office is a careless institution?"

"No."

"Could it be said that it maintains its independence?"

Dante nodded reluctantly. He now saw where Paola was headed.

"Taking all that into account, the most rigorous institution in the Vatican has been unable to find proof of Fowler's guilt, and you come into my office shouting that he's a killer, advising me not to trust him in the slightest?"

Dante leapt to his feet, furious. He leaned on Dicanti's desk.

"You listen to me, my pretty little girl. Don't think for an instant I don't see the way you're looking at that phony priest. Because of an unfortunate twist of fate we're obliged to hunt for a fucking monster under his orders, and I don't want you thinking with your skirts. You have already lost one coworker, and I don't want that American covering my back when we are face-to-face with Karosky. Then you'll see how he reacts. From all appearances, he is very loyal to his country and he's liable to take a fellow American's side when it comes down to it."

Paola stood up and, without losing her composure, smacked Dante in the face twice. *Whap. Whap.* Two slaps, absolutely on target, the kind that set the ears ringing. Dante stood there, so completely surprised and humiliated he had no clue how to react. He was transfixed, his mouth hanging open and his cheeks on fire.

"It's your turn to listen to me, Dante. If the three of us are joined at the hip for this fucking investigation it's because your Church doesn't want any light shining on a monster, a man who raped children and who was then castrated in one of its secret backwaters, a man who is now killing cardinals only ten days before they elect the next big shot. That and that alone is the reason why Pontiero is dead. I remind you that it was your people who came to ask our help. It seems that your organization functions stupendously well when it has to get its hands on information about a priest working in a Third World jungle, but it doesn't quite measure up when it comes to controlling a sexual delinquent who relapses dozens of times over the course of ten years, in full view of his superiors, in a democratic country. Since that's the case, drag your pathetic mug out of here before I start to think that your problem is that you're jealous of Fowler. And don't come back until you're ready to work on a team. *Capisci?*"

Dante recovered his composure long enough to take a deep breath and spin around. Fowler walked into the office at exactly the same moment, and the deputy inspector let out his frustration by flinging the photographs in his hand at the priest's face. Dante was so furious he slipped away without even remembering to slam the door.

But Dicanti actually felt better, for two reasons: first, for having the chance to do what she had many times imagined she would have to do; and second, for having done it in private. If the identical situation had presented itself with someone else present or in the middle of the street, Dante would never have forgotten being smacked down in public. No man would. There were still more ways to adjust the situation and create a semblance of harmony. She looked at Fowler out of the corner of her eye. He stood in the doorway, not moving, his eyes mesmerized by the photographs littering the floor of the office.

Paola sat down, took a sip of coffee, and, without raising her head from the Karosky dossier, said, "I think you have some explaining to do, Padre."

✝

THE SAINT MATTHEW INSTITUTE
Sachem Pike, Maryland

April 1997

Transcription of Interview #11 Between
Patient No. 3643 and Doctor Anthony Fowler

Dr. Fowler: Good afternoon, Father Karosky.

No. 3643: Come in, come in.

Dr. Fowler: I've come to see you because you have refused to speak to Father Conroy.

No. 3643: His attitude was insulting. In fact, I asked him to leave.

Dr. Fowler: What exactly seemed insulting about his attitude?

No. 3643: Father Conroy questions certain unchanging truths of our faith.

Dr. Fowler: Such as?

No. 3643: He says that the devil is an overvalued concept! It will be very amusing to watch when this concept sticks its pitchfork in his rear end.

Dr. Fowler: Do you think you will be there to see it?

No. 3643: In a manner of speaking.

Dr. Fowler: You believe in hell, yes?

150

No. 3643: With every bone in my body.

Dr. Fowler: Do you think you deserve to go there?

No. 3643: I am a soldier of Christ.

Dr. Fowler: That doesn't tell me anything.

No. 3643: Since when?

Dr. Fowler: Since there is no guarantee for a soldier of Christ that he will either go to heaven or hell.

No. 3643: If he is a good soldier, he does.

Dr. Fowler: Father, I want to give you a book that I believe will be of great help to you. It was written by Saint Augustine. It is a book which speaks about humility and inner struggle.

No. 3643: I will be happy to read it.

Dr. Fowler: You believe that you'll go to heaven when you die?

No. 3643: I am sure of it.

Dr. Fowler: Well, then you know more than I.

No. 3643: . . .

Dr. Fowler: Let me give you a hypothesis. Let's assume we meet at the Pearly Gates. God weighs your good acts and your bad, and the balance on the scale is even. And so he asks you to call on anyone you like to help dispel his doubts. Who would you call?

No. 3643: I'm not sure.

Dr. Fowler: Let me suggest a few names: Ryan, Jamie, Lewis, Arthur . . .

No. 3643: Those names mean nothing to me.

Dr. Fowler: . . . Harry, Michael, John, Grant . . .

No. 3643: Shut up!

Dr. Fowler: . . . Paul, Sammy, Patrick . . .

No. 3643: Shut up! I'm warning you!

Dr. Fowler: ... Jonathan, Aaron, Samuel ...

   No. 3643: Enough!

[The sound of a brief, confused struggle between the two men can be heard on tape.]

Dr. Fowler: The part of your body which I am squeezing between my thumb and forefinger is your trachea, Father Karosky. It goes without saying that it will be even more painful if you don't calm down. Signal with your left hand if you understand me. Good. Do it again when you have calmed down a little bit more. We can wait as long as is necessary. Already? Good. Here, take a drink of water.

   No. 3643: Thanks.

Dr. Fowler: Sit down, please.

   No. 3643: I'm better now. I don't know what came over me.

Dr. Fowler: Both of us know what just happened. Just as both of us know that the young boys on the list I read will not exactly testify on your behalf when you stand before the Almighty.

   No. 3643: ...

Dr. Fowler: You're not going to say anything?

   No. 3643: You don't know anything about hell.

Dr. Fowler: You think so? You are wrong: I have seen it with my own eyes. I'm going to turn off the tape recorder now and tell you something that I'm sure will interest you.

✝

UACV HEADQUARTERS
Via Lamarmora, 3
Thursday, April 7, 2005, 8:32 A.M.

Fowler took his eyes off the photographs scattered around the floor. Making no effort to pick them up, he merely glided over them. Paola asked herself if that represented an implicit response to Dante's accusations. Many times over the course of the next few days, Paola felt she was standing in front of a man as unreadable as he was polite, as ambiguous as he was intelligent. Fowler was a walking contradiction and an undecipherable hieroglyph. But at that moment she felt another emotion, blind anger, which her quivering lips could not conceal.

The priest sat down in front of Paola, resting his worn black briefcase against the side of her desk. In his left hand he carried a paper bag with three coffees. He offered one to Dicanti.

"Cappuccino?"

"I hate cappuccino. Makes me think of a dog I had whose vomit was that color. But all right." She took one of the cups.

For several minutes Fowler said nothing. Paola gave up the ruse of reading the Karosky dossier and decided to confront him. She had to know.

"And so? You're not going to . . ."

And she stopped in her tracks. Paola hadn't looked at Fowler since he had walked into her office. But when she did, she discovered that he was miles away. The hands that lifted the coffee to his lips were shaking and insecure. The room was cool, but tiny drops of sweat sat like pearls on the crown of his bald head. And his green eyes shouted that their owner had witnessed indelible horrors, and that, in his mind's eye, he was seeing them all over again.

Paola was silent. She realized that the apparent elegance with which Fowler had passed over the photographs was pure facade. She waited. The priest took several minutes to recover, and when he was ready, his voice was faraway, lifeless.

"It's difficult. You think that you've gotten over it, but then it turns up again, like a cork you try to sink in the bathtub. You hold it down and it pops back up to the surface. And that's where you run into it again."

"Maybe talking about it will help."

"Take my word for it: It won't. It's never helped in the past. There are some problems that cannot be resolved by talking."

"An interesting thing for a priest to say. Incredible for a psychologist. But appropriate for an agent of the CIA who was trained to kill."

Fowler did his best to keep from frowning.

"They didn't train me to kill, no more than any other soldier. I was trained in counterespionage tactics. God gave me the gift of perfect aim, that much is true, but I didn't go looking for it. And, to anticipate your next question, I haven't killed anyone since 1972. I killed eleven Vietcong soldiers, at least that I know. But all of those were killed in combat."

"You enlisted voluntarily."

"Before you judge me, let me tell you my story. I've never told anyone what I am about to tell you, so please, I only ask that you hear me out. Not that you believe me or trust me, because that is too much to ask at this moment. Simply, listen to what I have to say."

Paola nodded in assent.

"I suppose that all this information has arrived courtesy of our Vatican supervisor. If it's the Sant'Uffizio's report, it will have given you a very approximate idea of my history. I enlisted voluntarily in 1971, owing to certain . . . disagreements with my father. I don't want to blow you away with a horror story about what the war was for me, because words could never describe it. Have you seen *Apocalypse Now*?"

"Yes. Some time ago. I was surprised by how crude it was."

"A superficial farce. That film was a shadow on the wall, compared with what it was trying to describe. I saw enough pain and cruelty to fill several lives. But that's where I discovered my vocation. It didn't come to me in a foxhole in the middle of the night, with enemy fire whistling all around my head. It didn't come looking at the face of a ten-year-old kid wearing a necklace of human ears. It happened behind the lines, on a quiet afternoon spent with the regiment's chaplain. I knew then and there that I wanted to dedicate my life to God and his creatures. And that is what I did."

"And the CIA?"

"Don't jump so far ahead. I didn't want to return to the United States. My parents were still there. So I went as far away as I could, right up to the edge of the Iron Curtain. I learned many things there, but some of them—you are only thirty-four years old—you wouldn't know how to make sense of them. For you to understand what Communism meant for a German Catholic in the 1970s, you would have had to live through it. We inhaled the threat of nuclear war on a daily basis. The hatred that existed between the various groups was a religion unto itself. It seemed that every day we were a little closer to someone, either them or us, losing control. And that would have been the end of everything, I am certain of it. Sooner or later, someone would have pushed the button."

Fowler paused briefly to sip his coffee. Paola lit one of Pontiero's cigarettes. Fowler was reaching across the desk for the pack when Paola slid it a few inches farther away.

"They're mine. I have to smoke them all by myself."

"Don't worry about it. I wasn't going to take one, I just asked myself if you had suddenly picked up the habit again."

"It doesn't matter. I would rather you continue your story than we talk about that."

Fowler intuited the pain behind her words. He went back to his story.

"Of course. I wanted to continue to be part of the military. I love the companionship, the discipline, the feeling of a military life. If you think about it, it's not very different from the concept of the priesthood: it's a question of giving your life to others. Armies are not bad things in themselves; it's war that's evil. I asked to be sent to an American base as a chaplain, and as I was a diocese priest, my bishop went along."

"I'm a little vague on the meaning of diocese."

"It more or less means I am a free agent. I'm not tied to a congregation. If I want, I can petition my bishop to assign me to a parish. But if I think it's a better idea, I can undertake my pastoral labor where I prefer, always with the bishop's permission, understood as formal acquiescence."

"I follow."

"There, at the base, I worked alongside various members of the Agency who were giving a special instructional program in counterespionage activities for military personnel who did not belong to the CIA. They invited me to join them, four hours a day, five days a week, over the course of two years. It wasn't incompatible with my pastoral labors; it just cost me a few hours' sleep. So I accepted. And it turns out that I was a good student. One night, after class, one of the instructors pulled me aside with the proposal that I join the Company. That's how the Agency was known in its inner circles. I told him that I was a priest, that it would be impossible. I had a tremendous job in front of me with the hundreds of young Catholics at the base. Their superiors dedicated many hours each day to teaching them how to hate the Communists. I dedicated one hour each week to reminding them that we are all children of God."

"A lost cause."

"Almost always. The priesthood is a career for long-distance runners."

"I think I read those words in one of the interviews with Karosky."

"It's possible. We limit ourselves to making small points. Small victories. Every once in a while we achieve something a little grander, but that's few and far between. We plant a few seeds, with the hope that part of the crop will flourish. Typically the person who plants is not the one who sows, which can be demoralizing."

"Not to mention pissing you off."

"Once upon a time a king was strolling through the forest and he saw an old man, a poor man, bent over a furrow. He walked up to him and saw that he was planting seeds for chestnut trees. He asked the old man why he was doing it and the old man replied, 'I love the taste of chestnuts.' The king responded, 'Old man, stop punishing your bent back over a hole in the ground. Do you really not know that by the time even one of these trees has grown tall enough to bear nuts, you will not be around to gather them?' And the old man answered, 'Your Majesty, if my ancestors thought the way you do, I would never have tasted chestnuts.'"

Paola smiled, surprised by the fable's undeniable truth.

"Do you know what that anecdote teaches us?" Fowler paused before he went on. "That you always get ahead with goodwill, a love of God, and a good strong shot of Johnnie Walker."

Paola was a little abashed. She hadn't imagined the upright and proper priest with a bottle of whiskey in his hand, but it was clear he had been alone for long stretches of his life.

"When the instructor told me that some other priest could help the young men on the base but that the thousands of young people behind the Iron Curtain had no one to help them, I knew that what he was saying wasn't far from the truth. Thousands of Christians languished under Communism, praying in bathrooms and listening to mass in dark basements. They could serve the interests of my country and those of my Church at the same time, in those places where the two coincided. At that time, I really did believe they were in much greater agreement."

"And what do you think now? Because you've returned to active service."

"I'll get to that shortly. They offered to let me be a free agent, accepting only those missions I believed to be just. I traveled everywhere. In some I acted as a priest, in others as a normal citizen. My life was in danger many times, but it was almost always worth the risk. I helped people who needed my assistance in one form or another. At times that assistance took the form of a timely warning, a report, a letter; on other occasions it was necessary to organize a chain of communications, or to get someone out of a tight jam. I learned languages, and I even felt strong enough to go back to the United States. That was before what happened in Honduras."

"Hold on. You've jumped over an important part, your parents' funeral."

Fowler's face twisted into a look of extreme discomfort.

"I refused to take part. I merely arranged a few pending legal technicalities."

"Padre Fowler, you surprise me. Eighty million dollars is hardly a legal technicality."

"Ah, so you know about that as well. All right, yes, I relinquished control of the money. But I didn't give it away, as many people think. I used it to create a nonprofit foundation which works in various fields of social endeavor, inside and outside of the United States. It bears the name of Howard Eisner, the chaplain who encouraged me in Vietnam."

"You set up the Eisner Foundation?" Paola brightened. "In that case, you really have been around."

"I didn't create it. I just gave it a push, supported the finances. In reality, it was my parents' lawyers who did the work. Much to their dismay, I might add."

"Fair enough. But tell me about Honduras. Take all the time you want."

The priest regarded Dicanti with curiosity. Her attitude had quickly changed in a subtle but important respect: she was now inclined to believe what he said. And she asked herself what had provoked the change.

"I don't want to bore you with the details. The history of El Aguacate would fill an entire book, but I'll give you the essentials. The CIA's objective was to work on behalf of a revolution. Mine was to help Catholics who were oppressed by the Sandinista regime. A volunteer army was formed and trained, in order to undertake guerrilla warfare to destabilize the government. The soldiers were recruited from among the poorest Nicaraguans. An old ally of the United States government sold them weapons, a man of whom few suspected just how he would turn out: Osama bin Laden. And the command of the Contras fell into the hands of a high school graduate by the name of Bernie Salazar, a fanatic, as we later learned. Throughout the months in which the army was being trained, I went with Salazar across the border, on incursions which became a little riskier each time. I helped to get some compromised religious people out of the country, but I found myself progressively more at odds with Salazar with each raid. He starting seeing Communists here, there, and everywhere. Communists under every rock, if you listened to him."

"According to what I read in an old psychiatric manual, fanatic leaders quickly develop a heightened sense of paranoia."

"The case corroborates your book to the letter. I suffered an accident, which I only learned much later had been planned in advance. I broke a leg, which kept me out of any further border crossings. And the guerrillas started to come back a little later all the time. They no longer slept in the barracks, but in clearings in the jungle, in bivouacs. At night they were supposedly taking target practice, what was later revealed to be summary executions. I was laid up in bed, but the night that Salazar captured the nuns, and accused them of being Communists, someone warned me. He was a good kid, like many of those who threw their lot in with Salazar, but he was a little less fearful than the others. Only a little less, because what happened he told me in the secrecy of confession. He knew I wouldn't tell anyone, but it put me in the position of doing everything possible to help the nuns. We did what we could. . . ."

Fowler's face was utterly pale. He stopped long enough to swallow, not looking at Paola but somewhere outside beyond the window.

". . . But it wasn't enough. Today Salazar, like his young recruits, is dead, and the whole world knows that the Contras seized the helicopter and threw the nuns out over a Sandinista village. They needed three trips to do the job."

"Why did they do it?"

"The message was stark: 'We will kill anyone suspected of working with the Sandinistas. Whoever they are.'"

Paola sat without saying a word, reflecting on what she had heard.

"And you blame yourself. . . . It's true, isn't it?"

"It would be hard not to. I wasn't able to save those nuns. And I didn't take very good care of those young boys, who ended up killing their own people. My urge to do good was what dragged me there, but that wasn't what I achieved. I was just one more cog in a monster factory. My country is so used to it that it no longer bats an eye when someone we've trained, helped, and protected turns against us."

Although the sunlight was now full on his face, Fowler didn't blink. He merely squinted, turning his eyes into two green slits. He continued to stare out over the rooftops.

"The first time I saw the pictures of the common graves," the priest went on, "I was struck by the memory of the gunfire from the machine guns in the tropical nighttime. 'Target practice.' I'd grown accustomed to the noise. And then at some point one night, half-asleep, I thought I heard people crying out between the rounds, but I dismissed it. Sleep got the better of me. The next morning I told myself it was just my imagination. If, at that moment, I had talked to the base commander, and we had investigated Salazar more closely, we would have saved many lives. For that reason I am responsible for those many deaths, for that reason I left the CIA, and for that reason I was called before the Sant'Uffizio."

"Padre, I don't believe in God anymore. Now I know that when we die, it's all over. I think we go back into the earth, after a brief trip through the intestines of a worm. But if you in fact need absolution, I offer you mine. You saved the priests that you could before they fell into the trap."

A fleeting smile crossed Fowler's face.

"Thank you. You don't know how important your words are for me, even while I lament the profound break that comes across in such an affirmation from a longtime Catholic."

"But you still haven't told me why you decided to return."

"It's very simple. A friend asked me. And I don't like to let my friends down."

"So that is what you are now, God's spy."

Fowler smiled.

"You could call me that, I suppose."

Dicanti stood up and walked over to the shelves nearest her desk.

"Padre, this goes against principles, but as my mother likes to say, you only live once."

She pulled a thick volume of forensic analysis from the shelf and handed it to Fowler. He opened it. The first page had a signed dedication: "I hope this gift helps you to keep the faith. Maurizio." The pages of the book were cut out, creating three empty spaces, conveniently occupied by a half liter of Dewer's and two small glasses.

"It's barely nine A.M."

"Are you going to do the honors or do we wait for sunset, Padre? I feel proud to have a drink with the man who created the Eisner Foundation. Among other things, because that foundation provided the scholarship which sent me to study in Quantico."

It was Fowler's turn to be astonished this time. He poured two glasses of whiskey to the same height and raised his.

"Who are we toasting?"

"Those no longer with us."

"All right. For those who are no longer with us."

They drained their glasses. The liquid swirled down her throat, and for Paola, who never drank, it was like swallowing nails soaked in ammonia. She knew her stomach would be throwing tantrums all day, but she felt proud of having raised a glass with this man. There were some things you just had to do.

"What we have to be concerned about now is getting Dante back on the team. As you intuited, you owe this unexpected gift to your friend in the Vatican," Paola said as she gestured toward the photographs. "I ask myself why he did it. What does he have against you?"

Fowler broke out in laughter, which surprised Paola, who never before had heard a noise so theoretically joyful sound so piercing and sad.

"Don't tell me you haven't noticed."

"I'm sorry. I don't follow."

"*Dottoressa*, for someone so versed in applying reverse engineering to people's actions, you are demonstrating a radical lack of judgment in the case before you now. It's quite clear that Dante has taken a romantic interest in you. And for whatever absurd reason, he believes that I am his competition."

Paola was stone-faced, her mouth half-open. She could feel her cheeks turning a suspicious color, and it wasn't on account of the whiskey. It was the second time that man had managed to make her blush. She wasn't completely certain how he'd done it, but she wanted to feel it just a little bit more, like a child with a weak stomach who insists on getting back on the Ferris wheel a second time.

Providentially, from the point of view of getting out of a badly embarrassing situation, the telephone rang at exactly that moment. Dicanti grabbed it. Her eyes lit up.

"I'll be down immediately."

Fowler watched her, intrigued.

"Let's get a move on. Among the photos that the UACV developed from the Robayra crime scene is one with our Brother Francesco. We may have something."

✝

UACV HEADQUARTERS
Via Lamarmora, 3
Thursday, April 7, 2005, 9:15 A.M.

It was only a blur on the computer screen. The photographer had captured the interior of the chapel, and there in the background was Karosky, disguised as Brother Francesco. The technician enlarged that part of the image 160 times. Still, it was hard to make out anything specific.

"Not a whole lot there," Fowler interjected.

"Slow down, Father." Troi barged into the room, his arms full of papers. "Angelo is our forensic sculptor. He's an expert in image upgrade and I'm sure he'll find a way to get it in focus. Am I right, Angelo?"

Angelo Biffi, one of UACV's technicians, only rarely got up from his computer. His bottle-cap glasses were crowned by greasy hair; he looked to be somewhere in his thirties. He cloistered himself at a large, poorly lit table that served as his desk, and it reeked of half-eaten pizza, cut-rate cologne, and singed plastic. A dozen monitors of the very latest generation took the place of windows. Glancing around, Fowler decided that Angelo probably preferred to sleep next to his computers than to go home. He gave every impression of having been a lab rat his whole life, but even so he wasn't bad-looking. A timid smile had taken up a permanent perch on his face.

164

"You see, Padre, what I mean is, we, the department, or maybe it's only me—"

"Spit it out, Angelo. And have some coffee too," Paola said, leaning forward with the tray that Fowler had brought for Dante half an hour earlier.

"Thanks, *Dottoressa*. Wait, it's cold!"

"Don't worry, it's already hot outside. In fact, when you grow up you'll look back and say, 'This April is getting hot but not so hot as the one when Pope John Paul died.' Just wait and see."

Taken aback, Fowler stared at Dicanti, whose hand was resting on Angelo's shoulder in an attempt to calm him down. Even if she were going to pieces inside, Dicanti tried to camouflage it by making a joke. She had barely gotten any sleep, the bags under her eyes were larger than a raccoon's, and her emotions were a mess, sad and full of anger all at once. You didn't have to be a psychologist or a priest to see it. And in spite of everything, she was trying to help that kid feel more comfortable around a priest who intimidated him just a little. And at that moment Fowler loved her for it, but he quickly suppressed the thought. He couldn't forget the shame she had made him feel just a little while earlier in her office.

"Explain how you work to Padre Fowler," Paola said. "I'm sure he'll find it interesting."

When he heard that, the kid perked up.

"Take a look at the screen. We have, or I, OK, I designed special software for the interpolation of images. As you know, every image is composed of color dots called pixels. If a normal image contains roughly 2,500 by 1,750 pixels but we are only interested in a tiny corner of the photo, we'll end up with a few pointless splotches of color. Making it bigger simply turns it into the messy image you see now. Normally when a conventional program tries to enlarge an image it uses the bicubic method, what I mean is, it takes into account the color of the eight pixels adjacent to the one you want to enlarge. So at the end you get the same splotch magnified. But with my program . . ."

Paola looked at Fowler sideways while he leaned toward the monitor, staring. The priest had to force himself to pay attention to Angelo's explanation as he contended with the ordeal he had gone through just minutes before. Looking at those photos had been a very hard undertaking that had left him deeply upset; it was obvious to anyone who looked at him. And in spite of all that, he was forcing himself to like a timid young man he would never see again. Dicanti loved him for it, but she rapidly pushed the thought out of her mind. The embarrassment that had just taken place in her office was still on her mind.

". . . and taking into account the variables in the points of light, let's consider what a three-dimensional information program could bring to the project. It's based on a complex algorithm which takes several hours to work itself out."

"Damn it, Angelo, you brought us down here to tell us that?"

"But this—you'll see . . ."

"Don't worry, Angelo. Dicanti, I suspect that what this intelligent young man is trying to tell us is that the program has been working for several hours and will soon present its conclusions."

"Correct. In fact, it's coming out of the printer right now."

The humming laser printer directly in front of Dicanti produced a single piece of paper with an old man's face, his eyes shaded, but all in all a much more focused image than the original.

"Nice work, Angelo. Not strong enough to identify the man, but it's a point of departure. Take a look."

Fowler examined the features in the photograph closely. Troi, Dicanti, and Angelo watched and waited.

"I'd say it was him, but it's hard without seeing the eyes. The shape of the eye sockets and something else, something indefinable, tells me it's him. But if he walked by me in the street I wouldn't give him a second glance."

"So this is yet another dead end?"

"Not necessarily," Angelo suggested. "I have a program which can make a three-dimensional image out of a few pieces of information. I think we can infer enough with what we have. I've been working with a photo of the engineer."

"The engineer?" Paola asked out loud.

"Yes, the photo of engineer Karosky, the guy passing himself off as a Carmelite. You should see the look on your face, Dicanti."

Troi's eyes went on full alert, making unmistakable gestures of alarm behind Angelo's back. It finally dawned on Paola that Angelo had been left in the dark. Paola knew that the director had refused to let the four technicians looking for clues at the Robayra and Pontiero crime scenes go home. What he had done was give them permission to call their families to explain, and then put them in quarantine in one of the rooms where people took their coffee breaks. Troi could be hard when he wanted to be, but he was also fair: overtime he paid at three times the hourly.

"Ah yes, what was I thinking? Go on, Angelo."

Troi was no doubt divvying up the information at every level so that no one had all the pieces to the puzzle. No one had to know that they were investigating the death of two cardinals. Still, this obviously made Paola's work more difficult, besides which, it gave her serious doubts as to whether *she* had been made aware of all the elements in play.

"As I was saying, I have been working on the photo of the engineer. I think that in about thirty minutes we can have a three-dimensional image of his photo from 1995, which we can compare with the three-dimensional image we put together in 2005. If you come back in a little while, I'll have something more definite."

"Perfect. If it's okay with you, Padre, *Ispettore,* I would like to go over everything in the conference room. Angelo, we'll see you in a little while."

"Right, *Direttore* Troi."

The three headed up to the conference room, two floors above. No sooner had Dicanti walked in than she was overwhelmed by the terrible realization that the last time she had been in the room was in Pontiero's company.

"May I inquire what the two of you have done to Deputy Inspector Dante?"

Paola and Fowler exchanged quick glances. Their heads shook in unison.

"Absolutely nothing."

"That's good. I hope I don't see him storm out of here because of you two. It would be better if he was just pissed off by Sunday's soccer scores, because I don't want Cirin all over me, or the minister of the interior."

"I don't think you have to worry. Dante is fully integrated into the team," Paola lied.

"So why don't I believe it? Last night the guy saved your neck by a few inches, Dicanti. Want to tell me where Dante is now?"

Paola said nothing. She couldn't talk to Troi about the group's internal problems. She opened her mouth to say something, but a familiar voice got there first.

"I went out for cigarettes."

Dante, wearing his suede jacket and ironic smile, stood in the doorway to the conference room. Troi studied him slowly, skeptically.

"It's one of the very worst vices, Dante."

"We all have to die of something."

Paola watched Dante as he took a seat next to Fowler, as if nothing at all had come between them. Two fleeting, hostile glances were enough to convince Paola that things were not so smooth as they would like people to think. As long as they treated each other in a civilized manner for the next few days, everything would turn out well in the end. What she could not understand was how quickly her Vatican colleague had recovered from his anger. Something had happened.

"All right, then," said Troi. "This bloody case gets more complicated by the minute. Yesterday, in the course of going about our work in full daylight, we lost one of the best cops I have ever known, and nobody has a clue what's coming next. We can't even hold a public funeral, at least not until we come up with a reasonable explanation for his death. Which is why I want us to put our heads together. Tell me what you know, Paola."

"Since when?"

"Since the beginning. A quick overview of the case so far."

Paola stood up and walked over to the blackboard to write. She could think much more clearly on her feet, with something in her hands.

"OK, here goes. Victor Karosky, a priest with a history of sexual abuse, escapes from a private, low-security institution where he was subjected to excessive quantities of a drug which castrated him chemically while raising his levels of aggression. From June of 2000 until the end of 2001 there's no trace of his whereabouts. In 2001, using a fake name, he surreptitiously assumes the identity of a barefoot Carmelite in front of the Church of Santa Maria in Traspontina a few feet from Saint Peter's Square."

Paola drew a few lines on the blackboard and began to construct a calendar.

"Friday, April first, twenty-four hours before the death of John Paul the Second: Karosky takes the Italian cardinal Enrico Portini hostage in the Madre Pie residence. Have we confirmed that blood traces from both cardinals were found in the crypt?"

Troi nodded yes.

"Karosky takes Portini to Santa Maria, tortures him, and brings him back to the last site where he was seen alive: the chapel in the residence. Saturday, April second: Portini's body is discovered the same night as the death of the pope, although the Vatican Vigilanza decides to clean up the evidence, believing it to be the isolated act of a madman. Purely by luck, word does not get out, in good measure thanks to responsible parties in the residence. Sunday, the third of April: Argentine cardinal Emilio Robayra arrives in Rome on a one-way ticket. Our theory is someone meets him at the airport or en route to the Santi Ambrogio residence for priests, where he is expected on Sunday evening. We know he never arrived. Do we have anything useful from the airport's surveillance cameras?"

"No one has checked. We don't have enough personnel," Troi said, by way of excuse.

"We have more than enough."

"I can't bring any more detectives into this. The important thing is to keep a lid on it, complying with the wishes of the Holy See. Let's play it by ear, Paola. I will personally ask for the tapes."

Dicanti pulled a long face, but it was the response she had expected.

"Back to Sunday, April third. Karosky kidnaps Robayra and takes him into the crypt. Once there, he tortures the cardinal for more than a day, leaving messages on his body and at the scene of the crime. The sentence on the body is from the Gospels: 'And I will give unto thee the keys of the kingdom of heaven,' referring to the moment when the first supreme pontiff of the Catholic Church was chosen. This and the message written in blood on the ground, added to the severe mutilations of the body, leads us to believe the assassin has his eyes set on the conclave.

"Monday, April fourth: The suspect drags the body to one of the chapels in the church and calmly calls the police in his role as Brother Francesco Toma. Taking his mockery even further, he makes it a habit to wear Cardinal Robayra's glasses whenever he can. Vatican agents call UACV and *Direttore* Troi calls Camilo Cirin."

Paola paused briefly and looked directly at Troi.

"When you picked up the phone to call him, Cirin already knew who the criminal was, although he never suspected he was a serial killer. I gave it a good deal of thought and I believe Cirin knew the name of Portini's killer Sunday night. He probably had access to VICAP's database; the entry 'severed hands' would pull up a few cases. His network of contacts puts him in touch with Major Fowler, who arrives on the night of the fifth of April. Most likely the original plan did not include us. It was Karosky who brought us into the game, deliberately. *Why* is the real question in this case."

Paola drew the final line.

"Wednesday the sixth of April: while Dante, Fowler, and myself track down leads about the victims in their residence, Detective Maurizio Pontiero is beaten to death by Victor Karosky in the crypt of Santa Maria in Traspontina."

"We have the murder weapon?" asked Dante.

"Without fingerprints, but yes, we have it," Troi responded. "Karosky made several cuts with what could be a very sharp kitchen knife and beat his victim repeatedly with a candelabra found at the scene. But I don't have too many hopes along that line."

"May I ask why?"

"Because it isn't our normal procedure. Our job is to find out who the killer is. Typically, when we are sure of who he is, our work is over. But now we have to apply our knowledge to find out where the killer is. Certainty about his name has been our point of departure. For that reason, Dicanti's contributions are more important than ever."

"I tip my hat to *Inspettore* Dicanti. That was a brilliant chronology," said Fowler.

"Really sharp," Dante added, mocking all the way.

Paola could feel the resentment in his words, but she decided that it would be better to ignore the topic, for now.

"Nice summary, Dicanti." Troi congratulated her. "What's the next step? Pried into Karosky's head yet? Anything like what you've seen before?"

The profiler thought for a few seconds before she answered.

"All sane people are alike, but every one of these bastards is crazy in his own particular way."

"And what does that tell us, apart from the fact that you have read *Anna Karenina*?" Troi asked.

"Well, we would be committing a terrible blunder if we believed that one serial killer is exactly like another. You can try to search for rules of thumb, find equivalents, draw conclusions from similarities, but at the moment of truth every one of these pieces of shit is a very solitary mind living millions of light-years away from the rest of humanity. There's nobody home. They aren't human beings. They feel no empathy. Their emotions are turned off. The thing that makes them kill, that leads them to believe their ego is more important than anyone else's, the reasons they use to excuse their insanity—none of that matters to me. I don't try to understand them any further than is strictly necessary to catch them."

"Which is why we have to know what their next step is."

"Clearly, he is going to kill again. Most likely he'll hunt up a new identity for himself or he's already picked one. But there is no chance it will be as well rehearsed as that of Brother Francesco, which he worked on over several years. Maybe Padre Fowler can lend us a hand in this area."

The priest nodded his head, preoccupied.

"Everything I know is in the file I gave you, *Dottoressa*. But there is something I want to show you."

A pitcher of water sat on a side table along with some glasses. Fowler filled one of them halfway up and dropped his pencil in.

"It takes a tremendous effort for me to think like he does. Look at this glass. It's as clear as the water, but when I put a pencil in it, a pencil that looks like it's all in one piece now looks broken in two. In the same way, his monolithic attitude shifts at crucial moments, like a straight line that splits off and ends up in an unknown place."

"The point where it splits off is the key."

"Perhaps. I don't envy you your work, Dicanti. Karosky is a man who revolts against iniquity one minute, only to commit greater iniquities the next. What I do know is that we have to look for him around the cardinals. He will try to kill again, and he won't wait long. The conclave is getting closer and closer."

The group headed back down to Angelo's laboratory in a somewhat confused state. The young technician was introduced to Dante, who ignored him. Paola couldn't help but notice his rudeness. Dante was a very attractive man who was, at heart, rotten. His bitter jokes didn't conceal a thing; they were simply the best thing about him.

Angelo waited with the promised results. He hit the keyboard and three-dimensional images, conjured out of thin green threads on a black background, popped up on two screens.

"How about fleshing them out?"

"Sure. Now they'll have skin, rudimentary, but skin."

The monitor on the left displayed a three-dimensional model of Karosky's head as it was in 1995, the screen on the right the upper half of the head, as photographed at Santa Maria in Traspontina.

"I haven't modeled the lower half because with the beard it's impossible. You can't see the eyes too well either. In the photo they gave me, he's walking with his shoulders stooped."

"Can you copy the jaw from the first model and impose it on the new head?"

Angelo responded with a rapid flurry of pressed keys and mouse clicks. In less than two minutes, Fowler's request had been carried out.

"Tell me, Angelo, to what extent do you judge this second model to be trustworthy?" the priest asked.

The young technician was momentarily flustered.

"Well, you see . . . without assessing whether there was adequate lighting at the place . . ."

"That's out, Angelo. We already covered that," Troi interjected.

Paola started to speak, as slowly and comfortingly as she could.

"Listen, Angelo, nobody here is judging whether or not you've made a good model. We only want to know to what degree we can trust it."

"Well, somewhere between seventy-five and eighty-five percent. No more."

Fowler looked at the screen carefully. The two faces were very different. The nose was wider, the cheekbones stronger. But were they the subject's natural features or only makeup?

"Angelo, please, rotate both images on a horizontal plane and make a measurement of the cheekbones. Like that. That's it. . . . That's what I was afraid of."

The other four looked at him, holding their breath.

"What is it?"

"That isn't the face of Victor Karosky. An amateur applying makeup could never come up with differences like the one in the size of the cheekbones. Maybe a Hollywood professional could pull it off with latex molds, but it would be completely obvious to anyone who saw him close-up. He wouldn't be able to maintain the deception for very long."

"Which means?"

"There's only one explanation. Karosky has been treated by a surgeon and undergone a complete facial reconstruction. The man we are looking for is a ghost."

✝

THE SAINT MATTHEW INSTITUTE
Sachem Pike, Maryland

May 1998

**Transcription of Interview #14 Between
Patient No. 3643 and Doctor Anthony Fowler**

Dr. Fowler: Good afternoon, Father Karosky. May I enter?

No. 3643: Come in, Father Fowler.

Dr. Fowler: Did you enjoy the book I loaned you?

No. 3643: Yes, of course. *The Confessions of Saint Augustine.* I've already finished it. A very interesting book. It's unbelievable just how far innate optimism can take you.

Dr. Fowler: I don't understand.

No. 3643: But you are the only person in this whole place who can understand me. The only person who doesn't call me by my name, in an attempt to achieve a vulgar, unnecessary familiarity which denigrates the dignity of both parties.

Dr. Fowler: You are speaking of Father Conroy.

No. 3643: Yes, that man. The one who again and again maintains that I am a normal patient in need of being cured. I am a priest just as he is, and that dignity is what he constantly forgets when he insists I call him "Doctor."

176

Dr. Fowler: I believe that point was already clarified for you last week, Father Karosky. It's for good reason that your relations with Conroy are that of doctor and patient, and nothing else. You need help in overcoming a number of pyschological problems that stem from the suffering you endured in the past.

No. 3643: I suffered? I suffered at whose hands? Perhaps you too want to put my love for my saintly mother to the test? I beg you not to follow the same route that Father Conroy took. He has even stated that I will have to listen to some recordings that will remove all doubt.

Dr. Fowler: Some recordings.

No. 3643: That's what he said.

Dr. Fowler: I don't think you ought to hear those tapes, Father Karosky. It wouldn't be healthy for you. I will speak to Father Conroy about it.

No. 3643: As you see fit. But I am not at all afraid.

Dr. Fowler: Please listen, Father. I want to make maximum use of this session, and there is something you said a little earlier that very much interests me. About Saint Augustine's optimism in *The Confessions*. What were you referring to?

No. 3643: "And even if I appear laughable in your sight, you will come back to me full of mercy."

Dr. Fowler: I don't understand what strikes you as so optimistic in that passage. Is it because you don't have confidence in the goodness and infinite mercy of God?

No. 3643: The merciful God is an invention of the twentieth century, Father Fowler.

Dr. Fowler: Saint Augustine lived in the fourth century.

No. 3643: Saint Augustine was horrified by his own sinful past, and set out to write a string of optimistic lies.

Dr. Fowler: Father, but that string is the basis of our faith. That God pardons us.

No. 3643: Not always. They go to confession like someone who is going to wash his car. . . . Pah! They make me sick.

Dr. Fowler: That is what you feel when you administer confession? You feel nauseated?

No. 3643: I feel repugnance. Many times I vomited inside the booth, from the bile the person on the other side of the screen stirred up in me. Lies. Fornication. Adultery. Pornography. Violence. Theft. All of them, sneaking into this small space, contaminating it with their brutishness. They let it all spill out, until I'm drowning in it.

Dr. Fowler: But, Father, they aren't saying it to us. They are saying it to God. We are merely the transmitter. When we put on the priest's stole, we are changed into Christ.

No. 3643: Everything comes out. They arrive filthy and believe that they leave clean. "Bless me, Father, for I have sinned. I have stolen ten thousand dollars from my business partner." "Bless me, Father, for I have sinned. I raped my younger sister." "Bless me, Father, for I have sinned. I took photos of my son and posted them on the Internet." "Bless me, Father, for I have sinned. I put lye in my husband's food so he'll stop bothering me about being a good wife in bed. I'm sick of the way he reeks of onions and sweat." Just like that, day after day.

Dr. Fowler: But confession is a marvelous thing, Father Karosky, when there is repentance and an authentic attempt to change one's behavior.

No. 3643: Something that never happens. They always, always pile their sins on my shoulders. They abandon me, alone

before God's impassive face. I am the only one who in-
tervenes between their iniquities and God's vengeance.

Dr. Fowler: Do you really see God as a vengeful being?

No. 3643: His heart is as firm as a stone,

As hard as a piece of the nether millstone.

He maketh the deep to boil like a pot,

He maketh the sea like a pot of ointment.

The sword that layeth at him cannot hold;

The spear, the dart, nor the habergeon.

He surveys all with pride,

He rules over the fierce!

Dr. Fowler: I have to tell you that your intimacy with the Bible, particularly the Old Testament, always impresses me. But
the Book of Job was rendered obsolete by the truth Jesus
gives us in the Scriptures.

No. 3643: Jesus Christ is merely the Son; it is the Father who
renders judgment. And the Father has a face of
stone.

Dr. Fowler: I am very sorry to see that you have climbed so high in
the tower of your convictions. By necessity, the fall from
such a perch is fatal. And if you listen to the tapes in Father Conroy's possession, there is no question that that
is what will happen.

$$\dagger$$

HOTEL RAPHAEL
Largo Febo, 2
Thursday, April 7, 2005, 2:45 P.M.

"Saint Ambrogio Residence."

"Good afternoon. I'd like to speak with Cardinal Robayra," said the young journalist in her very worst Italian.

The voice on the other end of the phone was flustered.

"May I ask with whom I'm speaking?"

It wasn't much; the speaker's tone hardly changed. But it was enough to send a signal to the journalist.

Andrea Otero had spent four years working at *El Globo*. Four years in which she had blazed a trail through third-string press rooms, interviewed C-list personalities, and written stories for the back page. She was twenty-four years old when she joined *Globo,* and she had gotten the job through a personal connection. She started in the Culture pages, whose editor never took her seriously. She moved on to Society, whose editor never trusted her. And now she'd taken up residence in the International pages, whose editor did not consider her up to the job. But she was. It wasn't all about fame, or the courses you had taken. There was also common sense, intuition, the journalist's nose for a story. And if Andrea Otero had these qualities as much as even 10 percent of the extent she thought she did, she would be a journalist worthy of a Pulitzer. She didn't lack for confidence in herself. Her height of five feet eight inches, her angelic features, her blond hair and blue eyes—behind these was a woman of resolve and intelligence. So when her coworker who was going to cover the death of the pope tripped on the stairs of her apartment building on the way out to the cab to the airport and ended up with a broken leg, Andrea never hesitated when her boss proposed that she go instead. She caught the plane at the last second, the carry-on bag slung over her shoulder her only luggage.

Happily the streets around her hotel in the Piazza Navona were full of little stores selling the most basic necessities. And so Andrea Otero purchased several pairs of serviceable outfits and under-clothes, along with a mobile phone, all of them naturally charged to the newspaper. The last item was the one she was using to call the Saint Ambrogio Residence in order to set up an interview with candidate Cardinal Robayra.

"This is Andrea Otero, of *El Globo*. The cardinal promised me an interview for today, Thursday. But, sadly, he isn't answering his mobile. Would you be so kind as to put me through to his room, please."

"*Signorina* Otero, I'm sorry to say we cannot put you through to his room because the cardinal has not arrived."

"And when will he arrive?"

"He isn't coming."

"He hasn't arrived, or he isn't coming?"

"He hasn't arrived because he isn't coming."

"Is he staying somewhere else?"

"I don't think so. What I meant to say was, I guess he will."

"And with whom am I speaking?"

"I have to go."

The dial tone told her two things: the conversation was over and the person on the other end was exceptionally nervous. And so she had lied. Andrea was sure of that much. She was too good a liar herself not to recognize someone in her class.

There was no time to lose. In less than ten minutes she came up with the telephone number of the cardinal's office in Buenos Aires. It was almost ten in the morning over there, a prudent hour to make a call. She laughed at the bill the newspaper was going to get for her mobile. They were paying her little more than the minimum, so at least she had screwed them on expenses.

The telephone rang for a minute and then the line went dead. Strange that no one was there. She tried the line again.

Nada.

She tried the number of the main office. A woman's voice answered immediately.

"Archbishop's office, good morning."

"May I speak with Cardinal Robayra, please."

"Ah, señorita, he's already left."

"Left for where?"

"To the conclave, señorita. To Rome."

"Do you know where he's staying?"

"No, señorita. I'll connect you to Padre Serafín, his secretary."

"Thank you."

The Beatles played while she was on hold. How appropriate. Andrea decided to lie a bit just to keep things interesting. The cardinal had family in Spain. She wanted to see if she could pull it off.

"*Aló?*"

"Hi, I'd like to speak with the cardinal. It's his niece Asunción. The one from Spain."

"Asunción, how nice to hear from you. This is Father Serafín, the cardinal's secretary. The Eminence never told me about you. Are you Angustia's daughter, or Remedios's?"

She sensed a trap. Andrea crossed her fingers. A 50 percent chance of making a false move. Andrea was an expert in false moves too: she had a long history of putting her foot in her mouth.

"Remedios's."

"Of course, how stupid of me. I remember now. Angustia doesn't have any children. Unfortunately, the cardinal isn't here."

"When can I speak with him?"

Silence. The curate's voice became a touch cautious. Andrea could almost imagine him on the other end of the line, squeezing the receiver and twisting the cord with his index finger.

"What did you want to speak to him about?"

"Well, I have lived in Rome for years, and he promised me that the next time he was here he would visit me."

The voice on the other end became even more suspicious. He was speaking slowly, as if he were afraid of making a mistake.

"He left for Cordoba to take care of pressing matters in the diocese. He won't be able to attend the conclave."

"But at the main office they told me the cardinal had already left for Rome."

"Ah, yes, there's a new girl at the archbishop's office, and she's still unacquainted with how things work," Serafín fired back. He had obviously made that one up on the spot. "Please forgive me."

"You are forgiven. Will you tell my uncle that I called?"

"Of course. Could you give me your telephone number, Asunción? I want to put it on the cardinal's calendar. We might have to get in touch with you."

"He already has it. I'm sorry but my husband is on the line. Goodbye."

She hung up on the secretary just when he had something on the tip of his tongue. Now she was sure something wasn't right. But she had to confirm it. Lucky for her, there was an Internet connection in the hotel. It took her all of six minutes to find the phone number for the three main Argentine airline companies. She struck gold on the first try.

"Aerolineas Argentinas."

She made an effort to give her Madrid accent a passable Argentine stamp. It wasn't so bad. It was much worse when she had to speak in Italian.

"*Buenos días.* I am calling you from the archbishop's office. With whom do I have the pleasure of speaking?"

"My name is Verona."

"Verona, this is is Asunción. I am calling to confirm Cardinal Robayra's return flight to Buenos Aires."

"On what date?"

"He will be returning on the nineteenth of the coming month."

"His full name?"

"Emilio Robayra."

"Please wait while I check."

Andrea chewed nervously on the ballpoint pen in her hand, checked the condition of her hair in the mirror, threw herself on the bed, and tapped her feet to try to keep herself in check.

"*Aló?* My coworkers have advised me that you bought an open ticket going only one way. The cardinal has made the trip, which means that you can buy a ticket for the return flight at ten percent off. It's a special sale in April. Do you have his frequent flyer number handy?"

"One moment, let me check."

And she hung up, barely keeping a smile from taking over her whole face. But high spirits quickly passed into a euphoric feeling of triumph. Cardinal Robayra had gotten on a plane headed to Rome. But he never showed up anywhere. He could have decided to stay somewhere else. Yet, if that were the case, why did Saint Ambrogio and the cardinal's office lie to her?

"Either I'm crazy, or there's a good story here. A brilliant fucking story," she said to her reflection in the mirror.

Only a few days remained before they would choose the next man to sit on the throne of Saint Peter. And the great candidate of the poor, the advocate of the Third World, the man who openly flirted with Liberation Theology, had disappeared.

$\dagger$

DOMUS SANCTAE MARTHAE
Piazza Santa Marta, 1
Thursday, April 7, 2005, 4:14 P.M.

Paola stood at the entrance to the building with a look of surprise on her face. On the far side of the piazza, a long queue of cars waited at a gasoline station. Dante explained to her that, since the Vatican charged no tax, gas prices were 30 percent lower than in Italy. You had to have a special card to fill your tank at one of the city's seven stations, but even so the long lines were never-ending.

The three of them stood outside waiting while the Swiss Guards who covered the front door of the Domus Sanctae Marthae called the person inside the building to tell them that Paola, Dante, and Fowler would shortly be entering. Paola had a few moments to chew on everything that had happened that morning. Two hours earlier, at UACV headquarters, she had no sooner gotten out of Troi's clutches than she pulled Dante aside.

"I'd like a word with you."

Dante ignored the fact that Paola was glaring at him. He followed her to her office.

"I know what you are going to say to me, Dicanti. That we're together in this. Right?"

"That I already know. And I have also noticed that, like Troi, you call me *ispettore* and not *dottoressa*. Because *ispettore* is a lower rank than supervisor. It doesn't bother me in the least since your feeling of superiority never actually comes in contact with my doing my job. As in your little performance earlier with the photographs."

Dante turned red.

"I just wanted to let you know. Nothing personal."

"You wanted to put me on notice about Fowler? You've already done that. Is my position still clear, or must I be even more concrete?"

"I have had enough of your clarity, *Ispettore*." He dragged out the word, sounding a bit like a guilty child. Meanwhile one hand rubbed his cheeks. "You knocked the fucking fillings out. What I don't understand is how you didn't break a bone in your hand."

"Nor I, because you have a very hard face."

"I'm a hard guy in more than one sense of the word."

"I don't have the slightest interest. And I hope you don't forget that."

"Is that a woman's no, *Ispettore*?"

He was making Paola nervous again.

"What is a woman's no?"

"The kind they spell Y-E-S."

"It's the no they spell N-O, Mr. Ballsy Macho."

"Calm down. No need to get excited, Hot Pants."

Dicanti silently cursed him. She was falling into Dante's trap, letting him play with her emotions. But everything was fine. She would adopt a more formal tone, making her disdain impossible to miss. She decided to imitate Troi, since he always came out of these types of confrontations smelling like roses.

"OK, now that we have clarified that, I have to tell you that I've spoken with our North American counterpart, Padre Fowler. I have expressed my fears concerning your summation to him. Fowler made some highly convincing arguments, which in my judgment are sufficient for me to trust him. I want to thank you for the trouble you took to dig up the information on Fowler. It's a point in your favor."

Dante was surprised by Paola's cool tone. He had lost the match and he knew it.

"As the person in charge of the investigation, I have to formally ask you if you are ready to give your full support to capturing Victor Karosky."

"Of course, *Ispettore*." Dante spit the words out like red hot nails.

"All that's left is to ask you why you came back so quickly."

"I called my superiors to complain but they were no help. They ordered me to rise above personal animosity."

Paola's ear pricked up at that last phrase. Fowler denied that Dante had anything against him, but the deputy inspector's words indicated otherwise. Once before Dicanti had sensed that the two knew each other from some earlier time, in spite of the way they had carried themselves up to now. She decided she would ask Dante directly.

"Did you know Anthony Fowler before?"

"No, *Ispettore*," Dante said. His voice was firm, unhesitating.

"His case file showed up very quickly."

"The Corpo di Vigilanza is very well organized."

Paola decided to drop it. When she was ready to leave, Dante spoke three very flattering sentences.

"Just one thing. If you ever feel the need to call me to order again, I prefer the slapping method. I really don't care for formalities."

Paola asked Dante to show her the building where the cardinals were going to reside. And there they were. The Domus Sanctae Marthae, Saint Martha's House. Located to the west of the basilica, inside the walls of the Vatican.

From outside, its appearance was austere. Straight, elegant lines, without moldings, adornment, or statues. Compared to the marvels that surrounded it, the Domus stood out no more than a golf ball in a barrel of snow. It would have been difficult for the occasional tourist—and they weren't allowed into that restricted area of the Vatican in any case—to give the building more than a glance.

But when the authorization arrived and the Swiss Guards let them pass through the entrance, Paola discovered that the inside bore little relation to the exterior. Here was what looked like a fashionable hotel, complete with marble floors and tropical hardwoods. Traces of lilac wafted through the air. While they were waiting in the vestibule, Dicanti looked around. There were paintings on every wall, paintings in which Paola was able to recognize the work of the great Dutch and Italian masters of the sixteenth century. And none of them appeared to be reproductions.

"Holy shit." Paola was trying to limit her outbursts, but she was astounded. She only pulled it off when she calmed down.

"I know what you are feeling," Fowler said.

Dicanti recalled that Fowler's personal circumstances had hardly been pleasant during his stay at the Domus.

"It's a complete break with respect to the rest of the buildings in the Vatican, at least the ones I'm familiar with. The new and the old."

"Do you know anything about the history of this residence? You probably remember that in 1978 there were two conclaves, one right after the other, two months apart."

"I was a little girl, but I still have a few pictures in my mind from those days." For little more than a few seconds Paola let herself sink into the past.

Gelati in Saint Peter's Square. Mamma and Papa had limón, *I had chocolate and strawberries. The pilgrims were singing, there was happiness everywhere. Papa's hand, strong, with deep grooves. I loved to hold on to his fingers and stroll around while day turned into afternoon. We looked up toward the chimney and we saw the white smoke. Papa lifted me onto his shoulders. His smile was the best thing in the world. I dropped my gelato and I cried, but Papa just laughed again and promised me that he would buy me another one. "Let's have a cone for the health of the Bishop of Rome," he said.*

"The building was selected during the brief period between the two popes, when the successor to Paul IV, John Paul I, died suddenly thirty-three days after his election. There was a second conclave, the one in which John Paul II was chosen. In those days the cardinals resided in tiny cells near the Sistine Chapel. Lacking conveniences and air-conditioning, the heat of the Roman summer as heavy as lead, a few of the oldest cardinals went through a real calvary. More than one had to seek emergency treatment. Once he had put on the fisherman's sandals, Wojtyla personally decided that he would leave behind a facility so that when he died, none of this would happen again. The result is this building. Dicanti, are you listening to me?"

Paola emerged from her daydream with a guilty look.

"Sorry, I was thinking about something. Won't happen again."

Dante came back. He had gone in first in order to talk to the party responsible for security at the Domus. Paola noticed that he shunned the American priest, possibly just to avoid a confrontation. Both of them were straining to speak to each other in a normal tone, but Paola doubted that Fowler had leveled with her when he suggested the rivalry could be ascribed to Dante's jealousy. For now, even though the team was holding together with knives out, the best she could do was to maintain the farce and ignore the problem, something that Paola had never been very good at.

Dante returned in the company of a tiny little nun, who was

laughing and sweating inside her black habit. Introduced as Sister Helena Tobina, from Poland, she was Saint Martha's director, and she proceeded to deliver a thorough report of all the changes that had taken place in the building. The changes had been carried out in several stages, the last of them instituted in 2003. They walked up a wide staircase, whose every step was polished to a sheen. The building consisted of floors with large landings and thick carpets, with doors to the individual rooms on both sides.

"There are one hundred and six suites, and twenty-two individual rooms. All of the furniture dates from several centuries ago, and consists of valuable furniture donated by German and Italian families."

The nun opened the door to one of the rooms. A large one, some two hundred square feet, with parquet floors and a beautiful rug. The bed frame was made of wood, with an exquisite carved headboard. A bureau draped with fabric, a desk, and a bathroom made up the rest of the room.

"This room belongs to one of the six cardinals who has yet to arrive. The other hundred and nine have already taken theirs."

Dicanti mused that at least two of those who were absent were never going to show up.

"Are the cardinals safe here, Sister Helena?" Paola asked cautiously in response. She was uncertain to what extent the nun was aware of the danger that was hovering around the men in red robes.

"Very safe, my child, very safe. The building has only one entrance, with Swiss Guards on duty twenty-four hours a day. We have ordered the telephones taken out of the individual rooms, and the televisions too."

Paola found the precautions strange.

"The cardinals are incommunicado during the conclave. No telephones, no mobiles, no radios, no televisions, no magazines, no Internet. No contact whatsoever with the outside world under pain of being excommunicated." Fowler cleared things up for Paola. "Orders of John Paul II, just before he died."

"But it won't be easy to isolate them completely. What do you think, Dante?"

The deputy inspector stuck out his chest. It gave him great pleasure to calculate his organization's heroic undertakings as if he were carrying them out personally.

"You'll be happy to know, *Ispettore*, that we are using the most up-to-date technology in signal inhibitors."

"I'm not really familiar with spy slang. Mind explaining?"

"We have at our disposal electronic equipment that has created two electromagnetic fields. One here and the other in the Sistine Chapel. In practice, they operate like two invisible umbrellas. Underneath them, no apparatus which requires contact with the outside can function. Neither a directional microphone nor any kind of spy apparatus can work inside the cover. Give your cell phone a try."

Paola picked it up and saw that it was outside its roaming area. They went outside to the hallway. No signal at all.

"And what about the food?"

"It is prepared here, in our kitchens," Sister Helena said proudly. "The kitchen staff is made up of ten nuns, who throughout the day perform the different services provided here at Saint Martha's. At night, the only staff present are the people at the front desk, should some emergency take place. No one else is authorized to set foot inside the Domus, except for the cardinals."

Paola opened her mouth to ask a question, but it stuck in her throat. Just when she was about to speak, a terrible scream of pain reached them from the floor above.

DOMUS SANCTAE MARTHAE

Piazza Santa Marta, 1

Thursday, April 7, 2005, 4:31 P.M.

Gaining the man's confidence to get into his room had been easy. The cardinal had plenty of time now to regret that mistake. His regret was being spelled out in painful letters each time Karosky made a new cut on his exposed chest.

"Calm down, Your Eminence. It's not much longer now."

The victim fought back with less strength each time. The blood, which was soaking the bedspread and dripping in thick drops onto the Persian rug, carried his strength away with it. Yet he never lost consciousness for a second. He felt every blow Karosky gave him, and every cut.

The cardinal's chest was the culmination of Karosky's handiwork. He proudly contemplated what he had written. He held the camera with a firm grip and captured the moment. He couldn't leave without a remembrance. Sadly, the video camera was not available, but that one-use camera, a mere functional mechanism, served the purpose stupendously. He mocked Cardinal Cardoso as he advanced the film with his thumb.

"Say hi to the camera, Your Eminence. Ah, but you can't. In a second I am going to remove your tongue. I need your 'gift for languages.'"

Karosky was the only one laughing at his macabre joke. He put the camera down and brought the knife close to the cardinal's face while he stuck out his own tongue in a mocking gesture. And then he made his first mistake. He started to untie the gag. The man lying on the bed was terrified, but he wasn't so far gone as the other victims. He pulled together the little strength he had left and let out a loud scream that resounded through the hallways of the Domus Sanctae Marthae.

DOMUS SANCTAE MARTHAE

Piazza Marta, 1

Thursday, April 7, 2005, 4:31 P.M.

Paola reacted immediately when she heard the shout. She gestured to the nun to stay right where she was, and she hit the stairs three at a time, her pistol drawn. Fowler and Dante followed, one step behind. Their thighs nearly cramped with the exertion of climbing so quickly. Arriving on the floor above, they came to a stop. They were disoriented. They stood in the middle of the hallway, doors on both sides.

"Where did it come from?" said Fowler.

"I wish I knew," said Paola. "Let's stick together. It could be him, and he's a dangerous son of a bitch."

Paola chose the left side, across from the elevator. She thought she heard a noise in Room 56. Her ear was pressed against the wooden door when Dante motioned to her to move away. The stocky Vatican cop gestured to Fowler, the two of them piled on, and the door gave way easily. The two cops went in, Dante going ahead and Paola covering the sides. Fowler stayed in the doorway, his hands at chest level.

A cardinal was lying on the bed. He was very pale and scared to death but he was in one piece. He eyed the two cops fearfully and lifted his hands.

"Don't hurt me, please."

Dante looked over the room and lowered his pistol.

"Where did the noise come from?"

"The next room over, I think," the man said, pointing with a finger, his hands still raised.

They ran back out to the hallway. Paola stood to one side of Room 57. Dante and Fowler performed the human battering ram a second time. Their shoulders hit the door hard the first time but it didn't budge. On the second try, it gave way with a tremendous crash.

A cardinal was lying on the bed. He was very pale and very dead, but the room was otherwise empty. Dante crossed the room in two strides and stuck his head in the bathroom. He shook his head *no*. And then there was another shout.

"Help me! Help me, please!"

All three ran out of the room. At the end of the hallway, next to the elevator, a cardinal lay on the ground, his robes spread in an oval around him. They hurried over. Paola got there first, and she knelt at his side, but the cardinal was already getting up.

"Francis Casey!" Fowler exclaimed when he recognized his compatriot.

"I'm OK, I'm OK. He only pushed me. He ran that way," the cardinal said as he pointed at a metal door, distinct from the wooden ones to the rooms.

"Stay here with him, Padre."

"Don't worry, I'm OK. Catch that impostor," said the cardinal.

"Go back to your room and close the door," Fowler told him, barely able to keep from shouting.

The three quickly went through the door at the end of the hallway and hurried down the service stairs. The cramped space reeked of humidity and seemed to give off a bad smell from beneath the paint on the walls. The passageway was badly lit.

"Perfect for an ambush," Paola thought. "Karosky already has Pontiero's gun. He could be waiting for us at any turn in the stairs, ready to blow off two of our heads before we even know what's what."

In spite of this, they flew down the steps as quickly as they could, tripping more than once. They followed the stairs to the basement, one level below the street. The door there was closed with a heavy lock.

"He didn't get out this way."

They retraced their steps. Noises were coming from the first floor. They opened the door and walked directly into the kitchen. Dante walked ahead of Paola, his finger on the trigger and the barrel of his gun pointing straight ahead. Three nuns were rummaging about among the frying pans. They froze in their tracks, staring at the police officers, their eyes wide open.

"Did anyone come through here?" Paola shouted at them.

The nuns didn't respond. They simply stared straight ahead, bovine looks on their faces. One of them ignored Paola completely, slicing green beans and tossing them into a cooking pot.

"Did anyone come through here? A friar!" Paola repeated.

The nuns shrugged their shoulders. Fowler put his hand on Paola's arm.

"Leave them alone. They don't speak Italian."

Dante walked all the way through the kitchen until he came upon a very solid-looking metal door, six feet across. He tried to open it without success. He gestured at the door to one of the nuns while he held up his Vatican ID. She walked over to the him and slipped the key into a lock concealed in the door. The door made a buzzing noise as it opened on a side street off the Piazza Santa Marta. The Palace of Saint Charles was directly in front of them.

"Shit! Didn't the nun say there was only one exit in and out of the Domus?"

"Well, see for yourself. There are two," said Dante.

"Let's go back."

They ran back upstairs, from the vestibule to the top floor. There they found the stairway that led to the roof. But at the top, the door was bolted and barred.

"No one escaped through here."

Out of breath, they sat down in the dirt and dust of the narrow stairs below the door. Their lungs were pumping like bellows.

"Do you think he's hiding in one of the rooms?" Fowler asked.

"I don't think so. I'm pretty sure he slipped away," said Dante.

"Through where?"

"Through the kitchen definitely, when one of the nuns wasn't looking. There's no other explanation. The other doors have locks or they are guarded like the front entrance. Impossible by the windows, it would be too risky. Agents of the Vigilanza make their rounds every few minutes. And it's the middle of the day, for crying out loud."

Paola was furious. If she hadn't been so out of breath after running up and down the flights of stairs, she would have been banging the wall with her fists.

"I need your help, Dante. Get them to cordon off the piazza."

Dante shook his head emphatically. His forehead was soaked with sweat, dark beads of which were raining onto his leather hunting jacket. His hair, always so well combed, was a messy tangle.

"How do you want me to call them, my dear one? Nothing works in this fucking building. There are no cameras in the hallways; telephones and mobiles and walkie-talkies—none of them work. Nothing more complex than a lightbulb, nothing that requires waves or ones and zeros in order to function. Let's hire a carrier pigeon, say what."

"By the time you're down there, he'll be far away. No one is going to notice a friar in the Vatican, Dicanti," said Fowler.

"Can someone please explain to me how that fucker got out of this building? It has three floors, the windows are locked, and we had to break down the damn door. All entry points to the building are guarded or locked," Dicanti said as she banged on the door to the roof again and again, which answered her with a loud noise and a cloud of dust.

"We were so close," said Dante.

"Fuck, fuck, fuck, and fuck. We had him!"

It was Fowler who stated the terrible truth, and his words echoed in Paola's ears like a shovel scraping on a stone.

"What we have now, Dicanti, is another dead body."

✝

DOMUS SANCTAE MARTHAE
Piazza Santa Marta, 1
Thursday, April 7, 2005, 5:15 P.M.

"We have to take care of our business discreetly," said Dante.

Paola was livid. If she had had Cirin himself in front of her at that moment, she wouldn't have been able to control herself. She found herself thinking that this was the third time she wanted to knock the bastard's front teeth out, just to see if he would still maintain his calm air and that monotone voice.

After they had run into the obstacle at the top of the stairs, they turned back around and went down, all of them crestfallen. Dante had to walk over to the other side of the piazza to get his cell phone to work, and he spoke with Cirin about reinforcements and to request that there be an analysis of the crime scene. Cirin's response was that he could only allow access to one technician from the UACV, and he had to be wearing street clothing. Whatever equipment he needed to use he should bring in an ordinary suitcase.

"We can't let all this get out any further. You understand, Dicanti."

"I don't understand any of this shit. We are trying to capture a killer. We have got to empty the building, find out how he got in, collect evidence—"

Dante looked at her as if she'd gone mad. Fowler shook his head, not wanting to meddle. Paola knew she was letting the case slip through an unguarded part of her soul, poisoning her sense of well-being. She was trying to be as rational as she could, since she knew the way her character reacted. When something got under her skin, dedication turned into obsession. At that instant she felt her anger corroding her spirit like a drop of acid falling every few seconds onto a slab of raw meat.

They stood in the third-floor hallway, the same hallway where everything had happened. Room 56 was empty. Its occupant, the man who had told them to look in Room 57, was the Belgian cardinal Petfried Haneels, seventy-three years old. He was very much affected by what had happened. The building's doctor was tending to him on the floor above, where he would be staying for the time being.

"Luckily, most of the cardinals were in the chapel, participating in afternoon meditations. Only five heard the shouts, and they've already been told that a mentally disturbed person got in and went about screaming in the hallways," said Dante.

"And that's it? That's your damage control?" Paola was breathing fire. "To make sure that none of the cardinals realize that one of their own has been killed?"

"That part is easy. We'll say that he was indisposed and was taken to Gemelli with gastroenteritis."

"And with that everything has been resolved," Dicanti shot back, with a full dose of irony.

"Well, there is one more thing. You can't speak to any of the cardinals without my authorization, and the scene of the crime has been limited to Room 57."

"You cannot be serious. We have to look for prints in the doorway, in the points of access, in the hallways. You cannot be telling me this seriously."

"Just what do you want, *bambina*? A whole set of squad cars in the doorway? Flashes from thousands of cameras? Bellowing into the four winds is the one sure way not to catch your degenerate," Dante said, as arrogantly as he could. "Or are you only looking to wave your degree from the FBI in front of the cameras? If you're so good at what you do, it would be better if you showed it."

Paola refused to let him provoke her. Dante completely supported the theory that gave priority to concealing everything that had happened. She had to choose: either to lose time banging her head against a two-thousand-year-old granite wall or to give in and try to move as quickly as possible to make the maximum of the few resources at her disposal.

"Call Cirin. Tell him to have Troi send his best technical person. And put his men on alert for a Carmelite monk in and around the Vatican."

Fowler cleared his throat to get Paola's attention. He took her aside and spoke to her in a quiet voice, his mouth close to her ear. Paola couldn't help it, his breath gave her goose bumps, and she was happy that she had worn a jacket so no one would notice. She still remembered his strong, unwavering hold on her the day before, when she had thrown herself into the crowd like a madwoman and he had held her back. His good sense had anchored her. She wanted him to hold her again, but in that situation her anxiety was completely out of place. Things were complicated enough already.

"Those orders have assuredly already been given and are being carried out now. And forget about standard police procedure, because in the Vatican that's never going to happen. We'll have to play with the cards destiny has given us, however weak they may be." Then his tone changed. "All of which puts me in mind of an old saying: 'In the land of the blind, the one-eyed man is King.'"

"You're right, I shouldn't argue. . . . For the first time in this case we have a witness. And that's something."

Fowler lowered his voice even further.

"Talk to Dante. Be diplomatic for once. Tell him to let us have a free hand in speaking to Casey. Maybe we can get a useful description."

"But without a forensic artist—"

"That comes later. If Cardinal Casey saw him, we should be able to come up with a portrait, a quick sketch of the killer. The most important thing is to have access to his testimony."

"His name rings a bell. Is Casey the cardinal who made an appearance in the report on Karosky?"

"The same. He's tough, and intelligent. Let's hope he can help us with the description. Don't mention the name of our suspect. That way we will see if he recognized him."

Paola went back to join Dante.

"What, are you two lovebirds already done trading secrets?"

Dicanti decided to ignore the running commentary.

"Fowler has advised me to remain calm, and I think I'm going to follow his advice."

Dante looked at her distrustfully, as if he were surprised by her attitude. He had no idea what to make of this woman.

"Very wise on your part, *Ispettore*."

"'*Noi abbiamo dato nella croce.*' Right, Dante? We've run straight into the Church."

"That's one way to look at it. A very different way to look at it is that you have been invited into a country that isn't your own. This morning we did things your way. Now we do it ours. It's nothing personal."

Paola took a deep breath.

"Fine. I need to speak with Cardinal Casey."

"He's in his room, recovering from his ordeal. Denied."

"Dante. Do the right thing, just once. If you do, maybe we catch our killer."

The cop stretched his thick neck, first to the left and then the right. A few of his neck bones made a creaking noise. He was thinking things over.

"OK. But with one condition."

"Which is?"

"You say the magic words."

"Go to hell."

Paola turned around, only to walk straight into Fowler's glare of disapproval. He had been following the conversation from a short way off. She spun back around to face Dante.

"Please."

"Please what?"

The fat pig was enjoying her humiliation. All right then, here it was.

"Please, Inspector Dante, may I have your permission to speak with Cardinal Casey?"

Dante broke out in a smile. She had passed with high marks. He then suddenly turned serious.

"Five minutes, five questions. No more. I can play at this too, Dicanti."

Two members of the Vigilanza, both in black suit and tie, exited the elevator and took up position on either side of the door to Room 57, inside of which lay the body of Karosky's latest victim. They would guard the entrance until the specialist from UACV arrived. Dicanti decided to make use of the downtime to interview the witness then and there.

"Which is Casey's room?"

It was on the same floor. Dante led them to Room 42, the room next to the door leading to the service stairs. He knocked softly, with just two fingers.

Sister Helena opened the door. She wasn't smiling now, but a look of relief appeared on her face when she saw them.

"Ah, at least you're all right. I heard they chased the lunatic downstairs. Were they able to catch him?"

"Sadly, no, sister," Paola answered her. "We believe he escaped through the kitchen."

"Oh my God, through the delivery door? Blessed Virgin of the Olives, what a disaster."

"Sister, why did you tell us that there was only one access?"

"There is only one, the main door in front. The kitchen door isn't an access, that's just for delivery trucks to pull up to. A heavy door, with a special lock."

Paola was beginning to realize that Sister Helena spoke a different Italian than everyone else. She very much took her nouns to heart.

"The kill— I mean the assailant, could enter through there, though."

The nun shook her head *no*.

"The only two people with a key are the head of the kitchen and myself. And she only speaks Polish, as do many of the sisters who work here."

Dicanti deduced that the head of the kitchen must have been the woman who opened the door for Dante. Only two copies of the key. The mystery intensified.

"May we come in to see the cardinal?"

Sister Helena shook her head energetically. *No*, again.

"Impossible. He is, how do you say, *zdenerwowany*. In a nervous state."

"It will just be for a moment," said Dante.

The nun's face took on an even more serious look.

"*Zaden*. No, and no again."

It seemed she preferred to take refuge in her native tongue when replying in the negative. The door was already half-closed when Fowler stuck his foot against the jamb, to keep her from closing the door all the way. And then he spoke, a little hesitantly, chewing his words. *"Sprawiać przyjemność, potrzebujemy żeby widzieć kardynalny Casey, Siostra Helena."*

The nun's eyes widened into saucers.

"Wasz jzyk polski nie jest dobry."

"I know. I ought to visit your beautiful country a little more often. Haven't been there since the early days of Solidarity."

The nun shook her head and wrinkled her brow, but it was clear that Fowler had gained her confidence. She reluctantly opened the door and moved out of the way.

"Since when do you know Polish?" Paola whispered as they were going in.

"Just the barest outlines. Travel broadens the mind, as the saying goes."

Paola glanced admiringly at Fowler before giving her attention to the man stretched out on the bed. The room was dark, the Persian blinds nearly all the way down. Cardinal Casey lay there with a handkerchief or wet towel on his forehead. There was so little light it was hard to tell. When they drew close to the foot of the bed, the cardinal propped himself up on one elbow and sighed. The towel slid off his forehead. He was a heavyset man with sharp features. His hair, completely white, was knotted into a clump where the towel had soaked it.

"Forgive me, I . . ."

Dante bent over to kiss the cardinal's ring, but the cardinal stopped him.

"No, please. Not now."

The Vatican cop took a step back, a little unnerved. He had to clear his throat before saying anything.

"Cardinal Casey, we apologize for our intrusion, but we need to ask you a few questions. Do you feel well enough to respond?"

"Certainly, my children. I was just resting a moment. What a terrible thing to see myself assaulted here in this holy place. And the fact is, I have a meeting on several important issues just a few minutes from now. So please be brief."

Dante looked at Sister Helena and then at Casey. The cardinal understood: no witnesses.

"Sister Helena, please tell Cardinal Pauljic that I am running a bit late. If you would be so kind."

The nun exited the room, grumbling rather nasty things on her way out. Things certainly inappropriate for a religious person.

"Can you tell us how things happened?" asked Dante.

"I had gone up to my room for my breviary when I heard a terrible shout. For a second I was frozen in my tracks; I suppose I was trying to figure out if it was all just a product of my imagination. I thought I heard the sound of people racing up the stairway, and then a crash. I went out to the hallway, very much astonished. In the doorway of the elevator was a Carmelite friar, hidden in the indentation of the elevator doorway. I looked at him. He turned around, and looked at me too. At that instant I heard another crash and the Carmelite attacked me. I fell to the ground and cried out. You already know the rest."

"Did you get a good look at his face?" Paola broke in.

"It was almost completely covered by a thick beard. I don't remember anything specific."

"Could you describe his face and his physical complexion?"

"I don't think so, I only saw him for a second and my eyesight isn't what it was. Just the same, I remember that his hair was a grayish white. I knew right away he wasn't a friar."

"What made you think that, Your Eminence?" Fowler inquired.

"The way he was acting, of course. Standing there pressed against the elevator door, he looked nothing like a servant of God, absolutely not."

Sister Helena came back into the room, clearing her throat nervously.

"Cardinal Casey, Cardinal Pauljic says that, as long as is possible, the commission will wait for you before starting to organize the novena masses. I've set up the meeting room on the first floor for you."

"Thank you, Sister. Go ahead with Antun, because I am going to need a few things. Tell him that I will rejoin you in five minutes."

Dante took that to mean that their meeting with Casey was over.

"Thank you for everything, Your Eminence. We're ready to leave now."

"You don't know how sorry I am. The novena masses will be celebrated in churches all over Rome and in thousands of others throughout the world they will be praying for the soul of our Holy Father. It's an immense undertaking and I am not going to step back from it just because somebody shoved me."

Paola was about to say something, but Fowler discreetly grabbed her elbow and she swallowed her question. She too waved good-bye to the cardinal. Just when they were about to exit his room, the cardinal asked them a very compromising question.

"Does this man have anything to do with the disappearances?"

Dante turned around very slowly to respond to the cardinal's question, ladling thick syrup onto every syllable.

"Absolutely not, Your Eminence. It's nothing more than a provocateur. Probably one of those young people caught up in the antiglobalization movement. They frequently dress up in order to attract more attention, as you already know."

The cardinal sat up a little bit more, until he was now upright on the bed. He was facing the nun.

"There is a rumor running around among a few of my brother cardinals that two of the most preeminent figures of the Curia are not going to participate in the conclave. I hope that both of them are well."

"Where did you hear this, Your Eminence?" Paola was surprised. In her lifetime she had heard only one voice that was so smooth, so sweet and humble as the one Dante employed in his question to the cardinal.

"Ah, my child, at my age one forgets many things, such as who whispered what between the main course and dessert. But I can assure you that I am not the only one who knows it."

"Your Eminence, most assuredly it is only a baseless rumor. If you will forgive us, we must get busy looking for the agitator."

"I hope you find him quickly. Too many disturbances are taking place in the Vatican already, and perhaps this is the time to change the direction of our security policy."

Casey's veiled threat, as well concealed under a sugary glaze as was Dante's, did not pass unnoticed. It froze the blood in Paola's veins, and she was someone who detested every member of the Vigilanza she knew.

Sister Helena left the room with the others and continued down the hallway ahead of them. A heavyset cardinal was waiting for her at the stairway. It was Pauljic, and the two of them walked down to the next floor together.

As soon as Paola saw Sister Helena's back disappear, she turned around to face Dante, a mocking look on her face.

"It seems your damage control isn't working quite as well as you thought."

"I swear to you I don't understand it." Dante had a weary expression on his face. "At least we can hope they don't know the real reason. That will not be possible later on. As things stand now, even Casey could be the next man to wear the red sandals."

"At the very least, the cardinals know that something strange is going on. In all sincerity, nothing would make me happier than if the whole bloody mess blew up in your face so we could do our job the way it should be done."

Dante was just about to tear into her when someone came up the marble stairway. Carlo Troi had decided to send the one man he considered the best and most discreet of UACV's personnel.

"Good afternoon, everyone."

"Good afternoon, *Direttore* Troi."

The time had come to take a close look at Karosky's latest piece of theater.

✝

FBI ACADEMY
Quantico, Virginia
August 22, 1999

"*Come in, come in. I suppose you know who I am, yes?*"

For Paola, meeting Robert Weber made her feel the same way an Egyptologist would if Ramses II had invited her to tea. She walked into the conference room, where the famous criminologist was handing out grades to the four students who had taken the course. He had been retired for ten years, but his footsteps still inspired a reverential respect in the FBI hallways. He was the man who had revolutionized forensic science by creating a new method of tracking down criminals: the psychological profile. In the highly selective course that the FBI offered, the purpose of which was to develop new talents in various parts of the world, he was always in charge of giving student assessments. He made a tremendous impression on students, who were able to sit face to face with someone they greatly admired.

"*Of course I know you, sir. I have to tell you—*"

"*Yes, I know already. It's an honor to know me. Blah blah blah. If I had a dollar for every time I heard that phrase, I'd be a rich man.*"

The criminologist's nose was buried in a thick folder. Paola stuck a hand in her pants pocket and took out a crumpled bill, which she handed to Weber.

"*It's an honor to meet you.*"

Weber looked at the bill and started to laugh. It was a one-dollar bill. He put his hand out and took it. He smoothed it out and put it in his coat pocket.

"Don't wrinkle the bills, Ms. Dicanti. They are the property of the United States Treasury."

But he smiled, pleased by the young woman's quick-witted response.

"I'll remember that, sir."

Weber's face became serious, strict. It was the moment of truth, and every word that followed was like a hammer blow to his young student.

"You're weak, Ms. Dicanti. You slipped by on the minimum in the physical tests and target practice. You've got no character. You fall apart quickly. You give in right away. You put up roadblocks against adversity all too easily."

Paola was shocked. That a living legend knocks the stuffing out of you in less than a minute is a very difficult thing to accept. It's even worse when his hard-nosed tone reveals that he lacks even the faintest sympathy for you.

"You don't reason. That's OK, but you have got to make use of what you have inside. And to do that, you have to invent. Make things up, Ms. Dicanti. Don't follow the manuals to the letter. Improvise, and you'll see. And be more diplomatic. Here are your final evaluations. Open it after you leave the room."

Paola took the envelope from Weber with trembling hands and opened the door, grateful to be able to get out of there.

"One more thing, Ms. Dicanti. What is the serial killer's real motive?"

"His hunger to kill, which he cannot control."

The old criminologist shook his head.

"You'll find out what it is when you get to the place where you ought to be. You're not there yet. You're thinking just like the books again, young lady. Can you fathom the torment that makes a person commit murder?"

"No, sir."

"Sometimes you have to forget all about psychiatric treatises. The true motive is the body. Analyze his work and you will know the artist. The first thing you do when you enter a crime scene is get inside his head."

Dicanti ran back to her apartment and threw herself into the bathtub. When she had summoned sufficient peace of mind, she opened the envelope. It took her a little while to comprehend what she read.

She had received the highest score possible on all parts of the course work. And a valuable lesson too: nothing is what it seems.

†

DOMUS SANCTAE MARTHAE
Piazza Santa Marta, 1
Thursday, April 7, 2005, 5:49 P.M.

It was just over an hour since the killer had escaped. Paola could still feel his presence in the room, like someone inhaling fumes, metallic and invisible. If she was speaking with others, she was always utterly rational regarding serial killers. That was easy to do, voicing her opinions from inside a comfortable, carpeted office. And that was where she was, most of the time.

It was a very different thing to walk into a room, taking care not to step in the blood on the floor. Not just to avoid contaminating the scene of the crime. The principal motive for not walking around carelessly was that the damned blood would ruin a good pair of shoes forever.

And the soul with it.

It had been nearly three years since Director Troi had personally performed the work at a crime scene. Paola suspected he was coming to a degree of involvement where he needed to score points with the Vatican authorities. He really had nothing to gain with his Italian superiors. The whole subject had to be kept under wraps.

He had walked in first, and then Paola. The others remained behind in the hallway, staring ahead vacantly and feeling uncomfortable. Dicanti heard Dante and Fowler exchange a few words—more than a few of them, she thought, and not exactly civil in tone—but she made every effort to focus on what was inside the room and not on what she had left outside.

Paola stood by the door, letting Troi go through his routine. First the forensic photographs: one from each corner of the room, from above the body, from every possible side angle, and finally, one of every possible element the investigator might consider relevant. When all was said and done, more than seventy bursts of light illuminated the scene in shades of unreality, blanching the scene white for an instant before shutting off.

She took a deep breath and tried to ignore the smell of blood and the aftertaste it left on your tongue. She closed her eyes and counted from one hundred back to one in her head, very slowly, trying to match the rhythm of the decreasing numbers to the beating of her heart. From the wayward beat of one hundred to fifty was a smooth trot, with a heavy, precise drumbeat ending in zero.

She opened her eyes.

Cardinal Geraldo Cardoso, seventy-one years old, was stretched out on the bed. Cardoso was tied to the ornamental headboard with two towels, tautly knotted. His cardinal's hat, still on his head, was tipped to one side, lending him a perversely comical look.

Paola recited Weber's mantra slowly : "Analyze his work and you will know the artist." She repeated it to herself over and over, moving her lips silently until the words had lost all meaning. The words were engraving themselves in her mind, as if she were dipping a seal into ink and stamping it on a piece of paper again and again until no ink is left and the seal is dry.

"Let's get started," Paola said in a loud voice. She took a tape recorder out of her bag.

Troi didn't bother to look at her. He was busy collecting evidence and studying the shape of the various pools of blood.

The criminologist began to dictate into her tape recorder in exactly the manner she had been taught at Quantico: make an observation and an immediate deduction. What came out of those conclusions seemed to be enough for a reconstruction of how things had unfolded.

Observation: The deceased's body is tied at the hands in his private room, no sign of violence to furniture or other objects.
Inference: Karosky used some kind of subterfuge to gain access to the room, and then quickly and silently restrained the victim.

Observation: A blood-soaked towel on the floor. Looks wrinkled.
Inference: Karosky likely put the towel on the victim's tongue to keep him from shouting and then removed it so that he could continue with his macabre modus operandi: cutting out the tongue.

Observation: We heard a cry of alarm.
Inference: What most likely happened is that, once the towel was removed, Cardoso found a way to scream. The tongue is the last thing that Karosky cuts, before moving on to the eyes.

Observation: The victim still possesses both eyes, his tongue cut into strips. The cut looks like it was done under pressure; there is blood all around it. Victim's hands are in place.
Inference: Karosky's ritual began with the torture of the body, and continued with the ritual dissection. Cut out the tongue, pull out the eyes, cut off the hands.

Paola opened the door of the room and asked Fowler to join her for a moment. The priest's face recoiled when he saw the macabre spectacle, but he did not turn away. The criminologist rewound the tape on her recorder and they listened to the last point together.

"Do you think there is anything special in the order he goes about his ritual?"

"I don't know. The ability to speak is the most important thing for a priest: he administers the sacraments with his voice. The eyes have no overwhelming importance in a priest's ministry, since they don't participate in any critical manner in the fulfillment of his duties. But nevertheless, the hands do fulfill a crucial role: a priest's hands are sacred, always, no matter what he is doing with them."

"What are you trying to say?"

"Even a monster like Karosky: his hands are still sacred. In his capacity of administering the sacraments, he's no different than the holiest, purest priest. It may not make any sense, but it's true."

Paola shuddered. The idea that someone so abject could be in direct contact with God struck her as repugnant, terrible. She tried to remind herself that this was one of the reasons why she had rejected God's existence, imagining Him an unbearable tyrant in a cotton-soft heaven. Yet sinking more deeply into the horror, the deprivation of those who, like Karosky, were supposedly called to bring His work to fruition, produced a very different effect in her. She felt the same betrayal He must have felt and for a few seconds put herself in His position. More than ever she remembered Maurizio, mourning that he wasn't there to try to give some meaning to this wretched insanity.

"Good Lord."

Fowler shrugged his shoulders, without knowing what it was he wanted to say to her. And then he walked out of the room. Paola turned the tape recorder back on.

Observation: The victim is wearing a full-length robe, completely open. Underneath, a cotton undershirt and boxer shorts. The undershirt is torn up, most likely with a sharpened instrument. There are a number of cuts on his chest, which spell out the words *EGO TE ABSOLVO.*

Inference: In this instance, Karosky's ritual begins with torturing the body, and continues later with the ritual of carving. Cut out the tongue, pull out the eyes, cut off the hands. The words *EGO TE ABSOLVO* were also found in the Portini crime scene—according to the photographs Dante gave us—and Robayra's. An unusual variation.

Observation: There are bloodstains everywhere, splashes of blood on the walls. A partial print stamped on the floor, next to the bed. Looks like blood.

Inference: Everything at this crime scene is very strange. No way to deduce whether his style has changed or he's adapted to a new environment. His modus operandi is all over the place, and—

Dicanti pushed the stop button on the recorder. There was something that didn't fit, something terribly wrong.

"How's it going, Boss?"

"From bad to worse. I've taken prints from the door, from the night table, from the headboard of the bed, but there isn't much else. There are plenty of partial prints but only one, I think, might be Karosky's."

He pressed a piece of plastic onto the headboard as he spoke, making a halfway decent print of an index finger. He then compared the transparency with the digital impression on Karosky's ID card, that had come into Fowler's possession after Karosky fled Saint Matthew's.

"A light impression. Similarities at various points. At least I think there are. This ascendant line is characteristic enough, and this deltic . . ." Troi said, more to himself than to Paola.

Paola knew that when Troi recognized a fingerprint as a good one, that's what it was. He was famous, an expert in the field. Watching him at work, in his element, Dicanti deplored the slow ruination that had turned a forensic specialist into a bureaucrat.

"Nothing else, Doctor?"

"Nothing else. No hairs, no fibers, nothing. This guy really is a ghost. If he'd gone so far as to wear gloves, my opinion would be that Cardoso was killed by a spirit without a body."

"There's nothing spiritual about that severed trachea."

Troi looked at the cadaver with a breathless estrangement, perhaps reflecting on the words of his subordinate or extracting his own conclusions.

"No, not much. That's for sure."

Paola exited the room, leaving Troi to his work. But she knew that he wasn't going to come up with anything. Karosky was thoroughly prepared, and in spite of the pressure, he hadn't left anything behind. A disturbing suspicion continued to circulate in her head. She looked around. Camilo Cirin had arrived, accompanied by another man. A little man, terribly skinny and even fragile in appearance, with a pointed way of looking at people, as sharp as his nose. Cirin walked up to Paola and introduced Magistrate Gianluigi Varone, Vatican City's only judge. As far as Paola was concerned, he was not in the least bit sympathetic: he resembled a skinny, yellow a vulture in a jacket.

The judge signed a statement allowing for the removal of the body, which would be carried out with complete secrecy. The two agents of the Vigilanza who had been standing guard at the door had changed clothes. They were in black overalls now and latex gloves. They would take care of cleaning and sealing the habitation after Troi and his team left. Fowler was seated on a small bench at the other end of the hallway, calmly reading his breviary. When Paola untangled herself from Cirin and the magistrate, she went over to the priest and sat down next to him. Fowler could not avoid a sense of déjà vu.

"Very well, Dicanti. Now you know a few more cardinals up close and personal."

Paola smiled, saddened. How many things had changed in barely twenty-four hours, from the time when the two of them had waited together at the chamberlain's office. And yet they were not so much as even a step closer to capturing Karosky.

"I thought that macabre jokes were Deputy Inspector Dante's territory."

"Well, they are. I'm just here on a visit."

Paola opened and closed her mouth. She wanted to talk to Fowler about something that was disturbing her about Karosky's ritual, but she was still unable to put her finger on what was bothering her so much. She decided to wait until she had more time to give it serious thought.

As Paola would have occasion to confirm later on—and bitterly so—that decision was a terrible mistake.

✝

DOMUS SANCTAE MARTHAE
Piazza Santa Marta, 1
Thursday, April 7, 2005, 6:37 P.M.

Dante and Paola stepped into Troi's car, which was sitting outside Saint Martha's. He was going to drop them off at the morgue before heading on to UACV to work on determining the weapon of choice in each of the murder scenes. Fowler had just opened the door to the car when he heard someone calling his name at the entrance to the building.

"Father Fowler!"

The priest spun around. It was Cardinal Casey, who waved him over. Fowler retraced his steps.

"Your Eminence, I hope I find you in better shape now."

The cardinal forced a smile.

"We have no choice but to accept the proofs the Lord gives us. My dear Fowler, I wanted to take the opportunity to thank you personally for your timely rescue."

"Your Eminence, you were already in the clear by the time we arrived."

"Who knows? Who knows what might have happened if that lunatic decided to pay me another visit? You have my wholehearted appreciation. I will personally see to it that the Curia learns what a good soldier you are."

"It really isn't necessary, Your Eminence."

"My son, you never know when you are going to need a favor, or when unfortunate things are going to crop up. It's important to have money in the bank, as they say."

Fowler looked at the cardinal. He tried not to reveal what he was thinking.

"Of course, my son," Casey went on, "the Curia's appreciation could be even more complete. We could even call you back here, to the Vatican. Camilo Cirin seems to have lost his luster. Perhaps someone who could make sure that this scandal was utterly erased could fill his shoes. Someone who sees to it that it just goes away."

Fowler was beginning to catch the drift.

"Your Eminence, are you asking me to see to it that a certain dossier is lost?"

The cardinal smiled and shrugged his shoulders in a gesture of complicity both childish and extremely incongruent, given the subject under discussion. He was very close to getting what he wanted, or so he thought.

"Precisely, my son, precisely. 'A dead body revenges not injuries.'"

Fowler smiled with malicious pleasure.

"Well, well. A quotation from Blake. I never thought I would hear a cardinal reciting 'The Proverbs of Hell.'"

Casey pivoted; his voice became more inflexible. He didn't care for the priest's tone.

"The ways of the Lord are mysterious."

"The ways of the Lord are the the exact opposite of the Adversary, Your Eminence. I learned that in school as a child. And it has yet to lose its validity."

"A surgeon's tools will sometimes be stained with blood. And you are a very sharp scalpel, my son. Let's just say that I am aware that you represent more than one interest in this case."

"I'm a humble priest, nothing more," said Fowler, attempting to look stunned.

"I don't doubt it. But in certain circles they speak of your . . . abilities."

"And in those circles do they not also speak of my problem with authority, Your Eminence?"

"Yes, of that too. But I don't doubt that when the moment arrives, you will conduct yourself as you ought. You won't let the good name of the Church be publicly dragged through the press, my son."

The priest responded with cold, hostile silence. The cardinal gave him a few paternalistic slaps on the shoulder of his impeccably clean street clothes and then lowered the tone of his voice to just above a whisper.

"In times like these, who doesn't have a secret or two? It could be that your name turns up on other pieces of paper. For example, in the notes at the Sant'Uffizio. Once again."

And without another word, the cardinal spun around and walked back into Saint Martha's. Fowler got into the car where his friends were waiting for him. The motor was running.

"Are you all right, Padre? You look upset," Dicanti asked.

"I'm perfectly fine."

Paola studied him closely. It was a patent lie: Fowler was as white as a sack of flour. He looked like he had aged ten years in a minute.

"What did Cardinal Casey want?"

Fowler turned to Paola, a mirthless smile on his face. Things were quickly becoming unbearable in the car.

"His Eminence? Nothing. He merely sent his regards to a mutual friend."

✝

MUNICIPAL MORGUE
Friday, April 8, 2005, 1:25 A.M.

"I'm getting very used to throwing open the doors for you in the middle of the night, Dicanti."

Paola's response was a compromise between courtesy and shock. Fowler, Dante, and the coroner stood to one side of the autopsy table, Dicanti facing them from the other. All four had donned the mortuary's blue masks and latex gloves. Finding herself there for the third time in so few days made Paola remember something she had read when she was young, something about being sent back to hell, about how that consisted in doing the same things over and over again. Maybe hell was not stretched out directly in front of her but she was getting a close look at the evidence arguing for its existence.

Cardoso's body on the autopsy table looked even scarier than it had earlier. Just a few hours before his body had been awash in blood; now it resembled a pale doll festooned with ugly, raw scars. The cardinal was on the svelte side, and drained of blood, his face took on the look of a mask, sunken and accusatory.

"What do we know about him, Dante?" asked Dicanti.

The Vatican cop carried a small notebook in his jacket pocket at all times. He took it out and began reading.

"Geraldo Claudio Cardoso, born 1934, Cardinal since 2001. Well known as a defender of the workers, always on the side of the poor and the homeless. Before being named cardinal, he established his reputation in the diocese of San José. The largest factories in Latin America are in that district." Dante here mentioned two of the most famous automobile companies in the world. "He frequently acted as an intermediary between workers and ownership. The workers loved him, called him the 'union bishop.' Membership in various congregations of the Roman Curia."

This time even the coroner was quiet. He had cut up Robayra with a smile on his face, mocked Pontiero's inability to stomach the sight of blood. A few hours later the man he had made fun of was stretched out on his table. And the day after, another cardinal turned up. A man who, on paper at least, had done much good. He asked himself if the official version and the unofficial were in agreement, but it was Fowler who finally put the question to Dante.

"Is there anything in your summary besides press clippings?"

"Don't make the mistake, Fowler, of thinking that everyone in Our Holy Mother Church leads a double life."

"I'll try to remember that." Fowler had his game face on. "And now how about answering my question?"

Dante, simulating the act of thinking, twisted his neck again, first to the left and then to the right. Paola was sure he already knew the answer or at least was very ready for the question.

"I made a few calls. Almost everyone corroborates the official story. He had two unimportant run-ins, nothing worth digging up. Played around with marijuana as a young man, before he became a priest. Dubious political affiliations in the university, and that's it. Since becoming a cardinal he has had a few confrontations with colleagues in the Curia, owing to his defense of a group the Curia really doesn't care for: the Charismatics. The big picture is, he was a decent man."

"As were the other two," Fowler said.

"So it seems."

"Anything new on the murder weapon, Doctor?" Paola got a word in edgewise between the two men.

The doctor pointed, indicating the victim's neck and then the cuts on his chest.

"A short, smooth blade, probably a small kitchen knife but very sharp. In the previous cases, I reserved my opinion, but now that I've seen the molds of the incisions, I believe he used the same instrument on all three occasions."

Paola made a mental note of it.

"*Dottoressa*," asked Fowler, "what do you think are the chances Karosky tries something during John Paul's funeral?"

"Christ, I don't know. It's tighter than a drum around Saint Martha's by now."

"Of course it is," Dante crowed. "They're so shut in there they can't even tell if it's daytime without looking at a clock."

"Even though security was elevated earlier and it didn't mean much. Karosky has shown us his ability to adapt and his unbelievably cold blood. Truthfully, I don't have the slightest idea. I don't know if he is going to try something, although I doubt it. In this last incident, he was unable to complete his ritual or leave us a message written in blood, as he did the first two times."

"Which means we lost another clue," Fowler grumbled.

"Sure, but at the same time, that close call has to make him nervous and even a little vulnerable. But with a son of a bitch like this, you never know."

"We'll have to pay very close attention to the cardinals," said Dante.

"Not only protecting them, but looking for him. Even if he doesn't try anything, he'll be there, watching us and laughing. I'll risk my neck on that proposition."

SAINT PETER'S SQUARE
Vatican City
Friday, April 8, 2005, 10:15 A.M.

John Paul II's funeral took place with tedious normality. Everything was as ordinary as it could be at the funeral of the religious leader of more than a billion persons, at which some of the world's most powerful heads of state and royalty were present. But they were not the only ones who took part. Hundreds of thousands of people overflowed Saint Peter's Square, and every face told a story whose intensity was like the flames behind the grates of a fireplace. Several faces in particular will, nevertheless, play an important part in this story.

One of them belonged to Andrea Otero. She did not see Robayra anywhere, but the journalist noticed three things while she stood on a rooftop terrace, together with coworkers from a German television team. One, that looking through binoculars for half an hour gives you a splitting headache. Two, that the backs of the necks of the assembled cardinals all looked alike. And three, that there were only 112 red robes seated on those chairs. She counted them several times. And the printed list of electors pressed against her knees clearly stated that there should have been 115.

Camilo Cirin would not have felt in the least bit comfortable if he had known what Andrea Otero was thinking, but he had his own serious problems to deal with. Victor Karosky, the serial killer whose specialty was cardinals, was one of them. But while Karosky did not cause Cirin any trouble during the funeral, an unidentified plane that invaded Vatican aerial space in the middle of the funeral did. The anguish that overwhelmed Cirin during those moments when he recalled the September 11 terrorist attacks was no less than that of the three pilots who set off after the plane. Lucky for everyone, the situation resolved itself a few minutes later when it became clear that the pilot of the unidentified plane was a Macedonian who had flown off course. The episode stretched Cirin's nerves to the limit. A subordinate standing nearby later commented that it was the first time in fifteen years he had heard Cirin raise his voice to give orders.

Another of Cirin's subordinates, Fabio Dante, was mingling in the crowd. He cursed his luck because people pressed as closely as they could to John Paul's casket as it was carried past them, and many of those shouted, *"Santo Subito!"* in his ears. "Sainthood Now!" Desperately trying to see over the tops of people's heads and the signs they were carrying, he kept his eye out for a Carmelite friar with a bushy beard. He did not lead the celebrations when the funeral was finally over, but he was next in line.

Anthony Fowler was one of many priests giving communion to the assembled crowd, and more than once he thought he saw Karosky's face in that of the person who was about to receive the body of Christ from his hands. While hundreds of people filed up to him, Fowler prayed for two things: one was the reason he had come to Rome and the other was to ask the All Powerful to give him strength and illumination to face what he had encountered in the Eternal City.

Ignorant of the fact that Fowler was seeking the Creator's help in large part because of her, Paola scrutinized the faces from the steps of Saint Peter's. She had taken up position in a corner. She didn't pray. She never did. Nor did she give the people proceeding past her any special attention, because their faces very quickly blurred into one. She spent her time contemplating what motivated a monster.

Carlo Troi sat behind a desk full of television monitors with Angelo, the UACV's forensic sculptor. They were getting their feed directly from the RAI cameras in the plaza, before they went on the air. From that vantage, they staged their own hunt, for which they were rewarded with headaches as intense as Andrea Otero's. Of the "engineer," as Angelo continued to call him in his happy ignorance, they saw not so much as a trace.

On the esplanade, the secret service agents attached to George Bush came to blows with agents of the Vigilanza when they were denied permission to enter Saint Peter's Square. For those who know, even if only from hearsay, the way the Secret Service operates, what happened that day when they were outside looking in, was highly unusual. Never before had anyone ever denied them entrance so completely. The Vigilanza would not let them in. And no matter how much they insisted, outside they stayed.

Victor Karosky took part in John Paul's funeral devotedly, praying loudly. He sang with a beautiful, deep voice at the appropriate moments. He shed a very sincere tear and made plans for the future.

No one paid any attention to him.

VATICAN PRESSROOM
Friday, April 8, 2005, 6:25 P.M.

Andrea Otero arrived at the press conference with her tongue hanging out. Not just on account of the heat, but because she had left her press card in the hotel and had to yell at the dumbfounded cabdriver to make a U-turn in the middle of traffic to go back for it. Her carelessness was hardly fatal; she had left an hour early. She had wanted to arrive ahead of time so she could have a word with the Vatican spokesman, Joaquín Balcells, about Cardinal Robayra's "evaporation." All of her efforts to track him down earlier had been unsuccessful.

The pressroom was an annex to the large auditorium built while John Paul II was pope. Extremely modern, with room for more than six thousand, it was always filled to overflowing on Wednesdays, the day the Holy Father gave his audience. The door into the pressroom let out directly on the street, where it sat next to the palace of the Sant'Uffizio.

The pressroom itself had room for one hundred eighty-five people. Andrea thought she'd get a good seat if she arrived fifteen minutes before the hour, but it was obvious that more than three hundred journalists had had the same thought. And it was scarcely surprising that the press room was filled to capacity. Three thousand and forty-two accredited media outlets from ninety countries were covering the funeral, which had taken place that morning, and the conclave. More than two billion human beings, half of them Catholic, had said farewell to the deceased pope from the comfort of their living rooms that very morning. And here I am, she thought, me, Andrea Otero. If only her professors at journalism school could see her now.

Fine, she was in at the press conference where they were going to explain how the conclave functioned, but there were no seats to be found. She leaned against the wall near the entrance. It was the only way in and out, so when Balcells arrived, she would be able to make contact.

She calmly reviewed her notes on the spokesman. A doctor who had taken up journalism, a member of Opus Dei, born in Cartagena, Spain. According to all reports, deadly serious, and even something of a cold fish. He was nearly seventy years old and, from what an unofficial source told her, one of the most powerful men in the Vatican. For years he learned what he knew from John Paul's lips, before passing it on to the larger public. If he decided that something was secret, secret it stayed. There were no leaks with Balcells. His résumé was impressive. Andrea read the list of prizes and medals he had been awarded: knight of this order, prince of that, member of the Holy Cross of yet another. His achievements needed two pages in full, a different award on each line. He looked like a tough bone to gnaw on.

But I've got sharp teeth, damn it. She was busy trying to hear her thoughts over the din of voices when the pressroom exploded in raw cacophony.

First one sounded, the initial raindrop that signals the downpour, followed by three or four. Finally, a great outburst of ringing, a strident jungle of sound.

Dozens of cell phones seemed to be going off at the same time.

The noise lasted for some forty seconds. Journalists' hands went from typing on their computers to holding a cell phone, their heads tilted at an angle. People were starting to complain in loud voices.

"OK, everybody, we're on hold. Fifteen minutes, which leaves us exactly no time to edit the story."

Andrea heard a voice speaking Spanish a few feet away from her. She elbowed her way over and saw that it was a woman journalist, with brown skin and delicate features. Her accent led Andrea to believe she was from Mexico.

"How are you? I'm Andrea Otero, from *El Globo.* Listen, can you tell me why all the mobile phones rang at the same time?"

"Check out this message from the Vatican Press Office. They send us an SMS whenever there is important news. It's the latest innovation, the new way to keep us up-to-date. The hassle being the noise when we are all in the same place. The news that Balcells is going to be delayed is what just came in."

Andrea was impressed. Getting information out to thousands of journalists couldn't be easy.

"Don't tell me you haven't arranged a cell phone upgrade yet?" The Mexican journalist looked at Andrea as if her wig were askew.

"Well, not yet. Nobody told me anything about it."

"No sweat. See that girl over there?"

"The blonde?"

"No, the one in the gray jacket, carrying the folders in her hand. Go over to her and tell her you want to sign up for their cellular service. In less than half an hour they'll have you in their database."

Andrea did as she was told. She went up to the woman and mumbled all of her pertinent information in Italian. The girl asked her for her press card and typed her cell phone number into an electronic agenda.

"You are now connected to the main data bank." The young woman had a high opinion of the technology, but her smile was forced. "In about fifty minutes you will be given the service upgrade. I just need you to sign this form, if you would be so kind, authorizing us to send you the information."

The journalist scrawled her name at the bottom of the page the young woman had taken out of her file. She quickly scanned the fine print, thanked the girl, and said good-bye.

Otero went back to where she had been standing and tried to read more about Balcells, until a rumor circulated that he was about to arrive. Andrea focused on the main door, but the Spaniard had slipped in by an entrance hidden behind the stage he was now climbing. He calmly pretended to be organizing his notes, which gave the cameramen a second to frame their shots and the journalists time to sit down.

Andrea cursed her luck and once again elbowed her way to the front, this time as far as the stage, where the Vatican spokesman stood behind the dais. She had to push her way forward. While everyone else was taking their seat, Andrea got as close as she could to Balcells.

"Mr. Balcells, I'm Andrea Otero from *El Globo*, the daily paper. I have tried to get in touch with you all week without any luck—"

"Later."

The spokesman did not so much as glance at her.

"But, Mr. Balcells, you don't understand. I need to verify some information—"

"Miss, I already told you: later. Let's get started."

Andrea was knocked for a loop. He had never even looked at her once, which infuriated her. She had gotten very used to having men do what she wanted with just a beam from her blue searchlights.

"But, Mr. Balcells, I remind you that I represent an important

Spanish newspaper." She was trying to gain traction by mentioning that she represented the Spanish media, without the slightest success. Balcells shot her an icy look.

"What did you say your name was?"

"Andrea Otero.

"From which paper?"

"*El Globo.*"

"And where is Paloma?"

Paloma, the regular correspondent for Vatican assignments. Who had casually planned a trip to Spain for a few days and had had the extremely unfortunate circumstance of falling and breaking her leg before she got there, thereby giving her place to Andrea. A bad piece of luck that Balcells asked after her. Very bad.

"She couldn't come; she had a problem."

Balcells furrowed his brow as only a longtime member of Opus Dei is physically capable of doing. Andrea was caught off guard. She took a short step backward.

"Young lady, please take a look at the people behind you, if you would," Balcells said, gesturing to the packed rows of seats. "Those are your colleagues from CNN, the BBC, Reuters, and another hundred or so media outlets. Some of them were already accredited journalists here at the Vatican before you were born. And all of them would like to get this press conference under way. Please do us the favor of taking your seat right now."

Andrea spun around, ashamed and very flustered. The journalists in the front row chuckled at her expense. A few of them did indeed look about as old as Bernini's damn Colonnade. As she pushed her way to the back of the room, to the spot where she had left her bag with her laptop, she overheard Balcells joking in Italian with those ancient scribblers in the front row. Guffaws, hollow and nearly inhuman, were audible behind her back and she had no doubt the joke was on her. More people were turning around to look at her, while Andrea was turning red as far up as her ears. With her head down and her arms extended so she could make her way through the narrow passage to the door, she felt as if she were swimming through an ocean of bodies. When she finally got back to her spot, she didn't merely pick up her bag with the laptop and turn back around, she made a beeline for the door. The woman who had written down her information walked over and placed her hand on her arm.

"Just remember, if you go you won't be able to come back in until after the press conference. The door is locked. That's the way it works."

Like a theater, Andrea thought to herself. Just like in a theater.

She slipped out of the woman's grasp and exited the pressroom without a word. The door swung closed on her as she went out, slamming shut in a way that did nothing to diminish her overwhelming embarrassment. She felt a little better now that she was outside. She needed a smoke desperately, and she rummaged through all the pockets on her jacket, until her fingers found a pack of mints. Her consolation when she was out of her old pal nicotine.

"What a fucking time to give it up."

She opened the pack of mints and popped three in her mouth. Their taste was no better than fresh vomit, but at least they kept her mouth busy. They didn't help with the habit, but so what.

Andrea Otero would remember this moment many times in the future. She would remember standing in that doorway, leaning against the stones framing the entrance; she would remember trying to calm herself down at the same time she cursed herself for being so stupid, for embarrassing herself like a child.

But she wouldn't remember it for all that. She would remember it on account of the terrible discovery that nearly cost her her life, and which finally put her in touch with the man who would change her life, who she ran into thanks to the fact that she decided to wait for the mints to dissolve in her mouth before she hurried away, just so she could calm down a bit. How long does it take for a mint to dissolve? Not very long. For Andrea it was an eternity. Every inch of her body was begging to go back to the hotel and slide as far between the bedsheets as possible. She forced herself to stay where she was, if only because she could not bear to watch herself fleeing through the streets like a beaten dog, her tail between her legs.

Those three small mints would change her life—and very likely the history of the Western world—by the simple fact of being found in the right place at the right time.

There was just a little bit left of one of the mints, a thin sliver perched on her taste buds, when a messenger came barging around the corner. He was wearing a bright orange monkey suit and a baseball cap, and he had a bag slung over his shoulder. He was in a hurry. He walked right up to Andrea.

"Excuse me, but is this where they hold the press conferences?"

"It is."

"I have an urgent package for the following persons: Michael Williams of CNN, Bertie Hegrend of RTL—"

Andrea interrupted him, her voice reeking with contempt.

"Don't kill yourself, buddy. The press conference has already started and you will have to wait at least an hour."

The messenger looked at her as if she were an incomprehensible hallucination.

"No way. They told me that—"

The Spanish journalist found a kind of malignant satisfaction in piling her problems onto someone else.

"You understand. That's the way it works."

The messenger's hand covered his face. He really was desperate.

"You don't understand, signora. I've already missed a few deadlines this month. The urgent deliveries have to get to the intended parties inside of an hour, or they don't pay. There are ten manila envelopes here at thirty Euros each. I'm late on this job, my agency's gonna lose the Vatican route and I'll get kicked to the curb, no doubt about that."

Andrea softened up. She was a decent person. Impulsive, acting without thinking about it very much, and capricious, for sure. At times she achieved her goals with lies and a heavy dose of luck. But she was a good person. She read the messenger's name printed on the ID card hanging from a pocket of his one-piece. Another of Andrea's traits: she always remembered people by their names.

"Listen, Giuseppe, I'm sorry, but you couldn't open that door even if you wanted to. It only opens from the inside. See for yourself. There's no lock and no door handle."

Arms akimbo, one on each side of the growing belly visible even through his work clothes, the messenger grunted in despair. He was trying to think. He stared down at Andrea. She was sure he was stealing a look at her breasts—she'd gone through that disagreeable experience almost every day since puberty—but then she saw that his eyes were concentrating on the press badge dangling from her neck.

"Listen, I've got it. I'm going to leave the envelopes with you and we're done."

Her badge had the Vatican shield on it, and he must have thought she worked there.

"Look, Giuseppe—"

"Enough with the Giuseppe. Call me Beppo," the messenger said, rooting around in his bag.

"Beppo, I really can't—"

"Look, just do me this favor. Don't worry about signing, I'll sign the delivery slips. I make a different squiggle on each line and we're done. You just have to promise you'll deliver the envelopes as soon as they open the door."

"It's just that—"

But Beppo already had his hand on the ten envelopes in question.

"Each one has the name of the appropriate journalist. The client was sure they would all be here, so don't worry. OK, I'm taking off, I have just one more delivery to make, at the Corpo di Vigilanza, and another on Via Lamarmora. Ciao, bella, and thanks."

And before Andrea could say a word, this intriguing individual spun around and took off.

Andrea was left standing there, staring at the ten envelopes. She couldn't quite make sense of it. The envelopes were addressed to the ten most important media outlets in the world. Andrea knew four of them by reputation and had recognized at least two of them inside the pressroom.

The envelopes were half the size of a normal page, all of them identical except for the addressee. The thing that awakened her journalist's instinct, and then shortly set off all her alarms, was the phrase that appeared on all of them. In the upper left corner, written by hand:

Exclusive — Open Immediately

Andrea's moral dilemma lasted all of five seconds. She resolved it with a new mint, looking to the left and the right. The street was deserted; no sign of any witnesses to possible postal fraud. She picked one of the envelopes randomly and opened it, doing as little damage as she could.

"Simple curiosity."

There were two items inside the envelope. One was a Blusensbrand DVD, with the same phrase as on the envelope written in Magic Marker on the sleeve. The other was a note, written in English.

> THE CONTENT OF THIS DISC IS OF THE UTMOST IMPORTANCE. IT IS LIKELY THE MOST IMPORTANT NEWS OF THE YEAR, AND MAYBE OF THE CENTURY. SOMEONE WILL TRY TO COVER IT UP. LOOK AT THIS DISC BEFORE THEY DO AND DISTRIBUTE ITS CONTENT AS SOON AS YOU CAN.
>
> FATHER VICTOR KAROSKY

Andrea acknowledged the possibility that it was a joke, but there was only one way to find out. She slipped her laptop out of her bag, turned it on, and pushed the disc in. She cursed the operating system in every language she knew—Spanish, English, and the banal Italian of her guidebook—and when it had finally booted up, she saw that her DVD was a film.

Forty seconds into the film and she was overwhelmed by the urgent need to vomit.

UACV HEADQUARTERS
Via Lamarmora, 3
Saturday, April 9, 2005, 1:05 A.M.

Paola had been looking everywhere for Fowler. Still, it was hardly a surprise when she found him in the basement, a pistol in his hand, his dark jacket neatly folded on a chair, his clergyman's collar hanging from a peg on the wall, sleeves rolled up. He was wearing headphones to cushion his ears, so Paola waited for him to finish a round before walking up to him. His utter concentration fascinated her, the way his body completely assumed the firing position. His hands were strong, in spite of the fact that he was fifty years old. The barrel of the gun pointed straight ahead without wavering so much as an eighth of an inch.

She watched him empty not one but three rounds. He took his time firing, didn't hurry in the slightest, his eyes bearing down, his head tilted just so to the side. He finally noticed she was standing in the training room, which consisted of five booths separated by heavy wood, from which projected the cables holding the targets. The targets could be set at a maximum distance of forty yards by advancing them through a system of pulleys.

"Good evening, *Dottoressa.*"

"Kind of a strange hour for target practice, isn't it?"

"I didn't want to go back to my hotel. I knew I wouldn't get any sleep tonight."

Paola understood him perfectly. Being on your feet throughout the funeral was bad enough, but the night was guaranteed to give them no rest. Paola was going crazy trying to think of something useful to do.

"Where is my beloved Deputy Inspector?"

"Ah, he got an urgent call. We were going over the report on Cardoso's autopsy when he ran out, leaving me in the middle of a sentence."

"Very like him."

"Sure. But let's not talk about it. Let's see what the Army taught you."

Paola pressed the button that brought the paper target, the silhouette of a man in black, closer to her. The crude image had a white circle in the center of his chest. It took a while for the target to come back within range; Fowler had moved it as far away as possible. She wasn't in the least surprised to see that almost all the holes were inside the circle. What surprised her was that the last one had missed. That not all the shots were neatly inside the circle like a protagonist in an action film disappointed her.

But he's not an action hero, she thought, he's flesh and bone. Sharp-witted, cultivated, and a good shot. In some ways, the one shot he missed makes him more human.

Fowler kept his eyes on the target while he laughed, amused by his own failure.

"I am a little out of practice but I still like to shoot. It is an unusual sport."

"As long as it remains a sport."

"Still don't trust me?"

Paola didn't respond. She liked watching Fowler, without the collar, dressed only in his shirt with the sleeves rolled up and his black slacks. But the photos Dante had shown her of El Aguacate were still kicking around inside her head, splashing about like drunken monkeys in a bathtub.

"No, Padre. Not completely. But I want to. Is that enough for you?"

"It will have to do."

"Where did you get the gun? The depository is closed at this hour."

"Troi lent me his. It's his. He told me it had been a long time since he had used it."

"It's true, sadly enough. You should have known the guy three years ago. A real pro, the best sort of evidence analyst. He still is, but then his eyes were full of curiosity, and now that look is gone, replaced by the anxiety of the office manager."

"Is that bitterness or nostalgia in your voice, *Dottoressa*?"

"A little of both."

"Did it take you long to forget him?"

Paola looked as if she were taken aback.

"What did you just say?"

"Come on, don't be offended. I've seen the way he creates walls of solid air between the two of you. Troi is an expert at keeping his distance."

"It's a drag, but it's something he does very well."

Dicanti hesitated a moment before she went on. She again felt that emptiness in the pit of her stomach that looking at Fowler sometimes gave her. The feeling that she was on the top of the Ferris wheel. Should she trust him? She thought, with a sad, fleeting irony, that when all was said and done he was a priest and he was accustomed to seeing people at their worst. As was she, it might be remarked in passing.

"Troi and I had a fling. A quickie. I don't know if he stopped liking me or his mania about being promoted got the upper hand."

"But you prefer the second choice."

"I like to fool myself—in that and other things. I always say to myself that I live with my mother in order to protect her, but in reality I'm the one who needs protection. I suppose that is why I'm attracted to strong but inadequate personality types. Men with whom I will never share my life."

Fowler didn't respond. She had made herself very clear. They were standing quite close, looking at each other. The minutes ticked by in silence.

Paola read what Fowler was thinking as she stared into his penetrating green eyes. She thought she heard a quiet hum, an insistent noise, which she ignored. It was Fowler who pointed it out.

"You had better answer your phone."

And then Paola realized that it was the sound of her phone, which was now ringing furiously. She picked it up and became instantly enraged. She hung up without saying good-bye.

"Let's go, Padre. That was the laboratory. This afternoon someone sent us a package by messenger service. The envelope says it was sent by Maurizio Pontiero."

✝

UACV HEADQUARTERS

Via Lamarmora, 3

Saturday, April 9, 2005, 1:25 A.M.

"The envelope arrived almost four hours ago. Can anyone tell me why we didn't find out what was in it until now?"

Troi looked at her, patient but burned out. It was very late in the day to put up with a subordinate's nonsense. Nevertheless, he kept a tight grip on himself as he put the pistol that Fowler had borrowed back in its drawer.

"The envelope arrived with your name on it, Paola, and when it arrived you were at the morgue. The girl in reception put it in with my mail, and I only saw it later. When I realized who had sent it, I went looking for people, and at this time of the night that takes a while. The first thing to do was to call the bomb squad. Nothing suspicious in the envelope, as far as they were concerned. When I found out what was in there, I called both you and Dante. He showed neither hide nor hair. And Cirin never answered the phone."

"They are asleep. It is the middle of the night, for God's sake."

They were sitting in the fingerprint lab, a narrow space replete with lamps and large bulbs. The smell of the powder used to recover prints was everywhere. There were technicians who claimed to love the smell—one even swore he sniffed it before going to see his girlfriend because it was an aphrodisiac—but Paola found it unappetizing. The smell made her want to sneeze, and the dust stuck to her dark clothes and was hard to wash off.

"So all right, how do we know Karosky sent this message?"

Fowler was studying the script of the person who had written the address. He held the envelope up, his arms slightly extended. Paola suspected his sight was a little blurry close-up and that he must wear glasses to read fine print. She wondered how he would look with them on.

"This is his handwriting, that much is clear. And the macabre joke of putting Pontiero's name on the envelope, that's Karosky."

Paola took the envelope out of Fowler's hands, placing it on top of the large table that took up most of the space in the room, a sheet of glass for a surface, lit from below. Spread over the top of the table were the envelope's contents, in transparent plastic bags. Troi pointed at the first one.

"His fingerprints are on the note. Take a look at it, Dicanti."

Paola lifted the plastic bag with the note written in Italian and gave it a close look. Looking through the plastic, she read the message out loud.

Dear Paola:

I miss you so much! I'm in Mc 9, 48. It's steamy in here but very pleasant. I hope you can stop by and say hello sometime soon. Meanwhile, I've sent you a video of my vacation.

Kisses,

Maurizio

Paola recoiled in a mixture of anger and horror. She tried to hold back the tears, forcing them to stay inside. She would never cry in front of Troi. Maybe in front of Fowler but not Troi. In front of him, never.

"Padre Fowler?"

"Mark, chapter 9, verse 48. 'Where the worm dieth not and the fire is not quenched.' "

"Hell."

"Exactly."

"Fucking bastard."

"There is no mention of his having to flee the scene a few hours before. The disc was cut this morning. No wait, yesterday morning, according to the dates on the disc's files."

"Do we know the model of the camera or the computer it was burned on?"

"With the program he used, those details aren't recorded on the disc. No series numbers, no codes, nothing that could help us identify the operating equipment."

"Fingerprints?"

"Two partials, both Karosky's. But I didn't need them to know that. Seeing the content would have been enough."

"So what are you waiting for? Put the DVD in, Troi."

"Padre Fowler, could you excuse us for a minute?"

The priest instinctively understood the situation. He looked Paola in the eyes. She made a dismissive gesture, telling him that everything was OK.

"Why not. Coffee for three, Dicanti?"

"Two spoonfuls of sugar in mine, please."

Troi waited for Fowler to exit the room before grabbing Paola's hand. His fleshy, slightly moist hand repulsed her. How many times had she sighed, wanting those hands to touch her again? She had hated him just as much for his nasty attitude and his indifference. Now not even a spark from the fire was left between them. It had been snuffed out in a vast sea of green just a few minutes before. All she had was her pride, something she had in abundance. And she definitely was not about to give in to his emotional blackmail. She withdrew her hand and Troi let his drop.

"Paola, I just want to warn you. What you are about to see is going to hit you very hard."

Dicanti made a hard, humorless smile in Troi's direction and crossed her arms. She wanted to keep her hands as far from him as possible. Just in case.

"All of a sudden you are talking to me with the *tu* again? I'm very used to looking at dead bodies, Carlo."

"Not of your friends."

The smile that trembled on Paola's lips was as fleeting as a leaf in the wind, but her spirit never wavered.

"Let's see the video, *Direttore* Troi."

"That's the way you want it to be? It could be something very different."

"I am not a little doll you can treat any way you like. You rejected me because it was dangerous for your career. You preferred to return to your wife and your comfortable misery. I have my own misery now, thanks."

"Why now, Paola? Why now, after all this time?"

"Because I wasn't strong enough before. But now I am."

Troi ran his hand through his hair. He was getting the picture.

"You will never have anything with him, Paola. Even though he is what you want."

"You might be right. But that's my decision. You made yours some time ago. At this point, I'd rather give in to Dante's obscene leers."

Troi looked like he'd swallowed something distasteful. Paola relished seeing him look so uncomfortable; her angry outburst had penetrated her boss's ego. She had been a little hard on him, but he deserved it for the many months he had treated his conquest like a piece of shit.

"As you wish, *Dottoressa* Dicanti. I will go back to being the ironic boss, and you the pretty novelist."

"Believe me, Carlo. It's for the best."

Troi smiled sadly, like a child who had just lost his mother's breast.

"All right then. Let's see the disc."

As if he had a sixth sense, Fowler came in with a tray of something that could pass for coffee for someone who had never in their life tasted the real thing.

"Here you go. Venom from the caffeine machine. May I make the supposition that the meeting is about to get under way again?"

"It is indeed, Padre," Troi responded. Fowler observed them closely, unobtrusively. Troi seemed the sadder of the two, but there was something in his voice. Relief? Paola was obviously stronger, less insecure.

The director pulled on a pair of latex gloves and removed the disc from its sleeve. Technicians from the laboratory had rolled a small table in from the conference room. Sitting on top was a twenty-seven-inch TV and a cheap DVD player. Troi wanted to watch the film there because the walls in the conference room were glass, and anyone walking down the hallway would get a good look at Karosky's film. By then rumors about the case Troi and Dicanti were working on had circulated around the building, even though none of them came close to the truth. Not by a long shot.

The disc began to play. The filmed material started immediately, without titles or anything like it. The style was utterly crude; the camera was jumping about hysterically and the lighting was atrocious. Troi turned the brightness on the TV almost all the way up.

"Good evening, souls of this world."

Paola cringed when she heard Karosky's voice, the same voice that had tormented her over the phone after Pontiero was murdered. Nothing was visible on-screen.

"This film depicts the process by which I am going to eliminate the holiest men in the Church from the face of the earth, fulfilling my labors in the shadows. My name is Victor Karosky, a renegade priest of the Roman religion. Over the course of many years I abused children, protected by the stupidity and connivance of my senile superiors. For these good deeds I have been chosen by Lucifer himself for the stated task, at exactly the moment in which our enemy the Carpenter selects his chosen one on this ball of mud."

The screen changed from complete darkness to a series of shadows. A man appeared, soaked in blood, his head dropped onto his chest, tied up to what looked to be the columns in the crypt at Santa Maria in Traspontina. Dicanti just barely recognized him as Cardinal Portini, the first victim, the one whose dead body she had never seen because the Vigilanza had it cremated. Portini uttered a few quiet groans. Karosky was only visible in the tip of a knife which poked the flesh of the cardinal's left arm.

"This is Cardinal Portini, who is too exhausted to protest. Portini did more than his share of good in the world, which is why my master detests his stinking flesh. Now you will see how I put an end to his miserable existence."

The knife was pressed against the cardinal's throat. Karosky then slit it with a single cut. The screen went black again, and then a new picture appeared, with a new victim tied up in the same place. It was Robayra, who looked extremely afraid.

"This is Cardinal Robayra, quaking with fear. He carried a great light within him. That light will now return to its Creator."

This time Paola had to look away. The camera showed the knife as it emptied Robayra's eye sockets. A single drop of blood spotted the camera lens. It was the most horrible spectacle Dicanti had ever contemplated, and she felt that her stomach was one image away from heaving everything up. And then the film had a new subject, the one thing she feared most.

"This is Detective Pontiero, one of the followers of the Fisherman. They put him on my trail, but he was powerless against the Prince of Darkness. The detective is now beginning to bleed slowly."

Pontiero looked straight into the camera, but his face wasn't his. His teeth were set, but the life in his eyes had not yet been extinguished. The knife slit his throat agonizingly slowly. Paola looked away.

"This is Cardinal Cardoso, friend to the disinherited of the world, the bedbugs, and the parasites. His love was as repugnant to my Master as the stinking entrails of a goat. He too has died."

There was something wrong. In place of the filmed images, they were looking at photographs of Cardinal Cardoso on his deathbed. Three photos in all, all of them lusterless green. The blood was unnaturally dark. The three photos were on the screen for fifteen seconds, five seconds each.

"Now I am going to kill another saintly man, the most saintly of all. People will try to stop me, but they will end up exactly the same as those you have seen die before your very eyes. The cowardly Church has hidden it from you, but it can no longer continue to do so. Good night, souls of this world."

The DVD was nothing more than static now and Troi switched it off. Paola had turned white. Fowler clenched his teeth, furious. The three sat there for a few minutes without saying a word. They had to gather their wits after enduring that blood-soaked brutality. Paola, the one most affected by the disc, was nevertheless the first one to speak.

"The photographs. Why photographs? Why not video?"

"Because he couldn't," Fowler said. "Because cameras do not work in Saint Martha's, nothing 'more complex than a light bulb works in there.' I'm quoting Dante."

"And Karosky knew it."

"What did they say to me about that little game of diabolic possession?"

Dicanti once again had the feeling something did not fit. The video struck her as coming from very different directions. She needed a good night of sleep and rest in a quiet place where she could think. Karosky's words, the clues left on the corpses—all of it had a connecting thread. When she found it, she could unravel the ball. Until then, she was short on time.

Of course, my good night of sleep has just been blown to shit, she thought to herself.

"Karosky's crazed histrionics about the devil are not what bother me," Troi interjected, anticipating Paola's thoughts. "The most serious thing is that he's challenging us to stop him before he finishes off another cardinal. And time is flying."

"What can we do?" Fowler asked. "He didn't show any signs of life during John Paul's funeral. The cardinals are more protected than ever. Saint Martha's is sealed up tight, as is the Vatican."

Dicanti bit her lip. She was tired of playing by some psychopath's rules. Because now Karosky had committed a new error: he had left a trail that they could follow.

"Who brought this to our offices?"

"I've put two new guys in charge of following the trail. It arrived by messenger service. Tevere Express was the agency, a local company that operates in the Vatican. We haven't managed to get hold of the guy in charge of that route but the cameras on the exterior of the building took a picture of him driving up on his bike. The license plate is registered under the name of Giuseppe Bastina, forty-three years old. He lives in Castro Pretorio, on Via Palestro. Number 31."

"No phone?"

"Motor Vehicles has no number for him, and there's no listing at Information."

"Maybe it's under his wife's name," Fowler said.

"Maybe. But for now that's our best piece of evidence, which means we ought to take a walk. Coming, Padre?"

"After you, *Dottoressa*."

✠

BASTINA FAMILY RESIDENCE
Via Palestro, 31
Saturday, April 9, 2005, 2:02 A.M.

"Giuseppe Bastina?"

"Yeah, that's me." Giuseppe Bastina cut a curious figure, standing in the doorway in his underwear, a nine-month-old baby in his arms. It wasn't at all strange that a doorbell at that hour had woken the kid up.

"I'm *Ispettore* Paola Dicanti and this is Padre Fowler. Don't stress out; you're not in any trouble and nothing has happened to anyone in your family. We just want to ask you a few urgent questions."

They stood in the foyer of a modest but well-kept apartment. Someone had put out a doormat with a smiling frog, who welcomed visitors to the house. Paola hazarded a guess the welcome did not extend to them, and she was right: Bastina was fairly disturbed by their presence.

"No way this can wait till the morning? The baby has to eat and sleep at certain times; we're trying to keep her on schedule."

Paola shook her head.

"This will only take a moment. You made a delivery this afternoon, right? An envelope. To Via Lamarmora. Bring anything to mind?"

"Sure, I remember that. What do you think? I remember all my trips," Bastina said, touching the side of his forehead with his right

253

index finger. His left arm was still full of the baby, who had, for the moment at least, calmed down.

"Could you tell us where you picked up this envelope? It's very important; it has to do with an investigation into a series of murders."

"They called the agency, just like always. They asked me to swing by the Vatican post office, that I would find some envelopes on the desk in the lobby."

Paola was taken aback.

"More than one envelope?"

"Yeah, there were twelve. The client asked us to deliver the first ten envelopes to the Vatican pressroom. Then one to the Corpo di Vigilanza, and the last one to you."

"Nobody handed you the envelopes? You just picked them up?" Fowler was irritated by the man.

"At that time of day no one is at the post office. They leave the outside door open until nine, for anyone who wants to drop letters in the international box."

"And how did they pay?"

"They left a small envelope on top of the others. The small one had three hundred and seventy Euros, three sixty for the rush service and a ten-Euro tip."

Paola was losing it now. She looked at the ceiling in a gesture of hopelessness. Karosky had thought of everything. Another fucking dead-end street.

"So you didn't see anybody?"

"Nobody."

"And what did you do then?"

"What do you think I did? I made the run to the pressroom and then delivered the envelope to the Vigilanza."

"Who was supposed to receive the envelopes at the pressroom?"

"They were addressed to different journalists. Foreigners."

"And you handed them out to their recipients?"

"What's with all the questions? I take my job seriously. I hope all this isn't because I screwed up. I need the work, I really do, so please. My kid has to eat and my wife has another biscuit in the oven."

"Look, this has nothing to do with you, but it's no joke either. Tell us what happened and we'll leave. If not, I will see to it that every traffic cop in Rome can recite your career from memory. OK, Mr. Bastina?"

Bastina was cornered, and the baby started to wail, frightened just by Paola's tone.

"All right, already. Don't talk like that, you'll scare the kid. What kind of heartless person are you?"

Dicanti was very tired and irritable. She hadn't wanted to speak to the guy like that, in his own house, but the investigation had brought her nothing but obstacles.

"I'm sorry. So please, help us out here. It's life or death at this point. Take my word for it."

The messenger backed off a bit too. With his free hand he scratched the stubble on his chin and gently rocked the baby in his arm. Little by little the baby calmed down and stopped crying.

"I gave the envelopes to the lady in charge of the pressroom, OK? The doors to the room were already closed, and to deliver them by hand I would have had to wait a full hour. Special deliveries have to be taken care of within the hour following pickup or they don't pay. I've had a few problems on the job lately, you follow? Anyone finds out I did this, I lose the job."

"Nobody is going to find out from us, Mr. Bastina. Trust me."

Bastina looked at her and nodded.

"I'll try to believe it."

"You know the name of the woman in charge?"

"No, I don't. She was wearing an ID card with the Vatican coat of arms and a blue band on top. It said *Press*."

Fowler stepped a few feet into the hallway with Paola and started whispering in her ear again. She tried to concentrate on his words and not on the way his nearness made her feel. It wasn't easy.

"The card this guy is describing doesn't belong to someone who works for the Vatican. It's a press pass. The discs never arrived at their destinations. Do you know how I know?"

Paola tried to think like a journalist for a second. She pictured herself receiving an envelope while she was sitting in the middle of the pressroom, surrounded by all her rivals in the media.

"They never arrived at their destinations because if they had, their content would at this instant be splashed over every newspaper and television in the world. If all of those envelopes had arrived at the same time, the journalists would have had everything they needed sitting in their laps. They would have corralled the Vatican spokesman right then and there."

"Definitely. Karosky tried to send a message of his own to the press, but it backfired on him, thanks to the fact that this guy was in a big hurry and someone obviously didn't trouble their conscience before swiping the envelopes. Unless I am very wrong, this woman opened one of the envelopes and then took all of them. Why should she share this nice piece of luck that fell out of the sky?"

"Right now, somewhere in Rome, that woman is typing out the story of the century."

"And we have to know who she is. As soon as possible."

Paola took the urgency in Fowler's words to heart. They turned around and walked back to Bastina in the doorway.

"Mr. Bastina, tell us about the person who took the envelopes."

"Yeah, sure. She was a pretty girl with blond hair to her shoulders, twenty-something years old. Blue eyes. A light-colored jacket, beige pants."

"I can see you've got a good memory."

"For the fine-looking chicks." Bastina was a child of the streets and he was a little offended, as if they had questioned his worth. "I'm from Milan, *Ispettore*. Really, it's better my wife is in bed right now. If she heard me talking like this . . . There's a just a month to go before the kid is born, and the doctor says she has to take it really easy."

"Do you remember anything else that could help us to identify the young woman?"

"Yeah. She was Spanish, that's for sure. My sister's husband is Spanish, and you can always pick them out, trying to imitate the Italian accent. You get the picture."

Paola got the picture. She also knew it was time to take off.

"We're sorry we bothered you."

"Don't worry about it. The only thing I don't like is answering the same questions twice."

Paola spun around. She went on red alert, and had to restrain herself from yelling at the man.

"Somebody has already been asking you questions before? Who? What did they look like?"

The baby was crying again. His father rocked him in his arms and tried to calm him down, without success.

"Get lost, both of you! You're upsetting my kid all over again!"

"Tell us and we'll leave," said Fowler, trying to calm everyone down.

"It was one of your coworkers. He flashed the Corpo di Vigilanza badge at me. At least he had some identification. A short guy, thick shoulders. Leather jacket. Left here an hour ago. OK? Get out and don't come back."

Dicanti and Fowler looked at each other nervously. They took off at a clip for the elevator, trying to make sense of this new revelation as the elevator flew down to the street.

"Are you thinking what I am thinking, *Dottoressa*?"

"Exactly the same. Dante disappeared about eight o'clock tonight, using some lame excuse."

"After getting a call."

"Because over at Vigilanza they had already opened the package. And what they saw disturbed them. Why didn't we put the two things together before? Fuck, the Vatican makes a record of every vehicle that goes in and out. Standard procedure. And if Tevere Express works with them on a regular basis, it is clear that they would be able to pinpoint all of the employees, including Bastina, by his license plate."

"They followed the trail of the envelopes."

"If the journalists had opened their packages at the same time, in the pressroom, a few of them would have slipped the disc in their laptops. And the place would have exploded. No way for anybody to contain it. Ten well-known journalists . . ."

"But this way just one journalist gets the scoop."

"Exactly."

"One is a very manageable number."

Stories flashed through Paola's mind. A whole bunch of them, the kind that street cops and others passed quietly among themselves, usually when they were hitting the third round at a bar. Dark tales of disappearances and accidents.

"You think it's possible they—"

"I don't know. Anything is possible. It would depend upon the journalist's flexibility."

"Padre, do you have to keep dancing around the subject? What you are saying to me is, they pay her off if she hands over the disc."

Fowler didn't say a word. An eloquent silence.

"Well, then, it's better if we get there first, for her own good." She gestured to him to get in the car. "We have got to get back to

UACV as soon as possible. Let's start to look in the hotels, check the airline companies."

"No, *Dottoressa*, we have to go somewhere else." And he handed her an address.

"That's on the other side of town. What's over there?"

"A friend. He can help us out."

AN APARTMENT SOMEWHERE IN ROME

Saturday, April 9, 2005, 2:48 A.M.

Paola drove toward the address Fowler had given her, without knowing exactly where she was going. It was a long row of apartments and they waited in the doorway while Fowler pressed the buzzer.

"So this friend of yours . . . how exactly do you know him?"

"Let's just say it was my last mission for my old employer. The kid was fourteen years old back then, a real rebel. Since then I have been, how to say, a kind of spiritual counselor for him. We've never fallen out of touch."

"And now he works for your business, Padre?"

"*Dottoressa*, if you stop asking me tricky questions, I can stop telling you plausible lies."

Five minutes later, Fowler's young friend got up to let them in. He turned out to be another priest, and a young one at that. He led them into a small studio decorated with inexpensive furniture. It was very clean. There were two windows, both of whose Persian blinds were lowered all the way down. On one side of the room was a table some six feet long, with five hard drives and five flat screens sitting on top. Under the table, dozens of lights flickered manically, like an out-of-control forest of Christmas trees. On the other side of the room was an unmade bed. It was clear that its occupant had only gotten up a few minutes before.

"Albert, I want to introduce you to *Dottoressa* Paola Dicanti. We're working on something together."

"Padre Albert."

"Please, just Albert." The young curate's smile was very nearly a grin. "Sorry about the mess. Hell, Anthony, what brings you around here at this hour? I have no desire to play chess right now. And in passing, you could have told me you were coming to Rome. I knew you were back in action last week. I would have preferred to hear it from you."

"Albert was ordained last year. An impulsive kid, but a wizard with computers. And now he's going to do us a favor."

"What kind of mess have you gotten me into this time, you old screwball?"

"Albert, please. Try to show a little respect for the lady here," Fowler said, putting on a show of being offended. "We want you to supply us with a list."

"What sort of list?"

"The list of every authorized reporter working at the Vatican."

Albert looked serious.

"Not so easy to do."

"Come on, Albert. You're in and out of the Pentagon's computers the way some guys go to the bathroom."

"Baseless rumors," Albert said, but his smile betrayed him. "Even if it were true, one thing has nothing to do with the other. The Vatican's information system is like the land of Mordor. You can't get in."

"Then let's get going, Frodo26. I am certain you have already paid them a visit."

"Ssssh. Don't say my hacker handle out loud, ever, you nutcase."

"Sorry."

The young priest turned serious. He scratched his chin, where a few red zits had taken up fleeting residence. He turned around to face Fowler again.

"Is it really unavoidable? You know I'm not authorized. Goes against all the rules."

Paola resisted the temptation to ask who exactly gave permission for something like this.

"Someone's life is in danger, Albert. And we have never been men who played by the rules." Fowler shot a look at Paola that said, *Help me out here*.

"Could you give us a hand, Albert? You managed to get in before?"

"Yes, *Dottoressa* Dicanti, I've been there before. Once, and I didn't get very far. And I swear I have never been so scared shitless in my life. Excuse my language."

"Relax. I've heard the phrase before. What happened?"

"They caught me trespassing. That automatically activated a program which set two guard dogs sniffing at my heels."

"What does that mean? Remember, I know nothing about the subject."

Albert lit up. He loved talking about his job.

"There are two hidden servers which are just waiting for someone to slip past their defenses. At the moment I entered, they put all their resources on the job of finding me. One of the servers was going all out to locate my home base while the other started to put clips on me."

"Clips?"

"Imagine you're on a trail that crosses a gully. Your route is a series of rocks with surfaces above the water. What the computer does is to delete the stone I am about to rest my foot on and put spurious information in its place. A many-headed Trojan horse."

The kid brought his guests a chair and a small serving table to sit on. He clearly did not have visitors very often. He then took a seat in front of the computer.

"A virus?"

"A really powerful one. If I had taken just one step more, its lines of code would have erased my hard drive and I would have been in its hands completely. It's the only time I have ever used the panic button." The young priest pointed to a harmless-looking red button that sat to one side of the largest monitor. The button had a cable that descended into the thickets below.

"What is it?"

"It's the button that cuts the electricity to the whole floor of this building. Ten minutes later, the power comes back on."

Paola asked him why he had to cut the power for everyone on his floor and not just unplug the computer from the socket. But Albert was no longer listening. His gaze was directed at the monitor, while his fingers flew over the keyboard. Fowler answered for him.

"The information is transmitted in seconds. The time Albert loses in getting on his knees and unplugging the line could be crucial. Follow?"

Paola understood about half of what the men were talking about, and was interested in less. What mattered at that moment was to find the young Spanish journalist, and if this was how they did it, then so much the better. The two priests had obviously been in situations like this before.

"What's he going to do now?"

"He'll pull up a screen. I don't know exactly how he does it, but he routes his computer through hundreds of others, in a sequence which ends up in the Vatican network. The more complex and more widely spread the camouflage, the longer it will take them to find him, but there's a buffer zone that should never be crossed. Each computer only knows the name of the computer before it, the one which asked permission to connect. And it only knows that name while the connection lasts. In that way, if the connection is interrupted before they get to him, they won't come up with anything."

The rhythmic clicking of the keyboard went on for about a quarter of an hour. Every minute or so a small red dot appeared on a map of the world that filled one of the monitors. There were hundreds of these dots, covering the greater part of Europe, the north of Africa, the United States and Canada, Japan. Paola noticed that there was a greater density of red dots in the wealthier countries, and barely one or two in Africa, and a dozen or so in Latin America.

"Each one of the points you see on that monitor corresponds to a computer Albert is going to utilize, in sequence, in order to penetrate the Vatican's system. It could be the computer of a young man working at a university; it could be in a bank or a law firm. It could be in Beijing, in Austria, or Manhattan. The farther flung the geographical nexus, the more efficient the resulting sequence."

"How does he know that one of those computers won't be accidentally turned off, interrupting the entire process?"

"I keep records on each computer." Albert's voice was very distant. His fingers continued to fly over the keyboard. "I try to use computers that never get turned off. These days, with all the programs for file sharing, many people leave their computers on day and night, downloading music or porn. Those computer systems are ideal to utilize as links in the chain. One of my favorites is . . ." He mentioned a well-known figure in European politics. "The old fart likes pictures of young girls with horses. Every once in a while I slip in a photo of some golfers. The Good Lord forbids that kind of perversion."

"And you aren't afraid to substitute one sin for another?"

The kid laughed at Fowler's joke without taking his eyes off the instructions and commands his hands were bringing to life on the monitor. He finally took a breather.

"We're almost there. But let me warn you, we won't be able to copy anything. I'm using a system in which one of the computers is doing the work for me, but it erases the information copied to that computer as soon as a certain number of kilobytes have been used up. So you'd better have a good memory. From the moment they detect us, we have sixty seconds."

Fowler and Dicanti nodded. The priest took on the role of directing Albert in the search.

"There it is. We're in."

"Go over to the Press Department, Albert."

"Done."

"Hunt around for authorized press."

Barely two miles away, in the basement of a Vatican office building, Archangel, one of the Vatican's security computers, sprang into action. One of the many routines it performed automatically had detected the presence of an external agent in its system. It immediately activated its location program. The first computer activated another, this one named Saint Michael. Both were Cray supercomputers, able to undertake billions of operations per second, valued at more than $250,000 USD apiece. Both began to run through their calculation cycles searching for the intruder.

An alert appeared on the main monitor. Albert pursed his lips.

"Shit. Here they come. We've got less than a minute. There's nothing about authorizations."

Paola tensed up. She watched as the red dots on the map of the world started to go out, one by one. At the beginning there had been several hundred, but they were now disappearing at an alarming rate.

"Press passes."

"Nothing. Fuck. Forty seconds."

"Media outlets?" Paola suggested.

"Here it is. Thirty seconds."

A list appeared on the screen. A database.

"Shit, it's got more than three thousand entries."

"Arrange it by nationality and pull up Spain."

"Okay. Twenty seconds."

"Damn it, there aren't any photographs. How many names are there?"

"More than fifty. Fifteen seconds."

There were only thirty red dots left on the map of the world. All three leaned forward.

"Eliminate the men and arrange the women by age."

"There it is. Ten seconds."

Paola's hands were balled into fists. Albert took one hand off the keyboard and placed it on top of the panic button. Large drops of sweat fell from his brow as he typed with one hand.

"Here you are! At last! Five seconds, Anthony!"

Fowler and Dicanti memorized the names on the screen as fast as they could. They were still not finished when Albert hit the panic button. The screen and the whole apartment went pitch black.

"Albert," Fowler said in the depths of the darkness.

"Yes, Anthony?"

"You don't by any chance have candles, do you?"

"You ought to know I never use analog systems, Anthony."

†

HOTEL RAPHAEL
Largo Febo, 2
Saturday, April 9, 2005, 3:17 A.M.

Andrea Otero was very, very frightened.

No, sir, she thought, I am not afraid, I am fucking terrified.

The first thing she had done when she got to the hotel lobby was to buy three packs of cigarettes. The first pack of nicotine had been a blessing. Now that she was on to the second, things were a little less haywire. She felt a slightly comforting seasickness, something like a lullaby.

She was sitting on the floor of the room, her back against the wall, her arms clutching her legs while she smoked nonstop. Her laptop computer was on the other side of the room. It was turned off.

Considering the circumstances, she had acted correctly. Once she'd seen the first forty seconds of Victor Karosky's film—if that was his real name—she was on the verge of throwing up. Andrea had never been the kind of person to hold things back, so she looked for the nearest trash basket at full speed, one hand over her mouth, and coughed up some macaroni and cheese, her breakfast croissant, and something she didn't remember eating but that must have been yesterday's dinner. She asked herself if it was a sacrilege to vomit into a trash basket at the Vatican, and concluded it was not.

When the world stopped spinning around her, she walked back to the pressroom door while thinking that she had really made a racket and somebody was sure to hear it. No doubt, by now two Swiss Guards were ready to arrest her for postal assault, or whatever the hell they call the opening of an envelope that obviously was not intended for you. Because none of those envelopes were.

OK, Mr. Policeman, I thought it might be a bomb and I acted as bravely as I could. Stay calm. I'll wait right here while you go for my medal.

That wouldn't be very believable. Decidedly unbelievable. But the journalist had no need for an explanation for her captors because there weren't any. Andrea had put her things together calmly, left the Vatican as slowly as she could, giving a flirtatious smile to the Swiss Guards at the Arch of the Bells, the entrance journalists used, and then crossed Saint Peter's Square, which after many days was clear of people. She stopped feeling that the Swiss Guards were staring at her when she got out of the taxi at her hotel. And she stopped believing that they were following her half an hour after that.

And no, no one had followed her and no one suspected anything. She had thrown the nine unopened envelopes into a trash can in the Piazza Navona. She did not want them to grab her with all the incriminating evidence. And then she had gone directly to her room, not before making a stop at the nicotine kiosk.

When she felt sufficiently at ease, after inspecting the pot of dried flowers in her room for the third time without finding any hidden microphones, she loaded the disc into her laptop and started to watch the film again.

She managed to last sixty seconds on the first try. On the second try, she watched almost the whole thing. She made it all the way through on the third try, but she had to race to the bathroom to regurgitate the glass of water she drank when she got back to the room, as well as all the bile she was still holding inside. The fourth time, she managed to stay calm enough to convince herself that it was very real, and not a tape on the order of *The Blair Witch Project*. But, as we have already noted, Andrea was a very sharp journalist, which normally was both her great advantage and her major liability. Her intuition had already told her from the very first viewing that the film was genuine. Perhaps some other journalist would have given the disc a contemptuous once over, certain that it was a fake. But Andrea had spent days looking for Cardinal Robayra, and she suspected that the other cardinals were missing as well. Hearing Robayra's name in the film dispelled her doubts the way a drunken fart would blow through five o'clock tea at Buckingham Palace. Harsh, dirty, and efficient.

She watched the film a fifth time, just to get used to the images. And then a sixth time, to take notes, barely more than unconnected squiggles in a block. She shut her laptop down, sat as far away from it as possible in a sliver of space between the desk and the air conditioner. And she surrendered to the lure of nicotine.

"Definitely a bad moment to try to give up smoking."

Those images were a nightmare. At first sight the hostility they filled her with, the dirty way they had made her feel, was so profound she was unable to react for two hours. When the shock had worn off and she was able to think, she began to take stock of what she had in her hands. She took out her notebook and wrote down three points that would serve as the basis for her article.

> 1. A satanic killer is killing cardinals in the Catholic Church.
> 2. The Catholic Church, most likely in collaboration with the Italian Police, is keeping this hidden from us.
> 3. By chance, the conclave, where those cardinals will play a key role, is inside of ~~nine~~ days
> eight

She wrote down nine and then replaced it with eight. It was Saturday now.

She had to write a fantastic piece of reporting. A full report, three pages long, with summaries, pull-out quotes, sidebars, and a killer head. She couldn't send any images to the newspaper beforehand because they would take her off the story without a second's delay. The editor would no doubt drag Paloma out of her hospital bed so that the article would have the weight it deserved. Maybe they would let her have a byline on one of the sidebars. But if she sent the completed story to the paper, laid out and ready to send to the printers, then not even the editor in chief himself would have the gall to take her name off it. It was not going to happen, because in this case Andrea would also send a fax to *El Pais* and another to the daily *ABC* with the complete text and photographs from the article before it was published. And to hell with the exclusive. And her job, for that matter.

"Like my brother Miguel Angel says, 'All of us get laid, or we throw the whore in the river.'"

It was not exactly a simile appropriate for a young lady like Andrea Otero, but nobody butted in to insist that she was a young lady. It was hardly proper for young ladies to steal other people's correspondence as she had done, but she'd be damned if it mattered to her. She could already see herself writing the best seller *I Caught the Cardinal Killer*. Hundreds of thousands of books with her name on the cover, interviews all over the world, conferences debating her revelations. The shameless robbery was definitely worth the trouble.

Clearly, she thought, you sometimes have to be careful who you rob.

Because that message had not been sent by the senior executives of a newspaper. It had been sent by a heartless killer who probably was counting the hours until his message would be broadcast all over the world.

She considered her options. It was Saturday. Certainly whoever had sent the disc would not find out that it had failed to reach its destination until the morning. If the messenger service was open on Saturday, which she doubted, the killer would be on her trail in a few hours, perhaps by ten or eleven in the morning. But she doubted that the messenger had read her name on her press badge. He seemed more preoccupied by what lay immediately below, inside her shirt. Best-case scenario, if the service were closed until Monday, she had two days. Worst case, a few hours.

It was true that Andrea had learned that the sanest thing was always to act as if the worst case were the most likely. So she would put the story together right away. As soon as the editor in chief and the newspaper's director sent the article to press, she'd have to dye her hair, hide behind her sunglasses, and fly out of the hotel like a bee.

She got on her feet and told herself to be strong. She switched on the laptop and opened the newspaper's paste-up program. She wrote right into the template. She felt much better when she saw how her words would look in the text.

It took her three-quarters of an hour to prepare the three-page trial run. She was almost done when her cell phone rang.

Who the hell is calling me at this number, at three in the morning?

Only the newspaper had that number. She hadn't given it to anyone else, not even to her family. So it had to be someone from Editorial with an emergency. She got up and searched around in her bag until she found it. She looked at the screen, expecting to see the incredibly long display of numbers that appeared when there was a call from Spain, but what she saw instead, where the identity of the caller should appear, was a blank. It didn't even say *Unknown Caller*.

She put the phone to her ear.

"Hello?"

The only sound was a busy signal.

She hung up.

But something inside her told her that the call was important and she had better hurry up. She went back to the keyboard, writing faster than ever. The errors she let stand—she had always been a good speller, from age eight on—and never went back to correct them. They could do it at the newspaper. She was suddenly in a tremendous rush to finish.

It took her four hours to complete the rest of the article; hours searching for profiles and photos of the cardinals, news, biographies, and their deaths. The article had several images taken directly from Karosky's video. Some of them were so strong they made her blush. What the hell. Let them censor them in Editorial if they dared.

She was right in the middle of writing the closing lines when there was a knock at the door.

☩

HOTEL RAPHAEL
Largo Febo, 2
Saturday, April 9, 2005, 7:58 A.M.

Andrea looked at the door as if she'd never seen one before in her life. She took the disc out of the computer, jammed it back in its plastic slipcover, and buried it inside the wastebasket in the bathroom. She walked back to her room, her heart balled in a fist, wishing that whoever it was on the other side of the door would just go away. More knocks on the door, courteous but very forceful. Maid service was out of the question. It was barely eight in the morning.

"Who is it?"

"Signorina Otero? It's breakfast, courtesy of the hotel."

Andrea opened the door. She was surprised.

"I didn't order any—"

The man on the other side of the door never let her finish her sentence. There was no chance he was one of the hotel's elegant bellhops or waiters. Short and stocky but clearly fit, in a leather jacket and black pants, he had gone without shaving for a day or so. He was wearing a broad smile.

"Signorina Otero? I'm Fabio Dante, deputy inspector at the Vatican Corpo di Vigilanza. I would like to ask you a few questions."

In his left hand he held an ID card, with a very visible photo. Andrea looked at it intently. It appeared to be authentic.

"As you can see, right this second I'm very tired and I need to get some rest. Come back some other time—"

She shut the door as abruptly as she could, but the man on the other side wedged his foot in like an encyclopedia salesman with a large family to support. Andrea watched him force his way in the door.

"You didn't understand me? I have to get some sleep."

"It seems that it is you who doesn't understand me. I need to speak with you urgently. I am investigating a robbery."

Oh Christ, she thought to herself. How did they find me so quickly?

Not a muscle in Andrea's face so much as twitched, but inside, her nervous system passed from "alarm" to "total crisis." She would have to bluff her way out. Her nails were digging into her palms, the toes on her feet were curled into a ball. She opened the door all the way so the supervisor could enter.

"I can't give you much time. I have to send an article to my paper."

"A little early to be sending an article, wouldn't you say? The printers haven't even shown up for work yet."

"Right, but I like to do things with time to spare."

"Are we talking about some special news?" Dante asked, taking a step in the direction of Andrea's laptop. She stepped in front of him, blocking his way.

"No, nothing special. Habitual conjectures about who is going to be the next supreme pontiff."

"Of course. A question of great importance, no?"

"Of great importance, actually. But there is not a lot to say right this instant. You know how it goes, the usual human interest stories from here and there. There has been no new news for a while"

"And we would like it to stay that way, Signorina Otero."

"Except, of course, for this robbery you were talking to me about. What exactly was stolen?"

"Nothing so extraordinary. A few envelopes."

"What's in them? Something very valuable for sure. The cardinals' payroll?"

"What makes you think the contents were valuable?"

"Must be. Why else would they put their best hunting dog on the trail? Maybe it's a collection of Vatican postage stamps. I have heard that the philatelists will kill to get their hands on them."

"Actually, they weren't stamps. Mind if I smoke?"

"You ought to take up mints."

The deputy inspector's nose took in the air around him. "Advice which you yourself appear not to be following."

"It's been a long night. Smoke, if you can find an empty ashtray."

Dante lit up a cigarette and exhaled.

"As I was telling you, Signorina Otero, the envelopes do not contain stamps. It's a matter of some extremely confidential information, which must not get into the wrong hands."

"For example?"

"I don't follow. For example what?"

"Whose hands would be the wrong ones?"

"Those whose owner has no idea what's best for them."

Dante looked around in vain for an empty ashtray. He resolved the question by flicking the ashes on the floor. Andrea took the opportunity to swallow some saliva: if what he had just said wasn't a threat, she was a nun in a convent.

"And what kind of information is that?"

"The confidential kind."

"Valuable?"

"It could be. I expect that when I find the person who took the envelopes, it will be someone who knows how to negotiate."

"You are prepared to offer a lot of money for them?"

"No. I'm prepared to offer to let the person keep their teeth."

Dante's veiled threat didn't frighten Andrea, but the tone did. He spit out the words with a smile and the same tone he would use to order a decaffeinated coffee. And that was dangerous. She was suddenly very sorry she had let him in the room. She had one card left.

"Fine, *Ispettore*. It's been very interesting talking to you but I am going to have to ask you to leave. My photographer friend is due back any minute and he's a little jealous."

Dante broke out laughing. Not Andrea though, not at all: Dante had his pistol out and was aiming it at the center of her chest.

"Game's over, pretty one. There is no friend. Give me the discs, or we'll get a live look at what shape your lungs are in."

Andrea glared at the pistol.

"You're not going to shoot me. We're in a hotel. The police would be here in thirty seconds, and you'll never find what you're looking for, whatever that is."

Dante wavered for a few seconds.

"You know what? You're right. I'm not going to shoot."

He landed a left with terrible force. Andrea saw colored lights and a solid wall in front of her. It took her some time before she realized the punch had knocked her legs out from under her and she was staring at the ceiling.

"I won't take much more of your time, Miss Otero. Just enough for me to get what I need."

Dante walked over to the computer. He pushed the letters on the keyboard until the screen saver disappeared and Andrea's article appeared in its place.

"First prize!"

She managed to get halfway to her feet, one hand massaging her left eye. The cretin had lacerated the pulpy flesh under her brow, and blood was spilling everywhere. She couldn't see a thing on that side.

"I don't get it. How did you find me?"

"Signorina, you yourself gave us the authorization to do so by giving us your mobile phone number and signing the waiver." Dante took two objects out of his jacket pocket as he was speaking: a screwdriver and a small, shiny metal cylinder. He shut the laptop down, turned it over and used the screwdriver to get into the hard drive. He passed the cylinder over the drive several times, at which point Andrea figured out what it was: a powerful magnet, used in order to completely erase the article and all the information stored in her hard drive. "If you had carefully read the small print of the form you signed, you would have noticed that one of the provisions authorizes us to locate your mobile phone by satellite, 'in case of danger to your personal security.' A clause put there should a terrorist infiltrate the press, but which has turned out to be very useful in your case. Just be happy it was me you met up with, and not Karosky."

"Ah yes, I'm jumping for joy."

Andrea was on her knees. With her right hand she felt around for the heavy crystal ashtray that she had been planning to take home as a souvenir from the hotel. It was sitting on the floor next to the wall, where she'd been sitting and smoking like a demon. Dante came close to her and then sat down on her bed.

"Let it be said that we owe you a thanks. If it wasn't for your petty theft, the disgraceful actions of that pyschopath would be front page news all over the world at this moment. You wanted to take personal advantage of the situation, but you were unable to pull it off. That's a fact. Be smart and we'll leave things as they are. You won't get your exclusive but you will save face. What do you say?"

"The discs . . ." Andrea mumbled a few unintelligible words. Dante lowered himself until his nose was touching hers.

"What are you saying, Miss Charming?"

"I said you can shove them in your ass, you bastard," said Andrea.

She brought the ashtray down hard on his ear. The rock-hard crystal collided with Dante's head and the ashes flew in all directions. He cried in pain, his hand over his ear. Andrea sprung to her feet and pushed him over, and then tried to hit him with the ashtray a second time. But he was faster than she was. He grabbed her arm when the ashtray was an inch from his face.

"Well, well. So the little whore has claws."

Dante squeezed her wrist and twisted her arm until she dropped the ashtray. And then he gave her a straight shot to her stomach. Andrea hit the floor a second time, the air knocked out of her, feeling as if a heavy lead ball were pressing down on her chest. Dante massaged his ear. A thin thread of blood ran down the side of his neck. He looked at himself in the mirror: his left eye was half-closed, he was covered with ashes, and there were cigarette butts in his hair. He walked back over to the girl and dragged her to her feet. He was going to punch her in the chest. Had he done it, he would have broken a few ribs. But Andrea was ready for him. Just as Dante was pulling back for the punch, she kicked him in the ankle of his stationary leg. Dante lost his balance and fell onto the floor, giving her time to run into the bathroom. She slammed the door.

Dante got up, limping.

"Open up, bitch."

"Go fuck yourself, asshole." She said it more for herself than for him. She noticed she was crying. She thought about praying, but then she remembered whom Dante worked for and decided that maybe it wasn't a good idea. She leaned against the door, but it was no help. It flew open, pushing Andrea against the wall. Dante burst into the room, his face red and overwhelmed by rage. Andrea put up her fists. Dante countered by grabbing her hair and dragging her across the room; he pulled a fistful of hair out in the process. He was a brute who used every ounce of his strength to hold her down. All she could do was tear at his face and his hands, trying to break out of his hold. He began to bleed, and became even more enraged.

"Where are they?"

"Go fuck—"

"TELL ME—"

"Yourself!"

"Where they are!"

He pressed her face against the bathroom mirror, then pulled her head back and slammed it against the glass. A spider spread its web over the mirror, with a round glob of blood in the middle that quickly dripped down to the sink.

Dante forced her to look at her reflection in what was left of the mirror.

"Want to keep going?"

Andrea quickly decided she had had enough.

"In the wastebasket," she said in weak voice.

"Good. Bend down and get it with your left hand. And no more tricks, or I will cut off your nipples and shove them down your throat." Andrea followed instructions and handed the disc to Dante. He looked it over: it appeared to be identical to the one at the Vigilanza.

"Very good. And the other nine?"

Andrea swallowed hard.

"I threw them away."

"More bullshit."

Andrea felt as if she were flying out of the room, and in fact she was, for a distance of about four feet, carried by Dante. He threw her onto the floor.

"I don't have them, for fuck's sake. I don't have them! Go look for yourself in the damn garbage cans in the Piazza Navona, you fucking pig!" Dante moved closer. He was smiling. She was very close to the edge, breathing as quickly as she could.

"You don't get it, do you, bitch? All you have to do is to hand me the shitty discs and you'll be on your way home with a nice big strawberry on your face. But no, you think you're smarter than Mrs. Dante's kid, and that's not possible. So now we are going to get serious. Your chance to get out of this still breathing has just passed."

Dante straddled her, pinning her down. He took out his pistol and pointed it at her head. Andrea was terrified, but even so she looked straight back at him. This bastard would do just about anything.

"You're not going to shoot. You'd make too much noise." She said it with less conviction than the last time.

"You know what, you little cunt? Once again, you're right."

And he took a silencer out of his pocket, which he then screwed onto the barrel of his gun. Andrea was now face to face with certain death. But this time, it would be a little less noisy.

"Drop it, Fabio."

Dante spun around. He was caught off guard, and his face looked it. Dicanti and Fowler were standing in the doorway. Paola had her pistol out, and Fowler held the electronic key that had gotten them in the room. Dicanti's badge and Fowler's collar had played a crucial part in getting it. It had taken a while for them to arrive at the hotel because first they tracked down one of the four other journalists on their list. They arranged them by age, beginning with the youngest, who turned out to be a gofer for a television crew, with brown hair, as the very talkative receptionist at the front desk informed them. As talkative as the receptionist at Andrea Otero's hotel.

Dante stared at Dicanti's pistol, dumbstruck. His body was turned toward Dicanti and Fowler, but he hadn't lowered his weapon. It was still pointing at Andrea's head.

"Come on, Dicanti, you won't do it."

"You're attacking a member of the community on Italian soil, Dante. I'm a police officer. You're not about to tell me what I can and cannot do. Drop the gun or I'll find myself obligated to shoot."

"Dicanti, you don't understand. This woman's a criminal. She stole confidential information, property of the Vatican. She won't listen to reason and seems intent on throwing everything away. It's nothing personal."

"You said that to me before. And I've noticed you're very deeply involved in many 'nothing personal' assignments."

That was more than Dante could take, and it showed. He changed tactics.

"You're right. Let me take the girl to the Vatican, just so we can find out what she did with the envelopes she stole. I will be personally responsible for her safety."

Andrea knew what that meant. She had no intention of spending another minute with this cretin. She started to move her legs very slowly, getting them into position.

"No way," said Paola.

Dante's voice took on a steely edge. He directed his words to Fowler.

"Anthony, you can't let this happen. We can't let her throw everything out in the open. For the cross and the sword."

The priest stared back at Dante.

"Those are not my symbols anymore, Dante. And even less so if you tarnish them with innocent blood."

"But she's not innocent. She stole the envelopes."

Dante was still talking when Andrea finally got into position. She chose her moment and kicked with her foot. She didn't use all her strength, not because she didn't want to but because she wanted to hit her target exactly. She wanted to hit the son of bitch square in the balls. And she did.

Three things happened at once.

Dante let go of the disc as he grabbed his testicles with his left hand. With his right hand he cocked the pistol, his finger pressing against the trigger. His mouth was open, like a fish out of water.

Dicanti jumped across the room in three steps and rammed into Dante's stomach.

Fowler reacted a half second after Paola—either because his reflexes were a bit slower or because he was sizing up the situation—and beat a quick path to the pistol, which was still pointing at Andrea. He grabbed Dante's right wrist at almost the same time that Dicanti's shoulder barreled into Dante's chest. The pistol fired at the ceiling.

The three of them fell into a confused heap beneath a rain of falling plaster. Fowler, without letting go of Dante's wrist, pressed both thumbs down on the wrist joint. Dante let go of the pistol. He still managed to butt Dicanti in the face with his knee. She rolled over. She was out cold.

Fowler and Dante stood up. Fowler held the gun by the barrel, in his left hand. With his right hand he undid the latch and let the clip fall out. It made a loud noise as it bounced onto the floor. With his other hand he took a bullet out of the firing chamber. Two more rapid movements, and the firing pin was in his hand. He threw it across the room and let the rest of the pistol fall to the floor, where it came to rest at Dante's feet.

"Not good for much now."

Dante smiled, flexing his shoulders and dropping his head down.

"You're not much good for anything, either, Grandpa."

"Try me."

Dante threw himself at the priest. Fowler took one step to the side and threw a punch at the Vatican cop. It just missed his face, hitting him on the arm. Dante threw a hard left, and Fowler tried to dodge it, only to run into Dante's fist between his ribs. He fell down, gritting his teeth, out of air.

"You're a little rusty, old man."

Dante picked up what was left of the pistol and the clip of bullets. He had no time to find the trigger and put it back in, but he was not about to leave the weapon behind. Moving quickly, he forgot that Dicanti had a gun too, one that he could use. It was, at that moment, concealed between the rug on the floor and her body. She was still unconscious.

Dante looked around the room, in the bathroom and the closet. Andrea Otero wasn't in any of them and neither was the disc which had been tossed around during the tussle. A drop of blood on the window stopped him in his tracks, and for a second he considered the possibility that the journalist could walk on air as Christ had done on water. Or, more likely, crawl like a cat on all fours.

He soon realized that the room was at the same height as the roof of the building next to it. That building stood alongside the Convent of Santa Maria de la Paz. A beautiful cloister, built by Bramante.

Andrea had no idea who had built the cloister. But she raced like a cat over the red tiles glowing in the morning sun, trying as hard as she could not to draw the attention of the cloister's first morning tourists. She wanted to get across to the other side, where an open window held the promise of salvation. She was already halfway there. The cloister had two high peaks, and the roof was tilted at a dangerous angle above the stones in the patio, thirty feet below.

Dante's testicles were howling in pain but he ignored them, raised the window, and climbed out after the journalist. She looked back, saw him land on his feet on the roof, and took off, trying to get away even faster. Dante's voice stopped her.

"Don't move."

Andrea turned around. Dante was pointing the gun at her. A gun incapable of firing bullets, something of which she was unaware. She wondered if this jerk were crazy enough to fire his gun in broad daylight in front of witnesses. Because tourists had seen him now, and they rapturously watched the scene unfolding above their heads. Their numbers were slowly growing. A pity Dicanti was still out cold, because she was missing a vivid demonstration of what is, in forensic psychology, called the Bystander Effect. A many-times-proven theory which states that as the number of bystanders watching a person in danger grows, the probability that anyone will help the victim diminishes, while the number of people pointing with their fingers and telling others to watch increases.

Out of sight of the bystanders, Dante took short, slow steps toward the journalist. As he got closer, he could see that she had one of the discs in her hand. So she must have been telling him the truth, but it had been a dumb mistake to throw the other ones away. That disc was much more important now.

"Give me the disc and I'll leave. I swear. I don't want to hurt you," Dante lied.

Andrea was scared to death, but she put on a show of being brave and full of herself that would have shamed a Marine sergeant.

"What shit! Get lost or I toss it."

Dante stood in the middle of the roof, paralyzed. Andrea's arm was extended, her wrist bending back and forth. A simple flick and the disc would take off like a Frisbee. Maybe it would break when it hit the ground, or maybe it would ride on a light morning breeze and one of the spectators would grab it, and then it would evaporate long before he got down to the cloister. And with that, so long and farewell.

Way too risky.

Checkmate! What to do? Distract the enemy until the scales are balanced in your favor.

"Signorina," Dante said in a loud voice. "Don't jump. I don't know what has driven you to take this action but life is very beautiful. If you think about it, you'll see you have many reasons to go on living."

That's the way to go, Dante thought. Get close enough to help the madwoman with the face bathed in blood who jumped onto the roof and was threatening suicide, try to hold her down without anyone noticing how I snatch the disc, and then as we're rolling around on the roof she slips away. I can't save her. A tragedy. The people in charge will take care of Dicanti and Fowler. They'll know how to apply the pressure.

"Don't jump. Think about your family."

"What are you bellowing, you mastodon?" Andrea looked at him wide-eyed. "I'm not about to jump!"

The spectators down below were pointing at her. No one had called the police. There were a few scattered shouts of "Don't jump, don't jump." No one seemed to think it strange that her rescuer was waving a pistol. Or more likely, they couldn't make out what her intrepid savior was holding in his right hand. Dante silently rejoiced. He was getting closer and closer to the young reporter.

"Don't be afraid. I'm an officer of the law!"

Andrea only now realized what her pursuer was up to. He was less than six feet away.

"Don't come any closer, you creep. I'll throw it away!"

The spectators below thought they heard her say she was going to throw herself off the roof, since they barely noticed the disc she held in her hand. There were more cries of "No! No!" and a few tourists even went so far to declare eternal love for Andrea if she came down from the roof in one piece.

Dante's outstretched hand brushed Andrea's heel. She turned around to face him and then stepped back, slipping a few inches down the roof. The crowd—there were about fifty people standing in the cloister now, and hotel guests had begun to stick their heads out the windows of their rooms—held their breath.

Suddenly someone shouted, "Look, a priest!"

Dante turned around. Fowler had both feet on the roof, a roof tile in each hand.

"Not here, Anthony!" Dante yelled.

Fowler did not seem to be listening. He hurled one of the tiles, with devilishly good aim. Dante was lucky. There was just enough time to cover his face. If he hadn't, perhaps the crunch he heard when the tile struck his arm would have been the sound of his skull cracking. He lost his balance, fell onto the roof and started to roll all the way to the edge. By some miracle he was able to grab hold of the rain gutter that jutted out from the roof. He was dangling ten feet above the ground, his legs wrapped around one of Bramante's priceless columns. Three people left the crowd of useless spectators to help Dante, more of a broken puppet than a man, slide the rest of the way down to the ground. He was thanking them as he lost consciousness.

Fowler stood facing Andrea on the roof.

"Signorina Otero, do us the favor of climbing back into your room before you hurt yourself."

✝

HOTEL RAPHAEL
Largo Febo, 2
Saturday, April 9, 2005, 9:14 A.M.

Paola came back to the land of the living in the midst of a small miracle: Anthony Fowler was attentively placing a cold, wet towel across her forehead. But that bliss was short-lived, and in a second she was sorry her body didn't end at the shoulders. Her head was pounding like a jackhammer. She pulled herself together just in time to deal with the two cops who finally showed up at the hotel room, telling them they could go back outside, she had everything under control. Dicanti swore to them, and lied too: no one had tried to commit suicide; the whole thing was nothing more than a big mistake. The two cops nosed around the train wreck of a hotel room with wary looks, but they did as they were told.

Fowler was trying to put Andrea's forehead back together after her run-in with the mirror. Dicanti sent the two cops out the door and stuck her head into the bathroom just as Fowler was telling the journalist she was going to need stitches.

"At least four on your forehead and two on the brow. But right now you have no time to lose lying in a hospital. I'll tell you what we will do: you are going to take a cab to Bolonia right away. You will need four hours to get there. A doctor friend of mine will be waiting for you. He'll sew the stitches on your forehead and then make sure you get to the airport. You can fly to Madrid via Milan. You'll be safe there. See if you can avoid Italy for a few years."

"It would be faster for her to catch a plane out of Naples, wouldn't it?"

Fowler scrutinized Dicanti with utter seriousness.

"*Dottoressa*, should you ever need to get out of these people's clutches, avoid Naples whatever you do. The town is crawling with informants."

"I would say they have eyes just about everywhere."

"Sadly, you are right on that score. And I fear that crossing paths with the Vigilanza will have unpleasant consequences for both of us."

"Let's go see Troi. He'll take our side."

Fowler didn't respond. And then: "He might. Nevertheless, our priority right now is getting Miss Otero out of Rome."

The conversation Andrea was silently participating in did nothing to take the pained look off her face. The cuts on her forehead were still throbbing, even if, thanks to Fowler, they were bleeding a good deal less. Ten minutes before she had witnessed Dante plunge over the edge of the roof, and she had felt an overwhelming surge of relief. She had run toward Fowler and put her arms around his neck, taking the risk that both of them would tumble over the edge. Fowler had quickly sketched the situation for her: a very powerful element in the Vatican hierarchy didn't want this incident to see the light of day, which was why her life was threatened. The priest had passed over the minor detail of her deplorable theft of the envelopes, something for which she was grateful.

But not now. Now he was imposing his conditions, and the journalist wasn't pleased. She was thankful for her opportune rescue at the hands of the priest and the cop, but she wasn't disposed to give in to blackmail.

"I'm not thinking about going anywhere. I am an accredited journalist, and my paper is trusting me to deliver news of the conclave. And I want them to know that I have uncovered a conspiracy, operating at the highest levels, to hide the death of three cardinals and an Italian cop at the hands of a pyschopath. *El Globo* and other papers are going to publish some very powerful photos along with this information, and all of it is going to carry my name."

Fowler listened patiently before he answered.

"Signorina Otero, I admire your courage. You have more of it than many soldiers I've known. But in this game you need a good deal more than courage."

With her hand Andrea was holding the bandage that covered her forehead. She was gritting her teeth.

"Once the report is published, they will never dare touch me."

"Maybe yes and maybe no. But I don't want you to publish the report, either. It's not convenient."

Andrea looked at him, stupefied.

"What did you just say?"

"To make it simple: give me the disc."

Andrea got to her feet unsteadily. She was indignant, and held the disc pressed tightly against her chest.

"I had no idea you were one of those fanatics, ready to kill to preserve their secrets. I'm getting out of here right now."

Fowler pushed her back down onto the toilet.

"Personally, for me the most illuminating phrase in the Gospels is, 'The truth shall make you free.' And if it were up to me, you could take off at a clip, telling everyone that a priest with a long history of pederasty had gone mad and was walking around knifing cardinals. Perhaps then the Church would realize once and for all that priests are, always and only, men. But that has little to do with you and me. I am opposed to this getting out because Karosky wants it out. When a little time passes and he sees that his method hasn't shown results, he'll make a move. Then we can grab him and in the process save a few lives."

Andrea fell apart. It was a combination of exhaustion, pain, stress, and a feeling she found absolutely impossible to put into words. A sentiment composed of equal parts fragility and self-pity that welled up in her from time to time, when she realized just how small she was in relation to the larger universe. She handed the disc to Fowler, and her hands cradled her head. She started to cry.

"I'll lose my job."

The priest took pity on her.

"No you won't. I'll see to that personally."

Three hours later, the U.S. ambassador to Italy called the editor in chief of *El Globo*. He sent his apologies for the accident that took place between one of the embassy's official cars and the newspaper's special correspondent in Rome. As he told it, it had taken place the day before when his car was en route to the airport at full speed. Luckily for them, the driver had jammed on the brakes in time to avoid a catastrophe, and except for a small wound to the head, everyone was all right. It seemed that the journalist had insisted repeatedly that she had to continue with her work, but the doctors at the embassy had ordered two weeks of rest, for which they were offering to send her to Madrid on the embassy's tab. Of course, because of the great professional injury she had suffered, they were disposed to compensate her. One of the riders in the car had taken an interest in her and wanted to arrange an interview. They would get in touch in two weeks' time to finalize the details.

El Globo's editor in chief was a bit perplexed after he hung up. He had no idea how that rebellious, difficult young reporter had managed to snag what was probably the most difficult interview on the planet for the paper. He attributed it to a tremendous piece of luck. He felt a pang of jealousy and wanted to crawl back inside his skin.

He'd always wanted to visit the Oval Office.

✝

UACV HEADQUARTERS
Via Lamarmora, 3

Saturday, April 9, 2005, 1:25 P.M.

Paola walked into Tròi's office without so much as a knock, but she did not like what she found there, or rather whom she found. Camilo Cirin sat facing the UACV's director, and he chose that moment to stand up and walk out of the office, without giving Dicanti so much as a glance. She did her best to block his exit.

"Listen, Cirin—"

The chief of the Vatican Vigilanza deftly stepped around her and disappeared down the hall.

"Sit down, Dicanti," Troi said, still seated on the other side of his desk.

"I want to protest the criminal actions of that man's subordinate—"

"*Basta, Ispettore.* The inspector general has already given me a very useful summary of the events that transpired at the Hotel Raphael."

Paola's jaw dropped. As soon as they'd delivered the Spanish journalist into a cab headed for Bolonia, they headed directly to UACV headquarters to give their side of the story to Troi. The situation was no doubt complicated, but Paola still believed that Troi would back them up on the rescue of the journalist. She decided to talk to him alone, although naturally the last thing she'd expect was that her boss wouldn't even want to hear her version.

"He must have told you that Dante attacked an unarmed journalist."

"What he told me was that there was a difference of opinion, which was resolved to everyone's satisfaction. It seems that Inspector Dante was trying to calm a potential witness who was a bit out of sorts, when you two attacked him. Dante is in the hospital as we speak."

"That's absurd! It's not what happened at all."

"Cirin also informed me that he was no longer going to work with us on this case." Troi raised his voice several notches. "He was very disturbed by your attitude, which was hostile and aggressive toward Dante and the sovereignty of our neighboring country. Something which I myself can testify to, let it be said in passing. You will go back to your usual assignments, and Fowler will return to Washington. From here on out, only the Corpo di Vigilanza has the job of protecting the cardinals. For our part, we will immediately hand over the disc Karosky sent us, as well as the one which we recovered from the Spanish journalist, to the Vatican. And then we will forget it ever existed."

"And Pontiero, what about him? I still remember the look you had on your face during the autopsy. Was that faked too? Who will see that there's justice for him?"

"That's no longer our responsibility."

Dicanti felt so deceived and fed up she was physically sick. She was unable to recognize the man sitting in front of her, and whatever small ties of affection she might have felt for him were long gone. She asked herself with some sadness if that was why he had withdrawn his support so quickly. Perhaps it was the bitter finale to last night's confrontation.

"This is because of me, Carlo?"

"Sorry?"

"Because of what happened last night. I didn't think you were capable of this."

"Please, *Ispettore*, no delusions of grandeur. My only interest in this case is in giving the Vatican whatever they need as efficiently as possible, something I've observed you've been unable to do."

Thirty-four years of living and Paola had never witnessed such a discrepancy between a person's words and the look on his face. She couldn't hold back.

"You're a useless pig, Carlo. Seriously. It doesn't surprise me that everyone laughs at you behind your back. How did you end up this way?"

Troi turned red to the tips of his ears, but he managed to repress the explosion of anger that was making his lips tremble. Instead of letting rage get the better of him, he abruptly channeled it into a cold, measured verbal slap.

"At least I ended up somewhere, *Ispettore*. Be so kind as to leave your badge and your gun on my desk. You are suspended from your job and your salary for the next month, until I've had the opportunity to review your case carefully. Go home."

Paola opened her mouth but nothing came out. In the movies the hero always encounters the devastating turn of phrase that foreshadows his triumphant return, a phrase by which the tyrant strips away each and every one of his privileges. But in real life, she was speechless. She dropped her badge and her pistol on the desk and stormed out of Troi's office without looking back.

Fowler was waiting for her in the hallway. He had escorts: two policemen. Paola figured he had already received the fateful phone call.

"So this is how it ends," Dicanti said.

A smile lit up the priest's face.

"A pleasure knowing you, *Dottoressa*. These gentlemen have the sad duty of accompanying me to my hotel so I can collect my belongings before I head out to the airport."

Paola grabbed his arm, her fingers pressing the sleeve.

"Padre, can't you call someone? Just to get them to put this off."

"I'm afraid not." Fowler shook his head. "But I look forward to the day when I can invite you out for a good cup of coffee."

Without saying another word, he got up and walked quickly down the hallway, followed by the two policemen.

Paola held out. She was in her apartment before tears got the better of her.

†

THE SAINT MATTHEW INSTITUTE
Sachem Pike, Maryland
December 1999

Transcription of Interview #115 Between
Patient No. 3643 and Doctor Canice Conroy

[. . .]

Dr. Conroy: I see you have brought a book with you. *Enigmas and Curiosities*. Any tricky ones?

No. 3643: Beginner's stuff.

Dr. Conroy: All right, then. Tell me one.

No. 3643: They're too simple, really. I don't think you will like them.

Dr. Conroy: But I like riddles.

No. 3643: OK. If a man digs a hole in one hour and two men dig two holes in two hours, how long will it take a man to dig half a hole?

Dr. Conroy: That's easy. Half an hour.

No. 3643: [laughter]

Dr. Conroy: What are you laughing at? It's half an hour. One hour, one hole. Half an hour, half a hole.

No. 3643: Doctor, half holes do not exist. A hole is always a hole. [laughs again]

Dr. Conroy: Are you trying to tell me something, Victor?

No. 3643: Of course, Doctor. Of course.

Dr. Conroy: You are not a hole, Victor. You are not irredeemably condemned to being what you are.

No. 3643: But I am, Doctor Conroy. And I have you to thank for showing me the right road.

Dr. Conroy: What road?

No. 3643: I fought for so long to resist being who I am, trying to be something I'm not. But thanks to you, I've become who I am. Isn't that what you wanted?

Dr. Conroy: It's not possible. I couldn't have gone so wrong with you.

No. 3643: Doctor, you weren't wrong. You made me see the light. You made me understand that to open a heavy door, you need a strong hand.

Dr. Conroy: Is that you? The strong hand?

No. 3643: [more laughter] No, Doctor. I'm the key.

†

DICANTI FAMILY APARTMENT
Via della Croce, 12
Saturday, April 9, 2005, 11:46 P.M.

For a long time the door to her room was shut. Paola was inside, completely distraught. Her mother was away, visiting friends in Ostia for the weekend, a little piece of luck that greatly relieved Paola. She was at her lowest, and wouldn't have been able to hide it from her mother. If she'd seen the condition her daughter was in, Signora Dicanti would have tried to cheer her up, which would only have made matters worse. Paola needed to be alone as she plunged into the failure and desperation she felt inside. She didn't want anyone barging in on her.

She lay down on the bed, without bothering to remove her clothes. Noise from the street below and the faint light of an April afternoon both found their way into her room. That steady hum provided the background as she incessantly relived her conversation with Troi and the events of the last few days. Finally, she drifted off to sleep. Nearly nine hours after collapsing in exhaustion on her bed, the aroma of fresh coffee turned up in her dream, forcing her to open her eyes.

"Mamma, you've come back so soon—"

"You're right, I did come back quickly. But I'm not who you

think." The voice was firm, polite, speaking a forceful but slightly hesitant Italian: the voice of Anthony Fowler.

Paola opened her eyes all the way and, without realizing what she was doing, threw both her arms around his neck.

"Careful, careful. You'll spill the coffee."

Paola let go of him unwillingly. Fowler was sitting on the edge of the bed, looking at her with a mischievous smile. In one hand he held a cup he had taken from the kitchen.

"How did you get in here? And how did you manage to escape from the police? They were putting you on a plane to Washington—"

"Calm down. One question at a time." Fowler laughed. "As to how I managed to slip out of the hands of two fat and poorly trained public servants, I simply ask you not to insult my intelligence. As to how I got into the apartment, the answer is easy: a lock picker."

"I see now. CIA basic training, right?"

"More or less. Sorry for the intrusion, but I knocked several times and nobody answered. I thought you might be in danger. When I saw you sleeping so peacefully, I decided to make good on my promise to invite you to a cup of coffee."

Paola stood up, lifting the cup out of Fowler's hand. The only light in the bedroom came from the lamps on the street, which threw monumental shadows across the high ceiling. Fowler looked around the room in the half-light. On one wall hung her degrees: high school, university, the FBI Academy. Swimming medals too, and even a few oil paintings that must have been done at least thirteen years ago. Once more Fowler felt just how vulnerable this intelligent, energetic woman was; a woman who moved into the future borne down by her past. A woman who, in large part, had never abandoned her earliest childhood. Fowler glanced over the walls around the bed, trying to ascertain the line of sight of the person who slept there. At the endpoint of the imaginary line he drew from the pillow to the wall was a framed photograph of Paola in a hospital room, sitting with her father.

"It's good coffee. My mother's coffee is undrinkable."

"Just a question of an even flame, *Dottoressa*."

"So why did you come back?"

"Various reasons. Because I didn't want to leave you stranded in the wilderness. To stop that nut job from going about his business. And because I suspect that there is much more here than meets the eye. I feel like we have been used, you and me, by everybody. Furthermore, I suspect you have a very personal motive for wanting to keep at it."

Paola frowned.

"You're right. Pontiero was a friend and a coworker. Right now what I want is to bring his killer to justice. But I really doubt we can do anything about it. Without my badge and everything that comes with it, we are just two little clouds. The least little breeze and we will be blown away. And besides, they are probably looking for you."

"Quite possible, actually. I gave the two cops the slip in Fiumicino. But I doubt Troi would go so far as to issue an order for my capture and arrest. With the hullabaloo going on in the city now, it wouldn't do him any good, and how could he justify it, anyway? Most likely he's going to let me remain at large."

"And your bosses, Padre?"

"Officially, I'm in Langley. Unofficially, they have yet to object to my sticking around here a little while longer."

"At last some good news."

"The tricky thing for us now is getting into the Vatican, because Cirin will be on the lookout."

"I don't see how we can protect the cardinals if they are on the inside and we're out."

"I think we ought to start at the beginning. Go back over the whole imbroglio from the outset, because it's clear something has sailed right over our heads."

"How are we going to do that? I don't have the necessary papers. The Karosky file is sitting at UACV."

Fowler's lips curled into a roguish smile.

"God sometimes grants us small miracles."

His hand pointed in the direction of Paola's desk, at the other end of the room. Paola turned on the small desk lamp, which cast its light over the unwieldy pile of manila envelopes that was the Karosky dossier.

"Let me propose a joint venture. You concentrate on what you do best: a psychological profile of the killer. A definitive one, with all the facts we presently have at our disposal. I, meanwhile, will keep bringing you fresh coffee."

Paola finished off the first cup. She wanted to take a closer look at the priest's face, but he was sitting outside the cone of light cast by the desk lamp. And suddenly she was struck by the vague feeling that had overwhelmed her in the hallway at Saint Martha's, a premonition she'd ignored, putting it off until a later date. Now, after the long list of events that followed the death of Cardoso, she was more than ever convinced that her intuition had been on target. She turned her computer on, picked up a blank profile from among the papers on her desk, and started to fill it out compulsively, consulting the dossier from time to time.

"Let's have another pot of coffee, Padre. I want to see if a theory of mine holds up."

┼

PSYCHOLOGICAL PROFILE
OF A SERIAL KILLER

Patient: KAROSKY, Victor

Profile created by Doctor Paola Dicanti

Current location of patient: In absentia

Date of entry: April 10, 2005

Age: 44

Height: 6 feet

Weight: 187 lbs.

Description: Brown hair, gray eyes, healthy complexion, highly intelligent (IQ of 125)

Family history: Victor Karosky was born into a lower-middle-class family of immigrants dominated by a mother with profound problems relating to reality, owing to the influence of religion. The family emigrated from Poland, and from early on the lack of stability is evident in all family members. The father presents a typical portrait of irregular work history, alcoholism, and bad behavior, to which can be added the aggravation of repeated, periodic sexual abuse (intended as punishment) when the subject reaches adolescence. The mother was at all times aware of the abuse and incest committed by her husband, although it seems she acted as if she was not. An older brother escaped from the family household on account of the sexual abuse. A younger brother was left to die, after a long illness brought on by meningitis. The subject is locked into a closet, incommunicado, for long periods of time, after the "discovery" by his mother of the father's sexual abuse. When he is freed, the father has abandoned the household, and it is the mother who imposes her personality, in this case impressing upon the subject the Catholic teaching of fear of damnation, which is doubtless caused by sexual excess (always as defined by the mother). She dresses him in her clothes and even goes so far as to threaten him with castration. This produces a grave distortion of reality in the subject, equivalent to a serious conflict of unintegrated sexuality. The first signs of rage and antisocial personality start to appear, with a intense structure of agitated response. He attacks a schoolmate, and is sent to a reformatory. Upon leaving, his record is wiped clean, and at nineteen years old he decides to enter a seminary. They are unaware of any previous psychological counseling he may have undergone, and they accept his application.

Adult history: Indications of unintegrated sexual conflict are confirmed at nineteen years old, shortly after the death of his mother, when he engages a minor in heavy petting, an act that little by little becomes more frequent and extended. The ecclesiastical authorities in the seminary make no punitive response on their part to his sexual aggression, which becomes more refined when the subject is responsible for his own congregation. According to his file, there are at least 89 documented cases of sexual aggression against minors, of which 39 consist of sodomy with full penetration, and the remainder, petting or forcing masturbation and/or fellatio on the victim. The compendium of interviews with the subject allows us to deduce that, however strange it may seem, he was a priest fully convinced of his ministry. In cases of pederasty among priests, it is possible to identify their sexual drive as the motive for their entrance into the ministry, somewhat like a fox entering the hen house. But in Karosky's case the motives behind his vows are very different. His mother pushed him in this direction, even going so far as to use force. After the incident when he attacked a parishioner, the Karosky scandal could no longer be kept under wraps and the subject at last arrived at the Saint Matthew Institute, a rehabilitation center for Catholic priests with problems. There we find a Karosky very closely identified with the Bible, specifically the Old Testament. An episode of sudden violence against an Institute employee takes place just a few days after his arrival. From this incident we are able to deduce an overwhelming cognitive dissonance between the subject's sexual compulsion and his religious convictions. When the two collide, they produce a violent crisis, as in the case of the attack on the medical technician.

Recent history: The subject presents a portrait of rage, reflected in his displaced aggression. He has committed various crimes, in which elevated levels of sexual sadism are manifested, including ritual symbols and insertional necrophilia.

Profile of notable characteristics, manifested in his actions:

- Agreeable personality, medium-to-high intelligence
- Frequent lies
- Total absence of guilt or feelings toward his victims
- Complete egocentricity
- Personal, affective disconnect
- An impersonal and impulsive sexuality, harnessed to the satisfaction of egocentric needs
- Antisocial personality
- High levels of obedience

DOES NOT AGREE WITH ABOVE!!!!!

- _Irrational thought integrated into his actions_
- _Multiple neuroses_
- _Criminal behavior understood as a means not an end_
- _Suicidal tendencies_
- _Mission oriented_

✝

DICANTI FAMILY APARTMENT
Via della Croce, 12
Sunday, April 10, 2005, 1:45 A.M.

Fowler read Dicanti's new profile of the killer as soon as she handed it to him. He was not sure what to make of it.

"*Dottoressa*, I hope you don't mind me saying this, but the report is incomplete. You have just written a résumé of everything we already knew. In all sincerity, this isn't going to get us very far."

Dicanti stood up.

"You couldn't be more wrong. Karosky presents a very complex clinical portrait, from which we can deduce that the increase in his aggression turned a sexual predator, clinically castrated, into a killer several times over."

"That is, in fact, what our theory is built upon."

"And it's a complete waste of our time. Look closely at the characteristics in the profile, at the end of the report. The first eight constitute the definition of a serial killer."

Fowler went down the list, nodding his head.

"There are two types of serial killers: disorganized and organized. Not a perfect classification but it works. The first corresponds to killers who commit spontaneous, impulsive crimes, with a high probability that they are leaving evidence at the scene. They often know their victims, who they tend to chance upon in their usual neck of the

306

woods. They use weapons of convenience: a chair, a belt, whatever they can get their hands on. Sexual sadism appears postmortem."

Fowler rubbed his eyes. He was very tired, going on only a few hours' sleep.

"Sorry. Go on."

"The other kind, the organized, is someone who has great freedom of movement, who captures his victims by a show of force. The victim is a stranger who fits a specific criteria. The weapons and restraints employed match a preconceived plan, and he never leaves them behind. The body is abandoned in a neutral spot, in exactly the manner the killer wants. Fine. To which of the two groups does Karosky belong?"

"The second, obviously."

"Any observer could deduce that. But let's go further. We have the dossier. We know who he is, where he comes from, what he's thinking. Forget everything that happened in the last few days. Concentrate on the Karosky who entered the Institute."

"An impulsive character, who in certain situations exploded like a keg of dynamite."

"And after five years of therapy?"

"A different creature entirely."

"Would you say that this change was produced gradually, or was it all at once?"

"It was pretty sudden. I would pinpoint the change at the moment that Conroy forced him to listen to the tapes of his regression therapy."

Paola took a deep breath before she went on.

"Padre, I don't mean to offend you, but after reading dozens of the interviews between Karosky, Conroy, and you, I believe you are wrong. And that mistake sent us looking in the wrong direction."

Fowler leaned forward.

"No offense taken. I have a degree in psychology, as you know— but I was only at the Institute as a kind of punishment. My real profession is something else entirely. You are the expert criminologist and I'm lucky to have your insight. But I don't understand where you're taking this."

"Take a second look at the profile," Paola said, pointing toward it. "Under the heading, 'DOES NOT AGREE WITH ABOVE,' I have noted five characteristics which make it impossible for us to conclude that our subject is an organized serial killer. Criminology textbook in hand, any expert would say that Karosky is an organized anomaly, who evolved from the roots of his trauma, in this case the confrontation with his past. Are you familiar with the term cognitive dissonance?"

"It's the state of mind in which the actions and intimate beliefs of a person are at extreme odds. Karosky suffered from extreme cognitive dissonance: he believed himself to be an exemplary priest, while his eighty-nine victims would assert he was a pederast."

"Exactly. So then, as you put it, the subject, a committed Catholic, neurotic, impervious to all intrusions from the outside world, is in the space of a few months transformed into a serial killer, cold and calculating and without a trace of neurosis, after listening to a few tapes in which he comprehends for the first time that he was mistreated as a child?"

"Looking at it like that . . . it seems a bit far-fetched." Fowler was hesitant.

"Or impossible. Conroy's irresponsible act no doubt harmed Karosky, but it could never provoke such an overpowering change. The fanatic priest who covers his ears, infuriated when you read the names of his victims to him out loud, could not transform himself into an organized serial killer in the space of a few months. And let's recall that his first two criminal rituals took place at the Institute itself: the mutilation of one priest and the murder of another."

"But the cardinals died at Karosky's hand. He himself confessed it; his fingerprints were found at three of the crime scenes."

"No doubt. I do not dispute that Karosky murdered those men. That much is clear. What I am trying to say is that the motive that made him commit those crimes is not what we thought it was. The most important detail in his profile, the thing that led him to become a priest in spite of his tortured soul, is the one thing that has conditioned him to commit these terrible acts."

Fowler understood. He was extremely upset, and had to sit down on Paola's bed to keep from losing his balance.

"Obedience."

"Correct. Karosky isn't a serial killer at all. He's a hired assassin."

THE SAINT MATTHEW INSTITUTE
Sachem Pike, Maryland
August 1999

Solitary confinement was utterly quiet. Which was why the urgent, demanding voice that whispered his name filled Karosky's ears like an incoming wave.

"Victor."

Karosky jumped out of bed hurriedly, like a child. There he was, once again. Once more he'd come to help Victor, to guide him, to light the way. To help him understand and to channel his strength and his needs. Now he was able to endure the cruel interference of Dr. Conroy, who examined him just as he would a butterfly pinned under a microscope. There he was on the other side of the iron bars; he was almost sitting with Victor in his cell. Victor could respect this man, he could follow him. And the man in turn understood Victor and could give him direction. They had spoken for hours about what he should do. About how he should do it. About how he should act, how he should respond to Conroy's repetitive, bothersome interference.

Over the course of the long nights he thought about his own role and waited for his visitor's arrival. He only came once a week, but Victor waited for him impatiently, counting the hours and even the minutes one after another. While he went over their plan in his head, he had patiently sharpened the knife, trying not to make any noise. His visitor had gotten it for Victor. He could have given him a sharp knife, or even a pistol. But he wanted to temper his courage and his strength. And Victor had done what he asked. He had given the proofs of his loyalty and devotion. First he had mutilated the sodomite. A few weeks later, he killed the pederast, both priests. If he pulled out the weeds the way the man had asked him to, he would receive his reward in the end. The reward he wanted more than anything in the world. He would give it to Victor because no one else could. No one else could give him that.

"Victor."

He called out insistently to make sure that he was there. Victor crossed the cell with hurried steps and bowed down in front of the door, listening to the voice that spoke to him about the future. Of a mission, far away. In the heart of Christianity.

DICANTI FAMILY APARTMENT
Via della Croce, 12
Sunday, April 10, 2005, 2:14 A.M.

Silence followed Dicanti's words like a dark cloud. Fowler looked around, his hands gripping his face. He was both stunned and surprised.

"How could I have been so blind? He kills because he's been told to. Jesus Christ. And the messages, the ritual?"

"If you think about it carefully, they don't make any sense. The *Ego te absolvo*, written first on the ground and then on the victim's chest. The hands washed clean, the tongue cut out: it's the exact equivalent of the Sicilian practice of putting money in the victim's mouth."

"The Mafia ritual that indicates the victim talked too much, is that it?"

"Exactly. At first I thought Karosky was condemning the cardinals for some crime, something done to him or to their own dignity as priests. But the clues left in the crumpled pieces of paper never added up. In my opinion they were his personal contributions, his own finishing touches to a scheme dictated by someone else."

"But what's the meaning of killing them that way? Why not just get rid of them?"

"The mutilations are nothing more than an absurd disguise covering one crucial fact: someone wanted to see them dead. Just look at this."

Paola pointed at the flexible lamp on her desk. Its beam was directed onto Karosky's dossier. With the room in darkness, everything that did not fall inside its cone of light was in the dark.

"Now I get it. They forced us to look at what they wanted us to see. Fine, but who would want something like this?"

"The essential question when you want to find out who committed a crime is: who benefits? A serial killer erases the question with one swipe because he does it for his own benefit. His motive is the body. But in this case his motive is a mission. If he had wanted to give free rein to his frustration, his hatred for the cardinals, supposing that he possessed those things, he could have done it some other time when the cardinals were much more visible. And much less protected. So why now? What's different now?"

"Because someone wants to influence the conclave."

"So now ask yourself who would want to influence the conclave. And to answer that it's essential to know who they killed."

"Those cardinals were preeminent figures in the Church. Persons of great standing."

"With a simple connection between them. And our job is to figure it out."

Fowler stood up. He was pacing around the room now, his hands clenched behind his back.

"*Dottoressa*, it occurs to me who would be disposed to eliminate the cardinals and, furthermore, by this method. There is one clue which we have conveniently ignored. Karosky underwent a complete facial reconstruction, as Angelo Biffi took the trouble to show us. An expensive operation, one requiring a thorough convalescence. Done well, and with the necessary guarantees of discretion and anonymity, it could cost more than one hundred thousand dollars. That's not the kind of money that a poor priest like Karosky has at his disposal. Nor would it be easy for him to enter Italy, or to pay his expenses after he gets here. These questions have been relegated to the back burner the whole time, but they're crucial now."

"And they reinforce the theory that an unseen hand is in fact behind the assassination of the cardinals."

"Right."

"Padre, I'm not in your league when it comes to knowledge of the Catholic Church. Or the way the Curia works. In your opinion, what is the common denominator between the three dead cardinals?"

The priest mulled it over.

"Something that ties them together, something that would have been much more obvious if they had simply disappeared, or been executed. They were all ideological liberals. They were part of, how should I say, the liberal wing of the Holy Spirit. If you had asked me for the names of the five cardinals who most wholeheartedly supported Vatican Council II, those three would be on the list."

"I need more detail."

"Right. With the arrival of John XXIII to the papacy in 1958, it was obvious to everyone that the Church had to change course. John XXIII convoked the Second Vatican Council, a call to bishops all over the world to come to Rome to debate the pope about the state of the Church. Two thousand bishops responded to the call. John XXIII died before the Council was finished but his successor, Paul VI, finished the job. Shamefully, the initial reforms that the Council contemplated never went nearly so far as John XXIII had hoped."

"What are you referring to?"

"There were enormous changes inside the Church. It was probably one of the landmarks of the twentieth century. You cannot remember it because you are very young, but until the end of the sixties a Catholic woman was forbidden to smoke or even wear pants in public. It was a sin. And those aren't just random examples. It's enough to say that the change was great but by no means far-reaching enough. John XXIII tried to throw open the doors of the Church to the revivifying air of the Holy Spirit. And he only pried them open a little. Paul VI turned out to be a very conservative pope. John Paul I, his successor, was barely on the job for a month. And John Paul II was an apostolic Pope, strong and media savvy, who certainly did much good for humanity but who in everyday Church politics was extremely conservative."

"So the great reform of the Church still hasn't happened?"

"There is still much work to be done, there really is. When they published the results of Vatican II, the most conservative sectors of the Church were almost up in arms. And the Council still has enemies, people who believe that anyone who isn't a Catholic will go straight to hell, that women don't have the right to vote, and other, even worse, ideas. Even the clergy expects this conclave to give us a forceful, idealist pope, a pope who dares to open the Church to the world. And the perfect man for the job would no doubt have been Cardinal Portini, a hard-core liberal. Of course, he would never get the votes of the ultraconservative wing. Robayra would have been something else, a man of the people but a brilliant one. Cardoso had similar backing. Both were defenders of the poor."

"And now they're both dead."

Fowler's expression darkened.

"Paola, what I'm going to tell you now has to remain a secret at all costs. I'm risking my life and yours, and take my word for it, I am scared. This line of reasoning points in a direction I wouldn't want to look at too closely, much less follow." Fowler paused briefly to suck in some air. "Ever heard of the Santa Alianza?"

Dicanti's head filled up once again with stories of spies and assassinations, just as it had when they were visiting the messenger.

She'd always thought of them as the sort of stories told by a drunkard, but at that hour, sitting in her room with a man whose background was, to say the least, unusual, the possibility that they were real acquired a new dimension.

"It's the Vatican's Secret Service, or so they say. A network of spies and secret agents who don't hesitate to kill. Old wives' tales, used to scare rookie cops who just joined the force. Nobody takes it seriously."

"*Dottoressa* Dicanti, you can take the history of the Santa Alianza seriously, because it exists. It has existed for the last four hundred years, and it's the right hand of the Vatican for those assignments that even the pope himself cannot know about."

"I find that very difficult to believe."

"The motto of the Holy Alliance, the Santa Alianza, is '*La cruz y la espada.*' The cross and the sword."

Paola flashed on Dante in the Hotel Raphael, his pistol pointed at the journalist. Those had been his words exactly when he had asked for Fowler's help, and now she understood what he wanted to say to the priest.

"Oh, good lord. So you are . . ."

"I was, a long time ago. I served two flags, my country's and my religion's. I had to let one of them go."

"What happened?"

"I can't tell you, so don't ask."

Paola had no intention of pushing the point. What she was hearing came from the dark side of the priest, where a cold pain sank iron hooks into his soul. She suspected there was a great deal more there than he was letting on.

"Now I understand why Dante loathed you so much. It has to do with that part of your life, doesn't it?"

Fowler said nothing. Paola had to make a quick decision because they were short on time. She couldn't let them get sidetracked. She let herself listen to her heart, which she knew was in love with the priest; with each and every part of him, from the dry warmth of his hands to the afflictions of his soul. She wanted to rid him of all of that, to give him back the open smile of a child. She knew what she wanted was impossible: there were oceans of bitterness inside him, and had been for a long time. The priesthood was not only an unscalable wall for him. Anyone who wanted to get near him had to cross those oceans, and they would most likely drown. She realized then and there that she would never be his partner; but she also knew that he would kill before he let anyone do her any harm.

"It's okay, Padre. I trust you," she said in a whisper. "Go on."

Fowler sat back down. And he began to unfold a long and chilling history.

"They've been in business since 1566. In those uncertain times, Pius V was consumed by the rise of the Anglicans, and with heretics. As head of the Inquisition, he was tough, inflexible, pragmatic. The attitude in the Vatican was in those times much more territorial than it is now, although they enjoy even more power today. The Santa Alianza was created to recruit young priests and *uomos di fiducia*, trustworthy laypersons of proven faith. Their mission was to defend the Vatican as a country and the Church as a spiritual entity, and their numbers grew with the passing of time. By the nineteenth century they had reached the thousands. Some were mere informants, dreamers, sleepyheads. . . . Others, around five hundred of them, were the elite: the Hand of Saint Michael. The group of special agents who, posted throughout the world, could execute an order precisely and rapidly. They would invest money in a revolutionary group when necessary, engage in influence peddling, fabricate crucial information which changed the course of wars. To silence, to deceive, and at the furthest extreme, to kill. Every member of the

Hand of Saint Michael was trained in weapons and tactics. Originally, in population control, secret codes, disguise, and hand-to-hand combat. A Hand was capable of splitting a grape in two with a knife from fifteen paces. He could speak four languages. He could decapitate a cow, throw its decaying body into a well full of pure water, and place the blame on a rival group in an absolutely masterful fashion. They trained for years in a monastery on an island in the Mediterranean, whose name I won't reveal. At the beginning of the twentieth century, the training evolved only to have the Hand of Saint Michael nearly pulled out by the roots during the Second World War. An epoch bathed in blood, in which many men perished, some of them defending very noble causes and others shamefully in the service of causes far less so."

Fowler paused to take a sip of coffee. The shadows in the room had grown darker and longer, and Paola was overcome by fear. She sat down in the chair in the reverse position, her arms grasping the back while the priest went on talking.

"In 1958, John XXIII, the pope who initiated Vatican II, decided that the time for the Santa Alianza had passed, that its services were no longer required. And right in the middle of the Cold War, he dismantled the lines of communication between the various informants, absolutely prohibiting members of the Alliance from carrying out any action without his prior approval. And for four years it stayed like that. There were only twelve of fifty-two Hands left in 1939, and several of them were getting on in years. The pope ordered them to return to Rome. The secret location where they trained went up in flames mysteriously in 1960. And the head of the Saint Michael, the leader of the Holy Alliance, died in a car accident."

"Who was he?"

"I can't say, not because I don't want to but because I don't know. The identity of the head is always a mystery. It could be anybody: a bishop, a cardinal, an *uomo di fiducia*, a simple priest. It has to be a man, more than forty-five years old. That's all. Since 1566 until today the name of only one head has gotten out: the parish priest Sogredo, an Italian, originally from Spain, who fought Napoleon tooth and nail. And that piece of information is only available in very small circles."

"It isn't exactly strange that the Vatican refuses to recognize the existence of an espionage service, if it uses methods such as you describe."

"That was one of the motives that moved John XXIII to have done with the Santa Alianza. He said murder is not just, even in the name of God, and I agree. I know that a few of the campaigns undertaken by the Hand of Saint Michael hit the Nazis very hard. One of their attacks saved hundreds of lives. But there was one faction, very reduced in numbers, which operated completely on their own, and they committed terrible atrocities. I don't want to go into that now, and even less so at this late hour."

Fowler waved one of his hands in front of him, as if he were trying to chase away ghosts. In someone like him, whose economy of movement was almost supernatural, a gesture like that could only indicate an overwhelming case of nerves. Paola concluded he had had enough of this particular history lesson.

"There is no need to keep going. Just tell me what you think I need to know."

Fowler smiled gratefully.

"But that, as I guess you might imagine, was not the end of the Holy Alliance. The arrival of Paul VI on the throne of Saint Peter in 1963 came amidst the most fraught international situation the world had ever seen. Less than a year before the world had been a few inches away from atomic war. And a few months later, Kennedy, the first Catholic president, was assassinated. When Paul VI learned the news, he ordered the Holy Alliance back into action. The network of spies, although diminished by time, recovered. The tricky part was recreating the Hand of Saint Michael. Of the twelve hands who had been recalled to Rome in '58, seven were fit for service in 1963. One of them was put in charge of rebuilding the organizational structure to train new agents. The job took about fifteen years, but they succeeded in forming a core of thirty agents. Some of them had absolutely no prior experience, and some came from other secret services."

"Like yourself: a double agent."

"In fact, I was considered a potential agent. That's someone who normally works for two allied organizations, but in which the first is unaware that the second adds to or modifies the directives of the assignments in each mission. It was my job to use what I knew to save lives, not to take others. Almost every mission they sent me on involved getting people out: saving endangered priests in difficult places."

"Almost every mission."

Fowler nodded.

"We had a complex mission where things got bent out of shape. I stopped being a Hand that very day. They didn't make things easy for me, but here I am. I thought I would be a psychologist for the rest of my life, and look where one of my patients has led me."

"Dante is one of the Hands, no?"

"Years after I resigned, there was a crisis. Once again there are very few agents, from what I've heard. All of them work far away, on missions where extracting them would be very difficult. The only man available was Dante, and he is not known for his scruples. In reality, a perfect fit for the job, if my suspicions are right."

"So Cirin is the head?"

Fowler looked straight ahead, unperturbed. After a minute Paola decided he wasn't going to answer, so she asked him another question.

"But why would the Santa Alianza want to make a mess like this . . . ?"

"The world is changing. Democratic ideals are taking root in people's hearts all over the world, and I include in that group some of the very callous members of the Curia. The Santa Alianza needs a pope who steadfastly supports them or they will disappear. But the Alianza is a divisive idea. What the three cardinals have in common is that they were decided liberals; as liberal as a cardinal could be, when all is said and done. Any of them would have dismantled the secret service, maybe for good."

"Take them out of the picture, and the threat is gone."

"And in doing so you increase the need for security. If the cardinals just turn up dead, there would be a lot of questions. The Alianza would never be able to make it look like an accident: the pontificate is naturally paranoiac. But if you are certain about something . . ."

"A killer in a disguise. Jesus, this is making me sick. I am glad I put so much distance between myself and the Church."

Fowler moved closer to her and, kneeling down in front of the chair, took both her hands in his.

"Don't make that mistake. Behind this Church, made out of the blood and bricks you see before you, there is another Church, infinite and invisible, whose flags are raised towards heaven. This Church lives in the hearts of the millions of the faithful who love Christ and his message. It will be reborn from its ashes and fill the world. The gates of hell shall have no dominion."

Paola's eyes bored into the priest.

"You really believe all that?"

"I do believe it, Paola."

Both of them stood up. He kissed her tenderly and slowly, and she accepted him as he was, with all of his scars. Her anguish flowed into his pain, and came undone there, and over the course of the small hours of the night, they discovered what it means to be happy.

✝

DICANTI FAMILY APARTMENT
Via della Croce, 12
Sunday, April 10, 2005, 8:41 A.M.

This time it was Fowler who woke up to the aroma of fresh coffee.

"Here you are, Padre."

He glanced at her, puzzled by her formal tone. She looked at him unwaveringly, and he understood. Hope had given way to the clear light of morning, which already filled the room. He said nothing and she had no expectations. There was nothing he could offer her except pain. Even so he felt a little better, comforted by the certainty that both had gained from the experience, taking strength from each other's weakness. It would be easy to think that Fowler had strayed from his calling in those early hours of the morning, but it would be wrong. The truth was something else entirely: he was grateful to her for taming his demons, even if only for a short time.

She was happy he understood. She sat on the edge of the bed, a smile on her face. And that was no cheerless smile, because in the last few hours she had overcome a desperate obstacle. The new morning had not brought certainty, but at least her confusion had dissipated. Perhaps she was keeping her distance from him just to be on the safe side, to steer clear of any new pain. Yet even that, as easy as it sounds, would be wrong: she understood Fowler, knew that he kept his promises and was not about to surrender his personal crusade.

"*Dottoressa*, I have to tell you something, and it won't be easy to take."

"Go ahead, Padre."

"If you ever leave your career as a criminal pyschiatrist, don't open a cafe," he said, grimacing in the direction of the coffee she'd brought him.

They both laughed, and for a brief moment everything was perfect.

Half an hour later, showered and freshened, the two went over the details of the case. Fowler, standing by the window in Paola's room; Paola, sitting at her desk.

"You know what Padre? In the light of day, our theory that Karosky is an assassin following orders from the Holy Alliance has mutated into something weird and unreal."

"Very possibly. Nevertheless, in the light of day, the mutilations of the cardinals, and Pontiero, are still very, very real. And if we're right, we're the only two people who can stop Karosky."

Those words were enough to take the brilliant sheen out of the morning. Paola felt her soul become as tense as a tightrope. She was more than ever aware that it was their responsibility to catch this monster. For Pontiero, for Fowler, and for herself. And when she had him in her hands, she wanted to ask him who exactly was on the other end of his leash. In the mood she was in, she could barely contain herself.

"The Vigilanza is compromised, I understand that much. But the Swiss Guard?"

"Beautiful uniforms, but they are in fact harmless. They probably aren't even aware that three cardinals have died. I don't take them seriously: they are traffic police."

Paola rubbed her neck. She was disturbed.

"So what do we do now?"

"I have no idea. We have no clues as to where Karosky is going to attack, and since yesterday he's going to find it easier to kill."

"What do you mean?"

"The cardinals have begun the novena masses for the pope's soul. They are celebrated during the nine-day period after the death of the pope."

"You are not telling me—"

"I am. The masses will be held all over Rome, at San Giovanni in Laterno, Santa Maria Maggiore, San Pietro, San Paolo fuori le Mura . . . The cardinals say mass in groups of two, in the fifty most important churches in Rome. It's the tradition, and I don't think they will change it for anything in the world. If the Santa Alianza is involved in this, it would be the perfect moment for an assassination. The story has yet to become public, and as it stands the cardinals would rebel if Cirin tried to stop them from celebrating the novenas. No, the masses will take place, come what may. And it could be very bad, up to and including another cardinal who has already been killed without our knowing about it."

"Damn, I need a cigarette."

Paola looked all over her desk and felt inside her coat for Pontiero's pack of smokes. She put her hand in the breast pocket. Her fingers touched something tiny and inflexible.

"What's this?"

She pulled out a card a few inches long, with the image of the Virgin of Carmen printed on one side. The one that Brother Francesco Toma had given her when she was about to leave Santa Maria in Traspontina. The phony Carmelite, Karosky the killer. She was wearing the same black jacket she had worn last Tuesday morning, and the card was still there.

"How did I forget this? It's evidence."

Fowler walked over, his interest piqued.

"A devotional card. The Virgin of Carmen. There is something written on back."

Fowler read the text out loud. It was in English.

If your very own brother, or your son or your daughter,
or the wife you love, or your closest friend secretly entices you,
do not yield to him or listen to him. Show him no pity.
Do not spare him or shield him.
You must certainly put him to death.
Then all Israel will hear and be afraid,
and no one among you will do such a wicked thing again.

Paola translated it into Italian. She was livid, enraged.

"I believe it is Deuteronomy. Chapter 13, verses 7 through 11."

"Shit!" Paola said between clenched teeth. "It was in my pocket the whole time. It should have set off an alarm when I saw it was written in English."

"Stop beating yourself up. A friar handed you a card. Considering your lack of faith, it's no wonder you never gave it a second look."

"Maybe so, but we knew who this friar was a short time later. I should have remembered he gave me something. I was too busy trying to remember what I saw of his face in the dark. Even if—"

I tried to preach the word to you, do you remember?

Paola held her breath. Fowler turned around with the card in his hand.

"Look, Paola, it's just an everyday card. He stuck a piece of adhesive paper on back—"

Santa Maria del Carmen.

"Which is very helpful in locating the text. Deuteronomy is—"

Take it with you wherever you go.

"A pretty unusual source for a quotation on a card, wouldn't you say? I think that—"

It will help you find the right road in these uncertain times.

"If I tug a little on the corner, I can lift it off—"

"Don't touch it!" Paola grabbed Fowler by the arm.

Fowler blinked, taken aback. Not a muscle moved as she pulled the card out of his hand.

"I'm sorry I screamed at you," Paola said, trying to calm herself down. "I just remembered that Karosky told me the card would show me the way in uncertain times. I think it's a message, and he put it there to make fun of us."

"Maybe. Or maybe it's one more of his attempts to throw us off the track."

"The only thing we know for sure is that we are very far from having all the pieces to the puzzle. Maybe there's a clue here."

She turned the card over, held it to the light, smelled the paper. Nothing.

"The quote from the Bible could be a message. But what was he trying to say?"

"I don't know, but I think there's something else here, something we can't see at first glance. And I think I've got the perfect instrument for a case like this."

Dicanti rummaged around in a nearby closet. After a few minutes she pulled out a box, laden with dust, from the back of the small room. She laid it down carefully on her desk.

"I haven't used this since I was studying at the Institute. It was a gift from my father."

She opened the box slowly, reverently. She still remembered the advertisement for the device, about how expensive it was and how careful you had to be with it. She took it out and sat it upright on the desk. A standard microscope: Paola had worked with equipment a thousand times more expensive when she was in college, but none of them had she treated with the respect she showed this one. She liked feeling that way: the microscope was a touching connection to her father, and a rare one at that, especially for someone who constantly mourned the day she lost him. She fleetingly asked herself if she shouldn't treasure the glittering memories she had rather than holding on to the idea that he had been snatched away from her too soon.

The wrapping paper and plastic had protected the instrument from dust. She put the card under the lens and focused. With her left hand she moved the multicolored card around, slowly inspecting every speck of the image of the Virgin. Nothing remarkable anywhere. She turned the card over.

"Hold on. . . . There's something here."

Paola let Fowler look through the eyepiece. Fifteen times their normal size, the letters on the card were stupendous black chess pieces. There was a minuscule white circle around one of them.

"Looks like a perforation."

Paola took the microscope back from Fowler.

"I would say it was done with a pin. Appears to be done intentionally. It's too perfect."

"Where does the first mark appear?"

"In the *f* of *if*."

"Keep looking. Check to see if there are perforations around other letters."

Paola checked each letter in the first line of text.

"Here's another one."

"Go on, go on."

After eight minutes of looking, Paola had successfully identified twelve perforated letters.

If your very own brother, or your son or your daughter,
or the wife you love, or your closest friend secretly entices you,
do not yield to him or listen to him. Show him no pity.
Do not spare him or shield him.
You must certainly put him to death.
Then all Israel will fear and be afraid,
and no one among you will do such a wicked thing again.

When she had checked that there were no more perforated letters, Paola wrote them out in the order they appeared. What they read shocked them. And then Paola put the pieces together.

If your very own brother secretly entices you: the psychiatric sessions.

Do not spare him or shield him: the letters to the families of the victims of Karosky's sexual depravation.

You must certainly put him to death.

She recalled the one name that figured in all of it.

Francis Casey.

✝

AP NEWS FEED
April 10, 2005, 08:12 GMT

CARDINAL CASEY WILL CONDUCT THE
NOVENA MASSES IN SAINT PETER'S TODAY

ROMA (Associated Press). Cardinal Francis Casey will officiate today at the midday novena mass at St. Peter's Basilica in Rome. The North American cardinal will enjoy the honor of directing the ceremony on this, the second day of the nine-day mourning period for the soul of John Paul II.

Organized groups in the U.S. have not looked upon Casey's participation in the ceremony with approval. Specifically, SNAP (Survivors Network of those Abused by Priests) has sent two of its members to Rome to formally protest the fact that Casey has been allowed to officiate at the paramount church in Christendom. "We're only two people, and we will protest in a peaceful, orderly fashion and tell our stories to the press," said Barbara Payne, President of SNAP.

The organization is the principal group representing the victims of sexual abuse at the hands of Catholic priests, and it counts more than 4,500 members. Its chief activity is to locate and give aid to the victims, which it does in group therapy sessions that help the victims acknowledge what happened to them. Many of its members join SNAP once they have reached adulthood, after years of shameful silence.

Cardinal Casey, at present prefect of the Congregation for the Clergy, saw himself become involved in the scandal of priestly sexual abuse that exploded in the United States in the late 1990s. Casey, cardinal for the Boston archdiocese, was the most important figure in the North American Church and, many say, the strongest candidate to succeed John Paul II.

His career suffered a severe setback when it was discovered that for years he kept more than three hundred cases of sexual abuse in his jurisdiction out of the public spotlight. He frequently moved priests accused of the crimes of this nature from one parish to the next, hoping to avoid scandal. In almost every instance he limited himself to recommending "fresh air" to those so charged. Only when the cases were of the most serious kind did he send the priest to a mental health institution where he could receive treatment.

As the first serious charges began to surface, Casey agreed to settlements with the families of the victims, settlements whose large financial remunerations came with a vow of silence. After a period of time, the scandals became common knowledge throughout the country, and "highly placed Vatican authorities" found themselves forced to replace Casey. He was transferred to Rome, where he was named prefect for the Congregation of the Clergy, a position of some importance but which in any case would seem to be the last chapter in his career.

There are nevertheless some who continue to regard

Casey as a saint who used all his strength to defend the Church. "He has suffered persecution and calumnies for defending the faith," his personal secretary, Father Miller, said. But in the media's eternal horse race over who will be the next pope, Casey is given few chances. The Catholic clergy is in general cautious and no friend to extravagance. Casey can count on supporters, but short of a miracle it seems likely he will receive few votes.

04/10/2005/08:12 (AP)

THE SACRISTY, SAINT PETER'S BASILICA

Sunday, April 10, 2005, 11:08 A.M.

The priests who would celebrate the mass with Cardinal Casey were helping one another with their vestments in the auxiliary sacristy near the entrance to Saint Peter's, where along with the altar boys, they waited for the cardinal. The ceremony was to get under way in five minutes. They were forbidden to enter the main sacristy.

As of that moment, the museum was deserted except for the two nuns who served under Casey and the other cardinal who would be celebrating the mass, Cardinal Pauljic. There was also a Swiss Guard who stood watch in the doorway to the sacristy.

Karosky felt the comforting bulge that the knife and pistol made, nestled inside his clothing. He made mental calculations of his course of action.

He was at last about to carry off the prize.

The moment was at hand.

✝

SAINT PETER'S SQUARE

Sunday, April 10, 2005, 11:16 A.M.

"We'll never get through the Santa Ana gate. It's heavily guarded and the only people they're letting in are the ones with Vatican authorization."

Dicanti and Fowler had reconnoitered the entrances to the Vatican at a discreet distance, looking them over. Each one alone, so as not to draw attention. In fifty minutes or less, the novena mass in Saint Peter's would be getting under way.

A mere thirty minutes before, when Francis Casey's name had, with the force of a bolt of lightning, appeared on the devotional card of the Virgin of Carmen, they had undertaken a frantic Internet search. From the press agencies they were able to glean the time and the place where Casey would appear, in full view of anyone who might want to see him.

And there they were, in Saint Peter's Square.

"We'll have to go in by the main door."

"Won't happen. It's a classic funnel trap. Security has been visibly tightened everywhere except there, which is the entrance open to the public, so that's where they'll be waiting for us. And even if we managed to get in, we'd never get close to the altar. Casey and whoever is celebrating the mass with him will enter from the sacristy in

Saint Peter's. From there on out, the way to the basilica is clear. They won't use the main altar, which is reserved for the pope alone, but one of the secondary altars, and even then there will be as many as eight hundred people attending the ceremony."

"Will Karosky actually try to pull it off in front of so many people?"

"Our problem, *Dottoressa*, is that we don't know who is playing which role in this drama. If the Holy Alliance wants to see Casey dead, they are not going to let us stop him from celebrating the mass. If they are intent on catching Karosky, they are not going to let us warn the cardinal. He is their best bait. I'm convinced that, come what may, this is the final act of the tragedy."

"But at this stage in the drama there's no role for us. It's already a quarter after eleven."

"Not true. We'll find a way into the basilica, dodge Cirin's agents, and slip into the sacristy. We have to stop Casey from celebrating his mass."

"And how are we going to do that, Padre?"

"We'll take a route Cirin would never imagine in his wildest dreams."

Four minutes later they stood at the front door of a sober five-story building. Paola knew Fowler was right. Never in a million years would Cirin imagine Fowler knocking, of his own free will, on the front door of the Palace of the Holy Inquisition. The Sant'Uffizio.

One of the entrances to Saint Peter's is located between the building that houses the Sant'Uffizio and Bernini's Colonnade. It consists of a roadblock and a guard station. There are usually two Swiss Guards on duty. On this Sunday there were five, joined by a single Vatican police officer. He was carrying a file in his hand, inside of which were Fowler's and Dicanti's photos, a fact of which both were ignorant. The cop, a member of the Vigilanza, watched as a couple who seemed to match the descriptions crossed the open space in front of him. He saw them for only an instant before they disappeared, and he wasn't absolutely sure it was them. He was not authorized to leave his post, so he made no attempt to follow them and find out. His orders were to report back if those individuals tried to enter the Vatican, and to detain them, by force if necessary. It was clear to him that those two people were of some special concern. He pushed the button on his walkie-talkie and gave a description of what he had just seen.

Just short of the corner with Porta Cavalleggeri, and a mere sixty feet from the guard station where the cop was taking his orders, stood the entrance to the Palace of the Sant'Uffizio. The door was locked, but there was a bell. Fowler kept his finger glued to the buzzer until he heard the sound of locks being turned on the other side. The face of an aged priest squinted through a crack in the doorway.

"What do you want?" he said. His tone was thoroughly unpleasant.

"We are here to see Bishop Hanër."

"Who are you?"

"Padre Fowler."

"I'm not familiar with the name."

"I'm an old friend."

"Bishop Hanër is resting. Today is Sunday and the palazzo is closed. Have a nice day," he said as he brushed them off, like someone swatting at flies.

"Would you please tell me in which hospital or cemetery I can find the bishop?"

The old priest was taken aback.

"Excuse me?"

"Bishop Hanër told me he would never rest until he had made me pay for my many sins, so he must be either sick or dead. There is no other explanation."

The look on the priest's face changed a little, from hostile disinterest to slight irritation.

"It appears you know Bishop Hanër. Please wait outside." The priest shut the door in their faces.

"How did you know that this Hanër would be there?"

"Bishop Hanër has never taken a single Sunday off in his entire life. It would be a sad thing if he did so today."

"He's a friend of yours?"

Fowler cleared his throat.

"Actually, he hates me more than anyone else in the world. Gonthas Hanër oversees the day-to-day working of the clergy. He's an old German Jesuit who reins in the Santa Alianza when its overseas missions get out of hand. An ecclesiastical version of Internal Affairs. He put me on trial. He has a real aversion to me because I refused to say a single word about the missions they sent me on."

"But you were absolved?"

"Just barely. He told me that he had an anathema with my name on it, and sooner or later the pope would sign it."

"An anathema?"

"A decree of final excommunication. Hanër knows it's the one thing I really fear in this world: that the Church I've given my life to will prevent me from entering heaven when I die."

Dicanti gave him a troubled look.

"And so, Padre, why exactly are we here?"

"I have come to make a full confession."

✝

THE SACRISTY, SAINT PETER'S BASILICA

Sunday, April 10, 2005, 11:31 A.M.

The Swiss Guard tumbled to the floor as gracelessly as a drunk on the street, the only sound that of his ornate pike clattering onto the marble floor. His throat was slit from one side to the other, completely severing his trachea.

One of the nuns came out of the sacristy when she heard the noise. She never had the chance to scream. Karosky struck her on the face as hard as he could. The nun fell facedown on the floor. She was out cold. The killer took his time, dragging her by the right foot, which was nestled inside her religious garments. He felt around for the small of her neck. He chose the exact spot he wanted and put all his weight on the ball of his foot. Her neck made a dry cracking sound.

A second nun stuck her head into the sacristy with a confident air. She just needed a bit of help from her sister.

Karosky sunk his knife deep into her right eye. He threw her to the floor and dragged her over to the short hallway leading to the sacristy, where he had already deposited one of the bodies.

He surveyed his three corpses and then glanced at the door to the sacristy. He checked his watch.

He still had five minutes left to put the finishing touches on his work.

338

✝

JUST OUTSIDE THE DOOR
OF THE SANT'UFFIZIO

Sunday, April 10, 2005, 11:31 A.M.

What Fowler had said about a full confession made Paola's jaw drop. Before she could get a word out, the front door of the Sant'Uffizio swung open with great flourish. Instead of the elderly priest who had greeted them earlier, standing before them was a bishop. Slender in build, with immaculate blond hair and beard, he looked to be about fifty years old. He spoke to Fowler with a German accent loaded with disdain and heavy r's.

"Well, well. Look who turns up on my doorstep after all these years. To what do I owe the unexpected honor?"

"Bishop Hanër, I need to ask you a favor."

"I am afraid, Padre Fowler, that you are not in the position to ask me for anything. Some twelve years ago I asked you something, and you refused to say a single word for days. Days! The commission may have found you innocent, but I did not. Please be on your way immediately."

His index finger pointed in the direction of Porta Cavalleggeri. To Paola, his finger appeared so straight and inflexible, he could have drowned Fowler with it.

Fowler volunteered the rope himself.

"You still have not heard what I have to offer in exchange."

The bishop crossed his arms.

"Go on, Fowler."

"There's a strong possibility that there will be a murder inside the basilica in the next half hour. *Ispettore* Dicanti, who is here with me, and I are trying to stop it. Sadly, we can't get in. Camilo Cirin has denied us access. I ask your permission to pass through the palazzo as far as the parking lot so that we can enter the basilica without being seen."

"And in exchange?"

"I will answer all of your questions about El Aguacate. Tomorrow."

Hanër turned to Paola.

"Show me some identification."

Paola didn't have her police badge because Troi had made her surrender it. Happily for her, she still had the ID card that enabled her to pass in and out of UACV headquarters. She held it authoritatively in the bishop's face, hoping it convinced him.

Hanër took the card from Dicanti's hand. He studied her face and the photograph on the card, the UACV emblem, and even the magnetic band that identified who she was.

"Based on this, you can go in. I am inclined to believe, Fowler, that to your many other sins you have added concupiscence."

Paola turned away so as to avoid having Hanër notice the smile spreading across her lips. She was relieved to see that Fowler stared back at the bishop with the same serious expression. Hanër cleared his throat, making no attempt to mask his contempt.

"Fowler, where you're going you will be surrounded by blood and death. My feelings about you have not changed in the slightest. I don't have any desire to let you in."

The priest was about to respond to Hanër, but the bishop cut him off.

"Even so, I know you are a man of honor. I accept your petition. Today both of you will enter the basilica, but tomorrow you will meet me, and you will tell me the truth."

That said, he stepped aside. Fowler and Dicanti entered the building. The lobby was elegant, painted a cream color and bare of moldings or adornment of any kind. The whole building hovered in a Sunday silence, and Paola suspected that the only person inside was Hanër, as wiry and agitated as an épée. The man regarded himself as the agent of God's justice. She shivered just thinking what such an obsessed mind might have achieved if he had been around four hundred years earlier.

"I will see you tomorrow, Padre Fowler. And I will have the pleasure of showing you a document I am keeping for you."

The priest led Paola down a hallway to the floor underground, without looking back once. He was perhaps afraid that he would find Hanër there, standing next to the door, waiting for him to come back tomorrow.

"Very unusual, Padre. People usually exit the Church through the Sant'Uffizio, not enter it."

Fowler's expression was a combination of irony and sadness.

"I hope that if we capture Karosky, we aren't saving the life of a man who eventually is going to reward me with excommunication."

They came to the emergency entrance. A window looked out into the parking lot. Fowler pressed the bar in the middle of the door and stuck his head out as innocuously as possible. One hundred feet away, the Swiss Guards vigilantly watched the street. He closed the door.

"We'll have to make it quick. We have to get to Casey and explain the situation before Karosky can finish him off."

"How are we going to get there?"

"We'll exit the parking lot and keep going, staying as close to the wall as possible, walking in Indian file. At that point we are in front of the building where the pope holds his public audiences. We keep going, hugging the wall, until we get to the corner. We will have to cross on the diagonal as quickly as we can. Face right, because we have no idea if anyone will be looking for us in that area. I will go first, agreed?"

Paola nodded her head and started off, walking quickly. They made it to the sacristy without incident. An imposing edifice, attached to the side of the basilica. It was open all year to tourists and pilgrims, and its public spaces functioned as a museum that contained some of Christianity's most beautiful treasures.

Fowler reached out to the door.

It was half-open.

$$\dagger$$

THE SACRISTY, SAINT PETER'S BASILICA

Sunday, April 10, 2005, 11:42 A.M.

"Bad sign," Fowler said as quietly as he could.

Dicanti's hand moved toward her waist, and she pulled out her revolver, a .38.

"Let's go in."

"I thought Troi had taken your pistol."

"He made me turn in my automatic, which is standard issue for all cops. This little toy is only for emergencies."

They crossed the threshold. The museum inside the sacristy was deserted, the lights turned off in its vitrines. The marble lining the walls and the floors reflected the minuscule amount of sunlight that entered through a handful of windows. It was midday, but the galleries were practically dark. Fowler led the way without a word, silently cursing the crunching noise his shoes made on the floor. They passed straight through four of the museum's galleries without looking to either side. But in the sixth gallery, Fowler stopped in mid-step. On the ground a mere twenty inches in front of him, partially hidden in the shadows of the corridor he was about to enter, was an extraordinary sight: a white-gloved hand and an arm arrayed in vivid yellows, blues, and reds.

Rounding the corner, they discovered that the arm was connected to a Swiss Guard. He still clutched his staff with his left hand, but what had been eyes were now two empty sockets drained of blood. A little farther down the corridor Paola found two nuns in black habits and wimples, united in a last embrace.

Their eyes were missing too.

Paola cocked her gun. She and Fowler looked at each other knowingly.

"He's here."

They stood in the short hallway that led to the Vatican's principal sacristy, which was typically roped off, its double doors left wide open so the public could satisfy its curiosity by staring at the room where the Holy Father put his robes on before celebrating mass.

The doors were closed.

"I hope for God's sake we're not too late," Paola said, her eyes staring at the bodies on the floor.

The Swiss Guard and the two nuns brought the total of Karosky's victims to at least eight. Paola swore to herself that these would be the last. Without giving it a second thought, she crossed the open space between where she was and the door, stepping around the bodies. The pistol was in her left hand, and her right arm was raised, with the pistol resting on the forearm. She walked over the threshold.

She had entered an octagonal room with ceilings some thirty-six feet high, suffused with a golden light. Directly in front of her was an altar standing between columns, with an oil painting hanging above it: the descent from the cross. Standing against the sublime, wonderfully polished marble walls were ten armoires fashioned out of India wood and myrtle, inside of which hung the sacred vestments. If Paola had glanced toward the ceiling, she would have seen a cupola adorned with beautiful frescoes, through whose windows the light flooding the room entered. But Paola's eyes were watching the two men standing on the other side of the room.

She recognized Cardinal Casey first. The second was also a cardinal. He looked vaguely familiar, until at last she recognized him. Cardinal Pauljic.

The men were standing together at the altar. Pauljic, behind Casey, was almost done adjusting Casey's robes when Dicanti barged in, her pistol pointed directly at them.

"Where is he?" she shouted, her voice echoing in circles around the cupola. "Have you seen him?"

His eyes riveted on Dicanti's pistol, the American cardinal spoke very, very slowly. "Where is who, miss?"

"Karosky. The man who slaughtered the Swiss Guard and the two nuns."

Fowler entered the sacristy before her last word was out. He stood next to Paola. He looked at Casey, and for the first time, he and Pauljic exchanged glances.

There was fire, and recognition too, in those eyes.

"Hello, Victor," said the priest, his voice deep and hoarse.

Cardinal Pauljic, better known as Victor Karosky, put his left arm around Cardinal Casey's neck. With his right hand he took out Maurizio Pontiero's pistol and placed it against the cardinal's temple.

"Don't move!" Dicanti shouted, and the -ove echoed in succession throughout the room.

"Don't *you* move a muscle, Miss Dicanti, or we'll get a good look at the inside of the cardinal's head." The killer's voice hit Paola with the force of anger and fear simultaneously, the adrenaline pulsing through her veins. She remembered how angry she had been when, after she had taken a good look at Pontiero's body, the beast had called her on the phone.

She aimed carefully.

Karosky was more than thirty feet away, and at this moment only part of his head and his forearms were visible from behind Cardinal Casey, his human shield.

Even with a revolver and good aim, an impossible shot.

"Put the gun down on the floor, *Ispettore*, or I'll kill him right here."

Paola bit her lower lip to keep from screaming. She had the killer right in front of her, and she couldn't do a thing.

"Don't do it, *Dottoressa*. He would never hurt the cardinal. Isn't that right, Victor?"

Karosky tightened his grip around Casey's neck.

"Of course I will. Put the gun on the ground, Dicanti. Put it down!"

"Please, do what he asks," Casey groaned in a quavery voice.

"Excellent stage acting, Victor." Fowler's voice was shaking with rage. "Remember how it had seemed to us that it was impossible for the killer to have escaped from Cardoso's room, which was locked up tight? As hard as it looked, that part was easy. He never left at all."

"What?" Paola was stunned.

"We broke down the door. We didn't see anyone. And then a very opportune cry for help reaches us about some crazy attack taking place by the service exit. Victor was in the room, no doubt about it. Were you under the bed? Hiding in the closet?"

"Very astute, Padre. Now put down the gun, *Ispettore*."

"But this cry for help and the description of what his attacker looked like came from a trustworthy source, a man of faith. A cardinal. The killer's accomplice."

"Shut up, Fowler!"

"What did he promise you if you'd take his competitors out of the picture completely, in his search for glory he hasn't deserved for a very long time—"

"That's enough!" Karosky looked like a madman, with his face drenched in sweat, and one of the fake eyebrows he'd glued on dangling precariously over his eye.

"Did he come to see you at the Institute, Victor? He's the one who sent you there, isn't that so?"

"Enough of these absurd insinuations, Fowler. Tell the woman to put the gun down, or this madman is going to kill me," Casey said in a commanding voice. He was clearly desperate.

"Tell us His Eminence's plan, Victor," Fowler said, ignoring Casey. "You had to pretend to attack him right in the middle of Saint Peter's? And he would dissuade you from carrying it out, in front of all of God's people and the television cameras?"

"Stop talking, or I will kill him! I'll kill him!"

"You would have been the one dead. And he would be the hero."

"What did he promise you in exchange for the keys to the kingdom, Victor?"

"Heaven, you fucking son of a bitch! Eternal life!"

Karosky lifted the gun from Casey's temple, aimed at Dicanti, and fired.

Fowler shoved Paola to the floor and in the process her gun slipped out of her hand. Karosky's shot just missed Dicanti's head and instead hit Fowler in the left shoulder, shattering the bone into a dozen pieces.

Karosky let Casey go, and the cardinal scurried off to hide between two of the armoires. Paola, with no time to look for her gun, threw herself headlong at Karosky, her hands balled into fists. Her right shoulder smashed into his stomach and flattened him against the wall, but she did not succeed in knocking the air out of him: beneath his flowing robes he had worn extra padding to make himself look heavier. Pontiero's pistol bounced onto the ground with a hollow metallic echo.

Karosky beat Dicanti on the back. She cried in pain, but she managed to get to her feet and smash Karosky in the face. He looked dazed and came very close to losing his balance.

And then Paola made her only mistake.

She looked around for the pistol. Karosky seized the moment to hit her in her face, her stomach, her kidneys. He grabbed her around the neck, just as he had done with Casey. But this time he was holding a short object which he brushed back and forth across Paola's face. A common fish knife, but a very sharp one.

"Ah, Paola, you have no idea how much I am going to enjoy this," he whispered into her ear.

"Victor!"

Karosky turned around. Fowler was sitting up, one knee positioned on the marble floor, his left shoulder destroyed, blood spilling from his arm, which hung inertly, scraping the floor.

His right hand held Paola's revolver. It was aimed directly at Karosky's forehead.

"You're not going to shoot, Fowler." Karosky was breathing heavily. "We're not so very different. The two of us shared the very same hell. And in your vows you swore you would never again take a life."

Making a tremendous effort, his face flushed with pain, Fowler managed to lift his left hand to his priest's white collar. With a single gesture, he tore it off and threw it into the air between Karosky and himself. It spun in circles, the starched cloth an immaculate white save for one reddish splotch, where Fowler had pressed his thumb and torn it loose. Karosky watched it, hypnotized, but he never saw it hit the ground.

Fowler fired once, a single, deadly accurate shot that hit Karosky between the eyes.

The killer fell to the ground. From far away he listened to the voices of his parents, who were calling out to him. And he went to join them.

* * *

Paola ran toward Fowler, who looked pale as death and very lost. As she crossed the room, she tore off her jacket in order to use it as a tourniquet for Fowler's wound.

"Lie down."

"It was very bad before you got here, my friends." It was Casey's voice. He had recovered his courage sufficiently to get back on his feet. "That monster had taken me hostage."

"Don't stand there, Cardinal. Go tell someone—" Paola started to say, as she tried to help Fowler stretch out on the floor. Suddenly she realized exactly where Casey was headed: to the spot next to Karosky's body, where Pontiero's pistol lay on the ground. It struck her that she and Fowler were two very dangerous witnesses. She felt around for her revolver.

"Good afternoon," said Inspector Camilo Cirin as he walked into the room with three agents of the Vigilanza in tow. He hastened over to the cardinal, who was leaning over to grab the pistol on the floor. He immediately stood up.

"I was beginning to think you were never going to get here, Inspector General. You must arrest these two immediately," Casey said, pointing at Fowler and Dicanti.

"Forgive me, Your Eminence. I will be with you in a moment."

Camilo Cirin looked down. He walked over to Karosky, grabbing Pontiero's pistol on his way. He placed the tip of his shoe on Karosky's face.

"This is him?"

"That's right," said Fowler.

"Fuck, Cirin, a false cardinal," Paola said. "How did that happen?"

"He had very good references."

Cirin put things together at an incredible speed. Behind his impassive face there was a brain operating like a diligent machine. He instantly recalled that Pauljic was the very last cardinal named by John Paul II. Six months ago, at a time when the pope only rarely got out of bed. He remembered that the pope had told Samalo and Ratzinger about the naming of a cardinal *in pectore*, whose identity *he had revealed to Casey alone*, who would announce the papal choice upon his demise. He did not find it difficult to imagine whose lips had breathed Pauljic's name in the stricken pope's ear, nor who had acompanied the new "cardinal" to Saint Martha's for the first time, in order to introduce him to his intrigued brethen.

"Cardinal Casey, you have a lot of explaining to do."

"I have no idea what you are referring to."

"Cardinal, please."

Casey looked out of sorts, but he soon started to recover his arrogance and his unwavering pride, the very thing that had led to his downfall.

"Over the course of many years, John Paul prepared me to continue his work. You more than anyone know what can happen if the control of the Church should fall into the hands of those who lack the necessary discipline. I trust that in the present instant you will act as best suits the Church, my friend."

Cirin's eyes arrived at a summary judgment in a split second.

"I will of course do so, Your Eminence. Domenico?"

"Inspector," said one of the agents who had entered the room with Cirin. Both his suit and his tie were black.

"Cardinal Casey will go out now to celebrate the novena mass in the Basilica."

The cardinal smiled.

"Afterward, you and the other agent will escort him to his new residence: the monastery at Albergradz, high in the Alps, where the cardinal will be able to reflect on his actions in solitude. He will also have the chance to improve his mountain climbing."

"A dangerous sport, from what I've heard," said Fowler.

"Most certainly. Plagued with accidents," Paola added.

Casey didn't respond, and in his silence was revealed the depth of his descent. His head hung down, his chin resting against his chest. He left the sacristy without a word to anyone, accompanied by Domenico.

Cirin kneeled at Fowler's side. Paola held his head up with one hand, while pressing her jacket onto the wound with the other.

"Permit me."

He moved Dicanti's hand away. Her improvised dressing was already soaked and he put his own wrinkled coat in its place.

"You can relax. There is an ambulance on the way. Do you mind telling me how you managed to get into this circus?"

"We avoided your ticket booths, Cirin, in preference to those at the Sant'Uffizio."

Cirin, seemingly imperturbable, raised an eyebrow. Paola understood that that was his way of showing surprise.

"Ah, but of course. Old Gonthas Hanër, a man who never quits. I see that he has relaxed his criteria for admission to the Vatican these days."

"But his prices are higher," Fowler said, as he thought about the wrenching interview awaiting him the next day.

Cirin nodded. He knew what Fowler was trying to tell him, and then put even more pressure on the jacket wrapped around Fowler's wound.

"That could be arranged, I suppose."

An emergency medical crew entered the room, carrying a stretcher.

While the two medics attended to the injured man, inside the basilica eight altar boys and two priests carrying censers waited at the door to the sacristy for Cardinals Casey and Pauljic. It was now four minutes after twelve. The mass should have already begun. The more senior of the two subordinate priests was tempted to send one of the altar boys into the sacristy to find out what was going on. Perhaps the Oblate sisters, in charge of overseeing the sacristy, were having problems with the appropriate vestments. But protocol demanded that he stay where he was, keeping watch over the participants in the mass.

At the last moment Cardinal Casey appeared by himself at the door that led into the basilica. The altar boys escorted him to the altar of Saint Joseph, where he would lead the mass. The faithful perched closest to the altar during the ceremony talked among themselves, whispering that the cardinal must have truly loved the pope: Casey was in tears throughout the entire mass.

"Calm down, you're out of danger," one of the nurses told him. "We'll be on our way to the hospital in a minute. They'll run all the tests on you there, but don't worry, the hemorrhaging is under control."

The emergency crew lifted the stretcher, and at that instant it hit Paola: the alienation from his parents, the rejection of his inheritance, the terrible resentment. She stopped the two men carrying the stretcher as they were loading it into the ambulance.

"Now I get it. The private hell you two shared. You went to Vietnam to kill your father, didn't you?"

Fowler gave her a startled look. He was, in fact, so startled that he answered her in English.

"Sorry?"

"Anger and resentment are what brought you to Vietnam." Paola spoke in English as well, as quietly as possible in order to keep the others out of the conversation. "The deep hatred of your father, the cold rejection of your mother. The refusal to accept your inheritance. You wanted to cut every family tie. And the interview with Victor where you talked about hell. It's all in the dossier you gave me. It's been right in front of my face the whole time."

"Where do you intend to stop?"

"I get it now," Paola said. She leaned over the stretcher and gently placed her hand on the priest's shoulder. Fowler was in shock and wanted to cry out in pain, but he held his tongue. "I understand why you took the job at Saint Matthew's, and how it made you what you are today. Your father abused you as a child. That's the truth, isn't it? And your mother knew the whole time. Just like Karosky. Which was why he respected you. Because the two of you were on opposite sides of the same line. You chose to become a man, and he chose to be a monster."

There was nothing for Fowler to say. The men carrying the stretcher started toward the ambulance again. Fowler concentrated as hard as he could. He looked at Dicanti and smiled.

"Take care of yourself, *Dottoressa*."

In the ambulance, Fowler was fighting to maintain consciousness. His eyes closed for a second, but a voice he recognized brought him back.

"Anthony."

Fowler smiled.

"Well, Fabio. So how's your arm?"

"Pretty well fucked."

"You got lucky on that roof."

Dante did not reply. He and Cirin were sitting on a bench jutting out from the side of the ambulance. The Vigilanza deputy tried to fight off his typically cynical expression despite the fact that his left arm was in a cast and his face was covered with bruises. Cirin for his part wore his habitual poker face.

"And so? How do you intend to kill me? Cyanide in the serum bottle, a gradual loss of blood, or the classic shot to the back of the head? I personally prefer the latter."

Dante's smile was joyless.

"Don't tempt me. Maybe one day, but not now, Anthony. This is a round-trip. There will be a better occasion."

Cirin, his face unmoved, looked straight at Fowler.

"I want to thank you. You have been a great help."

"I didn't do it for you. Or for your cause."

"I know."

"In fact, I was certain you were behind all this."

"I know that too, and I don't blame you."

The three said nothing for the next few minutes. Finally, it was Cirin who spoke.

"Any chance you'll work with us again?"

"None whatsoever, Camilo. You tricked me once. It won't happen again."

"One last time. For old time's sake."

Fowler thought for a few moments.

"With one condition. And you know what it is."

Cirin nodded.

"You have my word. Nobody goes near her."

"Or the other. The Spanish girl."

"That I can't guarantee. We still don't know if she has a copy of the disc."

"I spoke to her. She doesn't have it, and she won't talk."

"Good. Without the disc, she can't prove a thing."

This time the silence in the ambulance lasted longer, interrupted only by the beeping of the electrocardiogram attached to Fowler's chest. The priest was letting go, little by little. Cirin's last words came to him as if through a fog.

"You know what, Anthony? For a while there I was sure that you were going to tell her the truth. The whole truth."

Fowler did not hear his own response, not that it mattered. Not all truths will set you free. He knew that not even he could live with his truth, much less put its heavy weight on anyone else's shoulders.

RATZINGER IS CHOSEN NEW POPE, ALMOST WITHOUT OPPOSITION

by Andrea Otero *(special correspondent)*

ROME.—The conclave, which gathered to choose Pope John Paul II's successor, came to a close yesterday with the selection of the longtime prefect of the Congregation for the Doctrine of the Faith, Joseph Ratzinger. Despite having sworn on the Bible to maintain secrecy, under penalty of excommunication, regarding election of the pope, the first reports from conclave members have already begun to slip out. It appears that the German cardinal was chosen with 105 votes out of 115 possible, many more than the necessary 77. Vatican sources state that the overwhelming support Ratzinger enjoyed was unprecedented, and even more so in light of the fact that the conclave took only two days to make its decision.

Experts attributed the unprecendented and swift election to the lack of opposition to a candidate who was, in the early going, very far behind in the race. Sources close to the Vatican indicated that Ratzinger's principal rivals (Portini, Robayra, and Cardoso) never managed the necessary votes at any time. These same sources further commented that those cardinals seemed "a little out of it" during the election of Benedict XVI.

EPILOGUE

The man in white robes was the sixth person to greet Paola. Two weeks earlier and one floor below, Paola had waited in a similar hallway, a bundle of nerves, ignorant of the fact that at that very moment her friend was slowly dying. Two weeks later, her anxiety about behaving properly was long gone, and her friend avenged. An enormous number of things had taken place in those ten days, not the least important of which were in Paola's soul.

The criminologist stood in front of the door adorned with red ribbons and wax seals that had been hung there to protect the office between the death of John Paul II and the election of the new pope. The supreme pontiff gestured toward the door.

"I have asked them to remain there for a while. They'll serve to remind me that this post is only temporary," he said in a weary voice, as Paola kissed his ring.

"Your Holiness."

"*Ispettore* Dicanti, welcome. I asked you to come so I can personally thank you for the brave things you did."

"Thank you, Your Holiness. I only did what my job required."

"No, *Ispettore*, you went far beyond what your job required. Sit down, please," he said, gesturing toward one of the throne-like chairs in a corner of the office. A gorgeous Tintoretto hung overhead.

"Actually I was hoping to meet Padre Fowler here, Your Holiness," Paola said, without disguising the urgency in her voice. "It has been ten days since I have seen him."

The pope took her hand and smiled in a comforting manner. "Padre Fowler is resting in a safe place out of harm's way. I took the opportunity to visit him last night. He asked me to send you his greetings and gave me this message: 'Now is the time for both of us, you and I, to let go of the sadness we feel for those left behind.'"

Those words were enough to provoke an intense emotional catharsis inside Paola, and she was no longer able to hold back her tears. She spent another half hour in the presence of the Holy Father, but whatever conversation may have taken place in his office is known only to the two of them.

A short while later Paola went out for a walk in Saint Peter's Square. It was a little past midday and the sun was a brilliant ball of light. She took out Pontiero's pack of cigarettes and lighted up the last one. Her face lifted toward the open sky, and she let the cigarette smoke escape from between her lips.

"We got him, Maurizio. You were right. And now get a move on, go into the fucking light and leave me in peace. And hey, say hello to my father for me."

ACKNOWLEDGMENTS

The author wishes to express his thanks to Antonia Kerrigan and Tom Colchie, the best agents an author could hope for. At Dutton, to Mitch Hoffman, editor of this novel (and even if she isn't going to read it until thirty-five, this book is for baby Ella too!) and Erika Kahn (now Mrs. Imranyi). And I can't forget to thank my *mano* James Graham, author of a classic New York novel and translator of the one hundred thousand words you just read. The efforts of these four people *went far beyond what their jobs required.*

Various people played key roles in the research for *God's Spy*: Julie Meridian *y* Alice Nakagawa in New York, and Dobbie *y* Mike Nelson in Maryland (thanks for letting me sleep on your sofa); masterly psychiatrists Carlos Álvarez and Thomas Hurt, who helped me to make detailed profiles of Victor, Paola, and Anthony; and Sor Fermina in Vatican City. To you, and to those who helped and who asked not to be mentioned, many thanks.

And, of course, to Katu and Andrea. For your aid throughout and your unconditional love.

AUTHOR'S FINAL NOTE

This is a work of fiction. Names, characters, places, and incidents are either the product of the author's imagination or are used fictitiously, and any resemblance to actual persons, living or dead, business establishments, events, or locales is entirely coincidental.

And after the inevitable disclaimer . . . For all of you who constantly ask me about a real-life version of Saint Matthew's Institute, or want to know more about the real facts behind the book involving the Santa Alianza, you can visit the website www.godspynovel.com, where you can learn more about these subjects, or even e-mail me your praises (or, eventually, imaginative insults, which are as good as praises).

Madrid, January 2003
Santiago de Compostela, February 2006